THE
ARCHER'S
PARADOX

DAVID BERGER

Email: tchrofengl@gmail.com
First Edition
David Berger Books
The Archer's Paradox / Written by David Berger, Land O
Lakes, FL 34638
Summary: Task Force: Gaea works to help Apollo heal
while facing an adversary from his past.
ISBN-13: 978-0-578-33543-8 (custom universal)
Printed in the United States of America. Layout by David
Berger. Cover by Don Aguillo.

DEDICATION

Friends do much to support you, share their energy with you, give of their heart, inspire you, and oftentimes, they don't even realize the impact they have. Just their presence in your life is enough. Some people you have only known for almost two decades, but when you think about them, it feels like you've known each other for so much longer.

Thank you, Michael D'Alessio, for being my muse, my friend, and my brother. Much love and appreciation for all you have done for me and been to me.

CONTENTS

ACKNOWLEDGMENTS

Thank you to the following people who have graciously let me make them a part of this story. You all are forever in my heart: Shawn Pinkerton, Matthew Skipworth, Dustin Dorough, Michael D'Alessio, Boston Blake, Brian Patterson, Steven Marin, Jayme Courtman-Bean, Scott Bean, Rusty Trimble and family, Thomas Coffin, Sybrina Augustine, and Brett Rudolph.

Many thanks go to Tyler Wing for suggesting I look into Don Aguillo as a cover artist. I cannot thank you enough, my friend.

I also want to thank Cyn Duby and Charlotte Lee for taking the time to read this labor of love. I appreciate your time and effort.

1 | GRIEF

Z eus' clenched fist hammered the arm of his marble throne, scattering bolts of lightning out into the world, followed by explosive thunder that shook the atoms of the air.

"My Shining One... Watch over him, Gaea! Lest you feel my..." More thunderbolts flew out from Olympos into the mortal world as he lowered his head.

At the news of Apollo being chained, a tenebrous pall had fallen over Olympos, dark clouds churning, roiling, invading the skies. Zeus' throne had taken possession of him, he who had slain the Titan king Kronos; grief became his robes, and a crown of despair weighed upon his brow.

"Neither the spirit of Ares nor the talent of Hephaestos can save you." Zeus' breathy words fell like his tears. "If only the compassion of your twin could free you from this torment, or the whimsy of Dionysos or fleet-footed Hermes."

Again, the heavy hand struck marble, sending bolts flying into the world. A peal of thunder ripped into the beyond.

"All of Gaea will mourn with me."

Gaea

Across the sea-blue globe, not even Poseidon could quell the maelstrom that battered shorelines and disturbed stone or grass or man-made constructs. Buildings cracked, vehicles spiraled away, and people took whatever refuge they could. No corner nor sanctuary could protect frail humanity. News reports from every country and continent that had the means to speak of this dominated the airwaves.

"For WEDJ in Columbus, Ohio, this is Janice Fielding. A storm that seemed to come out of nowhere has dumped more water in the Midwest than any storm seen in the last century. It's not an isolated incident, either. I'm standing downtown well inside the office building of Drobnis Industries, currently operating on a skeleton crew. Business has just about come to a halt as water started seeping onto the production floor through any crack or crevice near windows and doors. The glass-walled lobby is now in ruin, with rising waters running into the elevator shafts. Power has been out for about an hour. Once the portable batteries in our equipment run out of juice, we'll be unable to share any other updates. Emergency crews have been unable to get on the road, and it has been reported that the death toll is rising, but we have not received any confirmed reports. We'll try to share more if and when we can."

"This is Hassan Laayouni. Can someone hear us? I am sending this out on as many radio channels as I can. We are stuck in a desert bunker in Errachidia, Morocco. I have never seen anything like this *simoon* ever. Sandstorms don't get this serious. A few Task Force: Alpha operatives made it through to us with some water and food, but now they're stuck here with us. So many of us didn't make it before we had to close the bunker as the storm approached. We tried to bring in as many bodies as we could, but... we had to leave some out there."

"This is Ira Pincus for WMMI in Miami. Port cities like Miami have had to evacuate as quickly as possible, and all cruise ships close enough to port have been recalled. We have just learned that, unfortunately, the Prince Cruise Line ships Amazonia and Islandia were unable to make it back to port. All told there were 3,000 passengers and crew between both ships who are now considered lost at sea. Dear Lord… What a tragedy… Ships in port have been secured the best they can."

"—are doing what they can to prevent more damage, but workers in the downtown Sacramento area have had to abandon their offices. Military vehicles brought in to evacuate had not fared well, but they are moving as many as possible to shelters inland. Wait… I am now learning that lightning has struck one of the civilian transports, blowing out the tires and leaving them stranded on Interstate 80. Half of those on the transport are teenagers from Middleton Academy. We will report more as soon as we have more information. For KFOG, this is Sam Michaels."

"If anyone can still hear me, this is Dr. Hilda van Nordstrom at the Keller Research Station in Antarctica. Please! We are stationed below ground here with a crew of fifteen scientists, two of whom have succumbed to hypothermia and died while trying to aid a pod of killer whales from one of our rigid buoyant boats. Temperatures, normally around -45°C have dropped to -75°C or below, and we have no idea what's happening. Our instruments tell us that over ten feet of snow have fallen in the past two hours! By the poles, lighting and thunder just don't happen, and external cameras have shown bright blue lightning strikes hitting the surrounding ice. If anyone gets this, please send help!"

"*Scheiße!* Pardon! I am standing inside *Tonhalle Düsseldorf*, and I was almost blown over by the wind. We are seeing record weather here. The Rhine has flooded the streets, and cars are floating by. Wait… *Gott in Himmel*… five bodies… drowned just floated past. This is crazy. *Verrückt!* Where is this coming from? Almost no lights on here in this part of the city. Martina, I will hopefully have more for you as things progress. This is Dieter Zimmermann reporting for NDD 2, Düsseldorf. Are we off the air? *Verdammt!* I don't know how long we—"

⊙═╍═⊙

At the International Atmospheric Center in Gdańsk, Poland, reports had poured in from all over the globe, from the largest news outlets to the smallest radio stations, and record amounts of rain, snow, and even seismographic activity had baffled both meteorologists and seismologists. Padmini Joshi, head of Task Force: Alpha, met with the lead scientists to solve this catastrophe. She tried to call Dan, but cell phone service was spotty if at all. She shot a quick text message to him, but that came back as undeliverable. Even with satellite systems high above the earth, signals couldn't penetrate the storm. With so much chaos going on all around her, she locked herself in an empty office, put her head in her hands, and took advantage of the solitude to think.

Unaware of how much time had passed, she emerged to see the same frenzy as earlier, and one of her finest operatives was on the phone. She used her face to gesture a 'Who's that?', and the man held up a finger. A few minutes later, he made his way to her.

"That was a Russian scientist, Pyotr Markoff, in Varandey, north Russia. He has an outpost that tracks meteorological events with a new algorithm or something. He's narrowed the search parameters of a major part of this event around northeastern Greece. He said he's seen a higher occurrence of electrostatic discharges emanating from there. Any ideas?"

Padmini squeezed around her eyes with one hand, another hand on her hip. Exhaling sharply, she gave him a look.

"Northeastern Greece? How the hell would I even know what's there?" She held up her palm. "Sorry. Didn't mean to snap. This is beyond me. It's almost like something otherworldly is at work here. How can the entire world be experiencing storms?"

From across the room, another operative waved to get her attention. When she saw him, he mouthed the name 'Dan Fairmont'. She snatched the phone from him. The operative saw her face change from intently listening to wide-eyed to exasperated. She handed the phone back to him.

"Well? What did he say?"

With pale disbelief and a furrowed brow, she sighed. "Well. I was right. I don't know how, but I was. It *is* otherworldly. According to Dan Fairmont, this is caused by Zeus."

The operative's confusion prevented him from responding.

Padmini put her hand on his shoulder. "It would seem the king of the Olympeian gods? Dan's family?" That inquisitive lilt when she finished conveyed her own disbelief.

"So, what do we do?"

"Nothing." She threw up her hands. "Absolutely nothing. Dan said he'd take care of it, but I don't even know how that's even possible."

"Task Force: Gaea sure is peculiar." He scratched his head and returned to his desk.

◦━━✦━━◦

Dan paced around the Task Force: Gaea office conference room and leaned over the table, shaking his head. With every crack of thunder, without moving his head, he gave side-eye toward the windows. Cascading rain blocked the city view, and the charcoal gray clouds put a malevolent cast over the city. Like a cave, the room closed in around him, both hiding him from the world and drawing a focus to his own grief, the grief that mirrored his grandfather's.

"Dad, don't know if you can hear me. You once told me that you came to the mortal world to blend in. Being among people made you feel more like yourself. How ironic is it that now your absence has such a profound effect on the entire world? Zeus is doing what he does best, it seems. He wants the world to mourn along with him. And humanity has no real idea who you are too. Funny."

Vibrating on the table, Dan's phone moved around, and Aleta's picture popped onto the screen.

"What's up?"

"I have an idea on how to stop this. You at the office?"

"Are you at BioCorps?"

As soon as she nodded, he opened a sword portal to where she was.

"What's this idea?" His expression matched the pale ambient lighting through the rain.

Aleta smiled. "Oh, I think you're going to like this."

Olympos

"Have you spoken to him, my queen? Does he wish to destroy us all?"

Hera peered out at the tumultuous skies from the edge of the Hall of Prophecy, a lesser-used chamber on the other side of the mountain. The winds of Zeus' rage dared to move her red wavy hair, and lightning shimmered on her crown.

"My queen?"

"Aye, Aphrodite. We had words. Rather, I spoke, and he sulked."

The goddess of love stood with her sovereign, and this time, the air moved her incomparable blond locks as well. Like the living darkness itself, the clouds tumbled, striated with electricity.

"Poor Leto," Aphrodite uttered before she realized with whom she stood. "My apologies, my queen." She bowed her head.

"It is all right. Leto is still his mother. Besides, she and I have reconciled. What happened in the past cannot be held against her, especially with Zeus' roaming eye."

Aphrodite raised her eyebrows, and her eyes reflected the lightning beyond. "Hmm."

Hera laughed to herself. "That being said, you will appreciate this. When Zeus and I were mortal, I had thought he would have at least looked at other women but being the elderly Rakurai Saro had softened his desire. Well, for others, anyway. As Kujaku, I saw a side of him that I had not seen in a long time." She blushed a little.

Hera moved to the scrying pool, bracing herself on the stone rim.

"And now, as I see my husband grieving as if his son were dead, I would do whatever I could to help him. I am powerless to do anything, *anything*, Aphrodite. I must watch him consumed with so much remorse."

"My queen." A different voice came from behind her. "Wisdom knows there is nothing *to* do. My father allows himself to suffer."

"Aye, Athene. My husband feels the guilt of not stopping Python. We had all dismissed him as a minor threat since Apollo had dealt with him once before."

With Hermes' arrival, the others turned toward him as if he had news. His dour composure under his winged helmet revealed otherwise. Aphrodite extended a hand to him. His eyes conveyed to her how impotent that gesture truly was. An offering of love, no matter from whom, would not allay his own guilt.

"My heart is heavy as well." His voice had risen to uncomfortable levels. "But I do not sit on my throne and throw a tantrum that comes close to tearing Gaea apart. We stand here, at the farthest part of Olympos, and we share our melancholy as if it were the day's news? What purpose does this serve?"

"Silence! You will hold your tongue, messenger, or I will remove it from your ill-mannered mouth." Hera's eyes turned a bright red and smoldered a little.

Hermes straightened up and tightened his jaw as well as his grip on his caduceus. Even the snakes hissed.

"As *queen* of Olympos, you should be able to manage my father's rages. You've had millennia of experiences to know how to. Do not *dare* threaten me." He pointed his staff at her. "You apparently are just as impotent as we all are."

In a bright flash, he was gone.

2 | UNBOUND

I knew you would come."

A tall, lean man wearing a white chiton and no sandals sat by the fire, a smile spreading across his bearded face. He gestured for Danelos to sit.

"I figured. Doesn't your name mean 'forethought'? Humanity is in peril, Prometheos. You who created mankind surely have a stake in its survival." Danelos sat cross-legged opposite who he'd come to see. The Titan, even sitting, was taller than his guest, and he handed his friend a stone cup of wine.

Reddish-brown rock made up the cave, and the fire brought out more of the richer tones. Deep within the mountain, they could barely hear the storm that raged outside, something that was probably by design by he who built this refuge.

"I do not have the power to go up against Zeus while he rages. It would be a fool's errand." Prometheos tossed a twig into the flames and sipped his cup.

"You're his first cousin, right? Iapetus and Kronos were brothers. Surely, that puts you on par with my grandfather."

The Titan poked the flames with another stick, arranging the wood for the best fire. His deep, brown eyes reflected the oranges and reds, giving them an electric quality.

"Ah, that is a common misconception. 'Tis true that we are in the same line. However, when Zeus took Olympos, the mountain spirit infused him with greater power than all the gods. Even now, in this twilight of Olympos, his wrath wreaks havoc."

"He will *destroy* humanity. Look, I'm upset about my father's circumstances, but you don't see me taking it out on the rest of the world. Human lives will end because they can't stand up to the storm that Zeus brings. Innocent people will die, for nothing. They also don't understand why the storms come."

Prometheos stared off. "Hades can—"

"No, he can't. Once a soul enters the underworld, it's lost. The moment Hermes' staff releases it from the body, it must go."

"Eurydice?" The Titan smirked.

"You saw how well that worked out for Orpheos. It was only because of his *voice* that Hades relented. Come on, Prometheos. There must be something you can do. *You* are the father of mankind. Protect it. My friends and I are only four. And don't think I've forgotten about your 'twilight of Olympos' comment."

"You know the critics will say it is just another *deus ex machina*, yes? One more god stepping in to help?"

Danelos laughed and shook his head. "I don't give a damn about critics. The only one who can counter Zeus' power is someone on his level. You're the only one I know. His siblings won't stand up to him."

A niche carved in the back wall of the cave housed a small stone statue of a man about a foot tall. On one side of this niche was a burning iron torch. Prometheos lifted the statue out with both hands, cradling it like a newborn.

"This was the first statue of man I ever made."

Danelos was aghast seeing the intricate musculature and detail. If he wasn't sure it was stone, he would have thought it was breathing. "That… That looks like something Phidias himself would have sculpted."

Laughing, the Titan handed the statue to him.

"Who do you think inspired him? I knew if mankind were to exist, it would have to be physical beauty coupled with reason. You can thank your father for that. And that fire"—he pointed to the torch—"was the actual fire I left with humanity."

Danelos would swear he felt warmth from the statue as if it were in suspended animation, waiting to be released to exist in the world. He returned it to its creator.

"You remember what happened with the last Great Flood? That was Zeus punishing mankind for its evils. While it may be flawed, humanity has been left to its own devices for a long time.

Zeus doesn't care enough to wash it away again. Surely, there must be *something* you can do."

Before putting the statue back in its wall niche, Prometheos let his eyes rest on it for a moment. As soon as it was standing proudly again, Danelos thought he saw its chest rise and fall ever so slightly, but he convinced himself it was a trick of the torchlight.

"Perhaps… Perhaps there *is* something. As you say, my name does mean 'foresight'. I cannot protect humanity from the raging storm itself, nor can I protect Gaea, but I can augment humanity's ability to prepare for what is coming. Until the tempests abate, they can use that heightened awareness to seek shelter and protect themselves. They shall have my cunning and craft for however long Zeus' tantrum lasts."

With that pronouncement, Prometheos turned his gaze back to the statue and his eyes glowed red. In turn, the eyes of the statue did, and thus was set in motion the gift from he who stole fire from Olympos to gift mankind.

"It seems, yet again, I defy the Olympeian king to aid humankind against the folly of the gods."

Danelos smiled. "I knew you would think of something. Your power in this world is not what it used to be, but you have always been on the side of mortals."

Prometheos poured two more cups of wine, and they drank to mortality. The Titan wished he could do more. Opening a portal home, Danelos stepped through leaving humankind's benefactor to his solitude. Prometheos approached the entrance to his cave where the wind and storm ravaged the world.

"One would think your time as a mortal would have taught you more about compassion, Zeus. Your melancholy and selfishness may in fact destroy the world, and I fear there will be no Deucalion and Pyrrha to replenish those lost."

The son of Iapetos and Klymene returned to his fire.

3 | THE LESSON

In the early days of Olympos

Chiron, the centaur, normally had patience beyond measure, but even though the son of Zeus was young by immortal standards, he had the same arrogance as his father. Having taken to the bow when he saw his sister Artemis use it, Apollo's playful sibling rivalry sparked within him a desire to be the best archer he could be, but his youth and inexperience, coupled with his haughtiness and lack of wisdom, could frustrate even Chiron who had trained heroes such as Theseus, Heracles, and Achilles.

"Apollo, hold the bow as I showed you. Closer to your ear. Keep your left arm straight." He scraped his front hoof on the ground and swished his braided tail.

"I *am* keeping it straight," Apollo huffed. When his fingers freed the string, the arrow whistled across the field until it struck its intended target, although it missed the bullseye by a few inches to the left. "Gah! This is maddening! I am doing everything you have told me to do. How am I still missing the target? I am the son of Zeus. Should I not be able to do this by my very nature?"

The centaur chuckled to himself. "Indeed, you should, child, but you are letting your attitude guide the *bow* instead of letting the bow guide your *attitude*."

Apollo tried again, and this time, the arrow flew off a little to the right. He tightened his grip on the bow and, growling, set it aflame with a thought. Ashes of oak fell in a small pile at his feet.

Chiron folded his arms and his dark expression made Apollo cast his eyes to the ground. He didn't like to disappoint his mentor, and when he knew he had, he slumped down by a tree, wrapping his arms around his knees.

"What is wrong with me, Chiron? Artemis can use her bow so easily. I cannot even hit a simple target. Father will be ashamed of me."

Chiron stepped beneath the tree next to his charge who looked to be about ten. He tapped Apollo with his hoof.

"You rely on what you expect to be true rather than what you know in your heart to be true."

The young god looked up, his brow furrowing.

"In other words, you think because you are an Olympeian that you were born perfect. In reality—"

Apollo jumped up. "I am the son of Zeus! I should not have to *practice* how to do anything." Before he could vanish in a tantrum, Chiron's eyes became an iridescent green, and vines from the tree bound Apollo to it.

"What? How *dare* you—"

"Silence!" His voice shook the air. "Your father bade me guide you, Phoebos, and that is precisely what I intend to do. Now, reassemble your bow, and take an archer's stance. Now."

As the vines receded, the godling glared at his mentor, but Chiron's face didn't change. Apollo continued to bore into the centaur with a fiery gaze, but when he realized he wouldn't win, he conceded.

"Very well." He sighed hard. Opening his left palm, he conjured the bow back from its ashen pile.

"Now, take your stance. This time, when you aim, do not aim directly at your target. Aim just a little off."

Apollo looked back and raised an eyebrow.

"Trust me, child."

Zeus' son aimed the arrow directly at the center and seemed to think for a moment before poking his tongue through his lips as he let the shaft fly. As before, the arrow struck the target, but it didn't hit the bullseye. This time, it was Chiron whose ire flared.

"When you are ready to learn, I will be here, but until then, do not waste my time!"

Galloping off, Chiron didn't look back. Apollo seethed, but before he would take out his frustration on the bow, with clenched fists, he vanished in a burst of light. When he appeared, he was uphill from where Artemis was honing her own archery skills. He had merely wished to vent about the centaur, but he decided to watch instead. Even though they were the same age, she stood taller and with more intent. She *commanded* her bow. Nocking the bow, Artemis released it in one seamless motion. Each time, the arrow struck dead center. Each time. He moved to where he was standing directly behind her to see what she saw. Her stance was different from his, and she smirked. After watching her shoot a half dozen arrows, he shook his head.

Chiron was right, he thought.

He returned to his target, bow in hand. Remembering how Artemis stood, Apollo shifted his footing. This time, when he aimed, he turned a little. As he felt the string slide against his fingertips when he released the shaft, he held his immortal breath. The faint whistling of the fletching cut through the air, and when the arrowhead struck, the dull thud echoed in his ears. Even from that distance, he knew the arrow had hit its target, as before, but this time, it was just about dead center. Apollo nodded, smiling. Not wanting it to be a fluke, he proceeded to empty the quiver, and out of twelve arrows, ten hit bull's eyes. By the end of the second quiver, he had hit the center each time. He had just conjured a third quiver when a familiar face appeared. Chiron was under the tree and nodded.

"Chiron… Why does that work? I mean, it shouldn't."

The old centaur smiled. "It is called the archer's paradox."

Apollo stepped up to his mentor, unable to look him in the eye. "Chiron… I…"

"I understand, my boy. No apology needed. I am just happy that you now understand."

"I am starting to, Chiron. I have much to learn, but I am glad to have you as my mentor. You deserve better than my outbursts. Now, leave me. I have to practice." Apollo's stern expression bore the slightest smile.

Genuflecting, the noble teacher cantered off. Down the dusty road, a young goddess leaned against a cypress sipping nectar from a chalice.

"Did it work?" She opened her hand, and the cup dissolved into golden dust, whisked away by the breeze.

"Indeed. I knew he would seek you out. Your brother is nothing if he is not predictable. Did you speak with him?"

"No, but I could feel him behind me, watching. Chiron, why is my brother so stubborn?" Artemis laughed. "If he would simply listen—"

"I fear he takes after your father. You, however, are more your mother's child."

"That is why *I* am Father's favorite."

Artemis slung the bow over her shoulder with her quiver. Waving goodbye to her teacher, she headed toward Apollo's location. He was still emptying quiver after quiver into the target, and she noticed his satisfaction grew with each shaft hitting its target accordingly. Shaking her head and smiling, she vanished in a burst of leaves. Apollo looked over his shoulder and smirked.

"I hope you saw, dear sister, that I will master this archer's paradox."

With that, he let another arrow fly.

◦══✦══◦

Once he satisfied this desire, Apollo made his bow vanish before disappearing himself only to reappear in the main hall of Olympos. He was making his way to his chamber when his father spoke his name, and he answered the summons to the Hall of Tribunals just within the door.

"My son, sit with me." Zeus, at the top of the dais, patted the arm of his throne.

Bounding a few steps at a time, Apollo sat precisely where his father wanted him to be. The young god's smile illuminated his entire face and that of the king of gods.

"I hear from Chiron that you excel in your bow. Perhaps, later, you will show me what you have learned. It pleases me to hear of your successes."

Nodding, Apollo blushed. Zeus lingered on his son's face for a bit before his silver beard spread with a smile.

"Brothers and sisters you have many, and I do see so much in each that I admire. Ares has his strength of spirit. Hephaestos, his creative gifts. Your twin Artemis, her compassion for all creatures great and small." He chuckled. "Dionysos and Hermes, their... whimsical way. But, you"—Zeus patted his son's arm— "you have the light within you that radiates. You are the Phoebos, the Shining One."

The youth's face again reddened, and he leaned against his father's shoulder, staring out at the array of thrones surrounding Hesteia's fire ring within which glowed orange embers.

Zeus, too, stared out, beyond the columns into the wispy clouds that floated by. The essence of lilac and rose perfumed the breezes while father and son remained in silence. After a few moments with only the wind, in a soft voice, Zeus put the words, "I do cherish you, my son," out into the world.

4 | HOUSE OF THE RISING SUN

The Isle of Helios

Sunrise was late for the first time since creation.

On the first morning after Apollo lay chained inside Gaea's sacred vault, the chariot had not left the Island of the Sun to the East. Even though Helios now rode the chariot, after Apollo returned it to him when the son of Zeus married Alkinoë, the horses of the sun chariot had a kinship with their former driver. They understood the change in the cosmos, and their unease prevented their departure into the world. The bucking and frenzied whinnies in the stables reached Helios' ear, but when he investigated, the horses had broken free and flew rabidly above.

"Easy, Lampos! Asterope, calm, calm! Come down!" Helios addressed two of the five horses soaring over the field of Demeter from which they grazed, and then luminous Actaeon whinnied behind him, still on the ground. "Be still now. I need you to settle down."

Flashes in the sky, way in the distance, told Helios that the world beyond endured some great chaos by Zeus' hand. The horses could not be allowed to fly beyond the boundary of the island. He recalled Phaeton's ill-fated actions and knew the earth and mortality would suffer egregious harm. Helios had remained aloof from the world of Man his entire existence, but he knew how much mortals meant to Apollo especially, so he needed to regain control of the horses before irrevocable damage would be done. With Zeus ravaging Gaea, Helios feared the Earth Mother could only withstand so much. Calling to the horses had no effect; they simply were too distraught to listen. When Zeus and the gods defeated Kronos and his brethren and imprisoned them, the other Titans not involved in the Titanomachia—the Great War—were left to themselves, but their power had diminished. Helios' control would have to take another form.

Using a lariat made from Atlas' hair, Helios ensnared the thundering Bronte, the most agitated, and pulled him down. Not even the fiery hide of the steed could burn through that rope. Torch-like Lampos, the youngest and most whimsical, put up quite a fight, but eventually found himself roped with his brother. Starry-eyed Asterope came in on his own, seeing Helios preparing to rope him, but that left burning Phlegon and fiery red Æthion. The last two, neighing their frustrations, eluded Helios' attempts at capture. Helios held a golden apple aloft in each hand, and he patiently stood as the two steeds circled above, gradually getting closer. Apples from the garden of the Hesperides, a treat, had been known to lure the horses in the past. As soon as Æthion came close enough, Helios snatched his bridle and pulled him down. Seeing all of his brethren caught, Phlegon acquiesced but made Helios walk to him.

The Titan led them all back to their stalls. They were in no condition to drive just yet.

"Æthion, Phlegon, I am ashamed that you would join your brothers. You are the eldest. Heed me, all of you. Yes, your former master Apollo is bound within Gaea. It pains me as well."

Bronte started to whinny once more. A harsh look from Helios silenced him.

"Yes, he is bound, but that is for the safety of the world. Remember Phaeton. His rash behavior caused the very deserts to form. He could not guide you. Your antics have already delayed sunrise, and to be sure, the mortal world may feel it a bad omen, although Zeus' tempest may hide the sun's absence for a bit. Apollo trusts you to do your duty. I do as well."

He walked by each stall, giving each horse a gentle scratch or rub.

"Apollo's sons and their friends will make this right. I have faith in them, and you should too. Now, are you ready to usher in a new day, despite the sky?"

Each horse tossed his head up and down, scraping a hoof along the ground.

"Very well. You know your positions. Let us depart!" He opened the stalls, following them to the chariot, hearing a few random whinnies as he attached them.

Mortals and gods alike might question the tardiness of the dawn, and Eos herself would ask Helios about the delay, but the day would progress, and with it, new hope and possibilities for bringing Apollo back from the realm of madness.

5 | DESCENT INTO PSYCHOSIS

W rithing against the stone and pulling against the Earth-steel chains that bound him to Gaea, Apollo grunted and bellowed, his unintelligible mutterings absorbed into the living dark. A maternal voice made him respond with a glint of recognition, but his fractured mind could not reconcile whose voice he heard.

"*Phoebos Apollo, know that I am with you. Feel the warmth of my embrace. Rest upon my bosom, son of Leto. I had abandoned you, but now I am here. For all time, I am here…*"

Foamy spittle sprayed from his lips as he lurched to an up-right position, yanking against his confinement over and over again. His eyes, open and erratic, saw no detail of his containment, only light and shadow, but that was due to his Olympeian heritage. Any mortal in Gaea's adyton would see only blackness. Even the *Maniae*, the daimones of insanity, would keep their distance from him for fear that his frenzy would eclipse their own.

"*Be at ease, Apollo, be at ease. Those chains protect not only the mortal and immortal realms from your addled state, but they protect you as well.*"

Flashes of varied memories played in his mind, fragments of discontinuous images, emotional shrapnel left behind after Python's venom dissolved the tenuous barrier between Apollo's memories of the world in which he currently lived and those memories from a timeline known only to him and his son Danelos.

A remembrance bubbled forth as so many had before—a sun-drenched day when he saved an Arkadeian man from falling off a horse. The flashback to the man's grateful tears made Apollo smile, and he reached his manacled hands out—but another image came into focus where the same day occurred—and Apollo watched as the horse bucked, tossing the man to the ground. The sun god winced at the sound of neck bones snapping, reliving the pangs of shock and grief all over again as one of his own subjects died right before him. But which memory was true? Both couldn't have happened.

They had—to *him*.

A scream erupted from Apollo, one that in a normal cavern might have brought the stony walls down around him. He brought his knees to his chest, wrapping them with chained arms, and shrieked. Then, he stopped, remembering a spring morning where light drizzle coated everything, and the sounds of children playing in the palace garden echoed. He stood with Alkinoë, his hand in hers, from a balcony that overlooked the garden, both smiling at the sight of innocence: children from Tegea had come to play there at the queen's desire. She so enjoyed the sound of young ones scampering about. Giggles and songs clung to the air like perfume, and the dozen or so little ones hid among the shrubbery or collected petals that had fallen. He felt the queen squeeze his hand and looked over at the woman who had captured his heart. Locking her eyes to his, she placed his hand on her belly. At first, Apollo didn't know why, but then—a kick. Then, another. The third time made them both giggle just like the children playing beneath them. He took her hands in his and brought them to his lips, his eyes and hers sharing the love they had for each other.

In the dark of Gaea, Apollo wept again, smiling, reaching to caress the phantom of his wife's face locked forever in his mind. Again the memory shifted, and the day had turned to night. Both he and his wife sat in the throne room watching a performance of the royal dancers. Men and women, clad in a panoply of colors, glided across the marble floor while musicians played in the background. Lyre and flute joined drumbeats, constructing a musical milieu for the troupe gifted by Terpsichore, Mnemosyne's daughter of the dance. Agile bodies leaped and twirled, engaging in acrobatics, while a royal audience of ambassadors sat mesmerized. Alkinoë's eyes followed their movements, her smile faint so as not to distract her from the entertainment. Apollo glanced over and spotted the faintest wince, and the smile flattened, but only for a moment. Music and dance continued, and when he looked again at his wife, she twitched. When she saw him looking over, tears trickled down her face as she took his hand and placed it on her belly. At first, Apollo felt nothing more than the drumbeats reverberating through the floor, but when the music paused, there it was—a kick. They joined hands, their smiles augmented by the knowledge that soon, an heir would arrive, and they would have more reason to celebrate.

Curled in a fetal position, Apollo cried more, this time because he knew that both memories were laced with joy: the first, a recollection of Demetrios—later to be Danelos; the latter, the moment when he knew of Kidemonas—later to be Brandon. In the former timeline, he had but one son; in the current, he had two. *That* mystery, unlike so many others, he could wrap his mind around.

Peace washed over him, a tide of calm, and his tears ceased; his mind fell silent. He had no conscious thought, but something inside told him that the bombardment of memory would begin again, as it had since his arrival in Gaea's inner sanctum.

Even within the center of the Earth, a rumbling vibrated all around and made its way to him. Mother Earth knew all too well what that was, and—for the first time in a long while—feared that its source would be the undoing of the cosmos.

In the mortal world above, a sign of the shattered order came not just from the storms that mauled the Earth's surface, but also from the murders of crows that darkened every tree and roofline, squawking their lament. Sacred to Apollo, they added one more layer of cacophony, a Hitchcockian fear come to life for many, although these crows bore no malice to humanity.

6 | A HEART'S PLEA

Nothing would deter Alkinoë from her path, not even the storm that raged all around her. This place she had traveled far to see would be her best chance of seeking answers, on receiving the wisdom she yearned for. Marching through puddles along the path to the shrine did not deter or slow her, and neither did the scaffolding that circumscribed this holiest of places. With such a torrent, one that even the gods hadn't seen in millennia, no guards prevented anyone from entering what remained of the temple to Athene, the Parthenon.

Sodden yet steadfast, she made her way toward the center of the shrine where the statue of the goddess used to stand, knelt on the raw marble, and prayed.

"Daughter of Prudence, hear my plea. I kneel before you, in this holiest of places devoted to your grace, and ask for guidance."

As she spoke, rain cascaded down her face, running off her chin in a steady stream. Her words sputtered out into the tortured air, the percussive thunder rolling around as if it had become an angry, sentient being. Lightning illuminated the dark, gray clouds from within.

"*Please*, Athene. Please. I humble myself before you, bring myself to you in *this*." She raised her hands to the sky. "Perhaps it would be better if I were struck down here by the storm's rage so that I would not have to endure my pain."

The queen of Arkadeia slumped over, head in her hands. Then, she sat upright, her face to the sky.

"Goddess! What more must I do to earn an audience with you? Do you fear your father's temper so much that you would forsake me?" She raised both clenched fists as well as her voice.

Rain pelted her and collected in dancing pools at the base of the Parthenon. Weeks had passed since Apollo's imprisonment, insufferable weeks since she had last seen her husband. After meeting with Dionysos shortly after Apollo's fight with Python, she despaired because none of the other gods would respond to her pleas. Was it because of impotence? Was it because they felt ashamed? She had done everything she could to reach out to Olympos, even asking Danelos to take her there, but he wouldn't risk the wrath of Zeus, not when he mourned. She didn't fear the king of the gods. Had she still had her army in Arkadeia, she would have stormed Olympos if need be to get what she wanted. Left to her own, Alkinoë thought she would find answers in the one place she had always done so, but it seemed that even the goddess of wisdom herself had abandoned her.

"So, this is how it is," she muttered. "My husband has been denied to me. My son will not help me. And now, you have forsaken me. So be it."

By the time she reached the taxi, the driver had fallen asleep, but when she slammed the door, he jumped up.

"To the airport."

He saw her dripping in the back seat and was about to ask her something, but her expression in the rearview mirror made him think better of it. She had paid him well for his time, so he didn't see a reason to press his luck. Alkinoë didn't look back at the temple. Rather, she looked inward, but her thoughts brought her no comfort.

Olympos

On a white marble balustrade overlooking mortality, Athene stared down into the clouds, a white owl perched on her shoulder. A goddess approached, and the owl vanished into the sky.

"She has always devoted herself to you, Athene. Why did you forsake her?"

"Because, Aphrodite, what Alkinoë needs to do, she must do herself. I know what she would ask of me, and I am unable to help her."

"Solace, sister. She sought comfort from you, and I fear your abandonment will leave an indelible mark on her soul."

"Tread lightly." Athene's gray eyes remained on the clouds. "If there was anything that I learned from my time on Earth was that sometimes we need to find the answers within ourselves for them to motivate us to act. If I lose her because of my silence, then it is the will of the Fates."

In a mist, Athene departed, leaving Aphrodite to stare down at the mortal world.

"I know better than to defy you, dear sister, but I hope you have not made a grievous error."

1000 B.C.E., Mount Parnassus, Greece

Rushing through the stone courtyard of the house on the side of the mountain, a sparrow flew into the second floor gynaeceum, the part of the house reserved for women, and then transformed into a woman who, winded and crying, then fell onto the couch. One handmaiden comforted her, instructing another to let the woman's husband know she had returned. Once the woman had settled, she composed herself and found her husband in their bedchamber.

"Mestra, what's wrong?" He cradled her face, and then his expression soured. "It happened again?"

She nodded, pressing his hands against her cheeks. He kissed her forehead, and then pulled her close.

"I've told you before. People don't accept what they can't understand. I know you try to entertain the children by becoming animals, but mortals aren't used to being around people like you and me."

Mestra stepped back and laughed, wiping her tears. She pulled her hair back into its ivory clip.

"Yes, but *you're* the one who keeps getting into mischief. Didn't you impersonate the magistrate so you could manipulate—"

He smiled. "But that's different! You know why I do that. I have to remain vigilant."

She folded her arms playfully and pouted. Stepping behind her, he put his arms around her body, resting his head on her shoulder. His explanation played as it always did: atop this mountain, the Muses met, and when they gathered, *he* was sure to follow, with his penchant for music and dance. The only way to keep watch was to be other people, things, anything that could surveil the surrounding area. She turned in his arms, placing her hands on his shoulders.

"But, dearest, what do you hope to accomplish by all this surveillance? When you *do* see him, what's next? Are you going to spend the rest of your days watching him?"

He sighed, looking off. "I don't know yet."

Mestra stepped back, placing her hands atop one another on her belly.

"What happens when… when we have a mouth to feed, will you be off in the woods or scaling the mountain's highest crags? Can I… can *we* depend on you?"

His eyes widened, and he pressed a hand to his lips. Kneeling before her, he kissed her hands and then turned to press his cheek against her.

"I-I didn't know. Should you be shapeshifting in your condition? Is it okay with…?"

Her cheeks reddened. "It's fine. We're fine. But, my love, this obsession of yours… surely you must know that once he or she is born, you are needed here. I have servants, but there is no replacement for a father's attention and love."

As he stood, his face lost all expression. He kissed her cheek and left the room. Mestra sat on the edge of the bed and sighed, rubbing her belly.

7 | REINING IN THE STORM

Thrashed by hammering rain and buffeted by gale-force winds on the roof of the Task Force Division building, the Gaea team stood both slack-jawed and unsettled. Satellite transmissions had picked up the meteorological disturbance starting in northern Greece and radiating outward. Darkened masses of clouds had marched across the Atlantic like a phalanx, encroaching outward with full force. Dan and the others knew exactly when this began, and it would fall to them to stop it. Turning to his teammates, Dan's expression conveyed his thoughts: but, to stop this, they had to stop Zeus. Humanity would have to use Prometheos' gift to preserve their own lives. As the rain ran down Thyroros' blade, Dan gazed one more time toward the Atlantic before slicing a wide arc to the place he knew they had to go.

Sensing inhabitants, the Olympeian torches ignited, revealing a stony chamber within which sat a massive pool of viscous, sentient liquid. The ring of the pool shuddered with each rumbling, the watery substance rippling.

"This is the closest we should get to Zeus until we figure out a plan. We can't subdue him, not with the power we have. I'm open to suggestions. Hera?"

Sarah spun the ring on her finger.

"I doubt she'll go up against her own husband, even under these circumstances." She wrung out her hair and shook it out.

"For that matter, what god *would* go up against the king of all Olympos?"

Aleta wiped water from her face. "Can't we get the other gods to help?"

Arms crossed, Brandon narrowed his brow. "We can try to appeal to the other gods, but in the meantime, why not see if they'll help protect Gaea?"

"How?" Dan leaned on the rim of the scrying pool. "It would take the full pantheon to do that. The gods aren't as strong as they used to be. That's why *we're* here. Like it or not, it's up to us... somehow. Prometheos was a fluke."

Sarah paced around the pool, sliding her hand along the smooth stone. "Does he... have any weaknesses?"

Brandon sighed. "Tharmakondios. It *is* called 'the Bane of Zeus' for a reason."

Shooting him a scowl, Dan then relented, shaking his head. "I don't even know where we'd find that, and we don't have time to look. We need a more immediate plan."

A crack like a bomb detonating reinforced the urgency. They ruminated until Sarah suggested they just try to talk him down and volunteered herself. Brandon added that—no offense to Sarah—they would need a backup plan, or five, in case that didn't work. Snatching Brandon by the arm, Sarah marched toward the throne room while Dan and Aleta continued to strategize.

The majestic halls of Mount Olympos, empty of its inhabitants—presumably because they were as far from the mountain as possible—echoed with the endless, deafening clamor. Flashes of lightning cast misshapen shadows of statuary onto the marble walls, and even the hanging torches remained unlit as if the fire itself feared Zeus' wrath. By the time Brandon and Sarah reached the throne room, the winds whipped around while the dagger-like rain struck everything. The entry lay behind the thrones of Zeus and Hera, and when Sarah caught her first glimpse of Olympos' sovereign, she gasped. Electricity flared from the corners of his eyes. His fist pounded the arm of his marble chair, sending errant bolts out into the world below. He radiated raw power. She looked back to Brandon, his eyes fixed on his grandfather, who then nodded for her to advance, clenching and unclenching his fists. Taking a deep breath, she called her quarters, moving her mouth to form the sacred words. Brandon squeezed her shoulder, and she squeezed his hand in response. At the base of the dais leading up to Zeus' throne, she opened her palms, a gesture of peace. The winds didn't dare move a hair on his head, but her hair flew about.

"Lord Zeus! Please! Stop this." Her voice barely made it above the din. "I know you're grieving. But floods are threatening cities. Power outages are putting lives at risk. You once lived on Earth, among mortals. Rakurai Saro spent a *year* there."

Olympos' king remained unmoved. Sarah didn't have the depth of a connection with him, unlike Dan and Brandon or even Aleta. He had no reason to listen to her. This was like a mosquito trying to get the attention of an elephant.

"I feel so helpless. If I push him, he could end me with a thought," she muttered. "If I don't try, though…"

She pressed her palms together, lacing her fingers, lowered her head, and closed her eyes. When she lifted her head, her eyes had turned white, and her stature straightened. Extending her arms outward at her sides, in one swift move, she clenched her fists and swung them together in front of her. A wall of air surrounded her, and her hair settled. She spoke with the four layered voices of the Tetrastoikheia.

"Cease this, son of Kronos, or be bound."

Zeus didn't even acknowledge her but slammed his fist down once more.

Opening her palms upward, she summoned fire from the torches struggling to stay lit and, thrusting her hands forward, she created a flaming ring and surrounded Zeus with it, tightening it until his arms were bound against him.

"Do not defy the Tetrastoikheia!"

With her hands again clenched, two of the massive, marble thrones behind her ripped free from the floor and deconstructed into chunks that she manipulated to bind his arms to the sides of his throne. Zeus flexed against his restraints, grunting, but the binding held. With every attempt, the throne itself moved but remained intact.

"By Thalassa, by Khaos, by Hesteia, and by Gaea, we bind you. Water, air, fire, and earth, hold fast this son of Titans. Contain the power of the raging storm."

The incantation seemed to be working, and despite his best efforts, Zeus could not free himself. The voices continued as the throne room vibrated both from his attempts to break his bonds and the surrounding thunder.

"Be at ease. Quell thy heart. Find the peace that will ground you."

Brandon's mouth dropped. His eyes widened at her power, and the hint of a smile grew.

"Keep it up, Sarah! It's working!"

Then, Zeus stopped struggling. Sarah knew better than to relent at all, despite what seemed to be his acquiescence. Before she could anticipate what would happen, Zeus threw his head back and screamed. In one swift maneuver, he clenched his fists and pulled them free. Sarah committed once more to reweave the containment, but he ripped the fiery ring from around his body and stood. Glaring down at her, Zeus snapped on one hand. The wall of air around her fell. She didn't have time to reconstruct it when winds rushed past Zeus and flung her across the throne room toward the edge, and then she would plummet from the Olympeian mountain to the earthly one.

In centaur form, Brandon galloped as fast as he could. Readying his bow, he passed the throne of Demeter, turned, and shot an arrow with a rope attached to the stone. With a sweeping motion, he snatched Sarah out of the air before she went over the edge, but his hooves couldn't stop on the smooth floor. He lost his footing and slipped, Sarah in one arm, the rope in the other hand. His hind legs dangled over the edge, and he tried to gain any kind of purchase on the stone. It was no use. With the weight of his equine body and Sarah's, there was just too much inertia, and they both fell. Just then, a black cord caught Brandon around both arms. Resuming human form lessened the weight, and he looked up to see Dan gripping the rope with both hands. Making a large arc, Aleta swooped around and took Sarah's body. Brandon climbed the rope to reach the outstretched arm of his brother. Without stopping, Aleta flew back to the scrying chamber. As soon as Brandon was safe, both brothers managed to leave the throne room unscathed. Zeus had not wanted to battle and simply returned to his grief-stricken state, not bothering with them at all.

Lying unconscious on the floor of the scrying room, Sarah had grown pale from expending all that power. Aleta checked her vitals and examined her body for any wounds. As he stared at his teammate and friend, Brandon's eyes turned red. Dan turned to ask him something, but Brandon had left the room.

At the bottom of the dais, Brandon stopped. Taking a deep breath, he controlled his exhale and the amulet's peridot and emerald gemstones of Taurus and Leo glowed. With a leonine growl, he pounded the stairs, shaking the dais. Zeus didn't flinch. Brandon continued this a few times, but his grandfather remained uninterested.

"So much for the vaunted Zeus, lord of all Olympos, the killer of Kronos and vanquisher of Titans. When all of humanity is gone, you'll have no one to worship you at all. Is that what you want? You could help heal your son… my father… but you'd rather throw a childish tantrum!"

He raised his arms to bring them down again when a hand restrained him.

"No, Dan. Let me go!" Despite his best efforts, he couldn't free himself from his brother's grip.

"Brandon. Brandon! You're getting nowhere. His power is fueling your own rage. Stand down."

With a tug, Brandon extricated himself and glared at his brother before descending the dais. Dan took a few more steps up toward Zeus. He had never known his grandfather to exhibit such emotion before, even in the stories told of his younger days when he was more strategic, more prudent. When Dan returned to the scrying pool, Sarah had regained consciousness and sat up against the edge of the pool. Brandon, his arms folded, stood in the dark corner. His hard exhales could be heard through the rumbles all around.

"You do remember that *reason* itself is broken, yes? Apollo's absence has weakened it. That's why Zeus does this. It's not just grief. He knows his son isn't dead." Dan stared into the pool. "Living as a mortal exposed him to emotions that he had never felt before. They're more accessible now."

"Maybe if we do a multi-pronged assault, we—" Brandon stepped forward.

"Listen to yourself, Brandon. Assault Zeus? Do you have a death wish? He almost killed Sarah. I think the only thing that held him back is that he didn't *want* to kill her. Did you notice that he didn't do anything once you two were both safe? He doesn't care about anything except his own grief."

He went face to face with his brother.

"We don't have the power to stop him. This isn't some dragon or Gorgon. Even at our best… it wouldn't be enough."

"So, we do nothing?" Sarah stood with Aleta's help. "We stand by and watch the world around us drown? That's what's going to happen if we throw up our hands." Sarah got nose to nose with him. "What's *your* plan? Apparently, ours aren't good enough."

Sarah joined Brandon.

"My plan involves Aleta. If I'm right, she's the only one of us who has any chance to succeed. Let's head back to HQ. I'll tell you there."

He opened the portal into Quinn's office. Sarah brushed past him into the opening. In silence, Brandon followed, grumbling. Giving the chamber one last look, Dan stepped through, and the portal closed.

Thunder, fierce and incomparable, split the air all around.

The next morning, the luminous and concussive plague that infected the sky continued, leaving no airy molecule untouched. Before one jarring blast could subside, others would intrude, and streaks of light strafed the darkened sky with raw power. So much electricity caused blackouts all over the world. In the city below Aleta, if it weren't for portable generators in hospitals, and even those might fail with this much energy, many lives would be lost. Traffic lights flickered on and off, and street lamps even burst from the surges. The modern mortal world had never seen such chaos, and this monstrous tantrum had no mercy on those below. Not since Zeus flooded the earth to rid mankind of its evil millennia ago had Gaea received such an onslaught. Humanity would have to be at its absolute best to get through this.

Having recently learned she could transform into a white eagle, much like Aetos Dios who carried thunderbolts to the Olympeian king in ages past, Aleta soared over the Atlantic Ocean, waves reaching heights that could easily upend the largest of vessels. Her mission kept her focused on her goal, otherwise, her growing fear would cause her to panic. Gaea herself had no control over the skies, and she had left the preservation of her physical form and the skies that surrounded it in the care of the task force named after her. The gods themselves remained aloof, even in the best of days. Zeus was never known to care about the aftermath, and subsequent casualties, of his wrath. Of all on her team, Aleta stood the biggest chance of stopping him. While not the strongest of them, she understood the power he held perhaps more so than any with her intimate connection to thunder and lightning. It wouldn't be just stopping the storm; she had to stop the king of Olympos himself. Before she faced him, though, she had a few stops to make. Even Dan's voice shook when he had told her what she'd have to do.

Due to her wingspan in this avian form, she could fly faster than an ordinary eagle, and with the impetus to save innocents fueling her, she could cross the Atlantic in two days without stopping until she reached her destination. It would put her on the brink of exhaustion and possibly death, but she could do it. Not one part of the globe was safe, not even the home of those she sought. Seeing such energy unfold over the vast ocean would make anyone feel insignificant, at the whim of greater things. She didn't frighten easily but looking down into the stormy seas below made her wonder what creatures this weather would stir from the depths. Sarah had told her of the massive Carkharos, the mystical shark that guarded Ophion and Eurynome, but before her imagination would distract her from her mission, she rose a bit higher toward the clouds, squealing in response to the thunder.

Her world had been changed so long ago to where she was more like a fairy tale character she used to read about than the people who read them. Soon, her destination was in view, and she maneuvered to keep herself steady until she could land. Just before she reached the cave, she resumed her human winged form, stumbling through the opening. On her hands and knees, she retracted her wings and pushed herself against the stone wall. From her belt, she removed two water pouches, emptying them of their contents in a few swallows. Before she could face those she came to see, she would need to rest. Despite her altered DNA giving her avian characteristics, her healing wasn't as accelerated as Dan's or Brandon's. She didn't want to, but she would have to sleep a little before she could move on.

Waves of sulfurous heat woke her, and the stench made her eyes water. Aleta didn't know how long she'd slept, and her wrist-com didn't work well in magical realms, especially during this storm. She followed the soot-stained passage, using her wings to block the bursts of heated air that seemed to follow the sound of metal on metal. With no torch to guide her, she slid her hand along the wall, catching glimpses of where she needed to be from bursts of light at the far end. Percussive rumblings roared behind her, shaking the stone walls, and the warm, rough floor beneath her bare feet grew even warmer as she progressed, waves of hot, thick air pushing past her, taking her breath momentarily, leaving a metallic stench behind. Those she needed to find could smell her approach, even over the sulfur and smoke, each turning toward the much smaller woman carrying a silver javelin that they forged. They rose to more than four times her height, each of their muscled bodies clothed in black aprons. Three enormous heads, with one eye apiece, lowered toward her.

"May Gaea bless you and keep you, brothers of fire," Aleta shouted the greeting Dan advised her to use. "You know why I'm here?"

A gruff voice like stone scraping stone made her wince. "Aye. The sword bearer son of Apollo sent word, little bird. What you seek to do may very well get you killed."

"If you know what I'm here to ask about, then why haven't you done it yourselves?"

Brontês, the Thunder giant, knelt. "We are forbidden from entering Olympos. After Zeus freed us from imprisonment, he enchanted the mountain after we gave him the thunderbolt."

"Why can't you just use the incantation from here?"

"You must have him in your sight for the magic to work." Argês, the Bright One, replied.

Aleta smirked. "How inconvenient. So, what do I do?"

"Be certain that this is your will. If you fail, Zeus will know it came from us and destroy us."

"I won't fail." She puffed out her chest.

Steropês, the Lightning giant, summoned her up to a ledge in the cave where he could tell her. There would be no second chance. If this failed, Zeus would know he had been betrayed by the Cyclopes. Aleta wrinkled her nose at the pungent stench as the giant came closer to her, commenting to herself that even Boston's pollution was like perfume compared to this. She put her hands to her head.

"The pain…" She extended her wings to steady herself as she stumbled. "Why does it hurt?"

"A mortal mind is not meant for such knowledge. The language is beyond human comprehension. Once you use it, the pain will fade. You now have what you need. It will only work once."

Aleta stood taller, narrowing her brows. Grunting from the agony, she took deep breaths.

"Thanks. I hope it does." She took a few steps and then the voice grated again.

"Your deeds for our mother are known even here. You honor us."

Smirking, Aleta leaped off the ledge and placed herself in the storm-wrought skies again, but her next destination would be a shorter flight albeit a much more dangerous one.

Flying north, she had one more stop to make before she could confront Zeus.

Atop a naked crag near Thebes, Aleta pushed her way through the sheets of rain and wind to a small tholos. Assailed by the storm, she pushed against the tall wooden doors of the circular temple that creaked open into darkness. Once beyond the entry, the doors slammed shut, and a central hearth burst into flames. From a pouch at her hip, Aleta removed a bundle of herbs and tossed them in. Once consumed, the fire turned a shade of purple.

"You have come a long way, daughter of Amazons." Three female voices of different ages melded into one.

Hanging her head, Aleta knelt. "Yes, I come on a mission of—"

"We know why you are here. We three have seen what the threads reveal, could reveal, and Zeus must not be allowed to continue. Place your left hand in the fire."

After a deep breath, she complied. The purple flames did not singe or disfigure her flesh, but they were as hot as fire should be. Wincing, she held her hand in place leaning against the hearth while the symbols appeared.

"Withdraw your hand."

Examining her palm, Aleta saw ochre glyphs and markings, much like how henna stains the flesh. The symbols entwined around her fingers with intricate threads. On the back of her hand, there was a circle of symbols resembling the cycle of the zodiac, but these glyphs were unknown to her.

The triad of voices continued. "At the proper moment, you will know how to read this."

Engaging the torrent again, she made her way over mainland Greece toward Thessaly, the source of the rage. Streaks of electricity surged past her, and the thunder shook air and ground alike, stronger than before. She was near the epicenter. Since she had been to her destination before and knew how to traverse the

Nephelae or cloud nymphs that prevented mortals from scaling the heights of Olympos, she would need to think about her words carefully when confronting Zeus. Aleta circled around the rocky crags leading toward the mystical mountain, and when she met the Nephelae, she uttered the words taught to her by Dan, ironically invoking Zeus to get them to disperse: '*Lis'somai Zênos' Olumpi'ou, Nephelae—diaskorpistike!*"

Bolts of lightning raced from the tallest reaches of Olympos, almost coming close to scorching her as if in a warning. With the finesse of her avian form, she swooped and turned, eventually seeing her quarry. The throne room was an open space surrounded by columns with no ceiling. In the center was a rectangular fire pit, extinguished, with seats for each of the gods encircling it. At one end, the marble thrones of Zeus and Hera presided. Zeus slumped in his, unmoving, except for when his clenched fist would strike the marble arm, bolts of energy scattering into the world. Staring off, he didn't acknowledge Aleta's presence, if he even realized she was there. She took in her surroundings, as one does before going into battle, keeping him in her sights.

"Just what the hell are you doing? Are you trying to destroy the world?" She made sure to land at the far end of the hall. Her voice, however, rivaled the cacophony.

Aleta could tell he wasn't *with* her, not really. Moving from behind one colossal throne to another, each one three times as tall as she was, she focused on his expression, and it wasn't until she moved a few steps closer that his tears were obvious. They streamed down his cheeks and into his silver beard. She didn't even know Zeus cried. A few more steps...

"Those thrones... They will not protect you from me." His eyes were still elsewhere, and his voice labored to utter the syllables.

The heavens rattled, and Aleta wasn't even sure that Ouranos could have stood up to his own grandson, especially when he was in mourning.

"True. It was either that or waltz right up to you. You do realize you're going to destroy the world if this keeps up."

"Impertinent child." His fist crashed down, setting free more lightning. "What good is the world without my son?"

With no more thrones to hide behind, Aleta approached the foot of the dais. Still, he kept his eyes elsewhere, but by slight changes to his face, she knew he could see her.

"He's not gone. He's just—"

"Chained! Humiliated!" Thunder rose to meet his voice. "His mind has been splintered. He knows not why he is there, and he is treated no better than a stray dog. Imprisoned!" Punctuating the last word, his fist struck again. "I cannot free him without destroying the world."

Gaea had to give permission for anyone, even Zeus, to enter her adyton. If Zeus even tried to force his way there, it would tear the Earth apart.

"That was for his, and the world's, protection. You of all should know what could happen with a mad god running around. Maybe you've abandoned the mortal world, but I can tell you *he* hasn't. He's a part of it, and when he suffers, the world suffers. Your tantrum isn't helping, either."

"You *dare*!" This time, a bolt struck her in the gut, catapulting her back about twenty feet, slamming her into Hermes' throne. Had he intended to destroy her, only a pile of ashes would have remained.

Without thinking, she grunted and hurled her javelin, the lightning bolt striking him in the face. "That hurt! Is that what the king of the gods has become? A bully? I thought you'd changed."

Electric power arced at the corner of his eyes. Whatever he had been looking at, he shifted his gaze to her and rose. As he descended each step, the sky roared around them. Aleta stood her ground, even with the winds against her wings, gripping the javelin with two hands.

"You want to go, old man? I won't go down without a fight." Her voice sounded almost muffled.

She backed up as he moved toward her—a fruitless endeavor because if he really wanted to, he could end her with one mental gesture. Why he hadn't remained a mystery to her. That gave her hope. He threw his clenched fists out to his sides, sending lightning in all directions. And, again. She had no idea if they had wiped a country or continent off the map, or whether he was simply showing her he was still in control. What mattered to her, though, were the lives that could be lost on such a grand scale if he continued. The next bolt he threw, she intercepted with the javelin, and it pushed her back. She knew she couldn't continue that for long. This *was* Zeus, after all.

41

"Such hubris…" His voice was everywhere, even though he hadn't raised it. "That javelin… it was a gift to contain *my* thunderbolts. And you use it against *me*?"

"Zeus, please. We're doing everything we can to help Apollo. Ari has made it his mission to aid your son. He—"

"Will fail. You will all fail. 'Tis only the gods who have any hope of saving my Phoebos. You, however, have no hope." Another display of his power streamed from Olympos, and Aleta was only able to dissipate one strand of lightning.

In all her trips to this mountain and whenever she had had an audience with Zeus, she had never seen this much emotion. He could make the heavens and earth quake with a thought, but he had always been reserved when she and the others were around. Despite having lived his own mortal existence not long ago, with all its humility, he still retained some of the arrogance of being the son of Kronos, the god of gods, and the head of the Olympeian sovereignty. It was this arrogance and current uninterest in humanity that frightened her. He would throw away all the lessons he had learned as the man Rakurai Saro all for the sake of his son. It was no secret among the gods that Apollo was Zeus' favorite, despite how much Apollo implored his father not to speak that way. As if he could tell Aleta was thinking about Apollo, Zeus let out an ear-splitting howl followed by an outpouring of electricity. Taking flight, she threw herself in front of the biggest blast, letting the javelin take the brunt. She rolled backward a few times until she hit a column.

"Worry not, little one. Your end will be quick. I tire of this."

She saw the remotest hint of a smile and knew it was either that moment or never.

Holding up her javelin, she spoke the words given to her. "I hereby invoke the Rite of *Anaklisi*—The Revocation! By Argês, I call back the flash! By Brontês, I call back the thunder! By Steropês, I call back the lightning! Cyclopes Three, bestow your gift to me."

Zeus' eyes widened, and he growled as he summoned a thunderbolt. No energy came to his outstretched hand. He tried again, but nothing happened. He raised both hands, lifting his eyes to the apex of the heavens.

"The winds are denied to me? What-what have you done? You have denied me my power!"

42

"Not yet I haven't," she muttered. Then, in a tongue more ancient than Olympos itself, she looked at the glyphs on her left hand and spoke the other words in the ancient tongue of Fate, "I call upon Great Clotho, spinner of Fate to bind this son of Kronos. I call upon Great Lachesis, measurer of Fate to bind this son of Kronos. I call upon Great Atropos, she who cannot be turned, to bind this son of Kronos. Moirae Three, bind his essence."

Falling to his knees, he reached up again and gasped.

"You're still the king of the gods. Aeolos took back control of the winds when the Cyclopes' enchantment kicked in, and the Moirae have bound much of your power temporarily."

He lunged toward her, but she pushed him back with a lightning bolt. Zeus ripped, of all things, Apollo's throne from the floor and hurled it at her, but it crumbled with a bolt from her. "My power is who I am!"

"Then, that's pretty sad. You just don't get it, do you? You would have tried to obliterate Gaea to free Apollo, but it would've done nothing. Gaea outranks you, remember? The most you would have done is destroyed the mortal world, and then what? Look, I *get* it. You're in nine kinds of pain because your son is in chains. Let us do our job to help him. We'll figure it out, Zeus."

Immortal hands reached for another throne, but a filament of lightning wrapped around him, binding his hands to his sides. Aleta had indeed crossed a line, but she had no choice.

"I'll release you, but I beg you… stand down." She started crying.

From behind him, a figure materialized. Aleta froze, but one look at her face told her she had nothing to fear.

"Great Hera… I am so sorry about this. I—"

Hera held up her hand. "You did what you had to do." Her voice barely moved the air. "He will understand in time. Leave him to me."

With a nod, Aleta left Olympos. Looking back, she saw Hera take her husband in her arms, leaning his head on her shoulder. Then, she witnessed something few had ever seen in millennia: Zeus let someone console him while he wept. Perhaps he had learned something from mortality after all. Aleta had accomplished her task, and now she needed to assess the damage. On her way home, she realized she could use Zeus' power to undo whatever he had done, but it wasn't hers to use.

She also knew she couldn't control it. She just had to contain it until she could return it to Zeus.

8 | HEALING NO MORE

Beth Israel Hospital, Boston, Mass.

Floor nurse Joshua Adkins was filing patient information at the nurse's station terminal when he turned to check the patient ECPs, electronic chart pads. On top of each was a light: green showed normal vitals, yellow showed slight changes in patient status, and red—along with a high-pitched alarm—showed distress. This floor housed fifteen patients ranging from mild trauma and injuries to those recovering from basic surgical procedures. All lights were green. An intern, Katie Robinson, leaned on the counter.

"Hey, Josh. Dr. Williams told me you were going to show me the ECPs. I haven't had any training on them yet."

"Just a sec." He finished entering patient data and waved her behind the desk. "Okay, here's where we house them. They charge at all times they're not in use. This floor has fifteen patients in recovery, and each pad is linked to a patch on a patient's arm."

He pulled out a patch still in its packaging, and it was the size of a quarter.

"Notice the electrodes on the adhesive side. When you attach one, you peel off the backing and press it on the upper arm firmly for it to stick." He pulled an ECP from its charging station. "Then, you scan the code on the patch with the ECP to link it. It will then pull any data from the hospital computer and display it, like doctor's orders, meds dispensed, and patient history. The electrode is sensitive. Any change in the patient's status, and the pad will show it. Normally, this little LED on top will be green—"

"What happens when it's yellow?" Katie pointed to one of the ECPs.

"That's Anna Lowell in 12. She was just sent up here an hour ago. Call Dr. Moss." Joshua took the pad and trotted toward the room.

Dr. Angela Moss, the attending, arrived a minute later to see Joshua checking vitals by hand. She waved a penlight in Anna's eyes and then checked the ECP.

"How long has she been unconscious? She was awake when she arrived. Her car accident was minor, and her CT showed no head trauma or swelling. She had bruising from the airbag deploying and some minor lacerations from the glass."

"That's just it, Doctor, her lacerations should have started healing by now. They weren't deep." He pulled back one of the bandages to show blood trickling from the wound. "She wasn't given Heparin or any other anticoagulant."

"Start a CBC and PT/INR. Get me the results stat. While we're waiting, call the wound—"

Katie burst into the room moments after a patient alarm shrieked throughout the corridor.

"Dr. Moss, most of the ECPs just turned yellow, and Mr. O'Brien's in 9 just turned red!"

While Dr. Moss tended to the emergency, Joshua tapped the glass on the ECP to initiate the CBC and PT/INR, both of which could be done through the epidermal patch. Results took less than a half-hour. From the room phone, he paged one of the wound specialists, Dr. Rawleigh. While he waited, people shuffling through the halls, running from room to room got Josh's attention. It took ten minutes for Dr. Rawleigh to arrive, and he checked Anna's arm.

"The bandages have lost their efficacy. Get me Thrombin JMI spray. We need to keep this contained until we know the cause. She's not even a carrier of hemophilia, let alone one herself, so this makes no sense."

Once he returned with the Thrombin, the ECP beeped. "Doctor, the results are back on the tests. The results are... normal. How can that be?" Joshua scrolled through the screen. "All of the tests are normal."

"How the hell is she bleeding from her lacerations, and the test is normal?" He grabbed the pad from Joshua. "That's not possible. Josh-"

"Dr. Rawleigh, the patch is working fine since all of her vitals are coming through."

With the application of the clotting agent, Anna's wounds stopped bleeding, but just a little. While Dr. Rawleigh added the Thrombin to the chart to be administered *prn*—as needed, Dr. Moss returned and pulled him aside.

"Steve, we have a bigger problem. I've checked the patients on this floor, and they're all in various stages of subdued healing. It's as if their bodies aren't responding to their own healing processes. Mr. O'Brien went into cardiopulmonary arrest, and Dr. Shields is with him now. We should check—"

BEEP BEEP

Both Dr. Moss' and Dr. Rawleigh's watches read "Code Navy."

Normally, a Code Blue was for a medical emergency, but a Code Navy meant that there was a hospital-wide situation. Dr. Moss reached for Anna's phone and called the emergency extension.

"This is Dr. Moss... What? Understood... Dr. Rawleigh is with me. I'll tell him."

"What is it?"

"We have a complete hospital lockdown. No patients in or out. Every floor has reported patient issues, and we have to deal with the most serious cases first. Ms. Lowell here seems better for the moment. We'll keep an eye on her bleeding."

With the hallway emergency light flashing blue, both doctors began their rounds to those most needing attention. Floor nurses trailed behind, each keeping an eye on the ECPs.

Dan sat at the kitchen table poring over Task Force Division reports with the television on as background. When the news interrupted regular programming, he looked up.

"and hospitals all over Boston have gone into lockdowns, so no patients in or out until the situation is under control. According to Dr. Jordan Holland, Chief Administrator at Beth Israel Hospital, all patients are receiving the care they need, and when the lockdown is lifted, the hospital will inform the public. Massachusetts General and Brigham and Women's remain open for new patients at this time, but all other hospitals in the Boston area will be under lockdown until further notice. From an unnamed source within Beth Israel, 'It seems as if the patients have just stopped healing on their own, but we're working hard to help each and every one'. With the latest news, I'm Genevieve Osborn."

Dan called Brandon at Boston University.

"Hey. It's worse than we thought. Have you seen the news? Patients have stopped healing on their own. We need to do something. Get here now. I'm calling the others."

✦

Half an hour later, Sarah arrived, knocking once and then entering. Shortly after, Brandon arrived, grabbing a bottle of water from the kitchen.

"So, this isn't good." He took a swig. "What's the game plan?"

Dan sat straddling a chair, leaning his arms and head on the back. "What *can* we do? None of our powers can affect a worldwide disaster like this. If people just stop healing, who knows what the casualty count will be?"

"What I want to know is how this is possible. Living things, especially humans, have healed themselves since they came into existence, right? How can Apollo's absence affect that? He's still alive."

"Sarah, that's the $64,000 question." Dan crossed his arms.

She turned away, losing herself in thought. With Aleta on her way back from Olympos, she and the others would have to brainstorm what to do, and with Aleta being the only doctor among them, they didn't fully understand the ramifications of what could or would happen.

"Sarah, you're quiet. What're you thinking?"

"Think back to when Python bit your father. Don't you remember feeling something sort of wash over you, like a huge wave of energy?"

Brandon tapped the bottle on the table. "Come to think of it, I do remember that. Could that have caused this?"

"It's been a few weeks. I just don't know." Sarah shrugged.

Dan sat up. "What if... And bear with me... What if the trauma of what happened to Apollo sent a ripple, like a rock in a pond, throughout the world? Apollo *is* an Olympeian and basically the god of healing. He's also been inextricably linked to the mortal world since he chose to live here and not on Olympos. That link would explain why that surge of power affected the healing process. And, like any ripple, it'll dissipate. It has to, right?"

Brandon walked to the sliding glass doors that overlooked the city. "One can hope. We may have to just wait and see."

9 | DAMAGE

Aleta found the skies returning to blue with wisps of clouds replacing thunderheads once she left the heights of Olympos. Barely a breeze blew. She needed rest after this ordeal and used her wristcom to contact a hotel in Athens she had been to years earlier. Night fell, and the blackest of skies soon sparkled with a panoply of stars, but even the night couldn't hide the debris littering the streets. Broken street signs, tree branches, overturned cars, and much more had transformed the city. Police and street crews had started to work at clearing everything so that life could resume. The hotel's reserve generator had kicked in, so she could at least check in to her room, and the hotel staff gawked at this barefoot woman with her white sleeveless top and gray pants walking through the lobby of such a deluxe establishment. Fortunately, she had reserved a room on the third floor, so she could manage the stairs. Power had returned, but the elevators had sustained some damage.

Collapsing on the bed, she checked in with Quinn and let her know she would debrief when she returned to Boston. After a long, hot shower, she brewed some tea and looked out the window at a city where gods once walked and now, mortals would have to pick up the pieces of a god's rampage. Her phone rang, and the operator's voice was American giving her the code for a secure line. A few moments later, a familiar voice made her smile.

"How are you?"

"I'm… tired. I could sleep for a week, but I'll be fine. I hope you don't need me for a day or two." She sipped her tea. "Dan, Zeus was… All I can say is that I hope that binding enchantment lasts or I'm dead." Aleta noticed the markings on her hand were gone.

"It won't be for long, I hope. I've alerted the Task Force Division they will need to send teams out to help with recovery and repair. Believe it or not, I think Zeus was holding back."

"If complete chaos and property damage and unknown loss of life is holding back, then—"

"Trust me. If he had wanted to, he could have done a lot worse. Once the global agencies have assessed the damage and losses, we'll have a better idea of where we stand. Look. Get some rest. Eat something. I've arranged airline tickets for your return trip. Those wings of yours need a break."

"You'll get no argument from me." She rubbed a shoulder blade. "I'll see you in a few days. Keep me posted."

In the days and weeks to follow, civil engineers, Task Force teams, local law enforcement agencies, as well as many international organizations would do what they needed to do to bring the world back to some semblance of normality. Knowing that the danger had passed made it much easier to clear debris, begin the rebuilding process, and care for the injured and inter the lost. Those who knew the cause felt it best to say nothing to the public. The Global Atmospheric Organization put out a statement that a confluence of meteorological events, tied to the existence of solar flares, created the storms that spanned the entirety of the Earth. Once the solar flares dissipated, so did the storms. Those at the highest levels had no other explanation to offer, and the Task Force Division highly encouraged the GAO to make information classified to avoid further investigation.

Some of the hardest-hit places, rural towns with no infrastructure or organized aid, became the focus before larger cities and towns that had the means to address the consequences. Once thriving farms had become wastelands. Deserts in the American southwest had become flood zones. Flora of the region, normally requiring less irrigation, had drowned with the excess precipitation. Desert animal populations had been devastated with many species lying drowned on top of the sandy landscape once the waters receded. It would take time for Task Force: Eta to figure out how endangered species had been affected. Team leader Periklis Simonides put out a statement that the agency would collaborate with environmentalists to extrapolate just how much damage had been done to the ecosystems all over the globe.

Task Force: Mu reported that the cruise ships Amazonia and Islandia had been located in the Atlantic and had sustained some damage, with only minor injuries to passengers and crew. Reports from both captains confused officials because there were reports of a figure standing on the water's surface raising some sort of a pitchfork during the worst of the storm. Some believed the report was from storm fatigue, but others claimed that the figure was a bearded man.

Responding to some communiqués from Eta, Alpha, and other involved groups, Dan visited various affected locations, including the Sevier Desert in Utah. Sevier Lake had flooded the surrounding area, endangering the towns of Beaver, Milford, Eskdale, and a few others. Bearing witness to the devastation, his instinct was to help, but that was not why he was there. Other agencies and organizations, including FEMA and other task forces, were on the scene and doing everything they could. Apollo would be proud, Dan thought, seeing neighbors helping neighbors, putting aside whatever differences they had to help. The task of making things right was enormous. How would or could anyone repair the world, Dan asked himself. He considered appealing to Gaea, but the scope of what needed to happen was beyond her. Mother Earth sustained herself and those who empowered her through their worship. She didn't have the power anymore to sustain humanity, to help it heal, as she did for the earth itself. The rest of the world had forgotten she existed as a spiritual entity.

Being of the gods but half-mortal, Dan felt the ebb and flow of power, that electricity he had explained to the task force leaders, and he knew its limitations. No enchantment existed that, without the combined effort of the entire pantheon, would heal the earth itself. In his heart, he knew Gaea would do small things: helping seeds to germinate faster than usual or providing natural habitats for small animals to thrive and build up a population, but nothing on a grander scale like rebuilding a dam that collapsed from rising lake water or mudslides that washed through small towns, all but erasing them from the map.

At the edge of the enlarged lake, he crouched and touched the water's edge, hoping his connection to Gaea would give him solace. He and his team would have so much to do, probably more than they ever had before. This challenge came on many fronts. Ari would help with Apollo. Dan and his brother would balance what they could. Aleta and Sarah would be there to build what had been shattered. The damage had far-reaching consequences, more so than land or buildings or even loss of life. In his heart, Dan knew the very soul of everything he held dear was strung together with a tenuous thread, one that could snap at any moment. With reason itself untethering, it was only a matter of time before mortality would devolve into something Dan feared—a collective of humanity that no longer had the means to be strong in the face of adversity because it would lose the ability to have cognitive function and the means to think clearly. His greatest hope was that his father would recover so that the world could as well.

On Olympos, Hera did something she hadn't done in centuries: summoned Hades and Poseidon. Both of her brothers preferred their own realms to the lofty heights. If any could offer her advice on how to deal with Zeus, she knew they would be the only ones. While the almost impotent king of the gods slumped in his throne, his wife and brothers met in the Hall of Tribunals where accords were broached and acts of war declared. This time, they would meet to discuss the sovereignty of the mountain itself. Materializing from a swirling column of water, Poseidon arrived, followed by Hades in a black cloud. Their sister sat at the hearth, staring at the glowing embers, and her emerald eyes reflected them.

"It is true, then. The Amazon has bested our brother, neutering him like a wild dog." Poseidon smirked, tapping his trident on the marble.

Hera shot him a piercing look before returning her gaze to the smoldering ash.

"Come now, brother. We mustn't kick a cur when he's down." Hades was holding back a smile of his own.

"While you both have been beneath everything, I had to endure the tempestuous one." She shot her eyes in the direction of the throne room. "In some ways, I am grateful for Aleta. At least now when he pouts, he's quiet about it."

"As a father, I understand his grief. I too have lost children, and it is not something I would wish on my worst enemy. I know that Apollo is not forever gone, but none among us has ever lost his or her mental faculties. And to have balancing two timelines worth of memories… I cannot even fathom." Poseidon circled the hearth.

Hades nodded. "I will speak with him later. I am still untangling the mess that the Potamoi made of the underworld. At times, those rivers can be just as impetuous and petulant. I suppose that goes with their element."

Hera disappeared in a swirl of peacock feathers and reappeared on her throne.

"My fear is the power vacuum that Aleta created. If she truly wanted to, she could challenge Zeus' place. Not that having two queens here would be such a *bad* thing." Her lips curved upward ever so slightly.

Poseidon snorted. "Amphitrite would certainly be happy, that is certain. She and Zeus have never agreed completely."

"Persephone too. Something about our brother puts women off." Hades lifted his eyebrows.

Hera pursed her lips. "Not *all*. Anyway, what should we do?"

As Hera had intimated, the knowledge of Zeus' impotence would signal other immortals that perhaps another could sit on his throne. Without the pantheon at its fullest power, all any other deity had to do would be to rally enough support to attempt a coup. Hades didn't think that would happen, although his recent experience with the five rivers had given him pause for thought. One could conceivably take the throne but maintaining it was another matter altogether. Managing Olympeians and other immortals, as Apollo once retorted, was like herding chimerae. As powerful as Hera was, even she couldn't do what Zeus did in keeping the balance. That was one of his special talents that he had fostered over the millennia. She had been in charge many times before, but she didn't always *want* to be. As her husband's eye dallied, she had to take on the mantle of solitary sovereign, and she had a heavier hand than her husband, who could be swayed with gifts or a full chalice of nectar.

Hades reiterated that he would speak with Zeus since Poseidon didn't see the point and felt his brother would snap out of this gloom soon enough. With that, he swirled back to the seas. Hera suggested she might invite Aleta to see what her intentions were. The underworld king didn't think the Amazon wanted anything to do with ruling Olympos considering her allegiance to the United Nations. The Olympeian queen, however, knew just how tempting power could be. She'd be keeping her eye on Aleta just the same. In an uncharacteristic expression, she did feel concerned for Gaea's condition after her husband wreaked havoc. Olympos didn't have that kind of power, Hades reminded her. Gaea would heal as that was her nature. As for the mortals, he would tend to his newest spiritual arrivals just like any other. He lowered his head.

"You feel something for the mortals, brother." Hera tilted her head and raised a brow.

"And you do not? Is the heart of Kujaku Saro so cold, even after all she experienced?" Hades folded his arms.

The queen turned away. "No... I *do* feel for them. I *was* one of them. My concerns now are here, though, with my husband. Mortals do not worship Olympos. Our power has limits. You have a connection to the Arkadeian, Aristeides. Is there nothing—"

He spun around toward her. "Is there nothing what, sister? That man, the son of a simple temple caretaker who gave up one year of his life, has more nobility than a hundred mortals. Ari does what he does out of guilt, albeit misplaced guilt. There is nothing more he can do. His faith, and that of Apollo's team, cannot fuel enough power for us to fix anything. The Moirae alone know how this will all play out."

In a swirl of black smoke, he returned to the underworld.

Hera returned to the reverberant throne room by way of walking instead of magic. Slouching in his throne, Zeus' inward gaze settled in some unknown place. With a purposeful stride, she moved toward him, but then she stopped and sat at the fire's edge on the opposite side of the space, holding her husband in her eyes while she dragged a finger through the glowing embers. Flashes of past moments in that mortal year where Rakurai and Kujaku drank Sencha tea or planted vegetables in their garden, held conversations with vendors in the market in Osaka or wandered through the city to find her favorite ramen shop. Finding that balance that her husband liked to prattle on about so much was an endeavor she had not yet mastered—a human flaw that carried over into her immortal life. She toyed with the idea of summoning the pantheon to determine the next steps, especially with Zeus as he was. Then, she shook her head, rubbing her temple, remembering that it was like trying to get wild chimerae to walk in a straight line. There *had* to be another option. Taking her place on her throne, she willed it closer to his until the arms of the chairs touched before reaching over and cupping her ring-studded hand over his burlier one, caressing it ever so slightly. No matter what had transpired between them, he was her husband, and he needed her, even if he didn't know how to ask her for help.

Within the earth's darkness, Gaea called out to her sister, her own voice echoing all around until the spirit of Olympos emerged. Earth told Olympeia that the world was in peril, yet the mountain spirit knew well that Apollo's absence would be felt in all planes of existence. Gaea would protect and nurture Zeus' son with the restorative energy she exuded. Olympeia was troubled by the son of Kronos' grief-clouded mind, remembering that distraction leaves open the possibility of mischief. Earth could do nothing for him since his ailment came from his heart. In time, he would recover, whether Apollo's mind healed or remained fragmented. When Zeus killed his father, he took on the role of guardianship of the pantheon and the mountain on which they resided. To break that vow would bring the mountain itself crumbling to rubble. The pact of the three brothers sustained the mountain with both faith and reverence. Gaea, too, had faith in the four who protected all life under her name. They would have to persevere. Mortals and gods alike depended on them.

The Aegis would shield all from harm. The Talon would be a sign of strength. The Keeper of the Zodiac would nurture. And the Spirit who bound the elements would provide the life force to nourish all who needed it. That was their sacred pledge. They would assess the damage wrought and restore to balance what they could.

"We interrupt this broadcast with late-breaking news. After the United Nations and other global organizations have tallied those affected by the storms worldwide, buildings and manmade constructs were the greatest casualties. Civil engineers and construction crews will be busy for months, maybe even years, rebuilding what was lost. Task Forces Alpha and Epsilon will dispatch crews to those countries affected the most to start the rebuilding. The toll on human life, however, perhaps thanks to determination and peoples' will to survive, was much less than expected at around 4,000 presumed dead or lost. The total of injured reported is about

100,000. Considering the scope of the storms, that is far less than expected. We will keep you updated as more news becomes available. This is Diana Jimenez with WNN news."

10 | BLOOD AND GRAPES

On an Olympeian marble terrace overlooking the cosmos, Athene of the grey eyes watched humanity, turning when Aphrodite approached.

"Sister, tell me, what would you think if you saw Dionysos and Ares together?"

The goddess of love's alabaster face darkened. "Prepare."

"For what, exactly?"

"Nothing good can come from such a union. Surely, they see our brother's ailment as a sign of war and chaos to be loosed upon the mortals. Where are they now?"

Athene crinkled her eyes toward Gaea. "I cannot tell. Dionysos has hidden himself well. I just know they are together. The stench of blood and sour grapes will overwhelm us all soon enough."

"And with Zeus' power curtailed for the moment, I can only hope that Apollo's sons and their companions will be ever vigilant."

"May Gaea watch over them. I, too, will be on my guard for Dionysos and Ares lest they scar the earth."

Aphrodite put her hand to her cheek, remembering well her mortal year.

"As will I, Athene. As will I."

Even as the storm rent the skies across the globe, the gods of vine and war sat in a hole-in-the-wall bar on the corner of Manhattan's 8th Avenue and West 57th Street, closed due to the circumstances, but now the hidden refuge for these sons of Zeus. Dionysos, in business casual attire, sipped a glass of Shiraz, and Ares, in black jeans, boots, and a red T-shirt swigged an imported beer from its bottle. In a city without power, the establishment lay adorned with red votive candles, casting a pale glow over everything. Dionysos leaned back, swirling the glass, smelling the aromas, and examining the wine's legs.

"Amazing. For as much as I enjoy Olympeian nectar, I do so love wine crafted by mortals. This tastes of blackcurrant and chocolate. How about yours? What does that beer taste like?" His eyes never left the glass.

Ares took another swig. "Beer. Tell me again why you picked this venue?"

Dionysos closed his eyes and swallowed a mouthful of wine, swaying his head to the music. The jukebox, once a dusty piece of nostalgia simply part of the decor, powered by godly magic, played Foreigner's "Hot Blooded" in the background.

"Dionysos…"

"Yes, yes, Ares. I heard you. I am trying to savor this. I picked this place because it's so… mortal. Earthy. Pungent. Real."

"If you do not get to the point, I will—"

"Rest easy, brother. The gods cannot find us here. It is best, for now, that they do not know of my plan. We are a meddlesome bunch." He sipped his wine. "I need your help with something regarding our brother Apollo."

Ares finished the last mouthful of beer and moved to stand up.

"Sit down." When Dionysos wanted to, he could be almost as imperious as Zeus. "For as much as I revel in chaos, trust me, I need order and reason. A world only in chaos is boring. The fruit of the vine is certainly enticing"—he took another sip—"but without the sober truth, my influence is less than desirable. What is it Zeus prattles on about? Balance?"

Ares leaned in. "Think of all the wild, untamed energy you could draw from, brother. You could feast on it! Conflict, the turmoil, the unrest, the urges… you understand the human need, the desire, for impulsive behavior. Leave Apollo in his chains. I'm sure he'll be free soon enough."

"Brother. Listen. Those who act under the influence of my power do so with the aid of vulgar desire. The lifeblood of the grape and its kin erode the will and evoke lust. Again, without our brother's unabashed truth to provide a counterbalance, my power takes mortals to the edge. All I am left with are intoxicated fools. If mortals then return to their version of order and see just how mundane it is, they will continue to reach for the nectar of their choosing. I am appreciative of all—"

"You are a fool. Conquest. Deception. Manipulation... all a means to an end for those who follow my example. Bloodlust fuels me. With a swing of my blade, cities fall." Ares motioned his hand with a cutting action toward the table. "My battle cry deafens the weak, makes the timid wet themselves…"

"Ares, you make yourself the fool. Mortals do not fear you or fight for you. They have caused more wanton destruction and war all without even knowing who you are. Who among them worships at your altar? Who leaves you offerings? Declares their fealty? Wayward souls are as much mine as they can be yours. Apollo leads others to inflexible truths. He *needs* us. You see yourself as some sort of Earl of Conquest, a Duke of Decep—"

"So you claim. I am War." He gestured and another beer appeared.

"You plotted against him once before, so you know that a world without reason is folly. I know how to keep the cosmos from falling into unrelenting chaos. But I will need you by my side."

"An errand on behalf of Zeus' Shining One? Brother, pray, tell me how I must aid you. I need a hearty laugh."

"The Five Pillars of Arkadeia will keep order secure and constant. An enchantment exists…"

"Why have I never heard of these... pillars?"

"You care only for your own self-interests, war god."

"True. Tell me more." Ares swallowed half of his beer.

"Two pillars you know, Danelos and Kidemonas. The other three, sons of Apollo born to Arkadeia before Alkinoë's reign. They live in the mortal realm in secret. We shall locate them, warn them of the peril of a world without order, and hold faith to Khaos that they will heed our plea."

"Now you would have me be subservient? Put down the chalice, Dionysos. Why do you even need me?"

"Your good looks. Why do you think? All you need do is fold your arms and these children will acquiesce."

"You think them so fearful of our presence? How formidable would they be against that which Apollo cannot fight? Perhaps you put too much faith in these pillars. Where do they hide?"

"Leave that to me."

Dionysos threw the contents of his glass into the air. The wine moved around him, orbiting his body, and then coalesced into a sphere, the liquid taking the shapes of continents. His eyes flashed for a moment, and he moved his hand around the sphere, muttering. Three spots on the globe sparkled in the liquid.

"England. Japan. Iran. Are you ready?"

Ares had taken his last swallow just as Dionysos asked what was more of a rhetorical question.

North of the Jubilee Gardens on the south side of the Thames River in London thrived an art district that had been around since the turn of the century. What used to be trade merchants, pubs, and taverns catering to sailors, and a budding millinery industry in the late 1800s was currently blocks of quaint galleries, shops, and cafés. Landscaped garden parks combining both whimsical and formal English style lined the riverbank, offering patrons of the arts a place to enjoy a riverwalk or performances of local troupes of dancers and actors. Where the London Eye used to stand, a victim of a Stymphalian bird attack back in 2008, was a memorial for those artisans and craftspeople lost in the Culture War of 1964. As cameras appeared and the need for identity verification surfaced, riverfront property became prime areas for factories to build surveillance equipment. The galleries, speakeasies, and shops of the 1920s were torn down in 1964, much to the chagrin of creative society in London as well as other river-bound cities like Madrid and Paris. The arts community staged blockades and sit-ins, but they were no match for the firepower of armed unnamed militias forcibly removing people from their shops and homes.

All types of the arts fell to the scythe of an unknown entity, perhaps government intervention, and the tradespeople abandoned the cities for the smaller towns and villages. It wasn't until the 1990s when the community rekindled its love of art, music, and the like, bringing in legal muscle to shed light on the subversive activities by the river. While the original entity couldn't be discovered, those who ran the factories decided it was in their best interest to find another less populated location, like cockroaches scurrying out of the sunlight. By 2010, arts councils, craftspeople, and the city's leaders had rebuilt the area, brought in more galleries and shops than had been there in the 1920s, and established a firm grip on their part of the river.

Overlooking the Thames, the Arcady Gallery had a wall of windows reaching three stories, its glass treated to prevent sunlight damage to the art pieces within. Neoclassical columns of black marble ran down the inside, supporting balconies. Modern, postmodern, neo-Rococo, among other styles of all artistic media, hung from the walls, the ceiling, and sat on plinths throughout the first floor. Above the front door, in tile mosaic, a depiction of the Nine Muses and Apollo sitting on Mt. Helicon welcomed visitors. In the main foyer, Dionysos smiled as he enjoyed the inspired revelry of creative forms, drinking in the colors, textures, and sounds. Ares scouted the main floor for points of exit, objects that could be used as weapons, and groups of people that would probably become casualties of conflict, should it come to that. Normally, he wouldn't be quite so restrained or calculating, but his time as a mortal had given him a perspective on humanity he had never considered. He wasn't sure he liked it, either.

"Where is he, Dionysos? Let us do what we came here to do."

Dionysos smiled at those within earshot. "Can you not sound as if we are about to 'lay siege?' I am looking for him now."

"All of this, this culture makes my head ache. *She* will tell us what we need to know." He reached out to grab the arm of a woman who was serving hors d'oeuvres when his brother elbowed him.

"Down, boy. He's right there."

Making the rounds of his guests, a tall, slender black man with wavy black hair shook hands or kissed cheeks as he moved about the gallery. One would have to be blind not to notice him, but even the blind would sense his presence. Halfway across the main floor, he spied his two guests and had the slightest smile. He held his hands behind his back, his green eyes bouncing between Ares and Dionysos until he was close enough to extend his hand. Dionysos shook it first, noticing the man's copper wrist cuff etched with Olympeian glyphs. A marble-sized piece of the *omphalos* was embedded within the metal.

"Good evening, gentlemen." His voice had the richness of crimson and burgundy mixed with the faintest trace of an accent, part British, part something else. "Welcome to the Arcady. I am Keion Wolff, the owner."

When he shook Ares' hand, the war god squeezed a little harder, but Keion returned the firmness, much to Ares' surprise.

"You have quite the creative experience here, Mr. Wolff. The Muses would be proud." Dionysos moved his head all around.

Keion's smile warmed the room, and even Ares was taken aback by the man's composure and confidence. He gestured for his two guests to move to an alcove. Nestled in a curved niche was a marble table with three cobalt blue silk chairs.

"From the moment you walked in, I knew you were either connoisseurs of art," he moved his glance from Dionysos to Ares, "or perhaps men of purpose."

"You are most indeed your father's son, Onkios." Dionysos laughed and leaned back, crossing his legs. "You know who we are, I take it."

Keion sat up when a young man bearing a silver tray approached, depositing three drinks: a glass of Sangiovese, a bottle of Saint Bernardus beer, and a martini, each in front of its respective person.

"I wouldn't be who I am if I couldn't discern the truth, dear uncle. Onkios is a name I stopped using millennia ago, by the way. Taste the Sangiovese and tell me what you think."

Dionysos swirled the glass, smelled its aroma, and took an initial sip.

"By Zeus' beard, this is exquisite. A 1960 vintage. Only two bottles of it in the world still exist. I am impressed." He laughed. "*Sangiovese.* Blood of Jove indeed."

Ares wrapped his thick index finger around the bottle and took a hearty swallow. He raised an eyebrow.

"I am amused. Much better than the swill I drank earlier." He shot Dionysos a smirk. "If you know who we are, then you know why we are here."

Shaking his head, Keion sat back and sipped his martini. "I haven't the slightest clue, actually. But, since you mentioned my father, I assume your business concerns him. I have noticed a… difference in the energy of the world. Is he dead or worse?" He sipped again.

Dionysos and Ares shared a look. "Maddened, actually. He lies chained in Gaea's adyton, the victim of Python's venom."

"What do you need of me? Surely, this isn't a social call to bring me the news." He signaled the server for another martini. Keion's once vibrant mood had darkened slightly, but the only clue was the loss of his smile.

Using an economy of words, Dionysos explained the outcome of Apollo's melee with Python. He then mentioned the Five Pillars of Arkadeia, and that they knew of two others, Danelos and Kidemonas. The second martini arrived. Keion swallowed the contents, olives and all.

"What do I need to do?"

Ares crossed his arms and glared.

Dionysos rolled his eyes. "Oh, stop. A little late for that, I'd say."

"Wait. Were you under the impression that I would need convincing to help you? Is that why you brought Olympeian 'muscle'?" Keion howled.

Another look at Ares from Dionysos made Apollo's son slap his thigh.

"While it's been some time since I've seen my father, we had no bad blood between us. In fact, I've followed the exploits of my brothers in Task Force: Gaea ever since its inception. Having a chance to meet them would be extraordinary."

Ares finished his beer in one swallow. "I have to admit, brother. I did not anticipate *that* response."

"When all is in place, you will be contacted, Keion. Thank you for the hospitality. We have two more stops to make." Dionysos finished his glass.

In a blink, they were gone. Keion's smile returned with the prospect of meeting his brothers from Boston, and he resumed his socializing. Too many guests had been neglected already. As he approached a patron, he glanced at the mosaic and wondered if he would ever see his father again.

Dr. Ryuma Taiyo was in the middle of a consultation at Osaka University Hospital when his administrative assistant buzzed his phone. His curt replies to her were followed by him apologizing to his patient for the interruption. An hour later, the young man left, and Dr. Taiyo stepped into the lounge just long enough to signal the two men.

"Dr. Taiyo, thank you for seeing us." Dionysos noticed the man was blind and resisted the urge to extend his hand.

"Thank you? He made us wait an hour," Ares grumbled.

"Gentlemen, who are you, and why are you here? I know you're not patients since I don't have any appointments for a few more hours." Dr. Taiyo leaned against his desk and crossed his arms.

Dionysos sat and gestured for Ares to do the same. Muttering a growl, he complied.

"Doctor… Ryuma, we are, shall we say, family. Uncles, in fact."

"I see." He removed his dark glasses. "You're Olympeians." His response showed both recognition and annoyance.

Ares leaned toward Dionysos. "He catches on quickly."

"I'm blind, not deaf. Again, how may I help you?"

"I guess I am surprised that for a demigod who has not been in touch with his family in quite some time that you would know who we were."

Ares leaned forward. "Oh, for Zeus' sake, why do you prance around him as if he were some sort of delicate flower? Let us get on with this."

After the explanation, Dr. Taiyo rocked in his chair, taking in everything. Dionysos also informed him that another brother had already agreed to help once the plan was developed.

"Forgive me, but who are you again? I didn't catch your names?"

"Dionysos, and the brooding one next to me is Ares. You are being brusque with us because…"

Dr. Taiyo walked to the window. Dionysos noticed he didn't need a cane or any aid in walking despite his blindness.

"Your sister blinded me. I think that gives me a little latitude to be curt."

Laughing, Ares sat up. "If memory serves, you saw her making love to Adonis. Having been in Adonis' place, I would—"

"Enough, Ares." Dr. Taiyo growled. "Your adultery is known far and wide, even in the mortal world. How is Aphrodite these days? How long did it take you to untangle yourselves from Hephaestos' net? Isn't that how he caught you both?"

"Oh, I like this one, Dionysos! He does not fear me." He leaped up and took a few steps toward Dr. Taiyo. "Perhaps, he will be as brash when I remove his tongue."

"I take nothing from Olympos, Ares. I've been a doctor for quite some time once I learned how to live with my blindness. I fear nothing anymore."

The doctor, standing six feet tall, met Ares, nose to nose, and the war god was three inches taller. Neither flinched. Dionysos pulled his brother back by the shoulder, his eyes glowing bright red when Ares started to move back toward Dr. Taiyo.

"Stand down. Both of you. We do not have time for this posturing."

Dr. Taiyo put his glasses back on, and it was then that Dionysos saw the copper wrist cuff under the man's white lab coat. For a man who disdained the gods, he made no attempt to hide his connection to them. Dr. Taiyo realized Dionysos was looking at it.

"It's permanent. Just like my blindness."

"Ryuma, when we have the last brother with us, will you agree to help? I fear that without you, reason and truth will be in jeopardy, for god and mortal alike."

"I have no contempt for my father, Dionysos. He actually killed Adonis when Aphrodite blinded me. A bit extreme, perhaps, but I'm venturing that he was a bit different back then. When you have all the others assembled, let me know. I'll give you my answer then. In the meantime, can you take the warmonger and leave? I'd like to have time to eat before my next appointment."

"I am curious. What field of medicine do you practice?" Dionysos dragged his finger across a medical dictionary.

"Neuropsychology."

"I am sure you do your father proud. We will be in touch."

As soon as they were in the hallway, Ares turned to Dionysos.

"All of this had better be worth it, brother. I spent a year, like you, as mortal, and—"

"And, what, Ares? What did you learn? That they're boorish, arrogant, and cruel? Or that they disrespect the gods? That sounds a lot like you. What, Ares? I tire of your incessant childish need to berate humanity."

For anyone to stun the god of war into silence, one would think it would be Zeus or Hera, but Dionysos had done just that. Ares' tense expression slackened, and he lowered his head.

"I was going to say that my year as mortal showed me that humanity, while it can be all those things, and do not think that I am unaware of my own shortcomings, it can also provide us with hope. Yes, I said *hope*. For Ryuma to forsake us and lead a human life while being an immortal… That takes courage. I do recognize courage."

"Well, then you have just validated Apollo's existence as well. I know that you hesitate to help him because of your past with him, but he deserves a life just as you do, one free of pain and sacrifice. In all the years he has lived with Alkinoë here, how many times has he raised a hand against you? I will answer for you. None. He leaves you to your existence, I would imagine because he understands that you two need each other. Do you remember when he told us of that *other* life he led? You laid siege to Arkadeia and almost took the woman he loved from him."

"That was not me."

"True, it was another you. However, he remembered that event and did not bear any malice toward you in *this* lifetime. To him, you and that other incarnation were both gods of war, but he never once held that against you. For him to have two lifetimes of memories, even for a god… imagine the torment. I know you relish such things—"

"On the battlefield. I have not lifted a hand against him in centuries. I also have a warrior's respect for Alkinoë and would not dare go against her. I have seen Apollo's wrath, and for a god of reason, he can also bring destruction. You do me a disservice, Dionysos. I make you a pledge that I will be more open to this solution. But when our brother is whole once more…"

"As they say in the mortal world, 'all bets are off'. I know, Ares."

In the heart of Mashhad, Iran sat the Goharshad Mosque, and a few blocks away on Mosalla Blvd., nestled in between food markets was Café Aftab, a quaint coffee house that enticed tourists and residents alike. Seated at an outside table, a young man read *The Times*, a London newspaper, while sipping a cappuccino. He folded his paper and nodded at the server when Dionysos and Ares sat with him.

"Good day, gentlemen. How may I help you?" He folded his hands and smiled.

A server brought two more Turkish coffees and placed them by the newcomers.

"Were you expecting us?" Dionysos lifted the cup to sniff it, initially wincing from the strong aroma. After a sip, he nodded his approval.

"I see two men whose bearing seems... otherworldly... and I believe you come to see me for a reason."

Ares drank his coffee in one swig. "Are we wearing name tags?"

The man laughed and leaned forward, lowering his voice. "My *vision* is quite good. You are..."

Dionysos smirked. "Friends of your father." He leaned back and crossed one leg over the other.

"And the mystery continues." The man extended his hand. "Jamshid Motjaba."

"Can we get on with this?"

"Don't mind my brother Ares. He's not convinced we need to speak with you."

It was Jamshid's turn to smirk. "Well, I hope one of you would tell me why you've sought me out. I would imagine you don't get to Iran often."

"I need to remember not to underestimate my brother's children. I'm going to assume you know more than you're letting on. Apollo. Chained beneath the earth. Mind untethered and all that."

Jamshid's brow furrowed. "Then my dream has come to pass."

Dionysos raised both eyebrows, and Ares leaned forward on his elbows.

"I'm a seer. Like my father, I have prophetic or informative dreams. I saw the serpent lord attack Apollo and render him... inert. I thought it merely a metaphor, as many prophecies tend to be. What, if anything, can I do to help you?"

"Your zeal is unexpected, Iamos—"

"I go by Jamshid now. My lifestyle," he gestured around him, "requires a certain change of identity."

"Of course. As I was about to say, you are one of five sons of Apollo, and I believe you and your brethren will be able to keep the world from succumbing to a lack of reason, of order."

Bringing his hands to his mouth, Jamshid took a moment to absorb the information. Dionysos then noticed the two iron cuffs on the man's wrists. Ancient etchings of an Asulos Pistis, or divine pledge, were still visible. From his limited knowledge, Dionysos knew that Iamos was the eldest of the Apollonides, the sons of

Apollo, and the son of Evadne, an Olympeian seer. The man's black curls and smooth olive skin gave him the look of a man in his mid-twenties, even though he was thousands of years old.

"I am aware of two of my brothers from their activity in Task Force: Gaea. The others, I don't know."

Dionysos smiled. "We can have a rousing family reunion later, but right now, will you help?"

Grinning, Jamshid rubbed his hands together. "Of course. I imagine I could be quite helpful with Danelos and Kidemonas, especially with their ability to prophesy."

"Kidemonas, or Brandon as he calls himself now, hasn't manifested that ability."

Jamshid smiled. "He will. We all do, eventually."

"What did Apollo do to receive such loyalty?" Ares swallowed a second cup of coffee. "*My* children—"

"Ares, your children *avoid* you." Dionysos laughed. "Have you even seen any of them since your mortal year?"

The god of war glowered, a fire flickering where his eyes should be.

"Anyway. Jamshid, I normally would advise you to ignore my brother, but he does ask an intriguing question."

Smiling, Jamshid rested his elbows on the table and clasped his hands.

"When I was much younger, Apollo taught me about prophecy. My mother abandoned me in a field of violets when I was born, but I was reclaimed because my stepfather knew I was of divine birth. Later, when I became the seer in Olympia, I found my purpose. Had it not been for my father, I would have died in the wilderness. Every so often, an elderly man would come to visit the shrine and say nothing. He would simply watch me and eat bread and cheese. I knew it was Apollo who had not forsaken me."

"And now?" The god of war uttered only two words, but they were couched in disdain.

"Ares, before this calamity befell him, my father would appear to me in dreams and let me know he was still watching. If I can do something to help him, I will. Dionysos, have you informed my other brethren you were searching for their distant kin?"

For the first time, Dionysos had no response. He looked away for a moment and adjusted himself in his seat.

"I see. So, they have no idea we exist. That will certainly make for an enlightening meeting." Jamshid sipped his coffee.

Minutes passed, and neither Olympeian had anything to say: Ares, out of indifference, and Dionysos out of a mere loss for words. Jamshid suggested they arrange a meeting as soon as possible, especially since he could feel his father's dubious hold on reality dissolving by the moment. Without a contingency in place, the wave of confusion from Apollo's consciousness would gradually wear away at the order of the world. So as not to arouse suspicion around Jamshid, Ares and Dionysos were going to leave the same way they arrived, on foot. The last words of the god of the vine gave Jamshid a bit of hope.

"The sons of Apollo will meet soon. I hope your zeal remains constant. You will need it."

◦══◆══◦

1000 B.C.E., Mount Parnassus, Greece

Mestra's handmaidens mopped her brow as the midwife wrapped the newborn in swaddling, placing the crying infant in the mother's waiting arms. Once he lay against her chest, he settled into a softer cooing. Exhausted, both mother and son fell into a gentle slumber, with a handmaiden seated by the window should Mestra or her child need anything.

When Mestra's eyes opened, she didn't feel the extra weight of her child on her and jolted up, gasping. Once she saw her husband walking back and forth holding their child, her body eased, and she settled back onto her pillow.

"Isn't he beautiful, my love?" His eyes danced around, taking in his son. "He should be named Alekos, defender of men. He will grow up to be strong and fierce."

Mestra's cheeks puffed with her gentle smile. Alekos started to get fussy, so her husband placed him on his wife's chest. While he nursed, she hummed a tune she had heard from one of the handmaidens, and her husband watched, his own joy radiating from his face. With a gentle knock, one of his servants entered with news that made him nod. After a kiss on her forehead, he departed, and Mestra ceased her tune and her expression soured. She knew that nod all too well, and it signified that her husband's mission would take him away for days or weeks. Sighing, she resumed the tune, and a single tear dropped down her cheek.

11 | APOLLONIDES

Brandon deflected one of his brother's quarterstaff maneuvers. The basement gym of Dan's apartment building had a corner that they used for sparring.

"I feel so helpless."

Danelos kept his eyes on the keen advances of his brother, but he took a staff to the shoulder and let out a grunt. Like woodpeckers, their wooden staffs clacked together with speed and accuracy. Their training would do Athene proud. Sweat flew off limbs and spun off dripping brows. Occasionally, when their staffs struck one another, one would slide off as if the grip slipped.

"Yeah, me too." Turning around, Danelos swept across Brandon's legs, but his brother somersaulted out of the way.

Every few moves, one of them would hit the other's arm or side. For years, almost weekly, they had sparred with each other. It challenged them to maintain their skills since they didn't always go up against monsters or giants who could keep them battlesavvy. This day was different. Unspoken distraction would render bruised egos since they had accelerated healing of their own, seemingly unaffected by Apollo's absence.

"I hope we hear from Aleta soon. I can't do this all day." Brandon twisted around to deflect a strike, sweat flying off his face.

Their movements, calculated and matched, gave the appearance of an intricate dance to an onlooker, and one such individual sat in shadow, keeping watch on the timing of these two honed combatants. This presence hadn't gone unnoticed—these two would be unfit to call themselves warriors if they couldn't detect a hidden foe—and the brothers shared a few more blows before throwing their staffs like spears into the darkened corner. The weapons stopped inches from their target and fell to the concrete floor, bouncing in a dull clatter.

"Who's there?" Danelos took up a defensive posture, his eyes darting around.

Brandon followed his brother's lead, his fists clenched. In response to the inquiry, two towels flew toward them.

"Impressive, nephews. I think even Ares would be proud of such a mock melee."

Danelos patted himself dry and groaned. "What do you want, Dionysos?"

"Is that any way to talk to family?"

"You only show up when you want something, uncle." Brandon removed his drenched shirt. "Thanks for the towels."

When the son of Zeus entered the fluorescent light, he wore his traditional wine-dark tunic and held a pine-cone-tipped staff, his thyrsus.

"Are you training to go up against some Hadean creature? Some offspring of a Protogenos?" His mockery oozed.

"Don't you love when our uncle condescends to us? I feel all warm and fuzzy." Brandon rolled his eyes and swung the towel around his neck.

Danelos leaned on his brother's shoulder. "What amuses me is that we hardly ever saw him growing up, but now that Dad's been gone, we've seen him what... four times in as many months?"

"You have made your point. But my reason for coming will interest both of you. You two can sublimate your frustration through this farcical fighting, or you can actually do something to prevent your father's influence from disappearing entirely. Without Apollo holding the reins to truth and order, the world you live in—and I should say mine as well—will decompose like a rotting chimaera."

When neither Danelos nor Brandon responded, Dionysos took that as a cue to continue.

"Your father, clever immortal that he is, prepared a failsafe should he ever be compromised. He and I spoke on many occasions about the possibility of what actually did happen to him, although he did not know it would be at Python's hand, or fangs, as it were."

"So, what… you're saying he planned a contingency for his madness? How does that involve us? We're not powerful enough." Danelos crossed his arms.

Brandon stepped forward. "Plus, not that you would be aware, but mortals have lost the ability to heal properly. Aleta's checking things out on the medical end to see if there's anything we can do, but we're here, helpless, just biding our time until the world falls apart." He punched a pillar, cracking it.

Dionysos paced around the gym, eyeing the combination of Greek decor mixed with athletic equipment. With a casual finger gesture, he repaired the column.

"We Greeks do like our drama, don't we? I hope your friend is successful." He paused, checking his reflection in the wall of mirror that ran down one side of the gym. "Did you know you have brothers? Three, in fact, all born before your father married your mother."

Brandon started doing chin-ups. "Dionysos, what the hell does that have to do with what I just told you?"

"It does. I do think I may have something that will help."

"What does that mean? And, by the way, we're not that naïve to think Apollo didn't have relationships before Alkinoë. Do these brothers know about us?"

"They do, actually. Two are eager to meet you. The third… Let us say he's wary."

"So, what now?"

"Danelos, you do so have your father's scowl. I'm quite surprised he never told you about the other Apollonides. Regardless, you five have the power to regulate the flow of order." He removed a rolled parchment from the folds of his cloak. "This will tell you all you need to know. Good luck with Ryuma."

Dionysos departed into the shadows.

Brandon tossed the towel by his gym bag. "You ever get tired of the puzzles?"

Danelos unfurled the scroll. "Yeah." His eyes scanned the Olympeian glyphs. "We're living in one big Greek soap opera.

More fun than anyone should be allowed to have. Hey, look at this."

"Does that say what I think it does?"

"Mhmm. We have to go to Delos."

"Why?"

Danelos rolled the parchment and tucked it in his gym bag. "That's where order was born."

After the energy of the sword portal closed, Danelos and Brandon surveyed the ruins of their father's temple on Delos. The sun hadn't risen yet, but they could see random shattered columns jutting from the earth with grasses and wildflowers growing in places—chaos in order's womb. The idea that a temple to Apollo would have fallen to time unsettled both since they knew him as their father. To the rest of the world, the god Apollo was merely an idea or a concept. With the existence of Task Force: Gaea, humanity had gradually come to accept the existence of an "other" around them, but Apollo had wanted to keep his identity and role as downplayed as possible. Initially, he had put forth a glamour to protect his sons and their friends—their faces would always be obscured to cameras when acting on behalf of the United Nations. In the months before Python's attack, Apollo's mind had a harder time maintaining that, and eventually, the glamour failed altogether. Acting without a proverbial mask, the team would have to deal with being outed.

The current state of the temple pained Dan and Brandon, and they shared a look of shame mixed with regret.

"You sure they're going to show?"

"They'll show." Dan took in every single inch. "When I contacted them, they each said they would be here, although Ryuma took a little convincing. We have to trust them." He put a canvas rucksack on the ground.

"It's hard to believe that this used to be a vibrant place of learning and religious activity. You'd never know anyone had ever been here." Brandon crouched down and rubbed his fingers against the dirt.

"But *we* know." A man's voice from behind Brandon made him swing around.

Brandon made out a white lab coat and dark glasses on a slender man. When the man stopped, he shoved his hands in his pockets.

"Dr. Taiyo, I take it."

"And you must be Brandon." His words fell flat.

Neither man extended a hand to the other. Ryuma turned his attention toward Danelos.

"You are our youngest brother." Ryuma again did not attempt to shake hands.

Ignoring Dr. Taiyo, Danelos focused his attention on a tall, black man with wavy black hair approaching from another path. He had a regal bearing, something suited for a son of Apollo. Dan smiled.

Brandon wiped his hands together. "You know him?"

"I've seen his picture in many magazines since he owns the Arcady, a gallery I've heard of but have never seen. I had no idea you were related to us, Keion, although, given the circumstances, it makes sense."

Keion smiled and took Dan's hand in both of his, squeezing. "It's a pleasure to meet you finally. Your reputation," he turned his eyes to Brandon as well, "is known even by my patrons."

Fifteen minutes passed before Jamshid arrived, dressed in jeans, a T-shirt, and sandals.

"Gentlemen!" He sauntered toward them as if he'd known them his whole life. "Nice we can have this family reunion."

Danelos took in each of the men, reading them for anything off or questionable. Once he had finished, a faint smile appeared.

"What amuses you?" Ryuma narrowed his expression.

"Hmm. You know my face changed."

"I'm just full of surprises for a blind man."

"The reason why I smiled is that I see Apollo in all of you. You have his arrogance, Ryuma. And Keion has his confidence. Jamshid—"

"I have his good looks? His sense of humor?" Jamshid grinned.

"I was going to say you have his penchant for the casual." Danelos laughed a little.

Ryuma moved through the ruins, and the others by their expression noticed that he did so without a cane or any hesitation. Jamshid and Brandon got on as if they were old friends, comparing manacles. Keion and Dan spoke about the Arcady and how each had heard of the other. After twenty minutes, Dan assembled them by the ruins where the naos would have been and placed a small kylix on the ground he had brought in his rucksack, nodding for all of them to encircle it. He dropped kindling from an ash tree into the bowl.

"When do we light the wood?" The words fell out of Ryuma's mouth.

Dan tightened his jaw. "Do you hate Apollo that much?"

"You mistake apathy for hatred. I don't hate him. I just don't understand what we hope to accomplish. We're not gods, not really. How can we—"

"We're here for a bigger purpose. The power of a small group can effect change. My team has shown that. We're also Apollo's *sons*, making us linked to Olympos, and we're the only thing standing in the way of reason and truth just disappearing from the world. I don't think we can do this without you, but if your heart's not in it, then go. We'll figure it out."

Ryuma turned slightly and didn't respond, but he didn't leave either.

"In answer to your question, *we* don't light the fire. Just wait." Dan looked over at Brandon who nodded.

At sunrise, the newest of the sun's rays struck the ash, setting it afire. Dan stretched out his arms, palms up, and the others did the same, even Ryuma, although he was the last to do so. The flames grew until they seemed like they would consume the kylix and the men, but the sacred bowl held. Dan had shared the ritual with the others when he first contacted them, but as the youngest, he needed to initiate it.

"I am Danelos, son of Apollo, and I am a pillar for prophecy."

"I am Kidemonas, son of Apollo, and I am a pillar for reason."

"I am Iamos, son of Apollo, and I am a pillar for vision."

"I am Onkios, son of Apollo, and I am a pillar for truth."

Ryuma turned his face toward Dan.

"I am Erymanthos, son of Apollo, and I am a pillar for healing."

In unison, they spoke in ancient Greek:

"*We call upon Khaos, the All-Mother, to hear our plea.*

We bind ourselves to the world. We bind ourselves to the soul of Apollo."

Five strands of fire exploded from the kylix and each one encircled a brother. This was the first part of the rite—the naming. In the distance, leonine roars erupted around them, and five marble lions surrounded the men, each facing outward, an act of protection. In the past, marble lions sat facing the sacred lake near where Apollo was born. Now, these five guarded his sons during this delicate enchantment.

In unison, the men continued:
"We, the Five Pillars, shall stand firm.
On our shoulders shall rest Apollo's gifts.
From the North, we draw wisdom,
From the East, we draw knowledge,
From the West, we draw certainty,
From the South, we draw strength.
We, the Five Pillars, shall stand firm."

All five lions roared as the sun rose higher above the horizon. From different directions came five arrows of light, each striking the men in the chest with a dull thud, knocking them down. At impact, the illuminated shaft dissolved, giving each brother guardianship over one of his father's attributes. Ryuma reached for the entry point and felt something on his skin. When he pulled his shirt open, the Greek word *exakesis* had been burned into him. Jamshid found *pronoia;* Keion, *aletheia;* Kidemonas, *logos;* and, Dan, *profeteia*—all of the areas they had claimed. The fire extinguished itself. The sun, free of the horizon, blanketed them with its rays, but the ritual was not quite over.

Dan fell to his knees, holding his head and cringing as all the power of prophecy that Apollo held flowed through him. Even though Dan possessed the power to unlock prophecy, he had never known so much at once. To see this man of herculean proportions writhing and groaning would have put fear into the most courageous.

"The words... Ancient and new... Past, present, futu—Olympos, make it stop!" He leaned forward, rocking, moaning. "Make it stop… please, by all the gods…"

His brothers couldn't help him, and then he heaved until he vomited.

Overwhelmed by the force of reason filling his mind, Brandon, too, held his head, tears streaming down his face. Unable to form his own thoughts, he collapsed to the ground, shouting unintelligible words, experiencing all that Apollo understood.

His arms wrapped around his torso, Ryuma shivered, the power of healing that encompassed the world, the power that

Apollo kept in check, coursing through him. "Like electricity... a river of current that flows... by sacred Olympos..."

Keion, not seeming to be in pain, reached for the sky, his eyes bearing the sun's brightness, the golden light that shimmered down. "Clarity... Unfettered clarity... each sunbeam holds so much truth..."

His hands tried to grasp the light, but his fingers passed right through it.

On all fours, Jamshid shook his head, his dark curls hanging before his eyes, crying out as Apollo's foresight, his unending vision of the cosmos, pressed against the inside of the man's skull. Drops of blood from his nose splattered on the earth. Such power to be contained within one man, even if he were a demigod.

In just a few eternal heartbeats, each man recovered. One-fifth of Apollo's dominion resided within each brother, and once the transition dissipated, the sons of Apollo collected themselves.

"Well, if I had known it would be this unpleasant—"

"You would still have done it, Ryuma." Dan brushed himself off. "A moment of pain to help the world is a small price, trust me. Everyone else all right?" He pushed his hands through his hair and rubbed his chest.

The others grumbled their answer. With business concluded, Ryuma turned to leave, but Brandon put his hand on the man's shoulder.

"That's it? You're just going to go?"

"Did you want to hug now?"

Brandon jerked his hand back. "Never mind. I thought you might want to get to know your brothers a little before you take off for Japan. My mistake."

"Just let him go, Brandon. Jamshid? Keion? I know this great hole-in-the-wall restaurant on Mykonos." Dan pointed in the direction of that island.

Jamshid and Keion followed Dan and Brandon through the sword portal, and when Jamshid looked back, Ryuma was just standing there. The portal closed, and the four found themselves on Andronikou Street in late morning.

"Do you travel that way often?" Jamshid couldn't stop turning his head all around the town.

Brandon laughed. "Yeah. I should have a bazillion frequent portal miles by now."

Putting his hand across Brandon's shoulders, Jamshid squeezed a little. "I think we're going to get along fine, little brother."

Keion stayed with Dan as they approached the restaurant.

"You've lived quite the adventure, haven't you."

"You have no idea, Keion. When we have more time, I'll enlighten you. Here's the place." Dan knocked on the doorframe. *"Yassou, Niko! Eínai kaneís edó?"*

An elderly man's voice echoed from the kitchen, "Of course I'm here, Danelos. Where the hell else would I be? Just sit anywhere."

"We should probably sit in the back to avoid eavesdroppers." Dan gestured toward a table in the corner. "I met Niko when I was in college, and he was ancient *then*." He chuckled. "He may be ornery, but he makes the best moussaka in Greece."

As they sat, Keion leaned over to Dan. "Is he… family?"

"No, but he should be. Plus, he knows my… *our* father well. I figured here we could talk openly, and it wouldn't be a problem."

As they all got situated, a young girl came out with a tray bearing old jam jars filled with water. She placed them around the table without speaking, but when she realized Dan was there, she smiled. He whispered to her.

"What's his mood like today?"

"What's it always like?" Her giggle made the men smile.

Fifteen minutes after they started sharing life experiences, laughing, and telling stories about experiences with their father, a man silhouetted the door. The tiny restaurant darkened slightly. Dan looked over and smiled.

"Yasmina, can you bring over another chair, please?"

When the man reached the table, the server met him with a chair and a glass of water.

"Nice of you to join us, Ryuma."

Ryuma nodded, and the slightest smile appeared. "I was hungry."

Stories continued for another half hour, and then the food came.

"I don't remember us ordering anything."

Dan snorted. "Keion, in this place, Niko makes what he makes, and we eat. Trust me. You won't be disappointed."

Platters of moussaka, pastitsio, and dolmades came out first. Later, souvlaki followed, along with a dish of feta and olives. As the conversation advanced, Brandon kept an eye on Ryuma. The once-reticent, brusque man started contributing to the chatter, albeit in a controlled fashion. Keion laughed heartily, and Jamshid, who was finishing his third glass of ouzo, kept patting him on the back. Two hours passed, and another figure stepped into the restaurant, and this time, Dan rose to meet the guest at the door.

"Dionysos, what are you doing here?" Dan tried to keep his voice down. "I don't think this is a good time for you to be here."

Dionysos craned his head around Dan's broad shoulders. "Worry not, nephew. I am not here to stir up trouble."

"That would be a first." Dan looked outside. "Where's your partner in mischief?"

The wine god laughed. "Ares? How in Hades should I know? We're not conjoined. The last I saw of him, he was heading for Olympos. So tell me, how are my brother's boys getting along?"

Guiding Dionysos outside the restaurant, Dan glanced back to see Brandon squinting to see what was happening. The others hadn't noticed anything, and even Ryuma seemed to be enjoying himself.

"We performed the ritual. It would have been nice to know we'd be marked." He pried the tear in his shirt open enough to show Dionysos the word singed onto his chest. "Anything else we should know?"

"Nephew, your scowl is not quite as intimidating as Ares', and even his is laughable. As far as the mark, I was unaware of that. You of all people know that Olympeian enchantments come with… consequences."

Through the door came Brandon.

"Everything all right here?" He crossed his arms. "The guys asked where you went."

"I'm coming. Listen, uncle, thanks for your help, but we've got this now. Maybe you should go check on Ares?"

"So, I don't get to see them?" Dionysos' smile looked like that of a car salesman.

"No. Brandon, say goodbye to Uncle D."

Dionysos took a few steps toward the street and evanesced. As Dan and Brandon joined the others, Ryuma leaned in.

"What did *he* want?"

"Actually, he wanted to see all of you, but I didn't think that was wise. Not right now. Plus, despite what he thinks, he's a bit of a downer."

"You missed it, Dan. Ryuma has quite the sense of humor." Jamshid patted Ryuma on the back a few times. "Hilarious!"

Keion finished his glass, muttering. "Well, the ouzo helps."

By three p.m., the conversation had turned to more austere topics, namely the fate of Apollo.

"How is he? I mean, he's in the adyton, so I know Gaea's looking out for him, but have you seen him?" Jamshid popped an olive in his mouth.

Dan shook his head. "I can't bring myself to try. Also, it's not like a convalescent home. You can't just walk in. Gaea won't let anyone in."

Ryuma was sitting back. "Not even your mother? Is she all right?"

"If she's seen him, she hasn't said anything. Let's focus on the matter at hand." Brandon tapped the table. "Now that we're looking out for Apollo's areas of influence, what else is there to do? Dan and I are newbies to this life. You're the ones who've lived thousands of years."

His demeanor softened with familiarity and ouzo, Ryuma shared how he became blind. Having spied on Aphrodite making love to Adonis, the goddess blinded Ryuma—known then as Erymanthos—and Apollo, in the form of a boar, chased Adonis down, goring him. While he had lost his physical ability to see, he had retained a type of vision—intuition, to some—where he could move around without help. As the centuries passed, he mastered the skill. Back in the sixties, he wanted to reinvent himself, so he traveled to Japan, attracted by the ideas of purity in Shintoism. Wanting to separate himself from his past, he altered his appearance to look Japanese, changing his name as well. When he started seeing the Task Force division out in the world, his dreams revealed, in a vague way, the Gaea team; four people, empowered by the gods, somehow had managed to get themselves into the world of covert activities. Later, when he did hear the name 'Gaea' in reference to the U.N., he put things together. Instead of being proud that those connected with Olympeians existed out in the world, he felt increasingly apathetic. Ryuma was a son of Apollo, but he didn't have the power to change the world, not as that team did. Unlocking his true self required a desire to embrace his Olympeian heritage fully, and that meant relinquishing the life he had. Even as a doctor, something he fell into being a demigod of healing, he wasn't entirely comfortable with the "one at a time" approach to helping humanity. He'd kept his practice more out of boredom than a desire to heal.

Jamshid said he understood the feeling, loss as well as sense of separation from the world. Abandoned by his mother in a patch of violets, he was reclaimed when King Aipytos learned of the boy's ancestry and his fate to be a seer. Apollo taught his son the art of prophecy, and eventually, Iamos became the seer in Olympia. When the world no longer relied on seers, Jamshid moved to Iran where he changed his name and took on as a spiritual guide to those who needed help. He worked for charity, living much of his new life in a tent on the outskirts of Mashhad. In the modern era, he spent much time learning about the outside world, especially the machinations of mortals. Like Ryuma, when the United Nations started the Task Force Division, Jamshid felt like his father's hand was involved, but he didn't know how. As soon as the Gaea team made its debut, Jamshid said he'd followed their exploits, hoping he would eventually meet them, not initially knowing that two members were his family.

Of all the brothers, Keion, as Onkios, had known sovereign power, having been the ruler of Onkeion, a part of Arkadeia, and owner of a herd of horses. During this time, Apollo acted as a patron deity of the region, but he had not become the king, leaving the guardianship of its cities to individuals selected by oracular decree. When Demeter fled the advances of Poseidon, she hid among the horses until she could no longer disguise herself. When Poseidon found her, he mated with her, and their son, Arion, a stallion coveted by the gods for his swiftness and power of speech, drew much attention to Onkeion. Ashamed for his inability to protect Demeter, Onkios abdicated his rule and left Greece. From that point forward, Apollo dismissed the guardians, pulling all of Arkadeia under the sovereignty of a monarchy—a tournament of prowess would determine the rule, and men and women of the region competed. When Onkios returned to Arkadeia, summoned by dreams, he attended the coronation of Alkinoë. He returned to the outside world, eventually settling in London, and the urge to reconnect with his ancestry prompted him to open a gallery named after his home.

Dan's phone vibrated—it was Aleta. She wanted to let him know that whatever they had done had an almost immediate effect. From a contact at Beth Israel, she learned that patients had started to stabilize a little bit earlier. He told her to keep him posted in case this was a fluke as well as to check with other hospitals in Boston.

"Well, gentlemen, it seems our first collaboration is showing signs of success. That was Aleta. Patients are healing on their own. She'll let me know if anything changes." Dan noticed Ryuma smiling, and he knew it wasn't from the ouzo.

12 | ARI AND ESTEBAN

Centro de Salud Mental Aranzuela, Madrid
Atencion a Largo Plazo, Long Term Care
Room A121

Ari stood over the bed where Esteban Reyes, lost in a catatonic state, lay strapped in. After Esteban's encounter
with Nyx's daughter, Lismonia, Apollo had tried to heal
Esteban's mind. He had told Danelos he couldn't, that attempting
such a task might leave Esteban in a worse condition than he was
already in. So, he left Esteban in catatonia as a way of preserving
what was left of his mind. Danelos had told Ari of this, and when
Ari received the obol from Hades that enabled him to travel
through various states of consciousness, he knew he had to do
whatever he could to save the Olympeian. Whether it be the realm
of the underworld or the recesses of the mind, Ari believed he
could do what the other gods couldn't—to save Apollo, from
himself, if necessary. The first step, however, was getting aid from
an unlikely individual.

"Esteban, I know you can hear me. My name is Ari." He
gripped the obol in his right hand while he placed his left in
Esteban's. "If you can hear me, squeeze my hand."

Nothing. Taking a deep breath, he tried again, concentrating
on the coin hanging around his neck. The body, with its chest
rising and falling in shallow breaths, did not attempt to move in
response. Ari knew his ten minutes with Esteban would be up

87

soon, but he didn't know how to make the coin do anything. If he couldn't make contact, his trip from Boston would be a waste. He watched Esteban's eyes stay fixed on the ceiling, and he leaned over to whisper in his ear.

"I need your help. Your mind and Apollo's have touched. You're my only hope to help him. Without you, Apollo will be lost."

Ari turned to go, realizing his mission had failed, but then he had a thought. Taking the coin from beneath his shirt, he touched it to Esteban's lips. What felt like a tiny spark went up Ari's arm.

"Esteban Reyes, can you hear me? I need your help."

Although unmoving physically, Ari felt a presence growing in his mind.

"Esteban?"

The voice was soft yet present. "Sí. Soy Esteban. Who-Who are you?"

"Ari. I need your help. Apollo needs your help."

After a few seconds of silence, Esteban's voice replied.

"He left me here. Like this. I won't help him. He could have saved me, but he didn't."

"Esteban, please. I know you are angry with him, but try to understand, he had to leave you like this. His own mind was in danger of breaking down if he had helped you. I know you cannot understand all of this, but—"

"I *know* who he is. From the moment our minds touched, I knew. I know what he could have done too. Any conscious life would have been better than this. *No* life would have been better…"

Ari's heart ached. He placed his hand on Esteban's. The orderly would be returning shortly.

"If you help me, I will speak on your behalf with Apollo, once he is well, to heal you fully. Please, I do not have much time here. Without Apollo, the world will suffer. He is a god, and his mind has been shattered by evil."

"Then he will know what it feels like to be helpless, a stranger to his own mind."

"To save my friends, the man I love, and the world, I gave up a year of my life to the underworld. I was a pawn of Python, the one who destroyed Apollo. If I was willing to give up so much, surely you—"

"I'm afraid you came all this way for nothing. There's nothing I can do to help you. Now, go. ¡Déjame en paz!"

The clicking of the lock brought Ari back to full awareness. He didn't even wait for the orderly to say anything; as he reached the door, he turned back, hoping his last thoughts would get through.

"Think about it, Esteban. Please."

Just outside the hospital, Ari looked back at the building. He knew he had to do something to save Apollo, and that meant only one thing.

Standing in the throne room of the palace in the underworld, Ari paced. In Hades' realm, sound had different qualities, and unlike the smaller, more indistinguishable noises all around one might hear while standing in silence, Ari heard nothing. A place devoid of life was also devoid of certain sounds. He remembered that absence while he had tended to the ferryman's responsibilities. At first, it had unnerved him, but over time, he had come to find it comforting, as if nothing could penetrate that barrier to cause unease. A slight hissing made him turn toward the throne, and there, in a dissipating mist, sat Hades.

"You wished to see me?"

"Yes. Thank you for indulging me."

Hades broke into a small smile. "You are now my son and can always come here. I did not know when you would want to return here after what you had endured. But you seem troubled."

Ari explained about his visit to Esteban, emphasizing how much he wanted to help Apollo since he felt partially responsible for what had happened.

"Aristeides, you did nothing wrong, but I understand your desire to aid my nephew. I am not clear as to what you think I can do. No god has the power to fix that which Python has wrought."

"I know, but it is not *your* aid that I seek, at least not in helping Apollo directly. I have learned that this obol allows me to travel through different states of consciousness of which this realm is one, a place of death. I believe that I can, with Esteban, help Apollo. But… he was less than willing when I saw him in the hospital."

Hades leaned back, resting his chin in his hand. "Then, I am unsure of what you need."

"It took much of the money I had saved to travel to Spain so that I could convince Esteban to help me. With the obol, I can reach into his mind and communicate with him. He feels betrayed by Apollo, though, after the events with Lismonia, so he will not help me. If you were able, somehow, to get him to a hospital in Boston where I could visit him regularly, then I believe I can convince him to help me."

"What you ask has consequences. Plus, my power does not have the same reach in the mortal world as it used to. If I were to do this, and that is questionable, then you would have to be his guardian. I assume you think that once my nephew has returned, he will heal Esteban. Then, what? He will need a place to live and a means to support himself. Plus, bringing him to Boston against his will would mean he may wish to return to Spain. But, to whom? If you save his life, you are henceforth responsible for his life. Do you understand?"

Ari nodded. "Of course. I am certain Danelos will help me when that situation arises."

"Does he know what you plan to do?"

"Not yet. I am going to speak with him when I return to the mortal world."

"And, if he does not support this?"

"He will. He cannot afford not to do this when it could mean the safe return of his father as well as saving a human life, giving him back the quality of life he deserves. Apollo owes him that much."

The lord of the underworld sighed.

"All right. I will send word to you when this young man is situated. I do this because of all you sacrificed, and because of how much I care about you. Remember what I have said, Aristeides. He is *your* responsibility once he has regained his faculties."

Ari bowed, holding his palms together. "Thank you."

Once Ari left, Persephone ascended the dais and sat next to her husband, her pallid face holding a dour expression. She looked into her husband's eyes, and he turned away.

"Husband, you know that this may all go awry. If Ari does not succeed, order as we know it may wither and fade from the cosmos."

"Aye. That, however, is not what troubles me, but I cannot speak of it. Not yet."

13 | MINDSCAPE

"Dr. Luto, good morning. I'm Dr. Alvarez, the hospital administrator. Let's go back to my office."

A tall, striking man with short black hair and a closely trimmed beard put down the copy of *Life Coach* magazine, following the woman down the corridor. A few rooms down, she gestured for him to enter and closed the door. The brown leather chair creaked as he sat, and he placed his interlaced hands in his lap. Dr. Alvarez flipped through a manila folder with a label marked 'Esteban Reyes' and underneath, 'Dr. P. Luto, Psy.D.'

"I see that you would like to move a patient, one Esteban Reyes from Centro de Salud Mental Aranzuela in Madrid here to our facility. May I ask why? According to their hospital records, he seems to be getting excellent care where he is."

Leaning forward, Dr. Luto rested his elbows on his knees, his fingers still laced together. He smiled.

"I would like to try alternative treatments for this man's catatonia. Centro de Salud has been able to *maintain* him, but no one is seeking to *help* him. From my understanding, he has no family. There is a therapist I would like to bring in to help engage Mr. Reyes. I believe his information is in the folder."

Dr. Alvarez flipped a few pages. "Ah, yes. Dr. Ari Fairmont. He's a clinical psychologist, I see."

91

"Yes, one of the best. He asked to be assigned to Mr. Reyes. His credentials should be in order."

"I've not heard of him before. Has he been practicing long?"

"He gained his experience overseas, in Greece mostly. Grief counseling."

She looked over everything, and when she was satisfied, she signed the paperwork and handed the folder back to Dr. Luto. He stood to shake her hand.

"A pleasure. We're looking to have him transported by the end of the week. Thank you, Dr. Alvarez. I'll contact you when he arrives in the country to have the room prepared."

"We'll place him in D Wing. That's where patients with more serious conditions stay. He'll have a suite that includes a restroom as well as a seating area for any guests. He won't have to share a room, either."

Dr. Luto stepped out into the blaring sunlight of midday, shielding his eyes, and walked over to a young man sitting on a bench overlooking an arboretum on the hospital's property.

"Everything is set. I have you listed as a clinical psychologist. The paperwork I gave them will enable you to have unfettered access to Mr. Reyes. I hope you know what you're doing, Ari."

"I believe I can help Apollo, Hades. Esteban may not want to help me do this, but I can convince him. How do we arrange his transfer?"

"In a few days, I will remove him from the hospital in Spain, ensuring that the staff will remember that they released him into the care of Dr. Luto. He will then arrive here via ambulance where he will be placed in the suite that Dr. Alvarez is setting up. After that, it is up to you."

Ari smiled. "Thank you for this." He looked up and squinted. "You are okay in all this light?"

Hades laughed. "Before I chose the short straw and became the god of the underworld, I actually lived here on Gaea. And remember, very recently, I spent a year living in New York City as a life coach." He walked down the driveway. "I will let you know when Esteban is here. The rest is up to you."

In a few more steps, he vanished.

Ari returned his eyes to the sky. "Worry not, Apollo. I will help you gain control of your mind. I swear this to you."

A week later, Ari signed in at the main desk of Grove Psychiatric and made small talk with Nurse Gregory. This would be his first visit to see Esteban since his arrival, and it would also be the first time Ari had ever worn a shirt and tie. Danelos had taken him clothes shopping so he could have more of a wardrobe; for the museum galas as well as fancier nights out, he wanted Ari to have some more formal attire. He would have to dress the part of a clinical psychologist for this masquerade to work.

Isopropyl alcohol mixed with rose-scented air freshener hung in the air. The main foyer had a Mid-Century Modern aesthetic: clean lines, teak chairs, smoothness, and vibrant color. Even the clacking of Ari's shoes was crisp and precise. He entered Room 303 to see Esteban lying in his bed, as if simply asleep, the morning light showering him. Pulling up a chair, Ari loosened his tie and removed the obol from around his neck. He tightened his grip, the coin's edges against his palm and fingers, placing his other hand on Esteban's head. He closed his eyes, casting his thoughts.

"Esteban, can you hear me?"

Beyond silence. Beyond sound. Consciousness held no corporeal form and had no limits. Ari, however, could see into it. He could touch it. Death was one form of this consciousness, but so was the mind.

"Esteban, please. I know you are angry. You resent Apollo for leaving you in this state, but *we* can help him. Once we do, he will restore you. I am sure of it."

Moments passed, and Ari started to remove his hand from Esteban's head.

"¿Está sufriendo?"

Ari hesitated. "I-I am not certain if he is suffering, but he has lost his hold on sanity."

"Bueno. He should endure what it means to have no control."

"Is your heart that cold?"

Esteban didn't reply right away. Ari could see further into the consciousness and shivered as if a frozen wind had swept through the room. Something about Esteban made him tense up. Something dark.

"Do you know why I was placed in the hospital in Madrid?"

"No, Esteban. I do not."

A tingle ran through Ari's hand where it touched Esteban's head, a shiver of memory about to be revealed.

"When I was born, my parents knew I was different. El doctor said I was cold to the touch, and my pulse was thready. Padre González said he felt like my spirit wasn't entirely in this world. He feared I was tainted by something dark, or at least something he couldn't understand. I spent a month in the hospital and was released because my mother wanted me home. My father worked harder because he had a child, a child he wasn't sure about from the moment I had taken my first breath. Mi madre had named me 'Esteban' because she said she had dreamt of a crown the week before I was born. My last name, Reyes, comes from the word for 'king'. In my mother's eyes, I was royalty.

"Growing up in Madrid, I was the quiet child, the pensive one, one whose sadness was tangible. At school, my classmates said that a living shadow followed me wherever I went, so they nicknamed me *el sombro*. I was teased every day, and even the teachers couldn't stop it. When I turned 8, the first child went missing. People blamed me, saying I was a *maldito*, a cursed one. When I learned who had disappeared, I didn't even remember him. I had never had a problem with him. Why people blamed me, I will never understand.

"By the time I was 12, five more people had gone missing. Always at night. And each absence was blamed on me. I was still a quiet child, with no true friends, so people feared me. The name *El Maldito* followed me. That was when the dreams began."

Ari's skin tingled as if cold fingers lightly dragged all over his body. Whatever the source of the coldness was, it was alive. He hadn't imagined it.

"Tell me about the dreams."

"Oh, I was planning on it, Ari." Although Ari couldn't see Esteban's face in his mind, he felt as if the young man would be smiling.

"Dreams can do much to shape our destiny. I am curious to know."

"Well, Ari, the first dream had me in a desolate landscape, with the land as abraded as battle-torn flesh, and the sky void of stars. I looked all around me and felt the darkness as if it were an entity, a physical being. I knew this darkness. I reached out to it, and it enveloped my arm, but I felt no pain. It felt familiar to me. I knew it as *Tinieblas Eternas*."

Ari almost broke the connection when he heard that.

"The Eternal Darkness...Erebos." He whispered aloud.

Esteban didn't respond.

"I am not sure I understand what this has to do with the disappearances of the children. Erebos is not evil. Darkness is not evil."

"I'm not quite finished, Ari. You wanted to know, so I will tell you all."

Esteban's gelid tone immobilized Ari, but Ari still wanted to know why Esteban had been placed in a hospital.

"Other dreams like that one repeated over the years, and I remained reserved, speaking only when necessary, and keeping to myself in public. I would sit in the Plaza Mayor, always in shadow, watching the people pass, and I would wonder who might be next. The darkness in my dreams spoke about sacrifice and need, about hunger and sustenance. I didn't understand who or what could need those people, and my fears tightened my grip on my solitude.

"Then, the dreams changed. I would be walking through fields of white asphodels, their blossoms moving in a gentle, cold breeze. It was there I could hear the voice calling to me. The voice of darkness…"

The images of those fields were all too familiar to Ari. White asphodels grew in the underworld, across meadows where the spirits of ordinary mortals walked. He didn't remember anything about Erebos being anywhere near there, though, and this made his pulse increase. Esteban could tell something was different about him.

"What is it, Ari? Does this image disturb you? I know you were *porthmeos* of the underworld for a year, so why should the white asphodels irritate you. They're quite beautiful."

Ari knew Esteban was taunting him. Plus, Esteban referred to Ari as *porthmeos*, and only someone familiar with the Greek underworld would even know that word for ferryman. There was also that tone again, the implication that this young man knew much more than he was letting on. The two shared a connection, one that Ari couldn't quite figure out, even if Erebos *were* involved. Erebos was a Protogenos, and a primordial god had much more power than an Olympeian god like Hades. Before Ari could conjecture about this connection, Esteban continued.

"You remember the perfume of asphodel, do you not, Ari? The intoxicating sweetness, the scent that lingers in the meadows—"

"Esteban, how did you know I was the ferryman of the underworld?"

A pause. Ari felt his pulse against Esteban's where his hand touched the young man's head.

"My mother told me."

"Your... mother." Ari pulled his hand back, breaking the connection. This visit had revealed much, he thought, and he would have to digest all of this before he would continue.

<hr />

Danelos arrived home and found Ari lying back on the sofa, staring at the ceiling. Midday sun highlighted the edges of the blinds, leaving the apartment in dusky sepia tones. Putting his messenger bag on the table, Dan fell onto the sofa right next to his husband.

"Eisai kala?" He gave Ari a quick peck on the cheek.

Ari sighed. "I am fine. I had my first meeting with Esteban."

"Did it not go well?"

Ari turned to face Dan. "I learned quite a bit. Probably more than I wanted to. I will go back tomorrow to see what else I can find out."

Dan raised his eyebrows.

"Later. Right now, I need to talk to Hades." He pecked Dan's lips. "Worry not. I will keep you, as you say, in the loop. I may need your help."

After the front door closed, Dan fell back and smirked to himself.

<hr />

One of the benefits of possessing an obol as well as being the adopted son of Hades was that Ari didn't have to cross the rivers of the underworld or even enter it to communicate with the god. Sitting on a secluded bench by the Charles River, looking out at the skyline, Ari closed his eyes. Regulating his breathing, he pictured himself standing in the throne room of the god of the dead, and within moments, he was there—an astral projection of a sort. Hades materialized in his throne, his robes a dark Byzantine purple.

"How goes your investigation?" Hades leaned his head on his fist.

"That sounded almost mortal." Ari smiled. "I need to ask you something, and please do not couch your answer in some proverbial fog of mystery or shroud of misdirection."

Hades snickered. "I make no promises. Ask."

Ari explained all he had learned from his encounter with Esteban, and he wanted to know whatever Hades could tell him about the gods or other immortals who inhabited the realm of the dead. He felt that by understanding Esteban's past that he could try to convince the young man to aid him in his healing quest for Apollo.

"What you ask has no simple answer. This place has a hierarchy that begins with me and moves into the lower tiers of immortals. Nymphs, daimones, even creatures, like Cerberos, for example, have their place here. I have never taken a census of who resides in my realm, aside from the spirits. Why does it matter so much to you?"

"Esteban mentioned his mother told him about my role as ferryman here. How would anyone who was not tied to the gods know of such a thing? Who could his mother be?"

Hades' eyes didn't leave Ari, but he said nothing. No reaction. Then, he cocked his head and raised an eyebrow.

"I need you to do something for me when you speak with Esteban again. I need you to ask him a question, and his response will give me an idea of what you would like to know."

Hades gave him the question to ask, and with a solitary nod, Ari removed his consciousness from the underworld. Hades drummed his fingers on the arm of his throne, a habit he had picked up from his life as a mortal. Ari had brought a conundrum to him, one that could involve someone in his realm, and he wanted to know who.

Despite his interest in wanting to learn more from Esteban, Ari needed a few days to himself before he returned to the hospital. His conversation with Hades left him with more questions than answers, and he knew that the answers would come from Esteban. He wasn't sure, though, whether he wanted to know. Ideas floated around his mind, and his experience of being in the underworld gave him much knowledge, more than he thought he would have acquired. He kept reflecting on his life with Timaios, how he grew up in the Temple of Hades, and how he went from being the son of the temple caretaker to being the adopted son of the lord of the underworld himself. It was in these moments when he wished he could talk to Timaios the way he used to. The shade of his father was just that, and no matter what, Ari couldn't change the order of things. That was how things worked in death. Not even Hades could break the rules. While the son of Kronos held dominion over the underworld, it was Thanatos who created what it means to die a non-violent death. The Keres, on the other hand, presided over violent and cruel deaths, like that of Timaios. Ari tried to conceive how darkness, like Erebos, would be in league with Thanatos and take innocent people away. Was there more to the Protogenos than he had been led to believe? Danelos had told him that certain aspects of their existence differed from what truly was. By digging further with Esteban, Ari knew he would expose the mysteries that had been cast before him.

This time, when he approached Esteban's bedside, he wasn't going to let the young man catch him off guard. If there was a connection between Esteban and the gods somehow, Ari had had enough experience with them to be able to stand his ground. He also had to try a different tack, one that would provide equity in the environment. Taking a deep breath, he placed his hand on Esteban's head and closed his eyes. It didn't take but a moment for the link to establish itself.

"Tú has regresado, I see." Esteban's voice resonated with confidence.

"I have. I needed time to absorb what you had told me. But, if I am to continue this with you, I need to change the way this works."

The next thing Esteban realized was that he was in human form, standing in front of Ari in an ethereal place, with no visual boundaries, no objects, just space.

"Where have you taken me? How is it that I am standing here with you?"

"I need to tell *you* something. I am the adopted son of Hades, and I can move through states of consciousness. The last time we spoke, that disembodied state we were in did not work for me. I needed to see you as you are."

"But this is not how I am. If you open your eyes, you will see me lying in that bed in a catatonic state." Esteban scowled.

"True. I needed for us to see each other, though, in a way that would help bridge understanding. This way, you can share your thoughts with me so that I can experience them with you. Before, I relied on you to expose the truth. Now, I will see the truth exactly as it is. You cannot hide the truth in this place."

"Do you feel I have deceived you?"

"Not necessarily deceived, but purposely omitted certain details. I do not have time to spend listening to you spin your tale, Esteban. I swore an oath to help Apollo, and, by Olympos, I will do that. Now, continue telling me what you want me to know, starting with your mother."

In this version of consciousness, both Ari and Esteban could see each other as if they were in the same room, so every emotion, every facial expression, every hint at body language was visible. As Ari had said, Esteban could hide nothing from him.

"Bueno. The woman who bore me was my mother in a corporeal sense, but not in an ethereal one. There is a reason why I was born as I had told you, cold. I didn't understand just who I was until I had another dream, and this time, all was revealed to me, whether I wanted to learn it or not.

"In this dream, I walked hand in hand with a woman shrouded in black, the gentle chill of the underworld breezes alive. When I looked into her face, I saw the mysteries of the world, the darkness that I had always known to surround me. In the core of my heart, I knew that I was looking into the face of my mother. I asked her why I was who I was, and she told me that I had been born of love, but that mortal love required a price. To bring me into the world, in order for my father to have me in the mortal realm, she required others to join her in the darkness. She assured me that they did not pass into the underworld harshly. Their essence was absorbed by hers until they became a part of her."

Ari gasped. "Who-Who is your mother? I cannot sense anything about her, even seeing this unfold before my eyes as you tell it. She does not look familiar to me, yet I lingered in the underworld for a year. Tell me!"

"I do not know her name, Ari. She never saw fit to tell me. That was where my madness began."

"I have one more question. Hades bade me ask… Does the name Askalaphos mean anything to you?"

In the late evening, Dan sat on his balcony overlooking the Charles River. With the sun slipping below the horizon, his thoughts went to his father. Not a waking moment passed when he didn't wonder about Apollo chained within Gaea. Had something happened to his father, he would know, or at least he would think he would know. Gaea had reassured him early on that his father was well, as well as a madman could be. The idea of a god being held, bound to the earth literally, made Dan uneasy. His own oath to Gaea and Olympeia was through his Asulos Pistis, and the manacle showed that connection, but Apollo's current binding held no mystical connection. The metal that kept him in check was enchanted, but it didn't bind him the same way. It was a prison. The click of the sliding glass doors opening startled Dan.

"Ari, I didn't hear you come back. Did you have a better session today?"

Taking a seat next to Dan, Ari stared at the sunset, as much as mortal eyes could. He breathed deeply.

"Yes. Better. Although I am not sure by how much. I have two questions for you."

"Shoot." Dan creased his brow. "Are you sure you're okay?"

"First, does the name Askalaphos mean anything to you? And what do you know of the underworld? I mean, of the gods that exist there?"

"That name doesn't ring a bell. As far as the underworld, I suppose I know as much as you do, but you might know more since you spent time there. What is this about?"

"Esteban told me of a dream, one where he walked hand in hand with his mother through asphodel in Hades' realm. He said she never told him her name, and that intrigues me. How can he not know? Why would she not tell him? Hades asked me to ask him about someone named Askalaphos, but he did not answer. It was almost as if I had touched a nerve... or released a memory."

"I'm not sure why Esteban's mother wouldn't reveal her name. Other than Hades and Persephone, other *daimones* and nymphs reside in the land of the dead, but I'm sure Hades told you that. I only know that from what my father told me. You spoke to Hades, right? What else did he have to say?"

"If Hades knows something, he is not sharing it with me. If he does not know, then that worries me. What could exist in his realm that he is not aware of?"

"I see your point. That would be like Zeus not knowing, or not revealing, something about Olympos. Why does it matter who Esteban's mother is? How is that going to help my father?"

Ari placed his hand over Dan's. "I do not know, beloved. I do not know. But, where there is a mystery, there is also a truth. You taught me that."

Dan laughed. "I did indeed. Keep me informed about what you learn, and perhaps I can poke around a little. I hate to say it, but I might even ask Dionysos or Ares."

Ari raised his eyebrows and laughed.

"I know. The last resort, believe me."

"I go back tomorrow to learn more. Ever since I leveled the playing field, as you say, it has made this a bit easier."

"You seem to be taking in idioms well. But, you don't have to qualify each one with 'as you say'. Soon, I'll have you speaking in contractions." He chuckled.

Ari kissed the top of Dan's head.

"I *don't* doubt it. I am going to lie down for a bit. Wake me for dinner."

"See? I knew you could do it." Dan grinned.

1003 B.C.E., Mount Parnassus, Greece

Piercing shrieks from a servant brought Mestra to the marble steps at the entrance of her home at the base of which stood Mikos, the gardener, out of breath, a child draped over his arms. As he ascended, the shrill cries of the servant grew, yet Mestra's face remained stolid. When Mikos was a few steps away from her, she sat on the step where the man placed the body of her son on her lap. He placed the boy's arms on his body, and that revealed the two marks of an adder's bite. Alekos was aiding the gardener when the snake struck from under a bush. Despite how quickly the man ran, the venom was faster.

Leaping steps at a time, Mestra's husband sat next to her, cradling their son, and he pulled his wife to him. She remained stunned while he howled enough for both, rocking the boy's body, and caressing his cheek.

14 | DARKNESS AND LIGHT

The following day, Ari arrived at the hospital just as visiting hours began at 8 a.m. He had considered everything that Esteban, Dan, and Hades had told him, and he went into this visit with broader expectations. He wasted no time before making the connection. Again, Ari and Esteban stood in that void. At first, Ari said nothing.

"¿No tienes preguntas para mi hoy?" The construct of Esteban glared. "Have you decided to give up on me? I thought you were enjoying this game. Why create this elaborate environment if—"

"Yesterday, when I mentioned Askalaphos, you went silent. I believe you know who he is, or you think you might, and you are resisting telling me. Why?"

Esteban continued to scowl at Ari.

"The way I see this is simple. You can help me to help Apollo, or you can remain in this catatonic state in a hospital bed unable to interact with any*one* or any*thing*. I think you are enjoying this..." Ari gestured back and forth between him and Esteban. "No one came to visit you in Madrid. I checked the hospital records. Ever since the incident with Lismonia, you remained alone, the pungent scent of ammonia and bleach all around you in that sterile environment. You had to endure having a nurse bathe you daily since you could not do it yourself, clean your sheets, live off a feeding tube, do physical therapy to maintain your muscles, all in silence. Nurses and doctors would not speak to you because they did not

103

know what to say to a man who could not respond. All that time with no true companionship must have been hard on you. It has made you bitter."

"You have *no* idea—"

"Yes. Yes, I do. I spent a year of my life standing on a boat ferrying the souls of the *dead*. The *dead*! A year without conversation. A year without human interaction. A year of my life silent. I understand what that feels like, not to be able to reach out and speak to someone. It crushed a part of me, a part that I can never recover. But I did it because of someone I love. Between that, and the need to help make things right, I was able to endure. I am not the same man I was before that year began, and I would like to think I am better because of that, despite where I was."

"You're going to equate *one* year of your life, a year you willingly gave away, to my years... Years! It's not even remotely the same..." Esteban turned his head.

Ari sighed. "My point is that isolation is something I understand. If we work together to help Apollo, he will repay you, and I can think of no better compensation than to return your state of mind. He can free you from your isolation."

"He had that chance. He chose to leave me like *this*!"

Ari's ability to create the pseudo-physical construct of their bodies so they could see each other prevented him from interacting with Esteban as he would with a human being. Even though Esteban would surely reject any gesture of compassion, Ari's expression conveyed regret that he could not at least attempt.

"You are impossible! I am trying to *help* you. You would rather wallow in your bitterness and resentment. I see the man you truly are, Esteban Reyes. Unlike your name implies, you are no 'crowned king.' You are a petulant child who wants revenge. Very well. I will leave you to your silence. May the gods have mercy on you."

Ari's eyes popped open, and he yanked his hand from Esteban's head. He stared down at the young man whose eyes stared at the ceiling. Shaking his head, he got as far as the door when he heard a voice from inside his mind.

"Stop!" A few seconds later... "Por favor..."

For Esteban's consciousness to have reached him without being physically connected must have taken a great deal of mental energy. Ari hesitated before turning around, but he took slow steps toward the bed. His hand almost touched Esteban's head, but then he stopped himself.

"Can you hear me?" Ari thought.

"I can. You haven't made contact, though. How is that possible?"

"We have apparently surpassed that." Ari clenched his jaw. "What did you want?"

"Ari… mi madre. I do know her name. It's Orphne. I also know Askalaphos too. He's my half-brother."

"Why did you keep that from me? I have never heard of Orphne. Hades did not mention her, either."

"That's something you would have to ask *him* about. I'm not proud of who I am or who my mother is. I never asked to be the son of a nymph. She's one of the embodiments of darkness, and that would explain the reaction people had to me ever since I can remember."

"When I mentioned Erebos the other day, you had the chance to correct me, but you did not. Why?"

Esteban simply looked at Ari without responding, wrapping his arms around himself, and lowering his head.

Ari nodded. "You wanted me to think it was Erebos so that I would not question the will of a Protogenos. Esteban, I know you just said you are not proud of who your mother is but are you trying to protect Orphne for some reason?"

The construct of Esteban vanished. Ari opened his eyes and placed his hand on Esteban's head, but the physical connection didn't work. The young man's shallow breathing and slow pulse were normal. Nothing seemed off except that he couldn't contact Esteban. Ari didn't have time for this, he thought. The longer Apollo remained in his earthbound containment, battling his own sanity, the worse it could be getting. Since he was unable to pierce Gaea's boundary to enter the adyton, Ari would have to do the only thing left to him: find Orphne.

Once he was back at his apartment, he sent a text to Dan that read: "Going off the grid. Be back soon." Dan had told him that the Task Force used that expression whenever they went into an otherworldly place, like Olympos. To an outsider, Dan mentioned, it would seem as if he or one of the others was going wherever cell phone service was nonexistent or questionable. Ari had discovered that he could use the obol, in conjunction with a doorway, to enter Hades and appear in the throne room. Unlike Dan's sword, the obol couldn't let him go just anywhere, and using Hades' throne room as a nexus in the underworld gave Ari a frame of reference or anchor point.

Concentrating on the doorway to his bedroom, and clutching the coin, he walked through the opening, appearing in the black marble halls he had seen so many times before, and awaiting him were Hades and Persephone, each seated on a throne. Being more than just a projection of himself in this place made him shiver.

"Aristeides! I am so glad to see you!" Persephone shuffled herself quickly down the dais to the young man, pulling him into a tight embrace. Despite the warmth of her gesture, her touch was gelid.

"It is good to see you as well, Persephone." Ari laughed, returning the gesture. "I need to speak with you both, actually."

Taking Ari's arm in her own, she led him to Hades who gestured that he should sit on a marble bench next to the god's black throne. Hades moved his finger, and a spirit brought a tray with three chalices of nectar. Since Hades had adopted Ari, Ari would be able to have the drink of the gods.

"My husband has told me of your endeavor. Have you been able to sway the young man to help you?" Persephone sipped her chalice. "I so miss Apollo."

"Not yet. Soon, I hope. That is why I am here. Hades, as you suspected, Esteban is connected to an underworld nymph by the name of Orphne. He and I had begun exploring that when my connection with him broke, and he became silent."

Hades held the chalice before his face, staring off, and then finished the contents in one gesture. He stepped down from the dais and turned, his purple cloak swinging around.

"I had not truly suspected that Orphne was still here. After she bore Askalaphos to the river god Acheron, I had always assumed she vanished into the caverns. If she will see you, she may be able to help you. She is one of the *Lampades*, so follow the path through the asphodel until it enters the caves. You will know you are near when you see—"

"Torchlight. I am aware of the lampad nymphs, torchbearers for Hekate. My father told me tales of the nymphs when I was a boy. I did not realize Orphne was one of them." Ari pursed his lips. "Hades… Forgive me, but how is it that you are not aware of who resides in your realm?"

Hades put his hands behind his back and paced, each step precise as if attuned to an idea as it crossed his mind. Ari looked at Persephone, but she had nothing to say. He had never seen Hades at a loss for words, let alone so disturbed. Whenever Hades paused, Ari expected him to speak, but then he would resume his pacing. The longer it took for a response, the more Ari fidgeted. Persephone lifted herself as if to approach her husband.

"Hades?"

The son of Kronos turned toward them.

"Power is not absolute, not even here. Or Olympos." He took a few steps. "It's funny. When Zeus wanted us to gain perspective by living as humans, I don't think he understood the ramifications of such an act. The unknowns certainly concerned all of us. My brother always did like a challenge. I digress, though. My absence allowed other forces present here to establish a firmer hold. Hence, why the five rivers were able to form their alliance. My inability to sense who resides in my realm stems from others who also exist here, Nyx, for one."

"Why would Nyx care one way or another about a lampad nymph, even one attuned to darkness? Unless she…"

Hades nodded. "Yes, Persephone. I believe Orphne is Nyx's daughter. By whom, I'm not certain. Secrets fester here like algae. I'm fairly certain that Nyx wants to protect her daughter in a way she could not protect Lismonia."

Ari's eyes widened. "Orphne and Lismonia are sisters? By Gaea's grace…" Ari sat on the dais steps. "That explains so much. Lismonia would not harm someone close to her."

Persephone's cheeks looked even more pallid than usual.

"Husband… should we be sending Aristeides to seek out Orphne, then? One who—"

Ari jumped up. "I *have* to go. I need answers, and she is the only one who has them."

She implored Ari to think of another way, but the young man stood his ground. He crossed his arms and shot a glance over at Hades who put up his hands.

"This is between you and her, my boy. I know better than to get into a battle of words with the queen. She is most assuredly her mother's daughter."

After ten more minutes of their verbal volley, Ari turned his attention toward Hades.

"Through the asphodel until the caves, yes? Very well. I will come back here before I return to the upper world." He turned to Persephone. "Trust me. Please."

A heavy moment passed, but she nodded her assent.

Walking through the asphodel in bloom would take one's breath away if he or she had any breath to take. The perfume from the spikes of white flowers would intoxicate the spirits, keeping them sedate and aloof. To any mortals who dared to visit, the cloying scent caused headaches and dizziness. For Ari, who was under the paternal guidance of Hades, the flowers had no physical effect, and they made him almost nostalgic for the time he spent in this realm. When he acted as the ferryman, he would bring his skiff to this side of the river for the spirits to disembark, and the scent would waft across the meadow, teasing his nostrils. It provided a respite from the decay and fetid stench of the waters.

Halfway through the field, the gatehouse of the underworld sat where the judges of the dead decided whether the shade would go to Elysium, remain in the fields of asphodel, or be imprisoned in Tartaros. He had never met Rhadamanthys, Minos, or Aiakos, the three sons of Zeus, but their reputation as impartial was even known to some in the mortal world. To Ari's perception, the gatehouse looked like a stately temple of white marble striated with black and gold. From within, the hearth that burned with the First Fires glowed, that sacred flame that can only exist within Gaea, including Hades' realm. The trodden path meandering through the flowers gradually diminished, revealing dark earth and the gullet of the caves. The opening expanse measured close to fifteen feet with weighty iron rings bearing two iron torches. Ari took a deep breath and stepped into the living darkness.

Unlike the darkness of the mortal world, this tenebrous space was alive. Similar to Nyx, the form of Erebos had tendrils that wove themselves throughout the underworld, forming pockets of emptiness, but an emptiness that was sentient. To walk through Erebos felt like moving through a gelatinous cloud. Ari had a profound respect for the Protogenoi who resided in the underworld, especially because his father had taught him that these primordial beings held limitless—and frightening—power. Trusting his instincts and shuffling his feet across the ground to avoid rocks or bumps, Ari lost all track of time. For all he knew, days or weeks could have transpired. Sounds didn't travel in the cave, except his feet on the ground, and he had no idea what lay waiting for him.

Empusai, shapeshifting creatures sent out by Hekate to ward off nosy intruders into her shrine or sacred places, could be lurking somewhere, or maybe *lamiae*, vampiric spirits who indulged in pure flesh and blood, especially when mortals wandered through the underworld. Even being the ward of Hades wouldn't protect him.

Ari realized that he had come into this place basically unarmed. Should he encounter a problem, he would only have his brain and whatever skills he had picked up by training with Dan and the others. He would be no match for the denizens of this place. Surrounded by Erebos, the only sensation he could feel was his stomach grumbling. In his haste to begin his journey, he had forgotten to eat. Hades or Persephone would have had to conjure food for him since any plants that grew in this place would be poisonous to a living being, even the asphodel, although versions that grew in the mortal world could sometimes be eaten. He had no means to contact Hades, so he would have to endure his hunger. It was a distraction he didn't need.

To keep his mind focused, he repeated meditations he had learned from his father. Living in the Temple of Hades took its toll on both Timaios and Ari with so few visitors and a concentration of maintaining the shrine. Timaios had stumbled upon scrolls earlier in his life containing ancient poems that he would recite aloud while performing his tasks. As a boy, Ari mimicked his father, and it wasn't until he was older that the man told his son what they were. No one could tell Timaios where the poems originated, but they spoke of light and peace, something a caretaker of Hades' shrine would benefit from. Ari understood more than many about the grieving process, having seen the stages in so many who visited the temple in Arkadeia, but also because of his own father's death. His thoughts were interrupted by a smell, one that he knew well. At first, the scent was faint, but then its sweetness surrounded him.

"Myrrh. I must be getting close." Hearing his own voice, even a soft utterance, startled him. "Thank you, Father, for teaching me about these things. I miss you..."

The density of the darkness shifted, and his eyes perceived a faint glow, a gray flicker. The myrrh intensified, and waves of heat pulsed toward him. He turned a corner, and the illumination became a bit more yellow, like natural light. As the path opened into a chamber, Ari's eyes adjusted to seeing a dozen torches held to the cave wall by iron rings. Seated beneath each torch was a shrouded figure. In the center of the space was the fire behind which lay a wooden chair, not quite a throne, and Ari knew from his childhood stories that it was made from yew, a tree sacred to one goddess. His eyes moved from one torch to another, one shrouded figure to another, until he spied an animal seated by the fire, then another. The closer he got to the fire, the more attention one of the animals paid him. It walked toward him, a low growl vibrating the air.

"Hecuba, hush. He bears us no ill will." An old voice filled the chamber, one that sounded like a child, a woman, and a crone all at the same time.

A black dog crouched down, placing its head over its front paws. From behind the wooden chair emerged another shrouded figure, her covering an iridescent black that resembled the starry night sky. On her shoulder sat a polecat, and she scratched its chin. Taking her seat, she watched the polecat scamper down to the fire and tease the dog's ear.

"You are in a sacred place, Aristeides, son of Timaios. No one here will harm you."

Ari moved slowly around the fire to the chair, never taking his eyes off the woman. Her head covering obscured her face, and all he could see were her hands and feet. Curls of myrrh smoke rose, bringing sweetness throughout the chamber, intensifying the haze brought about by the fire. He got down on one knee and lowered his head.

"Gracious Hekate, I am honored to be in your presence."

"Rise, child. We have found you worthy of an audience, or you would not have made it this far. You seem familiar..."

Back on both feet, Ari removed a small parcel from his pocket wrapped in parchment and held it in the palms of his hands, outstretched.

"I bring you the offering of lavender and storax, *Hekate Aidônaia*, Lady of the Underworld."

The polecat jumped onto his arm, took the parcel in its mouth, brought it to Hekate, and then returned to the dog.

"You know the ancient ritual to honor one such as me, mortal. I see now. Your father taught you well. What brings you here?"

"I am on a great journey to restore the mind of Phoebos Apollo. I have encountered one who can aid me, and I have learned that his mother was one of your *Lampades*. It is she who I need to speak with, my lady."

Hekate revealed her face, one that shifted from child to mother to crone. Her eyes scanned the other figures seated around the chamber until she stopped on one.

"Orphne, this young man seeks an audience with you. Do you consent to such?"

The figure stood and removed her torch from its ring. When she reached Ari, she released the torch, and it hovered in place. She extended her hands.

Ari looked at Hekate first, but then placed his hands, palms down on Orphne's. The nymph took hold gently.

"You have met my son. How is he?" Her voice barely broke above a whisper.

Hekate raised hers. "A son? When did you leave the under-world?"

"Decades ago, by mortal standards, my lady. I had seen so many spirits enter Hades' realm, and I wished to see that other world." She lowered her hands from Ari's. "I took human form long enough to experience mortality. I-I met a man. He was kind to me, and we, as mortals say, fell in love. I conceived a child, but after he was born, I returned here. I knew that I had cursed his life. I did not know his mind would untether." Orphne lowered her head. "I deserve whatever punishment you deem worthy of me."

The goddess extended her hand. "Come."

Without hesitation, Orphne complied. Hekate lifted the nymph's chin.

"You violated the sanctity of this bond we share. I entrust twelve *Lampades* to walk with me, shining your torches to light my path. You and your sisters have seen more in your eternal life than many of the gods." Hekate let her eyes linger on the nymph for a moment. "But, punishing you would serve no purpose. You will aid this mortal."

"Yes, my lady."

"However… You will never leave this realm again."

Orphne returned to Ari who had felt the need to turn away from witnessing such a moment.

"Son of Timaios, how can I assist you? Is my son well?"

Ari sighed. "Esteban lies in a catatonic state, ever since his encounter with your sister, Lismonia. Through this," he touched the obol, "I can communicate with him. I believe he is the key to helping me. He resents who he is. It is his connection to this world that he claims put him in mental anguish. I do not know how much you know of him, but he spent years in a place of healing... an asylum."

"What did Lismonia do to him?"

"First, I must tell you that the man, his father, was no ordinary man. Lismonia sought the children of a god as her prey, and what saved him from oblivion was probably his heritage."

Orphne stepped back. "No..." She lowered her head. "Please. It cannot be he."

"I am afraid so. That man you met was a descendant of Zeus. Lismonia chose to attack those of Zeus' lineage, but because you, her sister, are Esteban's mother, Lismonia chose not to carry out her vengeance on the man. All of creation would forget that he existed, thus removing him from the world. Her victims then die by their own hand due to madness. Esteban claimed to know she was coming for him, perhaps because of their connection, and when she left him, he was in a catatonic state. He escaped oblivion. Apollo tried to help him, but he feared doing so would harm Esteban. Because of that, Esteban resents Apollo. I *need* him to help me."

"I can sense that you are a good man, Aristeides. I will tell you this, but it may not help. I was born to Nyx, and that is why I am a nymph of the dark. I do not know whether I have a father. It is my destiny to be a torchbearer for Hekate. That is why I did not stay in the mortal world."

Hekate threw herbs onto the fire. "It seems the allure of the mortal world has attracted even the gods themselves, my child. If one such as Zeus could be swayed—"

"My lady." Ari approached her. "You said I seemed familiar. That is because Python possessed my body. I have memories, foggy ones, of him, speaking with you. You used your magic..."

"Yes. That is how I know you. That wretched son of Gaea got what he deserved."

"I have a question, if I may be so bold to ask." Ari lowered his head a little.

Hekate didn't reply, but she didn't stop him either.

"My lady... Growing up in the Temple of Hades, I learned from my father that you are a goddess of witchcraft, of the crossroads. Of magic, and the moon. Some have even said you ruled this realm before Hades. But you are not evil. You even aided the gods during the Gigantomachia, when they fought the Giants…"

Ari pressed his hands together, brought them to his lips, and sighed.

"Why, then, did you help Python? He was malevolence incarnate, a being of decay."

With all three voices in unison, Hekate spoke. "Leave us."

The nymphs melted into the darkness, with Ari and Hekate alone.

"Heed me, mortal. I owe no one an explanation." She paused. "However, since Python manipulated us *both*, I will answer you. I do not side with human constructs like good or evil. I act to bring about balance, but I do not act out of malice." She stepped down from her yew throne and sat at the fire. "I am of Perses and Astraea, born to Titans. But it is only my mother whose story concerns you. Part of this tale you know…"

Hekate told Ari the story of Leto, one of Zeus' consorts, and how, pregnant with twins, she was forbidden by Hera to set foot on any land to give birth. Zeus had then set his wandering eye on Astraea, daughter of the Titans Coeos and Phoebe, but she rebuffed his advances, throwing herself into the Aegean Sea as a quail. Unable to traverse the vast expanse, she transformed into a floating island and called herself Ortygeia. When Leto sought refuge, the island form of Astraea took pity, knowing well the curse of Hera, and allowed Leto to use Ortygeia for her childbearing. The moment Leto set foot on the newly created soil, four pillars rose from the ocean floor, anchoring the once-hidden island. There, Leto first gave birth to Artemis who then helped her mother give birth to Apollo. When the young god spoke his first words, he named the island 'Delos,' meaning 'clear' or 'manifest', since his birthplace had become known to the world.

"Python knew that only ancient power such as mine could augment his own. I denied his request, but then… he threatened to destroy Delos… my mother. At first, I did not think he could do such a thing, but through mortals, he had amassed great power. With Gaea on his side, yet one more he had manipulated, he had access to arcane magic. I knew he could follow through on his threat. I reluctantly agreed to aid him."

Ari furrowed his brow and clenched his jaw.

"You are correct. He deserves his eternal fate, Hekate."

"Did Orphne give you what you wanted?"

"Indeed, she did. Thank you for allowing me an audience." He bowed his head. "I have asked *of* you, my lady. Is there anything I can do *for* you?"

The goddess of witchcraft pulled back her head covering. All three of her faces showed a faint smile.

"You thought to ask. Others would have taken their knowledge and left, without recognizing the need for balance. As for your question… there is something. I wish to reset the balance."

Ari heard Hekate's words and followed the path back to Hades' palace. He had started climbing the stairs when a coldness washed over him. Esteban, he thought. Something has happened to Esteban. He had wanted to speak with Hades and Persephone before leaving for the mortal world, but he knew he had to return. They would understand. They would have to. He brought himself back to the apartment within only minutes of his departure. Unfortunately, he had no means to travel to the hospital as quickly, so he would have to take a cab. He hoped he wasn't too late.

When he reached Esteban's room, the bed was empty, but not made, so Esteban was most likely still in the hospital. He asked the nurses if they had seen him, and one of them told him that a doctor had moved Esteban to the solarium. Fearing that something had happened to him, like one of Apollo's enemies wanting to stop Ari from helping him, Ari tore through the hospital, arriving at the solarium breathless, his eyes darting around. By the window that overlooked a pond, there was a wheelchair with Esteban, but no doctor. Only two other patients were there as well, one elderly woman and another young man with no legs below the knee in a wheelchair. A nurse sat at a table at the doorway.

"May I help you? Are you okay?"

"What? Yes. Yes, I am fine. Can you tell me who moved the young man by the window? He is my patient, and I had not authorized him to be moved." Ari craned his head to make sure Esteban was still there.

The nurse saw Ari's badge, and then touched her tablet. "When he arrived, Dr. Fairmont, I asked him to check in. He said his name was Dr. Andrew Paolo and that he was consulting with you on this patient"—she checked the tablet—"a Mr. Esteban Reyes. He asked that two visits to the solarium a week be added to his chart. He said you authorized that. Is that not correct?"

"Of course. Yes. I remember. Yes, I did authorize that. It has been such a crazy day. Thank you." He smiled at the nurse and tapped the table. "By the way, what did this Dr. Paolo look like?"

"About 6'2", short blond hair... wait, you said he was consulting with you. Wouldn't you know—"

Ari smiled. "Never mind. I am a little distracted. Thank you again."

How in Olympos' name could Apollo, or someone looking like him, have been here? Ari thought.

The wheelchair's head support had been raised, and for a moment, Ari expected Esteban to be aware. He leaned around to check, but Esteban was still lost. Sunlight gave the man's face a warmth it had been lacking in the hospital room.

"I am not sure I understand what has happened, my friend," Ari whispered into Esteban's ear. "Someone using a guise of Apollo's has moved you here, to this room. But, how?"

Ari sat on a bench and leaned toward Esteban.

"Why would whoever this was want you moved here? And, why two days a week? This does not make sense."

Turning his face to the window, Ari looked up and closed his eyes. As he felt his own face warm from the sunbeams, his thoughts jumped to something his father had told him long ago, something that helped a little boy, the son of the caretaker of Hades' shrine, feel better.

"Ari, this temple is a dark, dark place. So much sadness and death. What surrounds us is a thick blackness, a dense cloud, that lingers no matter what. Do you know what I do to make me smile? I think about the sun piercing that cloud and painting my face with light. Only then do I feel better. Only then do I feel healed of all my bitterness, my frustration, the pain of missing your mother... Remember that the sun heals all."

Then, Ari's eyes popped open, and he inhaled deeply as if he were trying to breathe in the sunlight. Those words of Timaios, like morning dew on the grass, clung to him, nurtured him. So much time had passed since he had heard those words, but he knew they spoke an undeniable truth.

"I think I am beginning to understand. Somehow, through his madness, Apollo has reached out to you, Esteban. I do not know how he did so. Perhaps through his own subconscious. This is a sign of good faith, a way to encourage your help. He knows that you are integral to his healing. This"—Ari pointed to the sky—"is his way of saying that he will heal you when we heal him."

After an hour, Ari took Esteban back to his room and placed him back in the bed. Drawing upon his connection through the obol, Ari created that space where both he and Esteban could see each other. The young man's eyes were closed, and he had the faintest smile. It seemed as if he were looking up, up toward an imaginary sky where an imaginary sun was radiating something alluring.

"It felt good to sense the sun again." He began. "It had been so long. In the Spanish hospital, I never did get to go outside. They kept me locked in that padded room, even before *she* came to me."

"I am not sure how, but Apollo exerted tremendous effort from his confinement to send you a message. I think you now know his intent." Ari smiled.

The manifestation of Esteban opened his eyes, his own smile fading. "How was your visit to the underworld? Don't look so surprised. I have come to understand that all states of consciousness are connected. I felt you move into that place, but then I couldn't see you."

Ari nodded. "Well, I feel I was successful. I had the chance to speak with your mother. I believe I understand now."

"What do—"

"You are a descendant of Nyx, Esteban. Orphne is her daughter. And... your father? He is related to Zeus. That is why Lismonia left you without using her full power, but she did try. That is why she was drawn to you. You are related to her."

"So, it is true, then..."

"Yes. Apollo could not undo what Lismonia had done because he was unable to do so. He did not merely leave you like this because it suited his whim. Now, do you see why we *must* work together? He was in your mind. You both have a connection. Through you, we can enter his consciousness and repair the damage, or try to."

This silence between them was alive, a palpable white noise that they could not hear. In the hospital room, Ari's skin tingled from the sensation, and he had never encountered it while talking to Esteban. It was as if he could feel the electricity of Esteban's mind working through the ideas.

"I-I think I'd like to try." Esteban's voice in Ari's mind had that optimistic timbre, with a bit of a lilt.

Ari's exhale was followed by tears. He opened his eyes and put a hand on Esteban's shoulder. "Thank you, Esteban. I will return soon so we can plan how to proceed. One way or the other, we will bring Apollo back."

15 | THROUGH A FACETED LENS

Gathered around the expansive walnut table of the Division boardroom, Twenty-five Task Force team leaders sounded like unintelligible white noise as they all made small talk before their monthly meeting. Just before the United Nations Secretary-General Jescha Benthe could gavel them to order, Dan found his seat and did the smile-and-nod to those next to him. Part of the agenda was to approve the minutes from the prior meeting, something that took barely a few moments, and then they reviewed the agenda: how to deal with the aftereffects of the global storms that ravaged every place of Earth. As he settled into his seat, a man in BDUs who stood at parade rest behind a large plant caught his attention. He didn't realize there would be a military presence for this meeting.

Padmini Joshi talked about how Alpha was dispatching teams to the hardest-hit communities to set up structures for cleaning debris, helping those in need, and set a plan to rebuild what had been destroyed. Epsilon's Seo-Yun Chung explored how Task Force civil engineers would work with local counterparts in planning interim measures before larger projects took place. She reiterated that funding was limited, but if the Secretary-General could address how the Reserve Fund could be tapped for some of this, that would be appreciated. Geological concerns came next, with Ige Ihejirika trying to articulate how Xi was working with the many African leaders to assess just what needed to be done. The type of storms that ravaged the continent hadn't been experienced before. While all this came up, Dan avoided making eye contact with anyone. Finally, the Secretary-General hammered her gavel and opened the floor to one more speaker before they could get into other items on the agenda.

"And maybe we could set up a committee to investigate possible reasons for this catastrophe."

Dan exhaled and put up his index finger.

The Secretary-General nodded. "The leader from Team Gaea is recognized."

With a dour countenance, Dan rose. "Thank you, Secretary-General. I've been listening to your reports, and my heart goes out to those whose lives have been irrevocably altered. While it may seem odd for me to speak since my team doesn't have jurisdiction over areas that directly connect to the people of this world, I think what I have to say will both explain a reason for these events and possible solutions."

Immediately, the assembled were abuzz with side comments and intense attention aimed at Dan, and he fidgeted a bit, not knowing if he should put his hands in his pockets, behind his back, or just hold them in front. The gavel struck three times.

"Ladies and gentlemen, please. Let Dr. Fairmont speak."

Nodding, Dan continued.

"Most if not all of you know my father, Paul Fairmont. If not personally, then at least by reputation. He's been an integral part of this division of the U.N. What some of you may not know, and I wouldn't know who at this point, is that he isn't simply Paul Fairmont." Dan took a slow, deep breath and exhaled for what seemed like minutes.

"My father is also known by another name. Apollo. He is an Olympeian god. Just what my team and I fight against is becoming less of a mystery, and most are inexplicable by mortal standards."

Hands shot up, with interjections by the other leaders, but Dan held up a hand.

"I will address your questions, but I need to finish. My father is the son of Zeus, the king of Mount Olympos. I know that this is hard to reconcile, but it *is* true. Back in the 1960s, he came here to this world with his family. He wanted to live more of a mortal existence. To do that, he took the name Paul Fairmont and became part of the United Nations first as an observer, then an ambassador, and later one of the architects of the Task Force Division. It wasn't until my team and I came to be that he helped us become one of you who seek to help the Earth. You may ask why I am telling you this. It's the reason why we are gathered here today."

A hand shot up, followed by a question blurted out by Robert Barns of team Kappa.

"Are you saying that your father caused the storms? If so, what are you going to do about it? What—"

"Bobby, I'm about to explain that. I get that you all have questions. This isn't easy to explain, so bear with me. A long time ago, Apollo fought a monster called Python, a serpent who was the son of Gaea, of the earth itself. Ancient stories would tell that Apollo defeated Python and was given the temple of Delphi as the seat of prophecy. Many of you may have learned this as children. But… Python was able to return. The details are complicated, but he took another form. Remember the incidents of decapitations months ago? That was Python's doing."

More chatter among the table, and again, the Secretary-General's gavel had to restore order. Dan had to raise his voice a little to compete.

"Please, let me finish. I hope this will all make more sense when I do."

Silence, like a curtain, closed over them.

"Without going into too much detail, Paul, er, Apollo and Python faced off. My father felt he had to bring an end to Python again, but this time, he was fighting another battle, one inside his mind."

Dan did the best he could to explain about the other timeline that existed, without telling them he remembered it as well, and that holding both sets of memories wore Apollo down, making it easier for Python to strike. He finished with the fact that his father was in a safe place, and that he was being tended to so that his mind could heal. Then came perhaps the most challenging part to explain to people who don't know much about the gods.

"With Apollo under watch, Zeus' grief took over. He lashed out, sending storms across the world. His recklessness… well, you know what that did." Dan's face paled.

This time dead silence and stares pressed down upon him, the pregnant pause of questions twisting in his heart like a dagger. He didn't know how to explain things to this room of mortals who had no frame of reference for the otherworldly. Team leaders sat back, arms crossed, or simply bore into Dan with eyes filled with rage from what had transpired.

Finally, the Secretary-General's soft voice cracked the silence.

"Well, Dr. Fairmont… I think I can safely speak for those assembled that we will need time to process this—"

"No!" a woman's voice erupted. "I don't need to process this. If what you say is true, and I can't say I believe that it is, what will *you* do about the damage and lives lost? Your team is supposedly one that deals with these 'magical' threats, so how will you deal with them? Do you even know the final death toll?" The leader of team Tau wiped tears from her cheeks.

"Radhika, at this point, the figures were about 4,000 lives lost and about 100,000 people injured. I haven't seen any updates." Dan choked this out, his voice cracking. "I… I don't know what to tell you. We, my team and I, are looking into ways to deal with the fallout of Apollo's incapacitation. I'm afraid, even though we stopped the storms, there is more to figure out."

Her expression morphed from rage to confusion.

"We noticed the storms had ended. How did you stop them? You're supposedly familiar with 'magic,' so what 'magic' can bring back those we've lost?"

"Talon learned of an ancient enchantment that could remove Zeus' power, temporarily, until he got control of his grief. We are also working on a way to help Apollo restore his sanity so the world will not be affected."

"I'll give you the benefit of the doubt, for the moment, but temporarily? If he is who you say he is, and you *can* remove his power, it should be permanent. How do we know he won't do something like this again once his power is restored? How will he make reparations? Again, I ask. What about those who perished?"

Dan put both his hands together and pressed them to his mouth.

"As much as it pains me to say this… they are… gone. The only one who has dominion over the dead is Hades, the god of the underworld. There are rules. He can't simply resurrect 4,000 people. If he did that, people would want others brought back who died before the storms. I'm afraid there is nothing that can be done. As for removing Zeus' power permanently? This enchantment won't last forever. I don't even know of anything that *could* do that. There needs to be balance, and for that balance to exist, Zeus will need to be the king of the gods. I know that brings no consolation to you all. It's beyond my power."

More questions, like volleys of arrows, flew at Dan, and he answered the best he could—with many leaders shouting their frustrations at him—but the one he needed to respond to was just how Apollo's absence would affect the world at large. Evgeny Dimitri, leader of the Rho team, raised a finger.

"Dr. Fairmont, we are aware of your team bios as well as your attributes. We've seen videos of your activities, so that evidence at least *seems* irrefutable. I never questioned too deeply. But, how would your father's absence affect *us*? We"—his hand swept across the room—"and most of the world don't even worship your gods."

"Evgeny, gods have spheres of influence, much like your Rho team's purview is the Middle East."

Dan pushed a button by his place at the table and projected a headshot, one from the Task Force Division database and website, on a screen behind the Secretary-General.

"Behind that suit and tie is a god who has slain giants." He drew Thyroros, and a dull humming passed through the room. "This sword used to be his. When I was 13, he gave it to me."

Held up, the edge of the blade glinted under the fluorescent light. Dan stepped back and swung a wide arc in front of him, and an opening to the Boston Common appeared. Sounds of parkgoers filtered into the room. Children played in the grassy areas. Cars honked. Even the smell from street food vendors wafted in. Those assembled gasped and some even stood up. With a mental gesture, Dan closed the aperture.

"If you can accept *that*, then surely you can accept my father's résumé."

Task Force: Upsilon's team leader, Célestin Georges, leaned an elbow on the arm of his chair, his chin in his hand. "So, Dan, what spheres does he influence?"

"Célestin, the gods tap into veins of power much like electric current. How they use it depends on their interest. Certain gods, like Zeus, due to being older, have access to more power. Think of it this way: spheres of influence are like different types of lamps. If the current weakens, some dim or just don't turn on. Apollo is tied to healing, music, reason, and prophecy. Some of these things affect humanity more directly than others. Even though healing has been around since life began, Apollo's presence in the mortal world has tied his energy to that of the world around him."

Nodding, Célestin crossed his arms and leaned back. "So, when hospitals talked about problems with patients healing all over the globe, that was him? How will that affect music or reason? And prophecy, well..."

"Yes, the hospital issues were connected to him. We have that one handled. Not sure about music. As far as prophecy, that's a bit more complicated. It's not something people generally put any belief in."

Radhika glared from across the table, clenching and unclenching her jaw. Dan noticed.

"Look. Of all the gods, only my father has spent any lasting time here on Earth, among mortals. He didn't intend for his power to be tied so closely that it would interrupt normal life. That must have happened over time." He took a moment to sip some water. "Anyway, without my father to be the regulatory force over his power, we had to take measures to make sure that the world would not continue to be adversely affected."

He opened his dress shirt and loosened his tie.

"Zodiak and I met with three others who have family ties, and the five of us have taken up the mantle of the spheres that Apollo cannot control. Each of us is a demigod, so it takes more of us to do this."

He showed the word burned on his chest: ΠΡΟΦΝΤΕΙΑ— prophecy.

"So, now there are others involved? What aren't you telling us? Are they new members of the Gaea team?" Team leader Birgitta Vanamo, of Task Force: Zeta, chimed in.

Dan shook his head. "They're not. Look, I can't explain everything to you right now. They're able to help, and that's all I will say. If you have individual concerns, I am sure that the Secretary-General would prefer that I meet with you privately to discuss them. With due respect to all of you, you don't share all of *your* data with the rest of us. You have your reasons. I have mine."

"One more question, Dan. Your father... where is he now?"

"I wish I could tell you, but you know how it is with immortals... classified and such."

He used air quotes when he said 'classified'. A glance showed that the man he had seen earlier was no longer by the plant, and he checked each exit door without losing his expression. Not a trace of him.

Dan continued. "As far as what the next steps are, the Gaea team will work on what we do best, examine extranormal options to fix what can be fixed. I would suggest, if I can be so bold, that the next steps for the rest of the teams are to do what you've been doing. If something unexplainable emerges, let me know."

After a few gavel strikes, the Secretary-General reclaimed the meeting to finish up. As soon as the meeting adjourned, Dan spied Radhika heading his way. Rather than deal with her, he maneuvered himself out of the building. He hadn't realized the time of day until he exited the building and saw the late afternoon sun against the glimmering golden dome of the State House. Once on the street, he scanned for the man he had seen earlier, but he was long gone. Dan surmised anyone dressed in BDUs had military training, and that meant he knew how to evade being seen. If things weren't bad enough, now his team would have to be more vigilant for another possible threat. After a quick update to Quinn, he headed toward the Government Center T station, but a sparkle from the northwest corner atop a university building across the street caught his attention. Of all the times he had left headquarters, he had never noticed that particular gleam. Dan stepped into the alley next to the building, looked toward the street for passersby, and assessed he couldn't quite jump to the top of the building without shaking it noticeably. Using Thyroros, he gained access via a portal instead; he'd been on the roof plenty of times to know what it looked like. From this vantage, he could see the Charles River. At the corner of the roof, the source of the twinkle became apparent: a silvery gum wrapper stuck on a camera aimed directly at the doorway of the Task Force building.

"This is new," he muttered, leaning over for a closer view. The size of a soda can, the camera's matte gray casing, whose purpose was to keep the camera itself obscured, shouldn't have reflected any light. The lenses normally didn't reflect, either. It was dumb luck that the wrapper was there.

He took photos with his phone from as many angles as he could reach, but the position of the camera itself made it impossible to get a good look up close. While he was up there, he set his eyes to nearby buildings to look for other cameras like this one, newer cameras that could pose a different kind of problem. The glare of the sunset made it more of a challenge, though. Dan messaged the team to meet since he was already nearby. It would be the most secure place to talk.

⊙━━◆━━⊙

"I asked Quinn to look at the pictures of the camera to see what, if anything, she could determine. Quinn?" Dan swiveled in his chair toward the team liaison.

Her fingers flew across the glass of her control panel, and a moment later, pictures appeared on the widescreen monitor.

"Well, kiddos, from the photos, this is a newer camera than the ones currently in use. It had to have been replaced within the last few weeks. Based on the coordinates from Dan's phone, satellite resonance imaging indicates the casing is a steel polycarbonate composite, resistant not only to the weather but also to tampering. Unlike other cameras, this one's wireless, with its emitter housed deep inside to prevent anyone or anything from messing with it. Where the signal goes, I have yet to figure out." She tapped the glass panel a few more times, zooming in on a spot. "This, though, was the most intriguing."

"What is it?" Sarah squinted.

"It's text, measuring 1/32 of an inch high. I'll see if I can zoom in."

With a few more taps on her panel, the image enlarged.

"That's the best I can give you, kiddos. A signal is messing with the scan. What do you make of it?"

Dan walked up to the monitor. "It looks like... Greek. And there's a symbol next to it. Quinn, can you zoom in a little closer?"

"I'll try, Dan, but if I do, the image may be blurry. How's that?"

"Hmm. A little better. I can make out some of the letters... ΠΑ... Ο... Τ... Σ." He shook his head. "The image... well, I think it looks like a feather of some kind. It's an icon. Perhaps a company logo?"

Using both hands, Dan brushed his hair back, resting his fingers on the back of his neck for a moment, staring at the image. His eyes started at the first letter and moved one letter at a time. Aleta joined him, putting a hand on his shoulder. She pointed toward the symbol.

"I've been staring at that feather. I can't make out what it is, but just from its proportions, it's not from an eagle. Too round.

Maybe we can find another camera where the imprint into the casing is deeper."

Dan smiled. "Feel like doing some recon? You'd be better than I would at this since you can get closer."

Aleta nodded. "I just have to avoid detection. I'll go out later today. You're okay with me in public? I mean, we don't have that glamour disguising us anymore."

"That ship has sailed. We've been outed. The best we can do now is damage control if we need to. I try to maintain a low profile, but it's becoming more challenging to do it. Even my students have probably figured things out, although they're reluctant to ask about it. Not sure how much longer I'll have that job." He laughed. "I can always go back to archaeology full time, but that would pull me out of Boston."

Aleta leaned back against the table. "I hear you. My role as a lead geneticist, and partial shareholder, could be in jeopardy as well. Dr. Forrester knows, but that's because we, um, dated." She raised an eyebrow and smirked. "No longer, but I know he won't say anything about my 'other' job."

Sarah went up to them, putting a hand on their shoulders. "That's why I work alone, my friends. Being a potter, I report to no one. And my kiln ain't talking." She winked.

Quinn had been tapping away at her panel. The updated haptic sensation was quiet, so it looked as if she were playing a silent musical instrument. A few minutes later, she threw another image on the screen.

"Here you go, boy and girls. From what our satellites can detect, this camera was installed about a week after Apollo went underground. There's no way to know who put it there… yet, but I can tell you that it's not the only one around. I put the specs for the steel polycarbonate composite into the system, and it kicked back multiple resonance frequencies. The bad news is, I don't know where. Something's blocking my scan, and to do that with our satellites, it has to be über powerful. The good news is, I'm detecting somewhere around a dozen MRFs in Boston alone. We might be looking at an upgrade to the cameras."

"Quinn, when were the original cameras installed?" Sarah checked out the data on the screen. "I mean, we've known about them for quite some time."

"Hang on a moment. According to public records, cameras went up back in the sixties when a company, one of the earliest technology companies, developed a line of surveillance items and sold them to interested parties. I'm pulling up a list of their initial clients." Quinn's eyebrows raised as her fingers tapped the relay.

"Quinn? You okay? What did you find?" Sarah sat up.

The team liaison officer pulled her hands from her console and sighed. "I'm not sure... hmm... on this list, one of the clients is the Task Force Division. Someone authorized a company named Argus Industries to put cameras up in major cities, first here in the American Conglomerate, and later, in other cities of interest all over the world."

Dan approached her desk. "Cities of interest? I'd also like to know who authorized—"

"I know. I'll get to the bottom of this. I know you're concerned that your father was involved. Right now, all I have are fragments. I'm not sure what that means yet. Let me work on some things for you. Why don't you guys take a latte break, and I'll buzz you later when I have something."

"The letters I saw on this camera wouldn't spell anything close to Argus Industries," Dan continued. "I want to know everything you can tell us. *Everything*."

Quinn couldn't see his face, but the emphasis on that last word gave her a chill. "Trust me. Your manacle will be a-buzzing. Now, get out so I can work. Shoo!" She flicked her fingers at them.

With all of her knowledge and expertise, Quinn took notes, flagged files, and made sure she would leave no kilobyte untouched. Apollo had meant as much to her as he had to Sarah and Aleta—a valued mentor, a consummate professional, and, on occasion, a cherished friend. She would do everything in her power to find out what she could. If he had been involved, she would want to know, as well as understand his reasons, but those would have to wait until he was better.

On Boston's south side in the Seaport district, from a black, unmarked sedan parked outside a weather-worn warehouse with exposed brick, a man appeared, passing the sign of what once was an eyeglass factory. Dilapidated wooden pallets leaned against a trash bin, a panoply of refuse strewn about. In combat boots, BDU pants, and a turtleneck—all black, the man scoped his surroundings as he sidled up to a gray metal door. As he leaned forward toward a glass square, a thin red light scanned his eye, and he swiped an ID card in a slot alongside the door. A small panel revealed itself, and he pressed his palm against the smooth surface. A pinprick-sized light changed from red to green, and the door's locking mechanism clicked. The air shimmered as a forcefield vanished. Taking one last look over his shoulder, the man entered. The forcefield returned.

Down a corridor illuminated by embedded quarter-sized lights, the man marched, his polished boots making almost no sound on the polished cement floor. At the next door, he repeated the palm and ID card routine, this time switching hands, and stepped into a steel-clad elevator. Once the door closed, the elevator car descended, the man standing at parade rest, with his hands behind his back, thumbs interlocked, just above his waist. His eyes faced directly ahead, even though no one else was with him. The ride took exactly one minute, and as soon as the doors opened, other voices became clear, with one man in gray immediately addressing him.

"Ah, here he is. Corporal, join us."

The man saluted Major Timothy McCallister and his adjutant, First Lieutenant Adrianna Harold.

"This is Corporal Rogers, Lieutenant Harold, one of our newest recruits, but quickly becoming one of our most proficient. What did you find out, Corporal?"

"Nothing yet, sir. From our original intel, we know that Paul Fairmont aka Apollo is off the grid, but we don't know where. The new cameras have detected no otherworldly movement matching his energy signature. I have heard rumors, though, from a few sources that he is held in a secure facility deep within the earth. The meeting with Fairmont's son and the other task force leaders proved unhelpful."

Major McCallister clenched his jaw, staring off. "Thank you, Corporal. Dismissed."

After his salute, the corporal returned to his duty station in the Intelligence Corps.

"This presents a problem. Let's take a walk." McCallister headed through the Intelligence Corps. area with his colleague, moving through secure sections, each time both having to scan palms and ID cards. Before entering the last door—matte black with no visible hinges or knob—McCallister stopped.

"Have you finished your briefing, Lieutenant?"

"Not entirely, sir. It was interrupted around the time we learned that Mr. Fairmont had gone missing."

"So, you don't know why we keep tabs on him, do you?"

She shook her head.

"Then, what I'm about to show you will require some explanation."

Making no sound as it opened, the door slid into the wall, and the temperature dropped. Adrianna rubbed her arms and scanned her surroundings, adjusting to lower light levels. Instead of a room, they had entered an earthen chamber carved from solid rock, supported along the sides with what looked like fluted columns made of the same material. Small torches hung in iron rings, casting a flickering light on the rough walls. Having left an austere, military establishment, they entered the inside of an ancient holy site. The top of the chamber disappeared into darkness, and at the far end seats of the same stone surrounded a lifeless fire pit the width of an average man.

"What *is* this place?" Adrianna stayed close to the major. "This was definitely not in the briefing."

McCallister didn't respond. Rather, he stopped at the fire ring.

"There's someone you need to meet. He'll continue your briefing."

As if on cue, a pillar of orange and red flame rose toward the ceiling. When it shrank back, a man was sitting in one of the stone seats, someone who looked familiar. In fact, she had just met him. He stood and then stepped down from the chair, the earth crunching beneath his boots. Standing in front of Lt. Harold, his expression remained stoic.

"Corporal?" She stood taller, her face equally expressionless.

Major McCallister smiled. "You do enjoy playing all the parts, don't you, sir?"

Without taking his eyes from the lieutenant, the corporal morphed into a slightly smaller man, lanky with a circle beard and close-cropped black hair. Saying nothing, moved around one side of the fire ring, and Adrianna couldn't be sure, but the fire appeared to lean toward him slightly, almost touching him.

"Lieutenant Harold." The man's voice had a distinctive accent. "Welcome to PANOPTES. I am Otto Wolf. Major McAllister assures me you are to be trusted." He held out his palm. "I certainly hope so."

She eyed the major who nodded once, and she then extended her arm, expecting to shake his hand. Otto took hold of her wrist with one hand, pushed up her jacket sleeve with the other, and then his eyes glistened. A tendril of flame meandered from the fire and, like a snake, struck Adrianna's bare wrist. Her pain reverberated throughout the chamber and melted into the darkness. Where the fire had touched her, blackened skin remained. She tried to pull her arm back but found she could not. Her free hand wiped the tears from her cheeks. McCallister leaned toward her.

"I'm-I'm fine. What the hell just happened? What did you do to me?"

Otto leaned over her wrist and blew. The burned skin fell away like paper sitting on her skin, revealing a symbol forever seared into Adrianna's flesh. Otto opened his fingers, and she retracted her arm, touching the mark. No pain.

"What is it?"

Ignoring her question, Otto walked around the fire ring to the opposite side and faced her. Adrianna couldn't tell whether his dark eyes reflected the flames or his eyes flickered on their own.

"One of the greatest skills any warrior has is that of surveillance. Keeping an eye on the enemy at all times means he cannot surprise you. The primary mission of PANOPTES is to surveil Apollo, whom you know as Paul Fairmont, a founder of the Task Force Division of the United Nations."

He paused long enough to lower himself into one of the stone chairs, his hands extending over the arms like the paws of a proud lion.

"He is tied to my past, and it is his presence that threatens what I do."

Otto paused, leaving a weighty silence, and Adrianna parted her lips to speak when his voice erupted once more.

"What do I do, you ask?" He grinned. "I am the antithesis of truth. I am deception incarnate. Like my father, I can assume whatever form I desire. Anything."

Pushing himself from the chair, he took strides around the fire ring.

With each utterance and step, he transformed into that which he spoke. "Apollo, Corporal Rogers, Hermes, the janitor, and… you."

He stopped toe-to-toe with her, a perfect reflection of her down to the wisp of her hair that hung from her bangs and the wrinkle her blouse made at the waist beneath her belt. Eye to eye, they stood, and with his eyes locked on hers, he slowly resumed his own form.

"You're asking yourself, 'Why do you want to watch Apollo?', am I right?"

Before she could part her lips to reply, he returned to his chair and continued.

"*He* is the source of reason in the world. He has, in fact, done nothing to me personally. It is his mere existence, though, that stands as an obstacle to my success." He leaned forward, his hands gripping the stone arms of the chair. "I want to end him."

McCallister shifted his weight from one foot to another. He had learned from prior experience that he was not permitted to sit in Otto's presence. Adrianna was the exception for this moment. The major had heard this many times, and he prevented his face from showing any emotion except enrapt interest. Anything else would be unpleasant for him.

"Mr. Wolf, may—"

Adrianna fell off the fire ring with the force of an unseen push, knocking the breath from her. She glanced back at the major who simply stared straight ahead. If her superior officer didn't dare say a word while Otto spoke, she should sit in silence until he was finished. She pressed her palms against her chest.

"Interrupt me again at your peril." Otto paused, his pupils turning a vibrant orange before returning to their natural brown. "Now, where was—no, never mind. The moment has passed. McCallister, you and your ward… get out. Another time, Lieutenant Harold."

With that, the fires leaped higher and receded, taking Otto Wolf with them. In silence, Major McCallister escorted his protégé back through the labyrinthine halls of PANOPTES. They shared a look, one that conveyed confidentiality. Adrianna went into the restroom, locked the door to a stall, and vomited into the toilet. Cleaning herself up, she rested her hands on the counter, stared into the mirror, and cried. A minute passed, she wiped her eyes, looked at her wrist marked with the strange design, and returned to her station.

Back in the cavernous chamber, Otto gazed into the fire. He pinched the bridge of his nose, closed his eyes, and took a deep breath. At his exhale, he made a sweeping gesture and the fire ring split down the middle, opening sideways to reveal a set of dark stairs. Once at the base, he took a few more steps forward. A table stretched out with an oil lamp that was burning already and two bronze urns, one smaller than the other. One read ΜΗΣΤΡΑ and other, ΑΛΕΚΟΣ. Otto knelt on the ground, pulling both urns closer to him.

"I wish you could see how close I am, dear Mestra, to achieving my goal. It's only a matter of time before Apollo is mine to do as I see fit. I have never stopped loving you. Alekos, my son, I wish you could be by my side. The Moirae snipped your thread too soon. Three years was not enough time to love you. I know I wasn't always there for you and your mother, but I hope you know that you were both in my heart."

Gently sliding the urns back, he dusted off his pants and returned to his sanctuary, the sides of the fire pit closing like a flower at the end of its bloom.

"Morpheos, I need of you. She must understand."

Adrianna dropped her keys in a wooden bowl on a table by the door of her apartment, took down her hair, and fell into the couch. It was only 7 p.m., and she felt woven into the fabric. Before she'd allow herself the balm of sleep, she downed a large glass of Chardonnay. With a dismissive gesture toward the TV, she stripped down as she walked toward the bedroom until she could place herself between the covers. The soporific effects of the wine took hold, and her deeper breaths of slumber began. Her clock's glow cast itself on the sprinkle of dust that descended seemingly from nowhere. The gift of the god of dreams was upon her.

Images came into focus, and a story unfolded.

Cries of a newborn child. A mother cradling the little girl, whispering the name, "Chione." News of the birth reached a warrior on a distant battlefield. Somehow, she knew his name was Daedalion, and the shields of his soldiers boasted vultures, dogs, and snakes. Whispers of Ares' name floated through the images.

Another scene coalesced. The girl Chione was older, with barely the kiss of womanhood upon her. A busy agora showed her ogled by merchants and farmers as well as soldiers and members of the priestly caste, shying away from lustful and hungry looks. A soft innocence, like a gentle illumination, surrounded her. Rumors spread that the girl was cursed.

131

A new glimpse into the girl's life showed her being wooed by a striking man, his golden curls like wisps of fire. Under a starry night, he caressed her cheek. His shining locks lured her like a moth, but one who enjoyed the attention. He whispered in her ear that their offspring would change the world, and Apollo seduced the fair Chione. She gave herself to him under Selene's moon. It was as if a whisper were narrating the story, and the words engendering the pictures in Adrianna's mind.

Deep, heavy darkness followed, and in her sleep, Adrianna pulled the covers up to her head.

From a vantage above, the gods' messenger watched Chione sleep. Then, on winged feet, he descended to her chamber, and waved his serpent-staff, inducing a deeper slumber. Thinking it was her earlier lover, she whispered Apollo's name, and this caused the god of mischief to depart, enraged.

In her own sleep, Adrianna left tear stains on her pillow, writhing in unease.

A wind swept through her mind, and then—a birth. The first boy's wisps of golden hair twinkled like that of his father... Philammon. The second boy's cries made the midwife shiver. Somehow, Adrianna knew that during childbirth of he who would be Autolycos, Chione relived the shame that Hermes had brought upon her.

Lyrical, lilting music filled her bedroom, with Adrianna tossing back and forth until the melody soothed her. Flashes of Philammon as a boy playing the lyre for Chione were countered by those of Autolycos thieving in the agora. When their mother would bring them to Apollo's temple, Philammon's eyes widened in admiration while his brother's narrowed in disdain for both god and child.

Bells echoed all around her. Fog and darkness swirled around until something shook Adrianna from her dream state—it was the doorbell.

16 | APPEARANCES

Adrianna checked through her door's peephole to see Major McCallister standing in the hallway of her apartment complex wearing a white polo shirt, a navy windbreaker, and khakis, attire she didn't usually see him in. Cinching her robe around her waist, she adjusted her hair in the mirror before opening the door. She couldn't imagine what the major wanted at 3:15 a.m., but she knew her duty assignment meant she had to be ready for anything at any time. She saluted, wondering how ridiculous she must look saluting her superior officer in a blue robe and bunny slippers.

"At ease, Lieutenant."

She closed the door once he walked in and wanted to excuse herself to change into more appropriate clothes, but he said she didn't need to follow protocol in this instance. He looked around, his hands behind his back.

"Nice place you have here."

"Thank you, sir?" She raised an eyebrow.

"Oh, come now, Adrianna. You don't have to stand on ceremony with me now. I'm not here on business."

She stood taller for a moment. "Then, I'll be back in a minute... sir."

In her bedroom, she threw on a pair of jeans, a gray sweatshirt, and her pink Chuck Taylors. She poked her head out to see the major checking out her bookshelf, pursing her lips and raising an eyebrow. Before she left her room, she tucked her sidearm into the back of her jeans, pulling the sweatshirt down over it.

"Thanks for waiting, sir. Can I get you something to drink?"

He put a worn paperback copy of Sun Tzu's *The Art of War* back on her shelf. "No. Thank you. Tell me, Lieutenant, what did you think about our friend, Mr. Wolf?"

"What did I think of him? Well... he was intense, sir. Seemed like he should avoid caffeine." She smirked.

Major McCallister laughed. "Too true, too true. You were going to ask him something before you, well, learned not to interrupt him. May I ask what?"

Adrianna walked past him into the kitchen, reaching for a glass from the cabinet. He stood and seemed intrigued by a piece of art on her sofa table. From there, he stood before a copy of a Picasso, leaning in and squinting. He raised an eyebrow, turning around to see Adrianna, her hands clasping her service revolver aimed at him.

"Who are you, and where is Major McCallister?"

"Adrianna, what—"

"I asked you a question. *Who* are you?"

He took a step. She cocked her head, insisting with both raised eyebrows.

"Very well. How did you know?"

Only Adrianna's mouth moved. "Major McCallister has been to my apartment before. You were a little *too* curious, Mr. Wolf."

The man who looked like Timothy McCallister didn't take another step, but his body shifted and shrank into the form of Otto Wolf. In the incandescent light of the apartment, his face had a softer, more affable bearing.

"I didn't realize how much shorter you were to Tim until just now." She lowered her pistol, putting it back in her jeans. "Why did you come here? I got the impression I'd messed with your mojo."

He laughed out loud, louder than one should at that hour.

"I was in a moment. Usually, when I speak, no one interrupts. You saw Major McCallister. He's fine, by the way. I just borrowed his appearance."

"I wasn't paying attention to him that much. I was, however, interested in your story." She sat on the couch. "I'm going to go out on a limb and say you're Autolycos."

"You're smarter than Timothy let on. Am I that transparent?" He sat on the other end of the couch.

"You should have picked a better *nom de guerre*. I mean, Otto Wolf... Autolycos. Doesn't lycos mean wolf?"

"I actually chose it because I didn't think most people, mortals anyway, would figure it out. I don't put much faith in mortality. Come to think of it, I don't put much faith in immortals, either."

Adrianna put up some coffee since she had a feeling this would take a while. Fortunately, she didn't have to show up to her post until noon, and she'd already had six hours of sleep. Otto asked questions about her life while the coffee brewed, and she gave clipped answers. Things for her were on a need-to-know basis; they'd be the same for him. She commented to him while she poured the cream into her mug that she still didn't trust him, no matter how much he tried to be charming. Otto laughed.

"Don't trust me. Remember who my father is."

"Have to say I don't know much about your family. My only exposure has been to Apollo or, rather, Paul Fairmont. Never met him, but I do remember reading about him in school."

"His human identity certainly *is* the best-kept secret that isn't kept, isn't it?"

She ignored the comment and sat on the arm of the sofa, bringing the coffee mug to her lips without ever taking her eyes off him. He chuckled, shaking his head.

"Adrianna, I'm not here to hurt you, in case you were concerned. You're far too important."

"Then, perhaps you'll continue to regale me some more. I'll keep my mouth shut this time. And I assume you had something to do with my dreams tonight?"

Otto laced his hands in his lap, sitting up and grinning. "Oh, you've already had them. Splendid. I had to convince Morpheos with quite a bit, but he does such good work. I hope it was illuminating." He sat back. "I'll even give you the abridged version. I tried to pluck a feather from Hera's peacock, one that had the eyes of Argus the watchman placed on it, and I was punished by cleaning her chariot. I managed a few feathers anyway."

"Huh. Magic feathers, I take it?" Adrianna muttered.

"Not really, but that's beside the point. I *stole* them."

Otto noticed the look on Adrianna's face.

"Hermes. God of thieves? Never mind. I despised him. Mischief was inherited. Anyway, I couldn't take my anger out on him, and I couldn't blame my brother. We don't choose our parents. But, Chione doted on him. She would never say anything to me about my father, but I know she took out her anger on me in subtle ways. I was the afterthought. As I got older, I decided the one to blame was Apollo. Had it not been for *him*, Hermes would never have taken interest in Chione."

"Let me get this straight. You're after Apollo because he loved your mother?"

"Adrianna, the competition between Apollo and Hermes was legendary. Maybe more so among immortals, I guess. But, Hermes always wanted what his brother had. I formed a cadre of spies as I got older to keep tabs on when Apollo came to mingle among mortals. If I could sow seeds of doubt about Zeus' 'shining one,' mortals would stop worshipping him."

"And what did the feathers have to do with this? I figure they're important?"

Otto laughed. "Oh, yes. Each spy wore one. It made people think we were on divine missions for Hera, so no one ever questioned our surreptitious skulking about, or our sitting on rooftops, or even asking people to hide in their homes when Philammon was around. In Apollo's sacred cities, like Tegea, we received no attention at all."

Taking a deep breath, Adrianna sighed, closing her eyes and shaking her head. She ran her fingers through her hair, pulled it back, and wrapped an elastic around the ponytail.

"Everything all right?" Otto leaned forward.

"Um, yeah. It's just a lot to take in. Hearing about Task Force: Gaea and its otherworldly mission…" She used air quotes around 'otherworldly'. "…even seeing some of the clips on television, didn't fully prepare me for what you're saying. I'm more of a down-to-earth girl."

Otto exhaled hard. "PANOPTES' mission is to find Apollo, to discredit him. Gods thrive on *attention*. Take it away, and it weakens them."

Adrianna pursed her lips.

"I don't expect you to say anything. The point of all the cameras you've undoubtedly seen is to let us know where and when he is."

He opened his palm, and a mug similar to hers appeared. He slurped from it before continuing.

She rubbed her temples. "Paul Fairmont has made many appearances at the UN, in public, and numerous other events over the years, right? He's been in your sights for decades. Just how have you tried to discredit him? I've never heard anything about that."

Waving his hand in a wiping motion, images of transparent newspapers appeared.

"The failed concord he worked on in the Greco-Roman Alliance in the 70s. Reports of his wife's philanthropy being a front for money laundering in the 80s. Alleged former lovers coming forward since the 1960s. Even how he manipulated the United Nations to make him a liaison to the Task Force Division when it started."

Adrianna laughed. "So, sensationalism? Did these even work?"

"For a few months at a time. Even a temporary stain on his reputation hurt him."

"And yet he seems to be doing just fine. His sons are in the spotlight, saving the world too. I'm just confused as to what *my* part is on this."

Adrianna excused herself. Otto took the opportunity to stretch his legs and peruse her book collection once more. On one shelf he glimpsed a few pictures sticking out between two books. Making sure she wasn't returning just yet, he sneaked a peek. The sound of a door made him push them back into place and take his seat. She had refilled her mug, sitting in the chair across from the couch.

"As for your part, that's on a need-to-know basis, and right now, you don't need to know that."

With that, he nodded and vanished in yellow smoke.

She muttered out loud, "Hm. He just wanted the last word."

At her desk, Adrianna sighed at the stack of manila folders. Major McCallister had told her one of her responsibilities as his adjutant was to screen the files that were to go to him. What he didn't share, however, was that they would be about an Olympeian god under surveillance by an ancient cult whose sworn mission was to destroy this god, by any means necessary. The first folder on the stack had eyewitness accounts of appearances of

Apollo, as Paul Fairmont, from a year earlier. This data needed to be entered into a database to discern any possible pattern in Paul's behavior. After reading three pages, Adrianna's eyes glossed over, so she went to the coffee station just outside Major McCallister's office to embolden herself to the coming task of working her way through the meticulously detailed accounts. A familiar voice came from the office, its door ajar.

"Lieutenant, how long before I see any of those files?" His voice had a distant, multitasking tone.

Nudging the door open with her hand, a cup of pungent coffee in the other, she saw her boss, his tie loosened but still within proper dress parameters, poring over other documents, his fingers tapping away at his keyboard.

"Just getting started, sir. I needed something to keep me focused." She lifted the mug toward him.

Without looking up at her, he replied. "Excellent. The files that you don't feel I need to see, just put them in the orange basket to be re-filed. Not every eyewitness account gives us reliable intel."

"Very well, sir." She started to leave.

"Lieutenant. I understand you and Mr. Wolf had a conversation earlier today. I assume he clarified some things?"

"Some. I could tell there was more to know, but he just," she gestured with her free hand like a small explosion, "vanished into thin air."

"Heh. He does that when he's finished talking. To be honest, I wish more people did that. If you have any questions, let me know. I can fill in the gaps for you."

"Yes, sir."

"Oh, one more thing. If you should ever reconsider and break your covenant, that tattoo on your wrist will eat you alive from the inside out."

Adrianna laughed until she realized he wasn't.

Back at her desk, she put the mug up to her lips long enough to take a sip. *Three sugars were not enough, she thought. I could clean my toilet with this coffee.* Within two hours, she had whittled down a stack of thirty files to eight that she needed to bring to the major. She dropped them in the plastic wall file on his door, now closed, put the rest in the orange basket, and stepped into the restroom. Another woman, a corporal, was freshening her lipstick just as

Adrianna closed the door to her stall. A minute later, the stall door next to her closed.

"Your experience in surveillance." A woman's voice spoke.

Adrianna waited a moment, thinking this other woman was on the phone.

"Lieutenant, that's why I need you."

"Are you talking to *me*?" Adrianna leaned toward the partition between the two stalls.

"Of course. Who do you think I'm talking to? Oh, my apologies." The voice changed to Otto Wolf's. "There. Better?"

Lieutenant Harold opened her mouth to chastise him, but then she remembered that the restroom was unisex.

"Yes." She paused. "Thank you." She rolled her eyes. "Are you sure it's safe to talk here?"

"Absolutely. I've kept my eyes on your, so to speak. Your history with computer surveillance, nanotechnology, and even covert ops. All necessary for PANOPTES to succeed."

"So… the grunt work?"

Otto chuckled. "You have to prove your worth."

The toilet next to her flushed, and she held back a laugh. The stall door opened. When Adrianna left her stall, the same woman she had seen when she walked in was at the sink, washing her hands. She looked over at Adrianna, winked, and walked out.

By the time she returned to her desk, a new pile of folders greeted her.

17 | ALKINOË'S QUEST

When Hellas Airlines Flight 3243 touched down at Athens International Airport, Alkinoë stared out at the tarmac, but her thoughts were elsewhere. A few months had passed since she last made this trip, when she thought by going to the Parthenon to speak directly with Athene she would be afforded some solace or information. She still couldn't get over that her patron goddess had ignored her pleas. Even though her experience as a monarch helped her to see the broader picture in most circumstances, she couldn't fathom why Athene would abandon her. Resentment had given way to incredulity. Anger had been quelled, yet her expectation of answers remained, something Apollo had said was a type of hubris from sitting on the Arkadeian throne. Life experience had shown her that this level of privilege was unfair, and no one demanded of the gods, no matter who her husband was. Logic told her this, but her heart still needed to process it. This time, though, she would take a page from her own past and reach out to wisdom a different way.

Once she boarded the ferry out of Rafina, a five-hour ride to Delos. Those whom she sought lived in a cave not far from her husband's temple, one that lay in ruins, much like her heart. The cool breezes from the Aegean Sea pressed against her cheeks, and she lifted her face toward the sun. Not one cloud besmirched the pale skies, and Alkinoë took that as a sign that her journey had been blessed. The last time she was in Greece, Zeus' wrath was abusing the earth, and the heavens had taken on a type of blackness not seen since the Titanomachia when the gods raged against their parents. Perhaps, she thought, that Athene had arranged for such a clear day. She laughed to herself. The name 'Delos' meant 'clear'—clear of Hera's curse and brought to light. Leto's offspring both embodied light: Artemis, the powdery illumination of Selene's moon, and Apollo, the strident beams of Helios' sun.

Past the isles of Andros and Gairos the ferry went, eventually bringing into sight Tinos and Siros. Alkinoë recalled her first journey to these islands thousands of years earlier when she had first gone to Delos right after her marriage to Apollo. He had wanted to show her the place of his birth, the river by which his sister had helped his mother bring him from darkness into light, and the majesty of the island once known as Ortygeia. Coveys of quail appeared not long after Astraea turned herself into the island and brought forth the birds to inhabit it. Many of the firstborn chicks became the island's first human inhabitants. When Leto stepped foot onto the island and it became a part of Gaea, the quails offered up their molted feathers to create a pillow for the newborn Artemis and Apollo. Once Alkinoë intuited she was near Delos, she sat up and craned her neck over the side of the ferry. Putting her hand up to shield her eyes from the sun, she squinted, a sense of relief on her face.

She disembarked and walked the quarter-mile toward the ancient site. Near the temple ruins, a slab of ancient marble jutted forth, flanked by eroded pillars. To the average person, it looked like a remnant of a temple, but no archaeological map showed such a place. Alkinoë unfolded a piece of paper and recited words in ancient Greek, words she had only heard once before from her husband's lips.

"With Gaea's grace and Athene's mercy, I kneel before this place of wisdom and prudence. Reach into my heart and find my purpose. That will be the key."

Winds gathered, swirling eddies of dust, and they moved with serpentine fluidity around her body. She hoped her innermost thoughts and feelings would be enough to grant her audience with those within. The dust entered her nostrils and her mouth, making her gasp, but she held firm. Within a few moments, the dust exited her body, and she regained control of her breathing. The wisps of air that held the dirt struck the marble panel, etching ancient glyphs, circumscribed by a deep circle. Markings filled the space, creating glowing pools. Luminescence dissipated, and Alkinoë took that as her cue. Without hesitation, she walked toward the stone and passed through it. Along the walls of the passage before her, leaf-fringed branches created a canopy. A wooden tapestry barred her way but untangled as she approached. The circular chamber that opened before her had massive branches from a myriad of trees growing upward toward an opening in the ceiling where the sunlight fell. Motes of dust created a suspension that gave the sunbeams substance. Lifting her head, she smiled at nine pairs of glowing eyes in the places untouched by light illuminating the space. Alkinoë had arrived.

Acknowledging within whose company she stood, she lowered her head. "I bid thee greetings, O Keepers of Wisdom and Prudence. Many thanks for allowing me to enter your sacred space."

From near the sun portal, flapping wings descended, alighting on a thick, gnarled oak branch.

"Lift your eyes, daughter of the Earth and Sky."

Alkinoë's face rose, and before her, its talons gripping the perch, sat a brown and white speckled Little Owl, its yellow eyes shimmering.

"O Great One," Alkinoë fell to her knees. "I am not sure I am worthy to be here."

"Had you not been worthy, you would never have been allowed to pass. You may call me Noctua, of Divinity."

As if on cue, the other eight owls moved into the shower of sunlight. One, a Short-Eared Owl, stretched its wings out before speaking.

"We recognize you, Queen Alkinoë. Your respect bears you out. I am Flammea… of Humility. Open yourself to us. You have nothing to fear from our ilk…" She paused. "Unless you bear untruths."

"What reason brings you before this *Koinovoúlio*? How may the wisdom of this parliament guide you?"

"And you are?" Alkinoë's voice regained its natural confidence.

"Otus, of the Deliberate." The Scops Owl cocked its head, its bright orange eyes like miniature suns.

The queen stood, taking in the enclosure. She rubbed her eyes as they became accustomed to the lower level of light and removed the elastic holding her long, black hair back.

"Otus, I am here because I need to know how I can see my husband. I need to know how he is. His absence has made my heart hollow." Alkinoë put her hands to her face. "I just need to know…"

A white-faced Barn Owl fluttered down to her, clasping its talons on a thick vine that traversed the trees.

"Child, we know of your pain. He who lies chained within the Earth Mother's bosom, who writhes in his own memories, has a strong energy that reaches us even here. I am Tyto, of Experience, and I know of yours."

"Can you help me?" Her voice quivered.

Tyto continued. "Daughter of Gaea, tell us what *you* have done to help yourself first."

Alkinoë walked around, touching the bark of a pine tree whose crest extended beyond the sun-soaked opening. She drew her fingers across the nubbly surface.

"I visited the Parthenon." She touched her forehead to the tree. "But, I was forsaken."

A Long-eared Owl flew down to a branch on the pine tree just above Alkinoë's head. Its feathery ear-tufts twitched as it spoke in a deep, resonant voice.

"Did she forsake you, or did you forsake her?"

"I have *never* given up on her. It is you who speak in untruths! I have been a most loyal servant and have been ever since I was a child." She glared at the owl.

"It would be best that you watch your tone. I am Asio, of Judgment, and when you are true to yourself, Alkinoë, then you will understand."

Her first impulse was to lash out, to retort in anger, and she clenched her fists. Before a word could leave her lips, she uncurled her fingers and turned away.

"Again, I ask you. What have you done to help yourself *first*?" Tyto fluttered his wings, pulled them in, and cocked his head.

For a short while, Alkinoë stared at the pine tree. Her mind drifted to other places and times as the owls waited. As embodiments of wisdom, they knew the value of patience. The queen's face was like parchment, telling the story of her soul by the expressions she made. Tyto's question had given her pause for thought, and it was that pause where she was reconciling her emotions with her reality.

She whispered her reply. "I-I have mourned. Grieved over my loss. Shed countless tears. Prayed to high Olympos." When she turned toward Tyto, the tears that pooled just above her lower eyelid caught the sunlight and twinkled. She blinked, the brine tracing the contour of her cheek before dropping to the ground bestrewn with pine needles.

"Did those things help you?" Flammea joined Asio on the branch.

"No…" Alkinoë wiped her tears. "No, they didn't. That was what led me to seek out Athene."

A large Eurasian Eagle Owl squawked as it circled from high above and landed on a thick birch branch seeming to jut from nowhere. Its brown mottled plumage showed a stark contrast to its orange eyes.

"You have shed tears for your beloved. You have offered prayers to the gods. You have tried to commune with wisdom's mistress, but you claim she has forsaken you. None of that has brought you solace. You have traveled a heart's distance to seek us out, Alkinoë. What power do you think we have that the daughter of Prudence does not? We are but wisdom's facets."

"I know you. I have seen you before." Alkinoë moved closer to the owl. "Why do I know you when I do not know your brethren?"

The hulking owl outstretched its wings to where the tips almost touched above its head, like a crest or display of majesty. His reply made her gasp.

"I am Bubo, of Balance. I was present the day you and Apollo wed."

"I-I remember that, of all the gods, Athene could not be present, and you… you sat on the oak tree that grows in the Great Hall of Olympos. You were your mistress' eyes that day."

Bubo lowered his wings. He spoke of how he had kept watch over her and Apollo from this place, and he had a special tie to reason and truth. He felt the searing pain when Python's fangs pierced Apollo, when that corrosive poison entered the son of Zeus, dissolving the barrier between the god's two sets of memories. That was the day that balance was broken. Of all those assembled in this place, he said he felt her pain in his heart. He asked again what she felt they could do that Athene could not.

"I'm not sure. I want to see my husband. I need to see him." She closed her eyes.

145

"Assuming we had the power to open a window into Gaea's adyton, what would seeing him do other than fueling your desire to be with him?"

Alkinoë sat at the base of the pine tree. Resting her cheek against her knees, she said she didn't know. Then, she asked Bubo if he had ever lost anyone he loved.

"No, Your Majesty. I have not. I am tied to wisdom in this world, and I can feel how your heart aches and craves peace. That is the closest I can come to feeling anything near to your loss. I do believe, though, that that gives me clarity and objectivity. One doesn't have to know pain to know that it hurts. I can see it on your face and how it radiates off you. Even when you smile, you cannot hide it."

"Perhaps... Perhaps, I am the one who needs balance, eh, Bubo? If I could be in that stony chamber with Apollo, to hold him, to cradle his face in my hands, to feel his immortal heart beating... I just want to know he is all right. Is that so wrong?"

A Tawny Owl—Strix, for Mortality—emerged from the shadows and her voice had the softness of down against the skin, a soothing timbre.

"No, sweet one. It is not wrong. You love him, perhaps more than you have loved anyone. You are a dichotomy. On one hand, you are a warrior who has fought in more battles than you care to remember, but on the other, you are a compassionate soul whose desire to bring love and care is almost unmatched. A few millennia have given you perspective, more than others in humanity. The window you wish to open will bring you more torment than succor. I believe that Apollo wants you to gather your strength. He needs you to be his anchor in this world. If you are adrift, how can he find you?"

She leaned back against the tree and sighed. A sensation on her knee got her attention, and she couldn't help but smile. It was a Great Gray Owl owlet. She held out her hand, and it hopped onto it. Its talons pinched her index finger, but she didn't care. It squawked as a baby would. Alkinoë caught Tyto's eyes, and the Barn Owl landed on her knee.

"I thought the *Koinovoúlio* was only nine? Who is this?" The queen stroked the owlet's feathers.

Bubo cocked his head. "Her name is Meleia. Her purview is hope. She has no voice yet, but she will, in time. She is not part of the parliament."

"Then why—"

"We want her to be your guide through your own wisdom. She is our eyes and ears in the mortal world. She cannot accompany you home through mortal means, but she will find you."

Alkinoë sat for a while in silence while Meleia stayed perched on her finger. In the owlet's eyes, she could feel the hope that wisdom brings to those ready to accept it, even though she was not quite able to do just that. It gave her something to strive for. A Eurasian Pygmy Owl named Glauca, for Intellect, while not in full view, offered the advice that the wife of Apollo create a plan for just how she would ground herself until Apollo had traversed the landscape of madness. She wanted Alkinoë to use her mind, one of her best attributes, to set a path of growth and strength. Glauca knew that Ari and Esteban were about to enter that landscape to help the son of Zeus find himself once more, no matter by how much.

"Will you continue to look for a way to see your husband, Alkinoë, either through a spectral window or in person?" A Boreal Owl moved across a branch into the light.

"I suppose I will have to think on that…"

"Aegolios, for Responsibility. Bear in mind this truth: if you break Gaea's law or try to, you will incur the wrath of not only the gods themselves, but also of the Great Mother. You do not wish to be an adversary to her. She protects her adyton like she would a delicate child. You would do well to remember that. Think on it, Your Majesty. Not even one such as you, with all the martial experience you have had, could stand against a two-pronged attack, especially of immortals. Betrayal bears a heavy cost, one that you would pay for all time."

"I shall indeed think on it, Aegolios. I swear it to you. To you all."

He continued. "Daughter of Gaea, we shall know if you transgress. Meleia will be with you, even if you cannot see her, and her eyes are bound with ours. We cannot stop you from pursuing what your heart yearns for. To betray wisdom is to isolate yourself from that which can sustain you in your darkest hours."

Alkinoë nodded. "I understand. If there is one thing I have learned about defying the gods is that it comes at a price. You have my word." Her lips quivered.

Tyto flew up to the lowest pine branch. "What is it, child?"

"I have given in to hubris, as if my needs are more worthy than those of others, including my children… and Athene's. Being among you has allowed my thoughts to gather. I know that Gaea keeps my husband safe. I shouldn't be worried *for* him, although I am worried *about* him. He used considerable power to keep those sets of memories apart, for thousands of years, and now that the barrier is gone, I'm not even sure I can imagine what he must be enduring. I am not meant to know that kind of torment."

A small ball of light, like a will-o'-the-wisp, appeared in the dark beyond the trees that made up the enclosure. Bubo told Alkinoë that the next part of her journey was to follow that light. As the guardians of wisdom, they would not lie to her. Meleia chirruped and clicked, something that Alkinoë took as acknowledgment. The nine owls came into the center of the chamber, all in full sunlight, and extended their wings. With a collective screech, they flew back into the shadows. Only Meleia remained, clicking.

"All right, tender one. I will see you soon." She kissed two fingers and placed them on the owlet's head.

Exhaling sharply, she moved toward the small wisp of light until she had left the enclosure of the *Koinovoúlio*. Soon, she no longer felt pine needles beneath her feet, simply earth. The ball of light was her only illumination, and she couldn't see past it. Ever since she was a child, she knew to put her trust in the magical and inexplicable. Her faith had been her shield and her pillar, and now it was literally a guiding light. The silence and still air let her mind wander occasionally, but the warrior in her needed to stay alert. She stopped when she realized she was so lost in her reverie that she had started humming. The tune was a prayer song she had learned from her nursemaid, and she hadn't thought about it since she was in Arkadeia. Continuing her movement, her humming became quiet singing.

"*When Eos' rosy fingers bring about the dawn,*
And 'Pollo's car moves the golden wheel across the sky,
Gaea's grace and mercy be upon you,
And, like the sparrow, you will fly.
On those tiny wings, to soar toward love's embrace,
Above the storms and over the seas you go,
Until you come upon true love's face,
A face you cherish and reverently know.
Reunited with your wingèd mate,
You will find mirth and hope,

Such is decreed by Fate."

When she had learned that song, she had no idea she would eventually, like the sparrow, find her true love in the son of Zeus. Alkinoë had also learned that sparrows were sacred to Aphrodite. Was she singing this song just then because she would again see her beloved? Was this, too, a sign from the gods to bring her hope? So many small things had transpired since she had arrived at Delos, things that made her smile. When she began the song again, even the Muses would envy her voice because it was fueled by love. She had no concept of how much time had passed since she left the owls, but singing the song lifted her spirits. Although she couldn't be certain, it seemed as if the small wisp of light had glowed brighter in response to the song.

Then, the wisp stopped. Before her, the darkness unfurled, revealing a meadow covered by trees, birds chirping all around, and a warm breeze replacing the still air. It took her eyes a moment to adjust, and she turned around. A pine tree whose trunk was about three feet wide stood where she had just been. Serenity replaced shadow. Through the forest, she spied a white-tailed doe and her fawn, neither of which seemed bothered by her sudden appearance. The heady perfume of grass mixed with wildflowers overtook her. Something about this place triggered recognition, but she couldn't place it. Beyond the meadow and through the trees, rolling hills of green speckled with flowers stretched. Outside of the forest, Alkinoë could see no structures or buildings, no roads or signs of civilization. When she tried to think of where she was, another thought crept toward her—she wanted to know *when* she was.

Across the landscape she stepped, knowing there must be some purpose for this, but the very idea of the situation was beyond her reach. On the other side of a hill, a river traipsed, its whimsy fringed occasionally by weeping willows and billowing lily clusters. She passed a tree stump—surrounded with intermingled bevies of fiery poppies, pale lavender, grape hyacinths, and daisies—alive with the buzzing of honeybees. Still, this place reminded her of somewhere, a place she couldn't name. A little ways ahead, an olive tree grew, its thick trunk and broad branches standing out among the flora. Alkinoë stooped by a brook next to it and cupped some water to her mouth. She sat beneath the tree, its branches laden with olives of purple and green, and every shade between them.

"Why can't I remember this place? It just feels so familiar..." She spoke in a low voice as if speaking louder would disturb the setting.

Leaning back against the wrinkled trunk, she closed her eyes, giving in to the desire to rest. Her encounter with the owls had taken much from her emotionally. She relinquished her will to that of Sleep itself and remained in his company until she heard what sounded like her name. The voice seemed distant... reaching. Alkinoë willed herself back to consciousness and sat up.

"Peace, sister." The voice was like a fawn's fur, silken and gentle.

Seated next to Alkinoë was a young woman in a dark brown tunic and leather sandals. Her russet hair was plaited down her back and tied with a hide thong. On her forearms were leather bracers on top of which were smaller hammered and inscribed metal bracelets. Resting on the hair above her brow was a string of tiny jasmine flowers, and dangling from the center of the strand, on her forehead, was a small silver crescent moon. Alkinoë and she shared a glance, and both smiled.

"Artemis. What are you doing here? Speaking of 'here', where am I?"

The goddess stood and helped Alkinoë stand, taking her sister-in-law into her arms.

"I am so, so sorry for what you endure. I do understand," Artemis whispered. She took Alkinoë's hand and walked toward the river. "Where do you think you are?"

"I-I'm not sure. The air smells of Greece, but untouched by humanity. When is this?"

The daughter of Leto put a hand on Alkinoë's cheek. "Long, long ago. Sister, you need to heal your heart for the coming journey. This place is the best for that."

"Journey? I don't understand." She shook her head and sighed. "But you're right. I do need to heal. Speaking with the *Koinovoúlio* helped."

They walked, hand in hand, across hills and through valleys. Creatures of all kinds showed their reverence for Artemis in their own ways: some through touch, and others through sound. Wispy, white clouds floated past them. The two stopped in a meadow where mountains lay in the distance, mountains that caught Alkinoë's attention. She unclasped her hand from the goddess' hand and stared out.

"That mountain. It looks like Mount Lykaion. But, that would mean this is—"

"Yes, my sister. This is Arkadeia."

"But, how?" She clenched her eyes as the tears flowed. "How-?"

"This is how the land looked before Apollo and Gaea created the Arkadeian people. You are standing in Tegea, many years before the city existed. This idyll remains a constant source of joy for me, as it was the first place I took up my bow. Like you, Alkinoë, I am tied to this place. Being here now doesn't threaten any sacred balance or change anything in history. You had not been home in so long, and I wanted to give that to you. The life force of this place can help replenish your spirit. Draw from it as you would from a well. Let its energies fill you up and augment your hope."

The eventual queen of *this* land reached down and ran her hands across the grasses like fringe. Where she stood would later become the city from which she would rule with her husband. Tegea had already existed for decades by the time she was born, so this landscape would look only a little familiar to her.

"I am home." With her eyes still looking out, she grasped Artemis' hand and squeezed. "Dear sister, this gift… it…"

Artemis smiled. "You deserve this, Alkinoë. I do love my brother, but he took you from this place and into the modern world, caused you to endure the pain of losing a son only to reclaim him decades later. Through all of that, you have loved him. Stood by him. When Python took him from you, from us, I knew that I had to come to you."

Her face toward the sun, eyes closed, Alkinoë let all her pain out. First, the tears trickled, but then as she remembered all that Artemis mentioned, all of what she wrestled with inside, her body wrenched, and she let out a howl that would tear the air itself. Her hands dug into the earth, and she pulled clumps of dirt, squeezing until blood dripped from her fingers. She opened her hands to see blood and dirt caked on them. Alkinoë screamed, pummeling the ground over and over and over. Artemis went to reach out, but she pulled back, knowing that this woman needed her release, something she had never been able to have.

Then, the earth shook.

"Daughter…"

The queen brought her hands through her hair, leaving traces of blood and dirt. Still, her pain poured from her eyes, an unending well of torment.

"*Daughter…*" The voice returned, and this time, the queen heard it.

"Gaea? Is that—is that you?"

"*Yes, Alkinoë. I am here. I cannot watch your pain.*" The words sounded like they were carried on the wind, fading in and out.

"Pain. Yes. My heart is missing a part of itself, Great Mother." She clasped her bloody, dirt-laden hands to her chest. "I am lost. So lost… so lost…"

"*You feel this more now because you sit at your birthplace, daughter. I come to you to help you heal.*"

Alkinoë's eyes widened, and she put her hands to her head.

"I feel him. *O Megalê Thea*, Great Goddess, his pain… his mania… his thoughts—"

"Sister, what do you see?" Artemis knelt by her side and put a hand on her shoulder.

"Blurred images. Memories? Emotions? They are dizzying to witness." She shook her head. "By all the gods, Gaea, he is in agony. Wait. His thoughts grow calm. I-I feel growing joy. Ecstasy." She smiled, nodding. "Love. I feel his love for me. For Danelos. For Kidemonas. He does indeed remember them. Us." She looked down at her wrists, her fists clenched. "The chains that bind him. So heavy. So heavy…"

She collapsed into Artemis' lap. The goddess stroked Alkinoë's hair and kissed her forehead.

"Sleep, fair one. Sleep…" She wiped her own tears. "*Chárin soi écho, Matêr Pantôn…*"

Thanks to thee, Great Mother.

When her eyes opened once more, Alkinoë found herself in a meadow surrounded by a perfect circle of trees, their canopy diffusing the light around her. The breezes whispered incomprehensible words, and on the branches, crows had kept vigil over her. Apollo's guardians. One flew down, and she let it perch on her finger. She brought it closer, and, instead of cawing, it uttered words in the ancient Olympeian language of the gods, a language few of the gods ever used, words that told her that they came from Apollo himself. This time when she smiled, it was of deep contentment.

"I am your forever love, too, *o sýzygós mou…*" She uttered the words *my husband* not out of duty, but out of reverence for their bond.

The crow vanished into the trees, and Alkinoë's eye caught another avian creature, one that she had just recently met. Meleia flapped her tiny wings and landed on Alkinoë's hand, squeaking its nascent voice.

"Yes, little one. I have found some hope once more." She kissed the owlet, releasing it back to the trees. Alkinoë noticed her hands were healed and clean. "If only your mistress would cast *her* eyes upon me."

"Mother Gaea was able to give you what I could not, sister."

In showering, auspicious sunlight emerged the one goddess Alkinoë had longed to see. The queen hung her head but said nothing.

"I know you are angry with me." The words of the immortal floated as if made of the air itself.

Rising, Alkinoë looked at Athene, her lips forming a gentle smile. "No longer. When Gaea shared Apollo's thoughts with me, she also told me that you didn't have the power to give me such a gift. My anger for you was misplaced. I was angry at myself, and at Apollo. Having peered into his mind, I saw that his love for me transcends timelines, and I know with certainty that what he did to protect my son he did out of that love and the unshakable love of a father. I lashed out at you because I *could*, sister."

Arrayed not in armor, but in a diaphanous pale green shift bound at the waist with a bronze belt whose buckle bore the countenance of an owl, Athene stepped from the shafts of light into the meadow. Her hair was wrapped into a coil on the back of her head and supported by a bronze sphendone that highlighted her face, bringing out her gray eyes.

"You have found your *own* wisdom."

"For now." Alkinoë raised her head to the canopy. "I have much to traverse. Being here has begun the healing that I could not begin in the modern world. My pain began here, and my redress had to begin here as well."

"Do you wish me to go?"

"Of course, not. Sit with me."

In the heart of the meadow, goddess and queen settled among the grass and flowers. Perfume from jasmine and rose wafted by, and Alkinoë inhaled.

Athene sighed. "Of all the mortals I have known, the love you have for another has been the strongest I have seen, sister. That you have it for my brother is… well… humbling. Aphrodite would be pleased."

"Why didn't you simply tell me you couldn't do what I wanted? Why did you remain silent?"

"Alkinoë, you were angry, and rightfully so. Nothing I could have said to you would have appeased you. Even if I had been able to help you, and did so, you would have wanted more. I needed you to find your own path, and you did. Gaea's choice came from her ceaseless love for you. You will mend those parts of you splintered by choices others have made. I know that you told Apollo that you had forgiven him his trespasses, even though in your heart's core, I know you had not. I think he knew that as well, but he did not wish to push you."

"Pallas… when I found out that Apollo had gone to see Python on his own, my first thought was that he did that because he *knew* Python would bite him. It is my most fervent belief that he wanted it to happen so he… he…" She pressed her eyes closed.

"Alkinoë?" Athene took her hand.

"He wanted to suffer… for betraying me, for betraying Kidemonas… He wanted to serve a penance because he believed that he had damaged a part of our love. That choice, to save my son from Lismonia, crushed his immortal soul, and the burden of keeping those sets of memories at bay had worn him down. He *chose* this."

The goddess gasped. "Great Mother Metis… you truly believe this." Athene grew pallid. "I could not believe he could, or would, falter. To think my brother would choose such a fate."

"My emotions have taken a wide path, and I had moved beyond his actions in my mind. They made sense to me. When I challenged myself to consider whether I could do the same thing… but in my heart? I couldn't force my heart to reconcile any faster than it can. And now, my husband goes between moments of clear sanity and muddled mania."

"What will you do?"

"I have no choice. Aristeides has taken it upon himself to save my husband, and I do believe he has the means to attempt it. Whether he succeeds or not is up to the Moirae. Neither of my sons, nor I, can transcend the barriers of the mind and spirit." She grabbed Athene by the hand. "Come. Before I have to return to the modern world, walk with me through my ancestral home."

They meandered across the untouched lands, places where a vibrant city would someday cover the rolling hills, silver brooks, and all the majesty of Gaea's splendor. With every footstep, Alkinoë felt the pulse of the Earth Mother, and she wanted the nurturing power to course through her and make her whole once more. A world rampant with sacred energy made her skin tingle. Seeing how Alkinoë responded, Athene smiled, having never borne witness to such pure joy. It warmed her immortal heart to see the effect of Gaea's grace on one she loved. They had traveled quite a distance, and both were distracted by their journey when they entered a valley. Alkinoë stopped and gasped. Stooping, she placed her palms on the earth.

"What is it?"

"I feel him. I *feel* him here, Athene. What is special about this place?"

Scanning the area to get her bearings, Athene touched Alkinoë's shoulder.

"This is Bassai. You feel him here because—"

"There will be a temple erected to him. To *Apollo Epikourios*. Apollo the Helper. How is it possible that I feel his presence when this temple won't be built for hundreds of years?"

"His presence in the future has left a tether that stretches back into the past. They are only felt by those who have a connection to the originator."

A hawk soared above them, squawking its approach, and it circled above before flapping toward the ground. Before it could land, it transformed into the one who had brought Alkinoë into this time.

"You did not realize, but you felt this innate urge to come here, to this one spot in all of Bassai. I wanted you to feel my brother's energy before I sent you back to your time. My hope, dearest, is that this visit will strengthen your resolve and give you focus to endure."

The queen nodded. "I believe it will. Thank you, Artemis and Athene both for your gifts." She looked out over the land. "And, thank you as well, Great Mother."

Athene embraced her. "Meleia will find you. Her wisdom will be your guide."

"Artemis, could you possibly… well, could you send me back to my home in Boston? The thought of that ferry back to Athens and then the flight home…"

Apollo's sister laughed. "Of course. May Gaea's grace be with you."

A circular portal opened, and Alkinoë could see her living room, and Dan sitting on the couch, his head in his hands. Wide-eyed, she sprang forward, and the portal closed behind her.

18 | SECRETS REVEALED

D anelos, what's wrong?"

Dan lifted his head up, puzzled.

"Mom, where have you been? You've been gone for days. You disappeared without saying a word."

Alkinoë touched his shoulder. "I was with Athene and Artemis."

"Well, that explains *that*, I guess." He slapped his hands against his thighs and stood. "The next time you decide to go off somewhere, could you tell someone? Please? A note? I have a hard enough time dealing with Ari and his hospital visits, and then you just go galavanting—"

"I don't believe I have to tell you anything at all. You may be the leader of your task force, but you—"

"But nothing. Sorry, but as the leader of that task force, it's my responsibility to keep people safe, and if you're going off on your own adventures, especially now, I'd like to be kept in the loop. In fact, I'm going to have to insist on it."

She straightened up, like a cornered animal. She wasn't used to being spoken to like that by anyone, let alone her son. His retort had caught her off guard. Alkinoë was about to reply, but Dan continued, walking around the living room, waving his arms, explaining to her just how dangerous it is for her to go off on her own, considering what had happened to her husband. He'd spent hours poring over details and events, trying to think if something else was at work, something bigger.

"I'm fairly certain something is up with those cameras too. Quinn's working on it. I have Aleta temporarily stripping Zeus of his power, my husband and a man in a vegetative state trying to figure out how to help my father, and now I have to worry about *you*. The only two who aren't concerning me right now are Brandon and Sarah, and that's only a matter of time!"

"You are just like your father," Alkinoë muttered, shaking her head.

"What was that?"

She raised her voice and pointed at him. "You are just like your father! By the gods, Danelos, you think just like him. You want to control everything and everyone around you, or you want to try. Your father couldn't control everything! He is an Olympeian god, a son of almighty Zeus himself, and look at what happened!"

"I am *not* trying to control anyone. If I am, I'm not very good at it. What—"

"Enough! Listen to yourself. You have worked yourself into a frenzy over things you simply cannot control." She paused, watching him pace and fume. "Do you trust Ari?"

"What?"

"Do you trust Ari? It's a simple question."

Dan took a deep breath. "Of course. Of course, I trust him."

"Then, let him do what he thinks is best. If you didn't think his plan had a chance of working, you would have tried to talk him out of it. Am I right?"

He pursed his lips and stared at her.

"Am I right?" She repeated slowly.

All he could do was nod slightly. Tossing his head back, he ran his fingers through his hair.

Alkinoë softened her expression and gently pinched his chin, looking up into his eyes.

"Trust him, Danelos. I do."

He closed his eyes and put his arms around her, holding her tightly.

"It's not that I don't trust him," he whispered. "It's that he's barely recovered from his ordeal with Python, and he's willing to jump right back into the fray. I don't want him to put himself at risk."

His mother put her hands on his cheeks.

"He adores you. He literally went to the underworld and back for you. If he needs your help, he'll tell you. I'm sure of that." She pulled his forehead to her lips. "I know you know that too. Remember, he's Arkadeian. We're pretty tough."

She took his hand, and he squeezed hers. Falling back onto the couch, he told her he was sorry for snapping, and that he loved her. He admitted that he felt like he was losing touch with reality because he couldn't change or affect anything. She reminded him that he was only one man, and despite his genealogy, he didn't have the power to do it all. He put his head back and closed his eyes for a minute.

"What did you do with Artemis and Athene? Girls' night out?"

She playfully slapped his leg and chuckled. Alkinoë told him the story, and as he listened, he sat up and leaned forward, cupping her hands in his. Dan grinned.

"What?" She raised an eyebrow. "You only smile like that when you have a secret. It's that mischievous smile I've seen so much on Hermes over the years."

"Well…"

"Spill it."

He sighed in that way he did as a child when he knew he'd have to tell her whatever it was he was hiding. Smirking, he leaned toward her.

"When I was little, Dad and I used to take walks in the Public Garden together. He'd put me on his shoulders, and we'd run around together. He'd bring a ball, and we'd play. I didn't know it then, but he was teaching me how to be a keen warrior. He taught me how to throw that ball, how to catch it, and, well… we just had some great father-son moments. I never really thought of him as a god, even though I knew he was."

"I remember those days." A warmth spread over Alkinoë's cheeks. "You would come home and tell me all about what you two had done together."

Dan nodded. "But, what I didn't tell you were the conversations we had." He paused. "We were sitting by the swan boats one day, and I looked up to see my father staring into the sunlight. Any normal man would have been blinded, but not him. I asked him what made him so powerful. Without hesitation, he said, 'Your mother.' I asked him what he meant, and this is what he told me. 'Danelos,' he said, 'I am not powerful because of my father, or my grandfather, or even being tied to Khaos herself. Those things make me a *god*. What makes me powerful is the love that I have for your mother, and the love she has for me. She is by far the wisest woman I know, but don't tell your aunt Athene that.' He laughed. 'She guides my immortal soul, and I never question her judgment. We may disagree from time to time, but I always come around.'"

Alkinoë's face froze, wide-eyed. Dan stroked her cheek with the back of his fingers.

"Mom, I couldn't agree more with Dad. You are the wisest woman I have ever known. I've even told Athene that." He chuckled. "Your power comes from your love. Your capacity for forgiveness and compassion is limitless."

She pulled her son into a tight embrace and rested her cheek on his shoulder. Both mother and son cried quietly, something they hadn't done since Apollo went to Gaea's inner sanctum. The serenity of the moment ended when Dan's manacle buzzed. It was Quinn. She let him know that she had information for him about the cameras and that Akmon was with her.

"You'd better go." Alkinoë wiped her eyes. "Danelos. Thank you."

"I love you, Mom."

"No mother has loved her children more than I love you and your brother. I'll be all right."

Stopping at the door, Dan turned around.

"I'll call you later. I'll bring Brandon over, and we'll do dinner."

After the door closed, Alkinoë caught a glimpse of something by the French doors that led out to the balcony. On a potted olive tree sat a tiny visitor. She stepped outside toward the balustrade.

"Athene was right, tiny one. You did find me."

Meleia chirped on the branch, fluttering her wings.

"Hope indeed." The queen uttered, staring out at the Charles River.

"About time you arrived." Quinn swung around in her chair when she heard Dan enter.

"Sorry." He pulled up a chair. "I was with my mother. What did you find?"

"I'll let Akmon explain."

Around the corner from the back of the office, the young man stomped, his husky frame still looking a bit awkward wearing modern clothing. He'd had his hair buzzed as short as Brandon's, so he looked more like a football player than the son of Hephaestos.

"Dan!" He wrapped his arms around Dan, forcing the man's breath out of him. "Good to see you. It has been a while."

"Good to see you, too, Akmon." As soon as Akmon let him go, Dan inhaled sharply. "What did—"

"Yes, I have things to tell you. Quinn has been teaching me about this incredible... what is the word... technology you have. It is hard to believe it is not magic. I wonder if even Heph—"

Dan put up his hand. "Akmon, what did you find?"

"Of course. Of course. We were looking for information about the cameras. I went back to where you said you saw the first one, and I touched it to see if I could tell what it was made of."

"Wait. I thought you could only tell what kind of metal something was."

"It seems, fearless leader, that his power has evolved." Quinn smiled. "The problem is that he doesn't know enough about modern-day materials to be able to relay their composition."

"Until now!" Akmon burst out, his demeanor more like an eager child.

"Until now." Quinn continued. "Sarah took him on a walking tour of the city earlier in the week, and she found that if he concentrated enough, he not only could see the individual substances that make something up, but he also could learn its name. The best was when they stopped for hot dogs from a street vendor, and with one bite, Akmon could tell the vendor exactly what was in the hot dog. Down to the chemicals, even though he didn't know how to pronounce them well."

Dan howled with laughter. "Seriously? What happened?"

Akmon's smile melted. "He was not pleased. In fact, he called me some words that made Sarah blush. One of them was this word, 'motherf—'"

"Okay! That's all I needed to hear." Dan shook his head. "Akmon," he patted Akmon's leg, "What did you find out about the camera?"

"Yes. Sorry. The casing is made from *steel* polycarbonate."

Rolling his eyes, Dan drummed his fingers on the arms of his chair.

"We knew that. What else?"

"Ease up, cowboy. Let him finish." Quinn raised her eyebrow.

Akmon continued. "Yes, we knew that, but what we did not know was that it is not ordinary steel. It's *Earth*steel."

"This is a joke, right? I mean, Earthsteel? That can't be right."

Quinn rolled her chair over to Dan.

"No joke. This means—"

"I know what this means. It means that whoever's behind the cameras is connected to the gods. There's no other way." Dan put his head in his hands. "Things just keep getting more and more bizarre. How the hell are the gods involved?"

"Dan, there's more." Quinn's voice dropped. "You won't believe what we've, well, what Akmon found."

"More? What more could there be?" He jumped up, putting his hands on the back of the chair, hanging his head. He muttered, "I really don't know how much more I can take."

Akmon brought a manila folder to Dan. Akmon didn't let go.

"Before you open it, just remember that we do not have all the information. I have many questions, brother."

Tugging it from Akmon's fingers, Dan scanned the report. When he reached a certain point, he tightened both his jaw and his fist, glaring at Akmon.

"I can feel that look from here. It's not his fault, you know. He just figured it out." Quinn tapped a little on her glass interface. "I just sent a message to the others. Priority Alpha. Before you say a word, we're going to need the whole team."

19 | MYSTERY

At the top of the curved marble stairs in the foyer building that led to Apollo and Alkinoë's condominium, Ari rang the bell, its chime echoing behind the carved oaken door. A moment passed, and he tried again. Trying the knob, he found it unlocked, so he announced himself as he walked in. The entryway table displayed Alkinoë's keys, so she was home, and it was unlike her to leave the door unlocked, even though Ari knew she could handle herself. Passing through the living room, he saw her on the balcony and gently tapped on the glass. Meleia fluttered back to her branch on the potted olive tree as Alkinoë stood.

"Ari, what a pleasant surprise." She waved him onto the balcony. "I didn't realize that I had left the door unlocked. Come sit. Is everything all right?"

He kissed her cheek and went to the tree.

"You have a visitor, I see." He rubbed the back of his index finger against the owlet's feathers.

"What brings you by? Did you try to call? I left my phone in the bedroom."

Taking a seat on a small marble bench by the tree, he kept looking up at Meleia. The owl cooed softly, opening and closing its eyes slowly.

Alkinoë watched his body language. "Can I get you something to drink?"

"No, thank you. I stopped by to see how you were. I realized we had not spoken in a few days." He rubbed his hands together.

She could sense something about him but took her seat over-looking the river.

"I'm doing well. Dan was here earlier, and we had a chance to catch up." As she would do with anyone in her presence, she sized him up.

"He mentioned he had seen you earlier today. We spoke a little while ago, just before he arrived at Quinn's office." He inter-laced his fingers, letting his joined hands rest between his legs.

Without shifting her gaze from the river, she asked if every-thing was all right and that he seemed troubled. Ari shifted his feet, and unlaced his fingers, putting his palms on the bench.

Alkinoë ignored his behavior. "Ari, why do you want to help my husband?"

He looked up with a start.

"What? What do you mean? Why would I not want to help him?"

She joined him on the bench and took his hands. "Look at me. Why do you want to help Apollo?"

Ari dropped his head. "I feel responsible. Python—"

She put a finger up to his lips. "Python did this to my hus-band. You didn't. I don't care whose body he used. *He* did this. Are you acting out of guilt?"

"No! Of course not. I-I simply want to help."

Unbeknownst to them, Dan had returned, and when he saw his husband and mother on the balcony, he was about to step out-side when he stopped, keeping himself hidden.

"You want to help my husband, and I am grateful for what-ever you can do, but please don't do it out of a sense of guilt."

Ari shook his head. "I am not. I do it because it is the right thing." He stopped as if to form a thought. "When Hades took me as his own, I felt as if I had found a family again. I know that Danelos is my family, as are you and Apollo, but I had missed my own father so much. Being Hades' son, even if adopted, makes me family to Apollo even more. He is the god of truth and reason, something I cannot live without. When I lived in the Temple of Hades, Apollo was the god I prayed to, and not because he was the Arkadeian king. I spent most of my childhood in a dark, sti-fling place, with the stench of death all around me. I needed light. That was why I went into Tegea to learn how to fight. Being there gave me the chance to visit Apollo's temple, to pray for guidance, and lift my spirit. When I followed Danelos here… when we met and fell in love… I felt as if Apollo had granted my prayer. My light *is* Danelos."

Dan pressed his fist against his chest while he looked at the man who held his heart. At the beginning of their relationship, whenever Ari saw Dan, he would press his fist to his heart as a sign of allegiance, since Dan was technically his prince. Over time, Dan adopted that gesture toward Ari to show *his* allegiance to his beloved.

"Let me ask you something." Alkinoë went to the balustrade. "Do you aspire to join Task Force: Gaea? I mean, you are Arkadeian-born, and you've trained to fight, and you possess that obol. You would be a tremendous asset to the team."

He joined her, and they both looked out at the river.

"No. I do not. I think that Dan wants me to, but I cannot. I can help, from the outside, in my own way. I do not wish to go on, as he calls them, field missions. My place is to support him. If I were on that team, my first allegiance would be to his protection. I would want to fight alongside him, to keep him safe. I do not need to consult Athene to know that that would be unwise. Do you understand?"

"More than you know. When I was queen, I learned through many poor decisions that my role was not to be side by side with Apollo. It was to support him, guide him, and even disagree with him. I had to be the one person who told him the absolute truth no matter how much it hurt me to do so, or hurt him. That is how I show my loyalty. He gets nothing but the complete truth from me."

Ari turned toward her. "I need to tell this to Danelos."

Alkinoë kissed him on the forehead. "My son is a lucky man. As are you."

Dan wanted to make his presence known, but this conversation wasn't intended for his ears. He went into the kitchen and returned with what he had gone there to find: his phone. Sneaking out, he headed back to Quinn's office with his heart a bit fuller. It wasn't until he was halfway back to the office that his smile shrank as he remembered what he needed to share with his team.

Exiting the elevator, familiar voices came from the end of the corridor, and a bit of laughter he didn't expect. Sitting at the conference table in Quinn's office, Akmon and Brandon arm-wrestled, and it was a standoff. Aleta sat beside Akmon, rooting him on while Sarah cheered on Brandon. By the time he got to the table, Brandon's hand had been pinned down by his opponent's.

"Let's make it two out of three. I need—"

"That'll have to wait, Brandon. There's a reason why Quinn summoned you." Dan tossed the folder on the table.

Sarah pulled it over, checking out the contents. "Are you kidding me?" She slid it to Aleta.

Aleta put her hand to her face. "What the absolute hell... This is what you found, Akmon?"

"I am afraid so. The image is a peacock feather, and that means this has something to do with Hera. When Quinn started her investigation, she called me in to see if I knew anything, as a fresh pair of eyes. That was when I decided to revisit the camera."

Aleta had her elbows on the table, her hands clasped. "How did you know it was a peacock feather? Quinn's research came up cold."

"Quinn gave me a camera which takes better pictures than those... what do you call them... cell phones. The imprint was not very deep in the casing, but I recognized the shape from something I had seen in Hephaestos' forge when I was there with Kidemo... er, Brandon. Why do we not just ask Hera about it?"

Aleta sighed. "It's not that simple, kiddo. We can't just waltz over to Olympos and ask the queen of the gods about these cameras. I'm not her favorite person right now, anyway."

Their conversation was more like a tennis match, with each suggestion being bounced around without gaining any purchase. Sarah offered to speak with Hera, but Dan didn't like the idea of her going by herself. He himself felt he was too emotionally scattered to go. Visiting Olympus wasn't something Brandon wanted to do either, even if conditions were favorable, and in Zeus' current diminished position, conditions were far from that. Dan deferred to Quinn for insight, but the Task Force liaison had only ever spoken to one Olympeian god, so she felt inexperienced in offering advice.

"It might be best to table this for the time being," Sarah suggested. "At least until we can figure out a better plan."

Dan nodded. "Agreed. For the moment, we can put this aside." He rubbed his temple.

"Something wrong?" Brandon patted his brother on the shoulder.

"Just a lot on my mind. Plus," he rubbed the scar on his chest. "I can feel my own energies taxed by using my body as a conduit for all things prophetic. How are you holding up?"

Brandon let out a sideways smile. "Eh. I'm all right. I get tired more easily. The last time I was at The Beanery, the baristas joked that they'd forgotten my name since I don't show up for my daily latte. Keeping myself artificially amped up is a recipe for disaster, especially since I'm the guardian of reason." He tapped his own scar. "I suppose it's a good thing we haven't had to fight any—"

"Uh uh. Don't say that out loud. The Fates are fickle." Dan chuckled, wagging his finger. "I talked with Jamshid, Keion, and Ryuma the other day, and we're all in the same boat. Ryuma tried to play it off, as he usually does, but I could hear it in his voice. Even though we can provide a more stable anchor for these aspects of Dad's power, it doesn't mean that it's not a burden."

"I meditate as much as I can. The other day, I was sitting in the lion enclosure, in a lotus position, while Brutus slept at my feet."

"Brutus is…"

"One of the lions. We're transitioning the habitats into larger enclosures to give our animals more freedom until we can get them back into the wild. I'm not a huge fan of most zoos, as you know, but ours is more a rescue for animals close to extinction. Task Force: Eta has its hands full dealing with hunters and poachers, so we're helping out however we can. Anyway, meditation helps."

"Do you really think that enchantment we did is doing anything? Seems like when I watch the news, more and more chaos creeps into the day-to-day than it used to."

"Dan, I don't know. I guess if it weren't working, we'd see catastrophe after catastrophe. Maybe it's my connection with the heavens, but I do feel the weight of things more than I used to. I'm starting to get an understanding of what Atlas deals with. Aleta tells me, from her conversations with the doctors she's talked to, that the power for people to heal themselves moves a bit slower. It's better, just not where it needs to be."

Aleta joined them. "I couldn't help but overhear that last bit. BioCorps has put out feelers to hospitals and other independent companies that deal with patients, and they have seen improvements across the board, albeit slow ones. What you're doing is helping. I just didn't realize how much Apollo's influence affected the world until recently. Stay strong, boys. We'll figure this all out. We'll figure out what's happening with Hera, too, but I don't think we should wait that long. When you're trying to diagnose a patient, you check everything out, no matter how hard or unpleasant it might be."

As Aleta went back to the others, Dan shook his head and exhaled.

"I can't help but think that last bit was meant for me, whether she intended it or not."

"You're going to have to suck it up and talk to Hera, team leader." Brandon tapped Dan's shoulder with his fist. "I have faith in you." He winked and joined his teammates.

"Thanks." Dan scowled. "But, I think you're right."

Drawing his sword, he took one more look at his team before stepping through a portal to Olympos. The austere marble walls supported by columns in each corner reminded him of the bleakness of his own spirit. He had let his emptiness with his father's absence press down on him like an invisible weight. It was fitting, then, that he put himself into the one room where he could gather himself before seeking out Hera: his father's chamber. Without Apollo's presence, the void was even more hollow, like a vacuum taking in all the life-affirming energy that entered it. At the center of it all lay the scrying pool, and he touched his finger to the mirror-like surface of the liquid. The waters of this pool were a part of Olympeia herself, and Dan had awakened the mountain's spirit to guide him in finding Olympos' queen. The ripples subsided, and the image of Hera sitting at the fire ring in the throne room came into focus. Her face made him think of his own mother's face and the heartache she had worn just after Apollo's absence. For Hera, however, hers, darkened by a cowl of shadow, read of a different god's predicament.

"I knew you would come." The queen of the gods pushed around the embers with a finger as Dan entered. "I do want to express my deepest sorrow for your father's fate. But I do not think that is why you are here." She turned her tear-strewn face toward him.

'No," Dan answered. "Thanks for the sympathy, but my father's fate is not why I've come. I'm sure you remember the surveillance cameras from the time you spent among mortals."

She nodded, her hand playing with the fire.

"We've just learned that they're being upgraded, and whoever is doing this is using Earthsteel as a component. That brings this into the godly sphere. On top of that, whoever has created these is marking them with this." He handed her a photograph. "From my recollection, you favor these birds. I've come to ask if you are involved with these cameras in any way."

Hera's eyes glowed red, the winds gusting around her, but she remained seated.

"You bring this trifling to me? Do you not see my pain? Why would I care that much about these cameras?" She took a fistful of embers and squeezed. "My husband has been stripped of his power by your winged friend." She threw the embers toward Dan. "He no longer commands the powers of the storm and sits in darkness, seething. I care not what mortals do to one another. If you—"

The sound of Thyroros crashing against the stone ring stopped Hera's tirade, and she swung her head around, her emerald eyes glistening.

"Enough!" Dan's voice took on the stentorian tone of his grandfather. "My world is threatened by forces I can't see, my father lies chained in darkness, my mother weeping for her loss, and you're concerned about Zeus having lost some of his power because he was throwing a tantrum that could have destroyed all of Gaea? Madness seems to infect many of the gods then!"

"You dare!" Hera clenched her fists that then glowed orange and red with arcane power.

Gritting his teeth, Dan growled, swinging the sword before him. "Yes! I *dare.*"

The Olympeian queen launched balls of energy the size of basketballs toward him, he deflected them with his sword, and they ricocheted at the thrones and pillars that surrounded them. The handiwork of Hephaestos was laying in rubble, and with each fireball, Dan turned the throne room of the gods into a pile of shattered marble and metal. Hera shrieked like a bird of prey, throwing continuous volleys of energy at him. Had she been more clear-headed, Danelos might not have been as successful at withstanding the attack. When dust and fire finally obscured the entirety of the chamber, the melee ceased. A summoned wind swept through and cleared the air, leaving Dan standing, still gripping his sword, his chest heaving, and Hera seeing what her anger had wrought. He sheathed his sword.

"This! Do you see *this!* This is the only throne that matters to me right now." He pointed at his father's, the only one he had left unmarred. "Look at what *your* anger has done, Hera. This is just one room on a vast mountain. Now, imagine if Zeus had remained unchecked when his storms were wreaking havoc. Not even Gaea herself could have stopped him, a parent grieving for the loss of a child. Aleta did what she had to do to protect the world. All of it. She can even return Zeus' power, assuming he won't turn around and smite something."

The goddess opened her palm and summoned another ball of fiery energy, her ire yet unquelled. Glowing like a small sun, the orb illuminated her face and her red hair, giving her a monstrous cast. Dan narrowed his eyes as he reached for his sword again.

"Stand down. I swear by all that is holy that I will use whatever power I can muster against you if I have to. Should you destroy me, you'll have to explain to Zeus why. When he does get his power back, you'll be on the receiving end of it. I guarantee it."

She lifted her hand as if to attack him, and then she closed her fingers, extinguishing the power.

"Thank you." He opened a portal back to Quinn's office. "Now, I have a mystery to solve, and you… well, you have a room to clean."

Brandon ran over to his brother, his mouth agape, witness to the marble dust and scorch marks on Dan's clothing.

"What the hell happened?"

Dan plopped himself into a chair. "I found Hera. We had words. She doesn't know anything about the cameras. We're back to square one."

"Okay. Well, while you were gone, Ari called. He and Esteban are going to try to contact your father."

20 | THRESHOLD

Ari had sneaked into Esteban's hospital room before visiting hours and stopped at the foot of the bed, staring at the young man. He had prepared for this day for a few months, and the journey needed to begin. Connecting with Esteban and being in his mind had been a two-fold experience: joining with the other mind necessary to move forward, but also being in someone else's mind to get the bearings needed to stay focused. Ari knew that Esteban and Apollo's mental landscape were entirely different, though, and he had planned for certain contingencies should the situation imperil them both. Since he and Esteban had found common ground, their rapport had grown as well. Trust was key for this journey, Hades had told him. Being in a human's consciousness was one thing but being in a god's was uncharted territory. One thing Ari knew for certain was that he had to start this process on this very day.

"All right, my friend. I hope you are ready for this. The first thing we have to do is connect with Apollo's mind." He said it matter-of-factly as if it were an everyday occurrence and pulled a chair closer to the bed.

Ari was aware that no one could visit Apollo in Gaea's adyton, and even getting into Apollo's mind would be a labyrinthine task. The power of the obol that Charon had given him would transcend all states of consciousness, and Gaea wouldn't be able to prevent Ari from traversing that ethereal realm. With his eyes closed, he focused on his breathing, as Brandon had taught him

171

to do, and put himself in a relaxed and transcendent state. Using his own heartbeat as a tether, he moved his mind farther and farther away until he breached the underworld. This kind of entry didn't require a canine watchdog; a consciousness was free to enter and leave if it were from a living person. Some stories claimed that Morpheos himself lived in the underworld and that is where all dreams originated. Through the thick, gelatinous darkness Ari moved, using only his thoughts of Apollo as a guide. What seemed like hours passed to him, and he had nothing along this path to look at—only the blackness of Erebos existed in this place. At times, his breathing labored, and he gasped as if he were drowning, but he gripped the sides of the chair and pressed on, pushing past the sensation. Sweat trickled down his temples. Then, he found himself in a cave-like corridor, the rock around him jagged and untouched by anything save for the darkness and underworld creatures. These subterranean paths had never seen light of any kind, even the lights of the First Fires. A wave moved over him that felt like crawling insects, and his arms bristled with goosebumps. He then twitched and cringed as if passing through a curtain of serpents, but nothing was there except his perception.

Next, he passed through a barrier of sharpened blades of all kinds, slices opening on his arms, legs, and face. Blood oozed from the wounds, and the pain pulsed through his body. He shivered and twitched. Then, as quickly as that feeling had come, it vanished. His pace slowed, despite his efforts, and he forced himself to move forward, even if by only small increments. Ari deduced he was close. He knew Apollo was just beyond the next boundary. Gaea wasn't going to make it easy for him, and that last barrier felt like acid was eating away at his flesh, forming pustules on his skin that burst with a stench to rival that of harpies who smelled of rotting human flesh. Ari gagged, vomited in a pail by the bed, but pressed on. With one final mental shove, he entered Gaea's inner sanctum, and there, on a stone slab, Apollo sat slumped over, chained. Whatever luster the Shining One had once given off had diminished, and he was gaunt and frail. Gliding closer, Ari reached out until he could feel Apollo, and when he made the connection, he pulled Esteban's consciousness in with his. Once inside, the two stood side by side within what they perceived was a temple, one that had been ravaged by time and neglect. Ochre pus oozed down the walls, eating away at the marble.

"We did it. We are here." Ari got his bearings. "That yellow liquid is Python's venom. Whatever you do, do not touch it."

Esteban leaned closer and scrunched his nose. "It smells like decay. What *is* this place? This can't be Apollo's mind."

"I am afraid so. Look around."

Within this mental construct of a temple, torches burned on the walls, but their fire was gray and barely moving. What should have been upright columns lay in fractured heaps on the floor, covered in that yellow liquid. On the wall, in one niche, lay a broken bow, its string hanging limp, with arrows missing arrowheads or fletchings. In another niche rested a withered laurel wreath. In yet another, the bones of a bird. Esteban craned his neck to see since the opening was just above his height.

"It is a raven, a sacred bird to him. All of these objects represent aspects of his influence, all deteriorated by Python. See that pedestal over there?" Ari pointed toward a cracked marble plinth. "That broken kylix has serpents painted on the outside. It represents *Apollo Epikourios*, Apollo the Healer."

"I-I thought serpientes were tools of darkness, like Python." Esteban narrowed his eyes.

"On the contrary, they have long been associated with the healing arts. Apollo's son and a god of healing, Aesculapios, walked with a rod entwined with a serpent that whispered secrets to him. Kidemonas, my beloved's brother has met him. Aesculapios is one with the stars as *Ophiokos*, the Serpent Bearer. It is he who watches over Python now."

Meandering through the shadowy chamber, they glimpsed other objects connected to Apollo—shields depicting wolves and dolphins—corroded by the venom. Esteban gasped, and when Ari looked up, he saw why. A broken chariot hung above them, skeletons of horses still attached with harnesses. Beyond, what would be the heavens had a few random specks of light, errant stars. They turned down an obscure corridor to find woven tapestries, ripped and worm-eaten, all depicting stories about Apollo's deeds.

"Do you hear that?" Esteban stared into the blackness ahead of them. "I thought I heard something."

Ari turned his ear. "No, I did not hear anything. We should keep going. We must find Apollo."

Even with no illumination, they shuffled down the corridor, occasionally coming across a barely lit torch. Turning and twisting, the passageway showed no signs of anything, unlike the earlier chamber. Ari stopped and touched Esteban's shoulder.

"I think I heard something this time. Did you?"

"Sí. It's faint, but it's coming from up ahead."

Without warning, another chamber opened before them, and this one had no columns or wall niches. In the center was a stone ring about ten feet across. When they investigated it, they saw what appeared to be oil, viscous and murky.

"A scrying pool. This represents Apollo's ability to see prophecy and into the outside world from Olympos."

Esteban reached toward the liquid when Ari yanked his arm back.

"No! We do not know what effect it will have to touch anything here. Besides, Python's venom is everywhere. That pool could be tainted by it. Even though we are not corporeal, we could be harmed by the poison."

Retracting his arm and cringing, Esteban took a step back. "Eso no sería bueno."

"No, it would indeed not be good at all," Ari muttered. "Let us continue."

Another darkened corridor stretched out before them, and the sound they had heard earlier grew louder. When the chamber opened again, the sound became clear—a child crying. In the corner, behind a column, they found a boy, about seven years old, weeping into his hands. Ari and Esteban exchanged a puzzled look before Ari knelt before the child.

"Are you… Apollo?"

The child continued to cry as if he hadn't heard the question, so Ari repeated it. Nothing. Ari touched the boy's arm at which point the boy shrieked and moved behind the column deep into the corner.

"Apollo… we are here to help you. Please. We have journeyed far to find you."

Still, the child sobbed. He had positioned himself so far into the corner that Ari and Esteban would be unable to get to him.

"What do we do?" Esteban tried to look behind the column, but it was too dark to see anything.

"We wait."

"For how long?"

"As long as it takes." Ari sat at the base of the column.

Both he and Esteban remained without speaking for a few minutes or a few hours—time had no structure with them. Ari had informed the floor nurse prior to his visit that he was trying some new therapies with Esteban and that he should not be disturbed. He told her it could be hours before he would come out from the room. A sound grew in the distance, one that they couldn't understand, especially over Apollo crying. Soon, though, the boy stopped and appeared from behind the column. Esteban tapped Ari's knee to get his attention. Apollo's face contorted, and he pressed his palms over his ears. Squeezing his eyes shut, he stood there.

"Apollo? Apollo, what is it?" Ari touched the boy's arm.

Young Apollo looked over at Ari, and his eyes shimmered before trickling tears fell.

"Are you in pain? Tell me what is wrong."

The strange sound came closer and then stopped. Esteban moved toward an arch between this chamber and another, a black space with intonations resembling two feuding swarms of insects. One would rise, and then the other, and this crescendo and decrescendo continued erratically for a few minutes. Once Esteban passed through the arch, the room illuminated slightly, like a slow sunrise. He waved Ari over. Ari lingered at the boy for a moment before joining his friend, and his face paled. This room was the part of Apollo's mind that dealt with other areas of influence: art, music, poetry, and history. Nine plinths lined the walls, three on each wall, with objects in various states of disrepair or corrosion.

"The Musai." Ari uttered. "Apollo kept company with the nine sisters. By Gaea's grace… look at them all. Urania's globe… Calliope's writing tablet… Thalia's mask of comedy… all damaged or eaten away by venom."

"And that sound?" Esteban examined each plinth. "I had no idea he was so complex. When our minds touched back in Spain, I saw only shards of images."

Ari spun around when he felt a touch on his arm. It was the boy, and his face looked pained.

"Voithíste me…," he whispered.

"What did he say?"

"He asked for help." Ari smiled, crouching down to the boy's height. "I will, Apollo. I promise."

The boy ambled through the room, his fingers grazing the objects on each plinth.

"Urania… Terpsichore… Melpo—" His finger went to touch the mask of tragedy, but Ari pulled it back.

"Óchi! Dilitírio!" *Poison.*

Apollo took a step back, looking into Ari's eyes. He turned again to the mask and blanched at the yellow pus dripping from it. The cacophonous sounds grew, and the boy pressed his palms against his ears once more. Ari and Esteban examined each of the plinths, seeing what degree of decay had infected each object. When they reached the end of the hall, a larger marble base supported one item in the greatest disrepair. Apollo had followed the two until he saw why they stopped. Practically coated in venom, the object had lost most of its shape, but the boy stepped closer and pointed since he couldn't reach it.

"Do you know what that is? I cannot tell." Ari saw a sparkle of recognition in the boy's eyes.

He nodded slightly. "Lyra…"

Esteban continued around the room, examining each symbol of a Muse. Despite how close he got or from what angle he stood, he couldn't see that much. Then, he smiled.

"I'll be right back." He headed back the way they had come.

"Where are you going? You will get lost if you are not careful!" Ari was about to go after him when the boy grabbed his hand. "All right. I will stay here."

Esteban returned with the torch from the scrying hall. He brought it closer to one of the Muse's symbols—the scrolls of Clio—and cringed as the pale light showed the acidic nature of the venom. It moved as if it were alive. While trying to see what was written on the scroll, he brought the flame close enough that it touched the scroll, and the yellow fluid burned away. He tried it again on another spot, and it had the same effect.

"Look!" Esteban called Ari over. "The fires burn away Python's venom. There isn't enough fire to cleanse this place, but it's a good thing to know, sí?"

Before they knew what was happening, Apollo jumped up, grabbed the torch with both hands, and ran back to the lyre. Despite how much he tried to reach it, he wasn't tall enough. Ari touched the boy's shoulder and took the torch. As soon as he brought the flame close to the lyre, it ignited the venom, burning it off, and extinguishing itself once the venom was gone. Ari took the broken lyre down and put it in Apollo's little hands. The boy embraced it and looked for strings. At that moment, the discordant sounds rose again, getting the boy's attention.

"Spasménos… spasménos…"

"Yes, the lyre is broken. I am sorry." Ari shrugged.

The boy shook his head and pointed in the direction of the noises.

"Spasménos!"

Esteban leaned into Ari's ear. "Do you know what he means?"

Shaking his head, Ari followed the sounds, with Apollo close behind, until they breached another chamber. There, the clamor overwhelmed Ari who returned to Esteban in the Muses' chamber.

"Where's Apollo?"

Ari shook his head as if to get the ringing to stop. "He must be in there. I could not stay."

"Funny. I don't hear it as loudly here." He took one step through the arch and returned to Ari. "I see what you mean. How can he stand it?"

"It is *his* mind. He did say whatever was in that chamber was broken, though, but I do not know what that means. We should go see if he is all right."

Esteban cringed. "Are you sure?"

Ari pulled his arm until they reached the threshold at which point they covered their ears and walked through. Aside from Apollo standing in the center of everything, the room was empty of objects. Apollo turned to them, still clutching his lyre, and had a blank expression. He took the damaged instrument in both hands and looked at Ari and Esteban.

"Spasménos. Anisórropos."

Despite the din, Ari made out the last word—unbalanced—and his expression changed. He knelt before Apollo, ignoring the noise, and pointed to the broken arm.

"Anisórropos." He waved Esteban over to him, shouting. "He said the lyre is unbalanced. I think this is how we help him regain his sanity."

"How?"

"We help him fix the lyre. Look. It has no strings. This has to be something important."

As Ari stood, he stumbled, trying to gain his equilibrium. He stepped into the neighboring chamber, with Esteban right behind him.

"It is time to go. We will come back."

Once back through all the thresholds, he pulled his consciousness back into his own mind and opened his eyes. The clock showed that three hours had passed. Esteban lay sleeping soundly, his forehead speckled with sweat. Ari squeezed his arm. Just as he passed the nurses' station, the floor nurse asked if everything had gone well with the new treatment. Ari smiled and told her he felt he was making a breakthrough, albeit a small one, but it was too early to tell. On the train ride back, he listened to the rumblings through the car as it went through a tunnel and emerged into the open air. Lost in his own thoughts, he jumped when a woman tapped him on the shoulder asking if he was getting off at Kenmore. Once back in his apartment, he took off his tie, kicked off his shoes, and collapsed on the bed.

When he awoke, he rolled over to glance at the clock: 9:15 p.m. He shuffled out into the living room to see Dan on the couch reading. He was so engrossed in his book that he didn't notice Ari until he was being kissed on the top of his head.

"Hey there. I tried to wake you a little while ago, but you just weren't having it. How did your day go?" He patted the couch.

Ari fell back against Dan's chest.

"It went well. I feel like I just finished wrestling the giant Antaeus and lost, though. Esteban did well too. I will tell you more, but I need to eat first."

Dan hopped up. "You rest. I'll make dinner. I haven't eaten yet."

While Dan puttered about in the kitchen, Ari paid attention to the clang of the pots, the clinking of the plates, and the chime-like noise of silverware as Dan set the table. As his eyes lazily moved around in thought, he stopped on a tapestry that hung on the wall across from the couch. He sat up and stared at it, a depiction of Apollo dancing with the Muses. In the god's hand was his lyre—unbroken and fully strung. He smiled and then lay back on the couch. Twenty minutes passed before Ari heard his name and opened his eyes. Dan asked where he was. At first, Ari didn't understand but then realized what Dan meant in his dreams.

"I was nowhere and everywhere at the same time." His words sounded like he was still in that other place.

Over their meal, Ari told Dan everything between forkfuls of salad and salmon. The fervor with which Ari spoke about his experiences made Dan smile, not having seen his other half so enthusiastic about something in quite a while. Finally, when Ari took a sip of wine, Dan found a moment to speak.

"I'm quite jealous of you. You get to interact with my father, even if he is only a boy in his mind. I can't begin to tell you how much this means to me."

Ari finished his mouthful. "This is important to me. That I can help your father, and one of my own gods, both empowers and humbles me." He reached across the table and squeezed Dan's hand.

"When do you go back?"

"Depending on how I feel, probably tomorrow. Making the connection is not without its discomfort, so I will need to get some rest."

"You're not overextending yourself, are you?"

Ari shook his head. "No, and I know the signs when I am fatigued. Trust me."

"I do. Why don't you let me take care of the dishes while you relax."

"I was going to do the dishes since you cooked."

Dan took plates off the table. "Nonsense. I won't hear of it. Go."

Fifteen minutes later, Dan found Ari sound asleep, fully clothed on the bed. Not having the heart to wake him, he pulled a blanket from the closet to cover him. Before he left the room, he kissed Ari on the forehead, and a vision popped into his head—danger. Something or someone would try to stop Ari and Esteban. Dan didn't know who or when, but his prophetic flashes panned out eventually. He had no idea who would, or could, stop Ari, let alone who would even know what Ari was doing. As he closed the door behind him, he made a phone call.

21 | OF HEART AND MIND

Ari had wanted to arrive early again, but his need to rest prevented that. As soon as the hospital allowed visitors, Ari returned to Esteban's hospital room. He watched the young man lay there motionless and at peace, as peaceful as one could be, considering Esteban's circumstances. Ari took Esteban's hand and made the connection. It gave Ari solace to feel the man's pulse alongside his own.

"Buenos días," Ari said.

"Hypíaine." Esteban laughed. "Did you rest well?"

"I did, thank you. Danelos seems concerned about me, but I woke up refreshed."

"I look forward to meeting him... someday."

"You will! I cannot wait for that, either. He is so grateful for all you are doing. Are you ready?"

"Sí."

After entering Apollo's mind, they tried to follow their original path, but they found that the mental chambers weren't the same ones. These new areas showed the same yellow pus everywhere, dripping from above in some places and puddling in others. One of the corridors between chambers had a torch of the First Fires, and Esteban snatched one from its wall ring as they walked.

"Tell me something." Esteban scrutinized the fires.

"Mmm?" Ari moved a few steps ahead.

"Everything okay? You seem distracted."

"Sorry. I am trying to get my bearings again. What did you want to know?"

"Well, how is it that this fire burns away the venom? If the torch is a construct of Apollo's mind, what can't he simply cleanse himself?"

Ari slowed a bit but kept moving forward. "I guess that he has the means to do it, but he does not have the ability. I think that is why we are here. First Fires originated with Khaos and has ancient, mystical properties. Regular fire, like that Prometheos stole from the gods, is not the same. Since Apollo is an Olympeian, the fires within his mind would more likely be First Fires, an extension of his godhood and immortality. The flames burn weakly because he himself has been weakened."

"How do you know so much?"

"Growing up in the Temple of Hades, I had much time to read. That, and my father would tell me stories he had heard from his father."

They meandered through empty chambers or those with objects neither recognized until they stopped at what looked like a wooden door.

"Strange. No other chamber has had a door before. This must be a part of Apollo's mind he doesn't want us to see." Esteban held the torch closer to it. "It actually looks like oak."

"He either doesn't want us to see what's beyond it, or he's trying to protect something."

"If we turn around, we'll have to go back the way we came."

Ari rubbed the obol between his thumb and finger. "Or, we go on in."

He pushed against the door, but it wouldn't budge. Again, he tried, but nothing. He motioned for Esteban to try with him, and they both pushed. The door wouldn't move. Esteban held the torch close to the edges of the door and grunted.

"No hinges. What do we do?"

"Well, we are here because of *this*." Ari removed the *obol* from his neck. "All of Apollo's mind should be open to us, but I do sense this is a well-protected place. I thought he knew that we were here to help him."

"Maybe we should just go back the way we came and go around?"

Ari ran his hands over the edges of the door, but the wood was flush with the marble. When he reached the floor, he jumped back.

Esteban sighed. "¡Mierda! The venom has permeated even this door. We need to get in there!"

"There has to be a way…" He muttered. "There has—"

"Ari."

"Just a moment. I think—"

"Ari! Look."

He turned to see the boy Apollo, still clutching the broken lyre. Ari crouched down.

"Hypíaine." He smiled. "Apollo, we need to get through that door. Would you help us?"

The boy stood motionless, his face empty of any emotion. He looked down at the lyre. "Spasménos."

"Yes, we know the lyre is broken. Will you please open this door for us? We are trying to help you." He kept his voice soft and steady.

Esteban moved closer to the door with the torch. "Maybe if we can destroy the venom, he'll believe us." He reached out to touch the exposed venom with the fire.

"Na stamatísei!" *Stop!* Apollo, his eyes flaring, held out his hand, and Esteban slammed against the wall, dropping the torch. "Kardía…"

Grunting, Esteban tried to pull himself free. Ari couldn't release him from Apollo's hold.

"Apollo! Ti káneis?"

"Why are you asking him what he's doing? You can see what he's doing. Tell him to release me." Esteban pulled against the containment, but he couldn't free himself. "Apollo! Estamos aquí para ayudarle! Let me go!"

Apollo went to the door and turned to face them. Shaking his head, he repeated the word 'kardía.'

"Esteban, I think I understand. Just do not say anything for a moment, and I will get you free."

Ari stooped down to be eye to eye with Apollo who held the lyre against his side.

"Apollo. This door. It leads to a chamber you want to keep safe. You keep saying *kardía*. Your heart lies beyond. That chamber is where whatever you remember about Alkinoë exists. She is your heart."

The boy didn't move at first, but a few moments later, he nodded a little.

"Let us help you… Parakaló." *Please.*

Apollo's tightened jaw relaxed. "Poios eísai?"

"I am Aristeides, your son Danelos' husband. This is Esteban, a friend."

"O gios mou…?"

"Yes, your son. You have Danelos and Kidemonas, among others."

With a glance from Apollo, Esteban became free and crouched beside Ari.

"Lypámai, Stefanos."

Esteban let out a little smile. "It's okay. No need to apologize. You're trying to protect something important to you, and you don't know me. But, as Ari has said, we are here to help you."

"Apollo, this torch flame burns with the Protí Pyrkagiés. The First Fires destroy Python's venom. Open the door, and I promise that we will make sure nothing happens to your *kardía*."

Extending his hand, Apollo pressed his small palm against the door, and light grew from the point of contact. As the light subsided, Apollo gasped.

"I kardía mou!" He jumped forward across the threshold, but Esteban grabbed him, wrapping his arms around him.

"No! There's venom in there. Look!"

The boy continued to shout about his heart, struggling against Esteban's grip.

"Ari, do something! Hurry! I don't know how long I can hold him."

Unable to speak, Ari stood horrified at the sight of crumbled objects and columns, dripping with the ochre phlegm-like substance. If one didn't know better, it looked like a beehive exploded and coated everything with honey, but this was not the by-product of bees.

"Ari!"

"What? Right! Sorry. Hold on!" At the threshold, Ari touched the venom with the fire, making it inert. He dashed around, continuing the cleansing.

Fortunately, much of the venom reacted like a fuse once ignited with the fire, dissolving large swaths of the caustic substance at once. What its absence revealed, however, made Ari pale. Once the poison had been expunged, Esteban let Apollo go. The godling burst into the chamber, saw the damage to most of the beloved treasures connected to Alkinoë, and fell to his knees, dropping the lyre. Seeing Apollo inconsolable made Ari weak, and he had to lean against one of the chunks of the column. This version of Apollo, with the maturity of a child that age, was unable to reconcile what he saw with what he felt.

"What do we do?" Esteban looked on, his mouth quivering. "I can't bear to watch him like this."

"I-I do not know. We eliminated all of the venom, but we cannot repair what the venom destroyed. It makes me wonder whether it will affect his memories of her."

Esteban held up the torch. "This isn't like normal fire, as you said. We've only used to burn away things, but… You told me once that First Fires originated with Khaos. Didn't she create the cosmos using this fire? Couldn't we then—"

"You are brilliant, Esteban! It is worth trying."

Esteban put the torch fire to a fractured marble statue of Alkinoë in full battle armor. "I may not know what it looked like whole, but if I concentrate on the idea of rebuilding this…" He pursed his lips as he stared at the statue engulfed by the gray fires.

About a minute passed, and Esteban exhaled as if he'd held his breath.

"It's not working!"

Ari joined him, and both held the torch and concentrated. Still, nothing happened. The flames grew a little, but the statue remained unchanged. They even tightened their grip on the torch. Ari's arms slackened and lifted a hand from the torch when a small hand put it back. A tear-stained Apollo contributed his hands and closed his eyes.

"Something's happening!" Esteban's voice startled Ari.

"The statue. It is repairing itself. Amazing…"

With Apollo's mind making contact with theirs, the statue of Alkinoë soon returned to its original state, looking as regal as ever. Around the chamber, they moved as a group, and eventually restored other items including another statue of the queen holding two infant boys, an Arkadeian scepter and crown, and a bust showing her modern appearance. Apollo brought his lyre to the torch: the arms grew back, the sounding chambers, and, finally, the smaller pieces like tuning keys.

"Wait." Ari examined the lyre. "Something is different. This is not like a typical lyre. The crossbar has two sets of tuning keys. That would mean this lyre takes two sets of strings?"

"Isorropiméni," Apollo commented, but his response caused Ari and Esteban to do a double-take.

"Yes, balanced. Wait... You-You're older? How did that happen?"

Ari's eyes grew wide. "He looks about ten years old now."

"¡Dios! And he's grown about six inches!"

Smiling, the young Apollo patted his lyre. "Epainó."

Shaking his head and smirking, Ari took in the new situation. "You are welcome. I wonder why you only speak Greek, but yet you understand English. Perhaps we have not reached that part of your growth. I think we should move on."

Esteban and Ari reached the next arch, but Apollo stared up at the statue of Alkinoë.

"Kardía…"

They couldn't see into the next chamber, but when they were about to step through, Esteban stopped.

"What is that?" He pointed at a mass of tangled threads that looked like a spider web, and it blocked their entry.

As Ari looked closer, he exhaled.

"Well, I feel better. This was not made by a spider. They are strings." He scrutinized one without touching it. "I think they are lyre strings, but some look golden, and others, silver and copper. Strange. I cannot see beyond too far, so I do not know what is in the chamber."

Once Apollo was close enough, he reached out toward the strings. The inharmonious noise they had heard earlier sounded again, and this time it was louder. Ari and Esteban covered their ears, and Apollo wrapped his hand around one of the silver strings. His eyes fluttered and took on a silver hue themselves. Ari tried to pull Apollo back, but a bolt of energy shot through his arm. The whole experience lasted about five minutes until Apollo opened his hand, severing the connection. He jerked the string, and it snapped off. With a moment's hesitation to stare at it, he then attached it to one of the tuning keys and then to the bottom of the sounding chamber.

"Wh-What was that?" Esteban shouted.

Ari gestured for Apollo to take a few steps away from the arch, and when they all did, the sound ceased.

"I do not know. Apollo?"

The god smiled a little, and his eyes jumped around as if he were still seeing something.

"Mia mními."

"Really? A memory of what?" Ari's heart pounded, and he grinned. "That is wonderful!"

Apollo extended the lyre toward them, and Ari touched the string. As if someone switched stations on a television, a scene appeared in Ari's consciousness.

"I am looking through his eyes." Ari's face was suffused with wonder. "Alkinoë wears a gold-trimmed ivory chiton and a golden cord around her waist. She has a thin crown, and her hair is braided down her back. I have not seen her look like this since I lived in Arkadeia. She is standing at the top of the steps to the palace, speaking to a crowd. The whole city of Tegea, and probably others, must be there. Behind them stands what looks to be Athene, Artemis, and Hermes. Alkinoë welcomes everyone to this occasion. Wait... It looks like Apollo's coronation as king of Arkadeia. I was not alive then to see it. She takes the crown off a pillow held by what I think is one of Apollo's high priests and places the crown on his head. She tells the people that they have sworn to uphold their vow to Arkadeia as well as their devotion to one another. They were married just a few days earlier, it seems. Alkinoë puts a golden belt around Apollo's waist, a belt she says was made by Hephaestos. The clasp brings together the insignia of a sun and earth. By holy Olympos... the *entire* city, for as far as one can see, cheers. Streaks of lightning fill the sky, and thunder rumbles all around. It would seem even Zeus himself condones such a blessing for the people..."

Ari wiped tears, reluctant to pull his hand away. Esteban put his hand on Ari's.

"This is a good thing," he said softly. "We need to help Apollo with more of these. The strings in that chamber are so erratic, though, that I wonder which memories are which. How do we know which ones are from that prior timeline? Would Apollo even know?"

As soon as he composed himself, Ari examined the woven metal strings.

"They do not seem to be in any pattern, and the colors confuse me. That memory of his I saw seemed like it could have happened in this timeline, but I would not know. I suppose we have to trust Apollo."

They both stared at the boy whose fingers brushed against the web. Apollo gripped another string and gasped. Within a few seconds, he dropped to the floor, shrieking, his hands pressed against his ears, the string still clutched in his grip.

"Ochi! I agapiméni mou gynaíka! Ochi! Ochi! Ochi…" He rocked in place, repeating, *No, no. no…*

Before Ari or Esteban could see to him, Apollo looked up, his face red and eyes feral.

"Den tha párete ti gynaíka mou apó ména, Áris!"

Ari cocked his head and furrowed his brow, reaching for the string. Apollo rambled on in Ancient Greek, and when Ari took hold of the copper string, his eyes widened.

"Ari, what is he saying?" Esteban touched Ari's shoulder, and the latter jumped.

"It is horrible. So horrible!" Ari clenched his eyes shut. "I-I cannot stop seeing it."

Using both hands, Esteban pried the string from Ari's grip, pulling him back.

His chest heaving, Ari took control of his breathing and stepped away from Esteban.

"I am better. Thank you. By sacred Olympos… it was unlike anything I have ever seen."

Apollo still rocked and spoke to himself.

Esteban sat and brought Ari with him.

"Tell me. What did you see?"

"I-It was Arkadeia. Ravaged. Utterly in ruins. Blood spatter stained the columns of buildings. Pools of blood gathered beneath the fallen soldiers and citizens. It was as if a wave from a sea of blood had washed over the city."

"And Apollo? What was he saying?"

"Alkinoë. She was strung up on the wall of the throne room. In chains. Her blood dripping onto the floor, pooling, and her head slumped forward. Apollo was saying that he could not take his wife from him."

"He who?"

"Ares." Ari swallowed. "This was not *my* Arkadeia. This had to be the other timeline. Esteban, every single man, woman, and child was slaughtered. I grew up in the Temple of Hades, and I had never seen so much death, so much wanton loss of life."

Looking over at Apollo, Esteban shook his head. "Seeing one's people destroyed once was bad enough, but to relive that memory down to the detail… No one should have to see that."

He sat by Apollo and put a hand on his arm. The boy, stuck in the heinous memory, had the expression of one who didn't know how to deal with such thoughts. This Apollo, in a ten-year-old boy's body, didn't have the tools to understand. Esteban pulled him over, pressing the boy's head against him. Heaving cries and tears came forth, his body shuddering.

"It's over, Apollo. I don't know if you can understand me, but this is a memory from a time that no longer exists. You have to be stronger than this. Please." Esteban held onto the boy.

Ari muttered, "You understand what this is like, Esteban. You have been there yourself."

He lifted Apollo, cradling his cheeks.

"Apollo, we need to keep moving. I know this memory is painful for you, but it is yours. Own it. Put it where it belongs. Do you understand?"

Ari's gentle smile and brown eyes soothed Apollo enough to where the god released his grip on the string and put it on the other side of the lyre. It was at that moment that Ari realized why the lyre had two sets of strings. He pulled the boy to him, holding him tightly, and repeating that everything would be all right. When he felt Apollo's arms squeeze his waist, he smiled to himself. *I will make you whole again, Phoebos Apollo. This I swear to you*, he thought.

"We don't have much time left today, Ari. We should continue." He squatted down to Apollo's eye level. "Is that okay with you?"

Apollo looked up, and Ari nodded. String after string Apollo touched, and with each memory, he put it on the lyre on the proper side. Esteban whispered to Ari that this would take a while, especially since there had to be more chambers with more strings, but then Ari reminded him that Apollo could continue this when they weren't there. The chamber they were in remained in the dark, except for the torch that Ari carried, and the young god seemed to know which memories were of the other timeline and which ones were not. Not all memories were as heart-wrenching to Apollo as the one about Alkinoë and Ares, and some weren't as joyful as the births of Kidemonas and Danelos. One string, in particular, elicited a gasp when Apollo touched it, and he clutched it to his chest.

"Adara…" That one word was heavy with grief for him, and he closed his eyes, inhaling deeply.

Ari reached his hand toward the copper string. "Who is Adara? May I see?"

At first, Apollo just stared at him, his fist pressed against him, but he exhaled and put the string in Ari's hand.

"It is an ancient memory. From early in Apollo's human penance. Somehow, I can tell. He is in a tent, and an elderly woman lies on a straw mat. An older man sits by her, holding her hand while another tends to her. This man… Ios. He is comforting his friend. Zotikos. I feel Apollo's profound sense of loss and confusion. It is a new heaviness for him, seeing this mortal woman suffer."

Esteban noticed Ari's face turn pale. "What happened to her?"

"She... had stepped on a harpy's egg." His eyes glossed with tears. "From what my father has told me, the poison of a harpy's egg would have killed her. Apollo… He… As a god, he would know death of mortals, but he had become close to these people. He is in Trapæzos. Part of this memory is a thought that the village was special to him because it is where he first went as a mortal. The memory fades…"

Apollo placed the string on the lyre and kept going. Something was happening as he confronted his past.

"Ari, is it just me, or is this room getting brighter?" Esteban looked around for a source.

Ari's eyes bounced all over the chamber. "Darkness signifies ignorance. The more Apollo reveals to himself, the more knowledge he gains."

Even though they had no means to measure time, both men knew that much of it had transpired. They were about to return to their bodies when they saw Apollo holding a string, a silver one. A huge grin spread across the god's face, and he even chuckled. His blond curls bounced. The moment lasted a little while. Esteban and Ari, too, found themselves laughing out loud, and they had no idea at what. Before they pulled themselves out of Apollo's mind, the room itself took on a warm glow, something they had never seen up until that moment.

"I am curious to know what he is seeing, but I do not want to pry. He is happy, though."

All Esteban could do was smile and nod before his mental presence faded.

Ari opened his eyes, and the sky had become a deep blue with only a sliver of light where the last remnant of the sunset could be seen.

"Are you still with me?" he thought.

"Sí." Esteban paused. "Ari... do you feel as I do that something darker is coming?"

"From within Apollo's mind?"

"No. From the outside world. As soon as my mind returned just now, I felt a ripple that made my heart flutter. I fear something is coming. No será bueno."

Ari took Esteban's hand and squeezed.

"Worry not. Whatever it is, I am sure Danelos and the others can handle it. Regardless of what may happen, we will finish our task. We have to."

With his hand on the door, Ari heard Esteban's voice once more.

"Ari, Lismonia didn't frighten me. But, what I feel coming... un espíritu maligno. I'm terrified. Will you protect me?"

Although Esteban couldn't see it, Ari smiled.

"I have picked up an expression of yours. Siempre, mi amigo." Always, my friend.

22 | AS ABOVE, SO BELOW

In a locked conference room at Task Force Division headquarters, Dan put out an alert call to his fellow team leaders. The walls of the room were constructed of foam over a fabric of interwoven metallic threads. Even without the use of soundproofing technology, the room was virtually impenetrable from surveillance, but with the added security of technoscience—lab-grown algae that lived within the metal fabric suspended in gelatin—the room was entirely protected. After the foreboding sensation he had felt from Ari, Dan knew he needed to check out every angle possible to make sure Ari and Esteban weren't in harm's way. He paced around the table, putting his fingers through his hair, while he waited for the operator to make the connections. A single television screen circumscribed the entire room. One by one, as the calls connected, images of team leaders appeared. A dozen faces finally populated the screen, so Dan made his inquiry.

"Thank you for taking time out for this. As I told you at the last face-to-face, we're trying to assess what will happen with my father's absence. I, unfortunately, don't have the means to do anything about it, but my husband Ari does. He possesses an object that allows him to traverse states of consciousness. Using it, he's trying to transcend mental boundaries and help heal my father from inside his mind. When I was last with Ari, I could feel something dangerous was lurking, connected to him, but I don't know exactly what that is."

Ekua Fujimoto, team leader of Task Force: Pi, was the first to reply.

"Dan, forgive me for asking this, but what does this have to do with us exactly? We deal with climate science and global warming."

Dan nodded. "I know. It's not something in your area of expertise. I bring it up because I'm asking you all just to keep an eye out for something odd that normally my team might encounter. You've known me long enough to know that I wouldn't ask unless it were serious."

"Is there something in particular? A person? Can you narrow down the parameters?" Task Force: Mu's leader chimed in.

"Angwusnasomtaqa, if I could, I would. I know your team covers oceanographic safety, but it's possible whoever, or whatever, is out there could travel by sea." He smiled. "By the way, your name means 'Crow Mother Spirit', I believe? One of my father's birds is the crow."

She nodded and smiled. "I knew that. The Hopi and your family share many similarities."

"Indeed." Dan returned the smile. "I know this isn't a lot to go on, and you all have so much you already do. I also don't know if this danger comes from within the Task Force Division itself, so I'm taking a risk here. I trust all of *you*. But we've just learned that the cameras we see every day have a deeper connection to my family, as it were. Back in the sixties, when this division was founded, the UN and this division arranged with SKOPUS to place those cameras all over the world. We've always assumed they were put in place for benevolent reasons, but now I have reason to believe they have a more sinister purpose."

Task Force: Omega's leader, Kristen Østergaard, lifted a finger.

"If I may, Dan? What proof do you have of this... SKOPUS... and its involvement? Can you please clarify 'sinister'?"

"Of course, Kristen. Quinn Reynolds, our team liaison, found the client list for SKOPUS, a document apparently buried deep within the system. I will have her send this document to all of you. As far as sinister? The camera housing is made from a steel polycarbonate composite. That by itself wouldn't raise any red flags, but under closer scrutiny, we've determined that the steel used is one only accessible by members of my family. It's called Earthsteel."

"Earthsteel?" Ige Ihejirika, leader of Task Force: Xi, asked, her fingers laced together, her thumbs supporting her chin. "As you know, we deal with geological issues, like seismic disturbances, but we also do a great deal of research into alloys and natural metals. I've never heard of this."

Dan drew his sword from the invisible scabbard on his back. The ringing of the blade as it became exposed made many leaders gasp.

"You all know my sword. Thyroros was made by Gaea in the First Fires of creation. This metal, called Earthsteel, is what many Olympeian metal weapons and ornaments are made from, including my brother's amulet and our manacles. It has specific properties that resemble normal steel, but it is indestructible by human means. It keeps its edge indefinitely, too. This is what was somehow blended with the polycarbonate housing of the newer cameras. That means that an Olympeian or someone within the family has access to it."

"If that's so, Dan, then how does that relate to us? Your team is the only one with such family connections, as it were. " Udo Afolabi, Task Force: Omicron's leader added, his arms crossed.

"Udo, as your team oversees the International Court, it's possible that whoever might prevent Ari from being successful would be under the Court's jurisdiction. Apollo's fate affects the *world*, not just Boston."

"Good point. I will pass along this alert."

Others expressed similar concerns, but Dan wasn't successful in swaying all of them. Those who dismissed his request still didn't understand the otherworldly nature of Apollo's influence. Before finishing the call, he reiterated that those with misgivings try to keep an open mind. Eleven team leaders disconnected, but Task Force: Kappa's Robert Barns remained.

"Dan, I've known your father for more years than I can count, and I think I knew he was… different… from the get-go. I was one of the first team leaders appointed, since our authority is international security, and if not for your father's diplomatic skill, this agency wouldn't be as successful as it is."

"Thank you, Bobby. I appreciate that. You would think after all my team and I have done that the others would understand just what's at stake, but I'm coming at it from a place of experience. They're looking at it from the outside. A place of skepticism."

"Quite true. For some, the idea of a magical world challenges some of their own beliefs, and to think that a Greek god truly exists, *and* influences the world, frightens them. It may even cause them to wonder just how much their own god or gods actually work. To think that reason and music are influenced by another culture's deity makes them question."

Dan plopped himself into a leather chair and put his boot-clad feet on the table. He stroked his circle beard and stared off for a moment.

"Give them time, Dan. They may yet come around. If not, I'll see what I can do to work on some of the other doubters. I've known them longer than you have." He chortled. "Longer than I would have liked, in some cases."

Nodding, Dan thanked him for his insight and disconnected the call. He sat in the absolute silence and gave himself the chance to ruminate over everything. With the walls keeping out every sound from the outside, he had no distractions. He wondered if this was what it sounded like in Gaea's adyton where his father was. The quietness of the absolute. He avoided setting up another conference call for the moment. He would try something else, something he had avoided doing because it would remind him too much of his father's predicament. Now that he had full access to his prophetic power, he knew of only one place where he might find some answers, and he'd been there not long ago. Delphi.

As the shimmering portal closed, Dan took in the neglected ruins of the once-great temple, dragging his fingers along the remnants of the past. In this place, he was most at peace. He could never tell that to Ari, but this sacred site grounded him in ways that nothing else did. It hadn't been that long since he was here, and yet, it felt like millennia had passed. Where the tripod of the oracle sat was nothing more than a crack in the earth now, with peacock anemones and chamomile growing through those openings where once the vapors would, along with chewing laurel leaves, give Pythia the visions of Apollo. Stale, weathered columns stood vigil over this quiet austerity.

"Dad, I wish I could have seen this place when it was vibrant and alive," Dan muttered. "Now, it's dead."

He removed his boots and socks where the entrance to the Temple of Apollo once stood. Of all the structures in this holy site, the cold marble here against Dan's bare feet made him feel close to his father. Sitting, he placed a small brazier, the size of a teacup, before him and ignited the frankincense and myrrh. He pressed his palms against what used to be the floor to his sides, closed his eyes, and tilted his head back, taking deep breaths through his mouth and exhaling slowly through his nose. Without the confines of the temple itself, the wispy incense was at the whim of the breeze. As if Aeolos, the god of the winds, were present, and suddenly aware of Dan's task, the air stopped moving. In ancient Greek, the words bubbled forth, as from a wellspring.

"Son of Leto and Zeus, O Shining One, if ever I needed your guidance, it would be now. Even with the mantle of leadership squarely on my shoulders, I falter. How am I to bring guidance and understanding when, like a yoke, I bear the burden of grief. Others look to me, to show them the way, but how can I find it when *my* light is darkened?"

Through his tightly clenched eyelids, tears broke free. It didn't take long for the great proverbial dam to splinter, and he sobbed. His release echoed throughout the landscape, and anyone who heard him would feel his anguish and loss. The last time he had this outpouring of emotion was when Ari left to spend his year in the underworld. Apollo had taught him that emotion gives strength to those who allow themselves to feel. Dan tapped into this and freed himself. He wasn't aware of how long he had been crying, but the air moved, bristling the hairs on his arms and the back of his neck. She had come to him.

"Gaea, I don't know what I could offer you to let me see my father." He drew Thyroros. "But I would give any part of myself for him."

From the ground, a rumbling approached, like a stampede, and her voice rose.

"*I know your love for him who is within. Know that he also feels it for you. Think not of what you desire, but what he does. Only the Moirae understand what is to come.*"

A zephyr swirled around him, girdling him with frankincense and myrrh.

"*Apollo is not the reason why you are here, my child. Your connection to this place, and his, lay bare your heart, now untethered. Speak what you truly wish to know.*"

Dan hesitated before answering.

"Great Mother… I saw danger around Ari, but not clearly." He paused. "The Moirae know what I don't. I can't protect him if I don't know what he needs protecting from."

"The son of Timaios braves his purpose, and peril does court his path, but understand that you are not he who can protect him. That, while he performs this task, is not your destiny."

Perhaps it was that the words came from Gaea, or that Dan had grown so much since meeting Ari, but he didn't reply as he might have in the past. She continued.

"In your heart, you understand this. For as much as you have faith in your father and your Asulos Pistis, your faith in Aristeides is the strongest, and that comes from a deep, resonant love. It will be your love for him that stays your hand and will save you both many times over. Submit to your love, my child. Remember."

"Wait. Why can't I see my father? Is it because he's chained? Is he not in a condition I can even look at him? Surely a window, even into your adyton, wouldn't break any rules."

Her voice was all around him now, even as high as the clouds.

Then, her reply would shake him to his core. *"What would that do for him? You ask for yourself, to assuage some guilt you feel for not being there to protect him from my son Python's fangs. Know this, son of Apollo and Alkinoë, when you understand yourself, you will find the eyes you search for."*

Left without the answers he sought, Dan let his frustration reign over his heart. He collected himself and took a road that headed southwest. When he reached Itea, a town on the shores of Kólpos Itéas that led into the Gulf of Corinth, he put his sword into a tidal pool and called upon its ancient power.

"O Keeper of Gateways and Prophecy, show me where I can find those I seek."

The etched words along the blade glowed white, causing the water to bubble, and when it ceased, he then saw two figures and knew how to find them. With the location embedded in his mind, he swung the sword. The scent of stale popcorn and musty ale buffeted him through the portal, causing him to wince before he stepped through.

"Why am I not surprised to find you both in a dive like this?" Dan turned a chair around and straddled it, crossing his arms over the top.

Dionysos took a healthy sip of Pinot Noir while he ogled the server. He turned to see who was talking to him, leaping out of his chair, arms outstretched.

"Nephew! Good to see you." He hugged Dan who hadn't even stood to greet his uncle. "You smell of incense."

Dan turned his head from the smell of his uncle's breath. "Where's your partner in debauchery?"

"That truculent old war hound?" He slurred his words. "Probably off trying to seduce…"

At that moment, the god of war lurched toward the table, a young woman sitting on his shoulder. Like his brother, Ares' eyes showed a distinct lack of sobriety.

Dionysos poured himself another glass. "Look who came for a visit! Ares, put her down. This isn't Corinth."

The war god shrugged his shoulder, and the giggling bar server slid down his chest. She leaned against him and winked at Dan.

"Another round?" She picked up her serving tray and the empty glasses on the table. "What can I get for you, honey?"

"Um… Jameson. Neat." Dan attempted to smile at her, but he was distracted by Ares who was putting fistfuls of pretzels in his mouth.

Ares leaned back and folded his arms. "What brings the mighty Aegis?"

Dan gave a quick summary of his visit to Delphi and his conversation with Gaea, seeing how his uncles had a liquid attention span. The server brought the drinks, and Dan threw a twenty on the tray. Giggling, she put it in her cleavage, winked, and left.

"My dear nephew, I'm not sure what you want from us." Dionysos examined the wine glass. "This Pinot is sublime. For a hovel like this."

Dan threw back his whiskey and put the glass on the table with just enough force to get Ares' attention.

"Look, I don't know what game you're both playing. This one," he nodded toward Ares, "isn't happy unless he's disemboweling someone. He and my father have *never* been what we'd call friends. And you? You didn't say one word about Apollo until very recently. I want to know what you're both planning. Now."

Ares continued to knock back his beer alternately with pretzels, ogling the servers, and grunting. Dionysos, on the other hand, was lost in his swirling wine. Dan growled, then jumped up and drew his sword. Ares smirked and reached to grab another handful of pretzels, but Dan flipped the bowl over with the tip of his blade.

"What part of my request was optional?"

The god of war rose, cracked his neck, and drew his own blade. Unlike Thyroros, which had an argent luster, Ares' xiphos was black as Erebos and exuded smoke.

"You wish to challenge me. Huh."

"Nephew, you shouldn't have drawn your sword." Dionysos signaled the server.

"If this is the only way to get you to listen to me, then so be it. Name the place."

Ares looked around and grinned, his voice deep. "Right. Here."

Dionysos sobered up and spun in his chair. "Here? Ares, there are innocents. I'm all for sport, but you're not known for being... tidy."

Taking steps around the table, both Dan and Ares circled, their swords looming over the wine god's head. Dionysos had seen his brother on the battlefield before. This would not end well. Dan kept his eyes locked on his uncle. At the fourth pass, Dionysos had seen enough.

"Not here." His eyes glowed orange.

In the next moment, all three appeared in what looked like a dark, abandoned parking garage. The only illumination came from small flickering bulbs by a dilapidated exit door.

"If you're intent on this, you'll do it here." Dionysos stepped into the shadows.

Ares and Dan resumed their circular movements, flipping their swords around. Finally, the war god swung his blade, re-sounding against Thyroros, and sparks flew. Dan was unmoved and returned the attack. The clanging of Earthsteel echoed, and both grunted and howled as their melee grew. For every move Ares made, Dan countered, until finally the son of Zeus let out a war cry and jumped onto Dan, knocking him to the ground. Strad-dling his nephew's chest, he raised his fist.

"You lasted longer than most."

Dan snarled. "Athene trained me."

With that, he kicked his legs up, wrapped them around Ares' neck, flipped the god off him, and jumped up. Ares landed on his feet, smiling, his eyes glazed over with bellicosity. His rage came off him in waves, pushing Dionysos farther away, but always within range to watch. More swordplay followed, and with every strike, spittle flew from Ares' mouth as he exuded animalistic sounds. His drug of choice was war, and the son of Zeus was inebriated beyond measure.

"What are your plans for my father?" Dan heaved out, sweat soaking through his t-shirt.

Ares howled, "Why don't you fall?" Each word was followed by a concussive sword strike.

Dan answered. "I fight for my father. What do *you* fight for?"

Flying toward his challenger, Ares knocked Dan down, sending Thyroros skidding across the concrete. The god leaned over, putting the edge of his blade against Dan's throat, and then went nose to nose.

"Blood."

In the war god's eyes, Dan saw fire.

"Éla!" Dan commanded his sword to him. "Go ahead, Ares. Slit my throat."

Ares took one step back and lowered his sword.

"Do it!" Dan moved to his knees and tilted his head back. "What's the matter, war god? Living among humans for a year softened you?"

He watched the rage and bloodlust leave Ares' eyes. The son of Zeus sheathed his sword and extended a hand.

"Yes. It did. Now, rise."

Dan lifted an eyebrow because he knew this could be a ruse. He saw the ire no longer on Ares' face, however; putting away his sword, he gripped Ares' forearm.

"Well, that was entirely disappointing." Dionysos returned from the darkness.

"Shut up, brother." Ares turned away. "Danelos, you know nothing of my relationship with your father. Unlike in that *other* timeline, we have always been rivals, but never once have I lifted a hand to hurt him. Not really." He faced Dan. "He never told you about our past, then."

Both of Dan's eyebrows rose, and he shook his head. "N-No… He didn't. I figured you both just avoided one another."

Conjuring two simple wooden chairs, Ares gestured for Dan to sit. He glared at Dionysos who simply rolled his eyes and vanished in a swirling of leaves. As before in the bar, Dan turned the chair around, straddled it, and rested his arms across the back. He then heard something he had never heard before—Ares sighed.

"Tell me about my father," Dan said, his chin on his arms.

"Things between us were more… complicated when we were young if you can believe that. As I'm sure you know, Zeus doted on your father from the moment he laid eyes on him. After Leto gave birth to your father and Artemis, she brought them both to the Hall of Tribunals. Quite an act of defiance, considering Hera had closed off all of Gaea from her. From all accounts, Leto was reclusive and soft-spoken, but she knew that Zeus would want to see his children. Hera was with child, attended by Eileithyia, Olympos' midwife, and when my mother saw the newborn twins, she gave birth to me right there, on her throne. Perhaps her own act of defiance. When I had been swaddled, she handed me to Zeus, but he was holding Apollo. With distant eyes, so I've heard, he instructed Eileithyia to tend to my mother and me. Hera never forgave him for that effrontery, not in front of the whole pan-theon. While she could hold no enmity for Apollo and Artemis, she dismissed Leto who never stepped foot on Olympos again.

"Apollo and I grew up in the same marble halls, and while he chose to stand at the balustrade and wonder at Helios' chariot, taking in that light, I preferred to hide in shadow. He had become known as *Phoebos*, the Shining One. My penchant for conflict was foretold by the Moirae. However, he found his sovereignty as he grew, a bit more whimsically. I remember when he discovered music. Hermes had just returned Apollo's cattle to him, at Zeus' insistence, and the messenger was playing an instrument he had made from a tortoise's shell. As soon as Apollo drew his fingers across the strings, the sound could be heard everywhere. Even *I* smiled. He was destined to create that magic."

Like a child enrapt, Dan listened. This was the most he had ever heard from his uncle, about any topic. Ares wasn't a talker—he had acted, always with reckless disregard. Now, he sat back in his chair, and his body had lost all of the tension he had shown earlier.

"That's not what I wanted to tell you. When I was ten years old, by mortal standards, Zeus had caught me tormenting one of Hera's peacocks. Castigation by Zeus is something not even I would wish on my enemies. One did not disappoint him. Ever. Thunder like you have never heard roared above us, and lightning flashed with every fist crashing down on his throne. I wanted to unleash my fury on him, although I didn't have much fury then. I remember tightening my jaw and clenching my fists. Other gods turned away in the hall, hearing me being upbraided. Zeus raised a thunderbolt. Watching that energy squirm in his grip, as if yearning to be set free... The memory still haunts me.

"I don't know if he would have thrown it, or if he was trying to intimidate me, but from behind, I heard Apollo. 'Father! No!' He jumped in front of me, his arms spread. Zeus roared for him to move, that I needed to be punished, but your father said Zeus would have to go through him to get to me. I did not dare raise my voice to Zeus, but your father did. Seeing Apollo's selfless act diffused Zeus' wrath, and I was let off with a warning."

"My father stood up for you? Wow. I had always been told he was a pompous ass back then."

"Oh, he was. Make no mistake. Your father's arrogance was only rivaled by our father's. But, at that moment, he stood his ground. I have to say... I was proud of him, but I couldn't tell him. I had been rescued by my brother, which made me look weak, and my rage flared. When he turned to me, I shoved him out of the way and stormed out of the hall. I poked my head back in to see him talking to Zeus who asked my brother why he'd come to my defense. Do you know what he said?"

Dan shook his head, even though Ares' question was rhetorical.

"He said, 'Father, you do not hide who you favor. I am no more worthy of your love than Ares, yet you smile in my presence and scowl in his. He is a son of Zeus. Treat him like one."

"My father said that? To Zeus?"

"I swear on my sword. Your father had quite the mouth on him. I think it was because Zeus favored him that he felt he *could* get away with speaking his mind. He would walk around Olympos saying, 'I simply speak the truth. If Zeus fears the truth, Olympos is doomed.'"

"That sounds exactly like my father." Dan laughed.

Ares' face darkened, and he leaned forward.

"I'm the god of war, Danelos. I have brought more devastation into the world than anyone could, but..." He hung his head.

"But?"

"When your father told me what that Ares did in that other timeline..." He shook his head. "I could never, *would* never, bring such destruction to Arkadeia. To your mother. I, above all, know that war has consequences, and most times, I haven't cared what they were. My goal, the only one, was to satisfy my bloodlust. Even at my worst, however, I wouldn't destroy a sacred city, risking a god war. How that Ares could is beyond my comprehension. I'm just grateful there's no way for me to see what your father saw."

"While I have memories from that other history, that happened before my birth as Demetrios. I'm grateful, too, to be spared that memory, as is my mother. From what my father told me, he and that Ares had quite a contentious relationship. As did I."

Ares sat up. 'Really."

"I, rather, Demetrios, was sent by Zeus to free Ares from Gaea's adyton." Dan sat taller, taking his arms down. "Wow. I haven't thought about that in a long time. I don't usually access those memories."

Ares chuckled. "How ironic."

"What is?"

"That version of you had to rescue *that* Ares from the very same place where your father currently sits. Perhaps it is my destiny to help *you.*"

"How would you do that?"

"I don't know. Yet." Ares took a deep breath. "Chaos and order need one other to exist. Without your father as the guardian of order, our future is unclear. As the god of war, I am only one type of chaos in the world, and Apollo's absence wouldn't fuel my bloodlust. Mankind, though, won't be able to resist filling the gap, and it's that that I worry about most." He saw Dan look off into the darkness. "What is it?"

"It's something I just remembered. The reason why Demetrios freed Ares and dumped him at Zeus' feet. Balance."

"In my younger days, I would say, 'To Hades with balance!', but my time on Gaea has taught me much. More than I can ever convey."

"It seems most of the gods aren't eager to share their experiences as mortals."

"It's... It's humbling. Frightening. Yes, I know that may sound surprising coming from me. To be exposed like that, though, without the power you've always known. Unable to extend your hand and call it forth. I used to think mortals were impotent because they could not do what we do, but now I understand. Humanity has many gifts. More than any other god, your father understands that. His decision to live among mortals still confounds many, but having been one, I can tell you I understand so much more."

Dan and Ares sat in silence for a little while, the flickering light bulb the only light around them. Now, this knowledge provided illumination. Out of nowhere, Ares laughed to himself, the way one laughs when he doesn't know what else to do.

"I've never told anyone outside of Olympos this. During my time on Gaea, I was a social worker."

The war god instinctively puffed his chest out, narrowed his brows, and closed his fists, perhaps preparing for Dan to laugh. On the battlefield, that posture would cause any hardened warrior to wet himself. This soul-baring confession would shatter whatever hard-worn image anyone would have of Ares. He watched his nephew's expressionless face for a reaction. Dan closed his eyes, and his exhale quivered. Moments crept along until he stood, and Ares followed suit. Dan took a few steps toward his uncle and did what the son of Zeus never expected.

He embraced Ares.

At first, Ares seemed unsure what to do, but then he closed an arm around his nephew. The hug lasted just a moment, and it left Ares speechless. Dan stepped back and wiped his eyes.

"Right after you said those two words, it dawned on me just how much an effect my father had on Olympos. Had he not shared his mortal experience with all of you… Well, it ultimately changed you in ways I would never have thought. I know that you didn't choose that mortal life, but you don't seem to resent it."

"On the contrary. It did exactly what Zeus said it would. It granted us perspective. Being among mortals and living as one are nothing alike. Danelos, and Zeus would hurl a thunderbolt at me for saying this, your father has done more for Olympos than any other god. He has always dared to be an instrument of change. Don't let Dionysos fool you, either. He understands. He may or may not tell you about his mortal life, but trust me when I say that he is different. We both want to help Apollo. Our roles in the cosmos demand it."

"We should return to the bar. The next round is on me." Dan smirked and opened the portal.

23 | RECKONING

Café Aftab in Mashhad, Iran had its busiest hours just before evening and this lasted until closing around 2 a.m. At a back table, at 6 p.m., Jamshid Motjaba could always be found, reading the newspaper or writing. Unlike most commercial coffee houses, this one was family-owned and had a certain quirky charm with its modern art pieces on the walls and mosaic tables created by local craftspeople. It attracted business people, students, and a few tourists, especially those wanting a more Irani experience. Jamshid, his hand lightly caressing his cup of Turkish coffee, stared off, beads of sweat dotting his brow. Under the table, his right foot tapped like a jackrabbit. He took a sip of the sweet, strong darkness and returned the cup to its saucer.

"Everything all right?" The server, a young girl with a soft, lilting voice, stopped by his table.

He didn't see her at first but glanced up when he did, nodding and smiling. When she left, he took another sip. Leaning over the table, he cringed, pressed his hand over his chest. His breathing increased, and the sweat dripped down his face. With a paper napkin, he dabbed his forehead. Without uttering a sound, he continued to endure this for about five minutes, and then everything subsided. Sighing, he finished his coffee and made a call.

"H-Hello? It's Jamshid. The visions... They're back, and with a vengeance." He rubbed his chest where the word *pronoia* had been seared into his skin. "Not sure what you *can* do. It's just-" He shook as if having a seizure, pressing his hand against the burn.

"Gah! It's hap-pening… now." He clenched his eyes shut. "Gods, the images… so many… so many."

It lasted a few minutes, and as quickly as it started, the seizure faded.

"I'm-I'm okay. It stopped. Yes, I'm fine. How many? Maybe ten times a day. The seizures have grown since that ceremony. No, there's no pattern. It's the connection to him. Being a demigod makes it harder." He nodded as he listened. "I will try that. Thank you, brother."

Jamshid threw 97,000 *rials*—about the equivalent of $3.00—on the table and left. In the restroom, he washed his face and hands, watching his reflection as he patted his face dry. A slight smile emerged. Before he rolled his sleeves down, he stared at his two iron cuffs, both about two inches wide, etched with ancient Olympeian. Indestructible and irremovable, they had retained their original luster from the day he received them. Normally, he would keep them covered to avoid questions, but after his conversation with Brandon a few moments earlier, he kept his sleeves rolled on his forearms. He would do what his brother had suggested, and he knew just where to go.

Traveling southwest from Mashhad, Jamshid found the ancient temple a few hours' drive away. The Bazeh Hoor Fire Temple would be the best place for what his brother had suggested. In ruins, the structure had four squinches, or arched openings, one on each side. He removed his shoes and unrolled a straw mat under the central dome. Out of instinct, he sat facing east, and held his arms out at his sides, then crossing them over his chest. He repeated this gesture three times, with eyes closed.

"It's been a long while since we've spoken, Gaea, *Megalê Thea*, O Great Goddess, and Olympeia, Evlogiméno vounó, O Blessed Mountain. These," he held his wrists before him, "have marked my Asulos Pistis for so many years, and yet, while I have never disrespected you, I have never submitted myself to your love."

He rested his hands, palms up, on his knees.

"For that, I humbly ask your forgiveness." He looked around. "This ancient temple, named Gate of the Sun, seems wholly appropriate since I am a son of Apollo."

Crossing his wrists on his chest once more, the iron clanking together, he closed his eyes and repeated the sacred mantra his brother had given him. The words, in a tongue that predated Olympos, were given to Brandon when he sojourned in Arkadeia by Gaea herself. An avid practitioner of meditation, he had used his celestial and earthly connections to bring him balance and unburden his spirit. He felt Jamshid could benefit from this as well. Since his arrival in this temple, Jamshid had not experienced any of his seizures, but they could return at any time. The sacred words flowed through his mouth, but they came from his core, and the more he recited them, the more they became as natural as the breaths he took.

His mind, body, and spirit moved closer to alignment. With each exhale, he felt himself taking command of his faculties in a way he hadn't before. Then, as he had experienced in the coffee shop and other times, the seizure grew inside his chest. He knew it was coming and had waited for the moment when his skin felt like fire. The mantra came out more forcefully as if the words themselves would contain the sensations and the subsequent flash flood of psychic imagery. Jamshid's mouth formed the language, his breath gave it life, and his will wrestled with the onslaught. He clenched his fists, pressing the iron against his chest, and the manacles grew hot, absorbing the energy from the inscribed word on his flesh. The wave crested and came down, buffeting him within in his mind, trying to wrest his will free and allow the pictures to control him. He pushed back.

Resisting ancient power, especially that of divine vision, can force that power to push harder. Jamshid had inherited his father's mind for seeing things that had yet to happen, and that differed from prophecy in that his glimpses into the future didn't give a path or direction to follow. Apollo used both his forward-thinking and his gift for prophecy to guide mankind, especially at Delphi. All Jamshid wanted to do was control the surges. He repeated the mantra, holding his arms before him, watching the inscription of his pledge to Gaea and Olympeia on the iron go white with each successive pass. Brandon told him to believe in the words, and they would give him the anchor he needed.

He had had no awareness of how much time had elapsed, and when he felt the seizure finally abate, he saw how dark it had gotten beyond the arches. Within the dome, although no torches or lights existed, he saw a gilded glow just bright enough to see light from shadow. For the moment, he had control. Being in this temple amplified his ability, and now that he had tasted what it felt like to master the seizures, he could try to do it elsewhere. Before his drive back to the city, he texted Brandon to let him know he felt better. He then asked if Brandon had been afflicted by anything similar.

⊙━━◆━━⊙

Brandon was riding the Red Line from Park Street to Harvard University where he was going to guest lecture when he'd received Jamshid's last text. His response was a simple, "Yes." He then followed it up with "On my way to Harvard. I'll call you later." As he watched the outside speed past him, he reflected back to just a week earlier when the weight of managing all the worldly *logos*—reason—nearly knocked him out of commission.

Climbing Mount Washington had been a passion of Brandon's ever since college when he joined the Appalachian Mountain Society, and he'd done it a few times since working at Boston University. Although climbing protocol suggested that one travel with buddies after he became Zodiak, he always tempted fate by climbing by himself. He did tell Dan when he was going just in case something happened, though.

The week after he and his brothers had gone to Delos, Brandon needed some alone time to reflect on his experience, so he drove the four hours to the Tuckerman Ravine Trail where the ascent began. While he could technically draw upon his celestial guides for strength or agility, he chose not to. An experienced hiker, he could reach the peak in three hours, but this time, he paced himself, focusing on his breathing and his body. This type of trip he called a full-body meditative experience. Most people, he claimed, would focus primarily on the sights as they hiked, but they rarely focused on how their bodies felt. Brandon paid attention to his breathing, heart rate, and even his gait not only to make sure his entire body benefitted from the experience but also to make sure his mind did as well. Everything was connected, he believed, and while it was okay to focus on the external, sometimes one had to focus on the whole picture. His mind, especially on this climb, seemed more labyrinthine than usual, and he wasn't sure whether or not he wanted to reach the center of it to go up against his "minotaur."

Views of the New Hampshire landscape, coupled with the crisp morning air, prompted deep breathing and his glassy-eyed reverie—this meditative trance-like state helped him open his senses to sights, smells, and sounds he would normally not experience. Unlike his brother, Sarah, and Aleta, whose power came from within, his power came from a connection to the stars. Mental acuity of a different sort, much like his father had had to maintain the barrier between two sets of memories, required energy and focus above the norm.

Brandon had gone about a mile along the trail when his concentration broke, causing him to stumble. He gripped his walking stick, a well-worn branch he'd fashioned many years ago, stopping himself from falling, his arm quivering. Blood flowed from his head, and he lowered himself to the ground. His forehead felt a chill from sweat. He took deep breaths through his nose and exhaled through his mouth a few times, and when he tried to stand, he couldn't. He knew he wasn't dehydrated, but he took two swigs of water from his canteen anyway. When the lightheadedness faded, he continued down the trail, retreating into himself to reestablish that state of mind.

As it was a weekday, he didn't see many other hikers. He pulled out his phone to text Dan, but just put it back. One dizzy spell wouldn't deter him, he thought. A mountain hike like this was child's play for him, having climbed Denali in Alaska twice, but he didn't feel the need to fly across the country to clear his head. At the halfway point, his legs buckled. He managed to land on his backpack so as not to injure himself, and he self-assessed before moving again. This wasn't like earlier, he determined. His inability to move his legs hadn't happened before, but even as he sat there, the feeling returned gradually. Trying to rule things out, he took a few handfuls of granola, thinking maybe low blood sugar was to blame. He decided it gave him time to appreciate where he was. The sound of crunching in his head as his teeth bore down gave him something to focus on. Outside of his head, the thrushes chirping coupled with the sound of wind through the trees created harmonies.

Brandon had always been cerebral, and his adoptive parents Max and Evelyn noticed at an early age that he would sit by his window, even at two years old, and observe, reasoning through what he saw. His love of nature began from the moment he was aware of his surroundings, and Evelyn would sit in the local park for hours with him as a toddler. As a teenager and adult, he preferred the quiet of his own thoughts to groups of people. Some called him shy, but he was more of an introverted extrovert. At Delos, *reason* chose him as its guardian because of this.

His third attempt to reach the summit had more success, and he had gone most of the way before another attack happened. This time, he lost his sight. He was on a switchback when his eyes simply shut off. Before his next step touched the ground, he stopped and found his center again. While he hadn't anticipated *this* particular thing happening, he wasn't surprised. He knew it made no sense to panic since that could only exacerbate the situation, and the other two attacks had subsided. Using one of the zodiac to help him crossed his mind, but he didn't know which would be the best one. What intrigued him more was that no light at all entered his eyes. Controlled breathing anchored him. Brandon had repeatedly told Sarah that he envied her calling Quarters because it provided order to a chaotic moment. She told him he could do it, too, but he didn't want to disrespect the deities involved. He preferred his own meditative mantras, most of which he kept secret. They were his bond with Gaea and Olympeia.

Like earlier, the symptom subsided. Each attack lasted no more than five minutes, but he knew he couldn't count on that for the future. More focused on reaching the summit than he had been, he widened his gait, and as soon as he arrived, he dropped his pack and sat. Without the need to move for a while, he retreated into his mind to find the source of these physiological oddities.

Just like Dan, Brandon drew strength from Gaea, so he placed his hands at his sides, palms against the cool earth. Still early in the day, a chill remained in the pine-laden air. He took stock of his breathing, his heart rate, and his connection to the world. In his mind, he passed images of arches made of marble columns, doorways of stone, and portals through sequoias—all symbols of passing the levels of his consciousness to his core. Dozens of entryways lay between his outer consciousness and his innermost mind. Finally, he entered a cave, and settled like a feather, floating to the ground he perceived. Being so close to his spiritual side made him vulnerable in the real world outside. His body was susceptible to attack, from an animal or person, as well as the elements. Situated where he needed to be, he opened his mind to the energy around him to tap into it.

A cacophonous cloud of voices rushed toward him, an unending cascade of sound expressing the need to think and process ideas. Brandon felt each voice on his skin like a pinprick so much so that he felt like he was wrestling with a porcupine. Humanity was trying to apply logic to its everyday situations, and he understood its struggle. Without Apollo of sound mind, the power to reason lost its balance and teetered. Gaea awoke and knew she needed to protect Brandon, so from where his hands touched the soil, rock grew over his skin, up his arms, across his torso, and over his head, encasing him in her living essence. If someone were to see him, he or she would perceive a rough seated statue. Brandon resisted, however, telling her he needed to feel the energy of the world's reason upon him so he could understand. His heart pounded in his chest, echoing in his ears, and he wanted himself to be pummeled by the onslaught, but Gaea persisted. Mankind struggled with the absence of Apollo, even though it didn't realize who he was or what his role was in their world. Brandon feared that the vacuum left by his father not being cognizant of this would damage everything. Then, he sensed another type of reason that suffered at the loss of his father's control—that of the gods. He heard their thoughts, felt their confusion, and understood so much: why Zeus had unleashed his wrath so strongly, why Hera lashed out at Dan, and even why Dionysos and Ares wanted to help Apollo. The other Olympeians as well fell prey to this, and the pall of disorder that hung over the sacred mountain made Brandon shiver.

The mountain spirit, Olympeia, gave off a different electricity than usual as well—not even the gods' home was immune.

Inside his earthen shell, Brandon's temperature rose, his muscles shook, and, like earlier, his legs went numb. Blood started draining from his head, but he knew if he lost consciousness that he wouldn't be able to fight. He pushed back against Gaea's aid, wanting to endure this challenge. His mental cave image only made the feelings more intense. It was as if the resonance of reason reverberated off the makeshift walls. Mother Earth couldn't protect him from this.

"I… I am Kidemonas, the son of Apo-" His attempt at a mantra was interrupted by a sharp sensation between his eyes.

Again, he tried. "I am Kidemonas, the son of Apollo and Alki-" He started hyperventilating.

Twice more he began, and each time his body prevented him from saying it. If his mouth wouldn't speak, he voiced the words in his mind. When he could finish the mantra internally, after a dozen attempts, he tried to say them aloud.

"I am Kidemonas, the son of Apollo and Alkinoë, a prince of Arkadeia. Gaea and Olympeia sustain my spirit. May balance be restored."

As he repeated the words, the stone casing cracked, then crumbled, around him. The essence of reason continued to strike him, the whole world's tries at logic crashing like an ocean wave. The ability or lack thereof to reason from billions of people assaulted him like a phalanx. His mantra became his shield, his sword, his ability to stave off the onslaught. Brandon took their energy inside him and sent it back toward them—he was the filter of control. He pulled himself back from the abyss of the cave, through uncountable doorways until he opened his eyes with a gasp. He got his bearings and the blazing sun beat down on him. His watch showed 3:42 p.m. He'd been in that deep trance for about six hours. Unconsciously, he touched the word *logos* cut into his chest. He hadn't quite recovered his faculties and could still hear the multitudes of voices in his head. A lingering image of his father loomed just beyond his periphery, but he had made it out of this ordeal.

"Man, I feel like I wrestled a hydra. And lost." He yawned. "My head doesn't feel right, either, but maybe that's the price I pay for bearing this responsibility. This must be what it felt like for him to keep those other memories at bay for so long."

He took one last look out toward the horizon before heading down the mountain. This excursion wasn't what he had imagined it would be, but it gave him a new understanding of what it meant to be a son of Apollo.

Osaka University Hospital had a reputation worldwide for handling a range of medical needs, and its neuroscience department had been rated at the highest levels. One of the doctors responsible for this accolade was Dr. Ryuma Taiyo, a neuropsychologist who had been with the hospital since the 1980s. He had revolutionized treatment for brain injuries and how they affect cognitive functions. Over the years, he had worked with renowned neuroscientists and surgeons globally, setting up clinical trials, seeking new treatment options, and putting Osaka University Hospital on the proverbial map when it came to how many patients it had successfully treated and helped to return to a normal, or relatively normal, life. He had been the attending physician for ten years before moving into the department chair of neuroscience position, a role he had enjoyed for the last six years. A shelf in his office boasted numerous trophies, plaques, and awards for his work in the community, his breakthroughs in neurotrauma, and his work with the United Nations and the Global Health Organization to treat underprivileged children.

At this moment, he sat in the dark on the couch in his office, facing what he knew to be the windows overlooking Osaka. Even though he couldn't see what lay beyond the glass, he knew the city to be robust and filled with possibilities. Opened slightly, the window allowed the outside air to bring with it the sounds of the city. In his lap, he held a woman's picture, its wooden frame cracked and abraded with age.

"Do you remember, Hyotaru, how we walked along the Yodo River? You told me what you saw, describing each nuanced color and scent, not realizing that I could intuit all those things. But, I let you tell me because it let me focus on your voice."

He placed the frame on the window ledge so that her picture faced downtown Osaka, and he leaned forward as if he were looking out over the expansive city.

"So much time has passed. How long has it been? A century? Maybe two? This city was all we had together, for as many years as we could share it." He sat back down. "Your mortality took you from me before I could find a cure."

He took a deep breath and smiled.

"Night is coming. I can smell it on the wind. You used to say that one who could know the sunrise from its counterpoint at dusk by its scent was truly a gifted spirit. I wish that were true. Since living in the ancient world have I walked without my eyes to see… to *truly* see… the world in which I live. Only because I am of Olympeian blood can I know anything about what lies beyond my dead eyes."

Ryuma moved effortlessly through the blackness of his office to the wall where a small black lacquered table sat. He poured genmaicha tea into a small cup and returned to his couch by the window, inhaling the perfume.

"I drink this tea for you, Hyotaru. You used to buy it when we went to the Kuromon Ichiba Market. You said it reminded you of your childhood. When you told me about the monk at the Shitennō-ji shrine who had given you your first cup, your eyes danced. Yes, I could tell. And I thought I could picture that moment with you in my mind."

He sipped the tea, cradling the cup in his hands as if it were a baby bird, delicate and in need of protection.

"I did everything within my power to help you. I can say that now. When I sat at your bedside, our hands clasped together as if we were one, I felt your life force fading. Before your spirit passed from your body, you mustered the strength to lift your hand to my cheek. It was so warm, but I knew it would grow colder. I did not need my father's gift for foresight to know that you were slipping away, like Eurydice from Orpheos, until your spirit would be among the asphodel."

He finished the tea, resting the cup next to the picture frame. Getting on his knees on the couch, he pushed the window open until the moon-kissed air fell into the office. Leaning on the window ledge in the direction of the city, he closed his eyes and smiled. He lifted his face toward the silver disk in the heavens surrounded by nascent stars and opened his eyes.

"Selene, I can't see your iridescence, but I know you are as resplendent as I remember before Aphrodite took my eyes. I can sense you here as well, Artemis. If your power extends into the underworld, convey my love for Hyotaru to her. She won't remember me since Lethe's waters have wiped clean her memories, but perhaps she'll have one moment, one quick glimpse, of when we walked by the Yodo."

Pouring another cup of tea, Ryuma turned his head back toward the picture frame, toward the woman he couldn't save, and he remembered all too recently how he had taken a vow to protect the healing powers of his father, and how he almost failed in doing so.

⊙━━◆━━⊙

A few weeks earlier, Ryuma stepped on the Midosuji Line of the Osaka subway at Nishitanabe Station after attending an early dinner with colleagues. He normally would have walked, but since he knew his friend and host Hideyuki was heavy-handed with the sake, he felt it best to take the precaution of the train. He remembered his father's words inscribed at Delphi, "μηδέν ἄγαν"—Nothing in excess—although he didn't always remember to adhere to them. The ride would last just over an hour to get home. Normally, he would read on the train, but he hadn't brought anything with him. Plus, the sake would make his fingertips a little numb, so their ability to read Braille would be hindered. He could suppress his godliness enough to enjoy the mortal pleasures. His mind drifted to a patient he was seeing, and that led him to think about treatment options. With healing in his thoughts, he was at home. This wasn't work to him; it was his passion. An advantage of Ryuma's blindness, having been caused by godly means, was that he had learned how to "see" by feeling the energy around him. Being a demigod also helped. This also enabled him to move around without a white cane. He used to use one, to make people more comfortable, but then he didn't care what people thought. He would rather they wonder how a blind man could get around. Ryuma could see inside his patients to know how best to attempt to cure them. His eyes looked normal, too, and he kept his face lowered on the train following Japanese cultural norms.

As the train filled with passengers, his facial expression changed as he read the energy around him. After a few stops, people occupied every seat while others crowded around standing, paying attention to their own thoughts or quietly conversing with companions. Ryuma's brows furrowed, and he sat up. Turning a little to his left, he felt pressure against his chest, like a wave preparing to crash down. In his mind's eye, he knew an older woman, around sixty, sat there. Whatever it was about her that pushed against him made it hard for him to breathe. He pressed a hand against his rib cage, taking labored breaths. His throat seemed to close, and his lungs ached.

"Asthma," he thought. "I feel her asthma. How is that even possible?"

While he wrestled with that, a dull ache crawled up his right arm, and he squeezed it with his other hand. Seated next to him, a young man in his early twenties read a newspaper. The sensation moved across his chest and into his heart. Then, a sharp pain lodged there for a few seconds before lessening.

To himself just at a whisper, Ryuma said, "He has… ischemic heart disease. How am I feeling this?"

He then remembered the word imprinted on his chest—*ex-akesis*—the ancient word for healing. When diagnosing a patient, he had always been able to sense the illness or what was happening in the brain, but he'd never felt the problem in his own body. This empathic connection had never manifested itself. At the same time that he experienced the intermittent heart pain and the breathing difficulties, he winced at pressure in his sinus cavity. It tightened until he pressed his fingertips just below his eyes. He was facing straight ahead at an elderly gentleman who was rocking, his eyes clenched shut.

"Sinusitis," Ryuma thought. "He's in so much pain." The same sensation occurred in his own head.

Sweat soaked through his dress shirt and ran down his temples. He gripped his knees and controlled his breathing as much as possible. The asthma-afflicted woman leaned over to him.

"Daijōbudesuka?" *Are you all right?*

"Genki desu. Arigato." *I am fine. Thank you.* He hid his pain with the gentlest smile.

She leaned back and crossed her hands in her lap, occasionally looking at him. When a new passenger boarded, Ryuma gasped, digging his fingers into his chest with one hand and gripping the seat with the other. His eyes fluttered. A teenage girl with headphones held onto the metal pole in front of him.

"Acute myeloid leukemia." The words exploded in Ryuma's mind. "Stage four."

As a doctor, he had taken the Hippocratic Oath. The first line, '*I swear by Apollo the Healer, by Aesculepios, by Hygieia, by Panacea, and by all the gods and goddesses, making them my witnesses, that I will carry out, according to my ability and judgment, this oath and this indenture,*' was a part of him. He was of that very lineage to which he swore to heal. Sitting on this train, surrounded by people afflicted, more people than he ever thought would be, choked his spirit like a serpent. Something else was inside him, however, aside from his innate ability to detect illness. Through the asthma, the sinusitis, heart disease, and leukemia, another presence had taken residence inside him.

The power to heal.

Part divine ichor and part blood, Ryuma's own life fluid now carried an electric current beyond that which a human body would produce. This energy charged him with Apollo's divine gift, the same one the son of Zeus had passed on to his son Aesculapios and his offspring. It was a fire that burned hot inside Ryuma, a fire unlike the First Fires of creation and those of Prometheos. These flames burned away sickness, allowing the regenerative healing process to begin. The moment he realized he could heal these people on this train, Ryuma's first thought was to touch these four people. He could change their lives forever, make them whole once more. Nothing else mattered at that moment. All the

218

symptoms of their illnesses faded behind the power of his desire. He pressed his feet onto the floor, ready to stand and move across the crowd.

He then remembered Hyotaru, his beloved, whose eventual death from amyotrophic lateral sclerosis tortured his soul every waking moment. When she lived, over a century earlier, no one knew what this was. Ryuma, then a neurologist, had no experience with it, and medicine hadn't advanced enough to know how to treat it. Watching her deteriorate all but made him quit medicine. Even though he now practiced neuropsychology, he retained his prior specialty, among many others—one advantage of being an immortal healer. He used to punish himself with the uncertainties of his inability to help Hyotaru. Her life's thread had been cut by the *Moirae* when it was supposed to be, and he could have done nothing about it.

That was when his epiphany struck—he couldn't heal these people. No matter how much pain they endured, or would endure, when would his healing others end? It would have to be all or none. How could he heal these four and not the others he had yet to experience? Surely others on this train suffered as well. How could he not walk through Osaka Prefecture, or Japan, or travel the world, and heal all those who suffered? If not them, then who, he thought—he could heal *himself*.

Lifting his trembling hands toward his face, he recalled seeing Aphrodite in Adonis' embrace, the last thing he ever witnessed before she struck him down. He was comforted that Apollo took the form of a boar and gored Adonis since he couldn't do anything to his own sister. Within his fingertips, Ryuma could restore that which she had stolen from him. All of the world would be open to him. A thought burst through. It was Hyotaru's voice, with the resonance of a 13-stringed koto, when they had walked along the Yodo River.

"If you could see this, Ryuma, you would see true magic. The way the deep blue-green waters move, each droplet in unison, a fluid collective that marches on, ever progressing, with one purpose. Afternoon sunbeams ignite the surface with a shimmer. It's like the gods themselves reached down and touched the river, igniting it. As it reaches Osaka-wan, it impregnates the bay, and the living waters spread, like tiny swans."

He lowered his hands, closing them into fists. If he could see the river for himself, what his eyes would render would pale into insignificance compared to Hyotaru's inspired words. Everything he remembered coming from her was poetry set aloft. She would be ashamed of him for what he was about to do. The train car jostled as they neared Shin-Ōsaka Station, and Ryuma came out of his reverie. He had touched the fire within and knew its power, and that opened the path for others' maladies to register within him.

"If I won't use it," he thought, "I need to suppress it. Bury it. It won't do *me* any good, and it's not mine to use. It belongs to Apollo. I'm simply its custodian for a while."

From hangnails to pimples to diverticulitis, he felt every single thing within a fifteen foot radius on the train. He knew the train would stop soon, and if he didn't shut off this empathy, he would be no better off than Apollo now—a healer without the ability to heal—walking through the station and the city. As soon as the train stopped, he pushed his way to the closest restroom and vomited. Once his insides stopped churning, he cleaned up and walked home, but he knew he wasn't finished dealing with this.

He crossed his apartment's threshold, and the emotions rose like magma in a volcano. Ryuma managed to keep himself contained until he fell onto his bed, at which point he let out a scream that would undoubtedly frighten his neighbors. Curling up in the fetal position, he sobbed, pressing a pillow against his face to contain the outpouring of such primal emotion. This catharsis lasted throughout the night until he finally wore himself out. His alarm went off at 5 a.m. In a tangle of sheets he awoke and shuffled to the kitchen. Still groggy, he drank two full glasses of water before falling into his armchair in the living room.

For the first time in his existence, he'd had a dreamless sleep.

"Hyotaru…" He exhaled.

⚬━◆━⚬

Returning his thoughts to the present, Ryuma finished the last of the tea and put the picture frame back on the credenza behind his desk. Night had blossomed fully over Osaka, and with it came the crushing silence he endured every day. After a gentle knock on his office door, a middle-aged woman with her black hair in a bun and white lab coat poked her head in.

"Dr. Taiyo? Are you still here?"

"Yes." He clicked his desk lamp on. "What can I do for you, Dr. Yokota?"

"I heard movement, and I was concerned. Everything all right?"

He nodded slightly, his face showing no expression.

She cocked her head and smirked. Sitting in the chair in front of his desk, she put her clipboard down.

"You were thinking about *her* again, weren't you? Is today the day?"

"Exactly to the day. It's been… a long time."

After a few awkward moments, she leaned forward.

"Ryuma, I've known you for almost twenty years. I think I can safely say that *this* is why you keep people at arm's length. Even me."

"What are you talking about?"

"Ever since we met, you've been distant. Over the years, while we've worked together, that has never changed. You finally told me about Hyotaru, but it took ten years."

He sat back and looked away.

"Look. I consider you a friend, and If I'm crossing a line, so be it. You can't close off the world around you without sacrificing a part of yourself. This acerbic side you show has closed more doors than you think. I've seen you bearing the weight of her death for so long that even I begin to feel the remorse. Let people in, or you will walk this path alone." She picked up her clipboard. "Well… I just wanted to see if you were all right. I have rounds."

She had just reached the door when she heard him.

"Mizuki. Wait."

Ryuma moved toward her, unable to face her.

"You're right. I keep people at a distance to avoid being hurt. But, it also prevents me from seeing those who care." He bowed. "Thank you for your honesty."

She bowed in return and left.

24 | UNDERSTANDING

The Arcady Gallery held some of the world's most intriguing art treasures, from all cultures, and it had the added benefit of being one of the most secure buildings in the world. When Keion Wolff opened the gallery, he used the considerable wealth he had acquired from his immortal life to hire security specialists who had developed unique methods to ensure the safety of his pride and joy. On top of that, knowing that humanity had inherent immutable flaws, he also brought into play his godly background to use magical wards to augment the human technology.

Keion walked the levels of the gallery each day, mingling with potential clients or simply visitors to London. The wall that overlooked the Thames was entirely of enhanced glass so that the sunlight could shine in, but it would do no damage to the artwork. A few parts of the wall displayed stained glass that filtered a rainbow throughout. As the sun set, he would gaze out at the river, the beams bringing out the golden ochre of his eyes. An advantage of being the son of Apollo—no need for sunglasses. His hands clasped behind him, he took in the city, once nicknamed "The Smoke," but no hazy hubris prevented the sun from casting its rays anymore. Without the hindrance obscuring the true London, the vibrant, pulsing city was laid bare for all to see. That was what mattered to him the most—truth. After his experience on Delos, with the word *aletheia* a part of his flesh, Keion was coming to terms with that responsibility of being the guardian of something so precious and so unsettling at once.

On the north side of the gallery on the top floor, which was simply a walkway that circumscribed the building, leaving the openness for ceiling art to descend toward the bustling patrons, he encountered a young man and woman standing before a painting. They didn't seem to blink as they took in the entire canvas.

"*The Matchmaker* by Gerrit van Honthorst. Stunning, isn't it?"

The man smiled but kept his eyes on the painting. "Absolutely."

Keion leaned in. "Are you familiar with chiaroscuro?"

They both shook their heads, figuring his gentle smile and dancing eyes would enlighten them.

"The dichotomy of that which is obscured with that which is brought to light. It has some ancient origins, but it became popular in Europe in the 1400s. Van Honthorst, who was Dutch, completed this in 1625. His mastery of the oils brings out this style."

"How remarkable." The woman took notes on a small pad. "The revelation of the woman, with so much detail to her clothing and expression in vibrant blue, ivory, and gold, is juxtaposed with that of the men, ensconced in shadow. And that one man's expression-"

Laughing, Keion nodded to her. "The light reveals the truth, while the darkness hides it. Compare her expression to the man's on the left."

"Almost sinister by comparison." The man squinted as he got closer. "Perhaps he doubts the woman's ability to find a match?"

The woman, still writing, smirked. "Couldn't you say that the darkness also reveals truth?"

Keion moved to the other side of the painting. "Of course. Darkness is the absence of light, but it is no less a truth. Perhaps we are discussing different kinds of truth, then."

Their conversation lasted a little longer and culminated with him shaking the man's hand and kissing hers. He directed them toward a server with a tray of champagne flutes and invited them to enjoy as they perused the rest of the gallery. As he watched them approach Monet's *San Giorgio Maggiore at Dusk*, he reflected back on his own encounter with truth, and the burden of being one now yoked to its care.

The day after he returned from Delos he spent in bed, resting his mind and body. The experience of being with his brothers, while exhilarating, was also exhausting. Not one to be entirely lazy, he dragged himself out of his loft in the late afternoon and meandered until he reached the Thames by Westminster Bridge. A weathered wooden bench by the river became his vantage for the oncoming sunset. A couple walked on the path behind him, and he sensed their approach before they were within earshot. With arms wrapped around each other, they seemed almost conjoined. They shared no words, but as if he had heard some, Keion turned his ear toward them.

"He doesn't love her," he thought. "His behavior hides his true feelings. And…" He turned around fully. "…she adores him."

Keion took the path in the direction where the couple had come, passing cyclists and ponderers and those rushing by. Each time, he learned a truth that rose to the surface. One man, impeccably coiffed and dressed in an Italian suit, with a body like Adonis, radiated self-esteem. A young girl walked past him, earbuds separating her from the world, and her truth—she was homeless. The way she was dressed and even her gait belied her outward self. For some, their thoughts shot out to him like a radio signal. For others, their intangible, unknown truths radiated like fire. Even looking at structures showed inconceivable realities. One three-story brownstone shop looked faultless, but behind the façade, he knew the truth behind it. It hadn't met building codes and would collapse within six months due to shoddy materials. He texted a friend on the city's building commission to check it out. When asked how he knew, Keion simply said, 'Trust me'. His friend replied, 'Good enough for me.' He had developed *that* kind of relationship with people.

Across the river sat what was once the Houses of Parliament, now a museum to the range of politics throughout England since the Beaker folk of the 3rd century BCE. The Great Bell, originally Big Ben, had been silenced decades earlier. Now the austere clock face kept time, but in silence. Keion didn't need to be tied to the greater "truths" of Apollo to know why this government moved away from a parliamentary system and became a full monarchy— the bicameral system had become ineffectual for them for two reasons: other countries of the world had joined distinct alliances or conglomerates, strengthening their position, and the prime minister had engaged in corrupt relationships with criminal organizations, threatening the validity of her position. The queen, Ida I, along with smaller, vocal factions within the parliament, convinced other members of Parliament to consolidate power under a monarchic umbrella, transforming the parliamentary government to a set of advisors for the queen, thus enabling a more democratic monarchy. She would act more like a president, moving her from figurehead to actual leader, but it wouldn't be an absolute monarchy.

Decades earlier, Keion had stood in this very spot and wondered about the policies arbitrated within those walls, but at this moment, with access to his father's ability to discern truths, nothing happened in those buildings that registered with any intensity. The path then took him into more congested areas of pedestrian traffic, and—like Ryuma—he was bombarded with thoughts and lingering truths that only one with his gift could see or understand. With each step into the crowd, the sound of revelation grew like a hornet's nest, and it became a white noise of indistinct voices. Where his focus went, the truths sought him out. Deception clung to humanity like a dark, damp heavy blanket, making it hard for him to breathe. Pockets of lightness released his lungs for mere seconds before others' hidden natures pressed down. Keion wrapped an arm around a light pole, his eyes rolling back in his head, and he used every ounce of energy to keep himself from passing out.

In his mind, he stood at the edge of a craggy cliff that loomed over a great canyon, both bottomless and limiting at the same time. Within that emptiness, the palpable truths of the cosmos emerged. Keion was aware of his heart rate, his breathing, the sweat coating his body, and he pushed back against the wave that could crush him from inside this vast, gaping imaginary pit. The sensation of the cold metal of the lamppost against his arm and chest reminded him he was still in the mortal realm, but his spirit was not.

"H-How does Apollo manage all this… at once?" he asked himself, his lips barely moving.

A sea of truth rose before him. The deeper he looked, the more ethereal they became until he breached a boundary he was never meant to go beyond: that of the gods. His connection to Apollo was the key to a lock unintended for one such as he. An icy breeze swept over him, and the cosmological truths of Olympos and beyond coalesced. A maelstrom engulfed him, a swirling, churning cauldron of reality and truth clutched at him, pulling, tugging... the avian nature of the gods became clear—an eagle, a dove, a crow, and a bevy of winged creatures flocked together, constructed of light and darkness, love and war, conflict and peace.

He gasped, his breath sucked out as the ancient power of the gods pulled at his lungs. In this discord, his eyes moved forward from his body deep into the earth. Beyond the canyon. Beyond the layers of rock. Beyond Hades and Tartaros.

The next Truth he witnessed was something no one else had ever seen: Apollo in Gaea's adyton.

His father's power gave him access to the one place not even Danelos could see. The embodiment of truth's custodian chained to Gaea made Keion inhale, reclaiming the breath he had lost. There, seated on the rough stone, was the outline of a god, contracted and impotent. The illumination of truth itself inside him allowed Keion to see where his father was, although he couldn't see whatever expression Apollo had. He reached out, but his fingers were insubstantial, almost vague, and they ached to make contact. It had been millennia since he and his father had been in the same place together. Then, the connection retracted, placing him back within his own body. The sensation of someone touching him on his shoulder, a small hand, gave him the focus to collect himself. As soon as he regained his awareness, he was still holding the lamppost, but he had slid to the ground. The hand belonged to a little boy. Keion's golden eyes registered a vibrant truth within the child—compassion.

"Are you okay, mister?"

As if the boy had the power to control everything around him, he had pulled Keion back. One sole spirit acting for the benefit of another, without bias, had been like Ariadne's string to Theseus, a tether to the world. The one thing that Keion didn't have was the power to control how he could perceive these truths. He wondered how he could walk through such a widespread city and not be overwhelmed.

"Thank you..." Keion patted the boy's shoulder, getting his bearings. "Where're your mum and dad?"

Just then, a woman, smiling, stepped up.

"Paul, the man's all right. You're a good boy for checking on him." She tousled the boy's short, brown hair. "We were walking by, and he saw you clutching the post. Before I knew what was happening, he ran over and patted you on the shoulder. You sure you're okay?"

Laughing a little, Keion nodded. "I am, thank you. Low blood sugar, I think." He crouched down. "You, sir, are a shining example for others."

He felt a wave come from the woman. Her truth—love—was largely for the boy, but he sensed she was a caring soul to others, too. As they parted, he waved at Paul, realizing the similarity to his own father's names, both his Olympeian one and the one he took to live in the mortal world. A sign, perhaps. Somehow, that encounter was enough to quell the raging inside his mind. Just knowing that someone else acted on his own truth without a second thought gave Keion the power to suppress Apollo's ability.

Lingering at *San Giorgio Maggiore at Dusk*, Keion marveled at Monet's skill at rendering color, light, and shadow. How the gradients blended, becoming a panoply of images, and the liquid nature of the Thames, much like the sea of truth he had seen in his mind, helped him to comprehend the inexplicable nature of Truth.

○══╪══○

Below Otto Wolf's military stronghold in the heart of Boston lay a compound covered by layers of earth, a mystical hub for all of his other clandestine activities, the ones even Major McAllister didn't know about. He had put this subterranean base of operations as far from the sunlit upper world as he could, and even the unnatural light within was dim. Unlike the offices at the surface, these walls, painted a unique shade of tan, displayed black art frames containing shifting images, with no two looking identical. Corners of hallways had rounded edges. Doors slid open and closed with an almost indistinct whoosh, and when closed, they blended so that the edges were imperceptible with the rest of the wall.

Secrecy was ensconced in every aspect of this space.

At the heart of this garrison was a stone chamber no larger than ten feet square with a wall niche that housed a statue to the only Olympeian Otto had ever held in any regard. On each side, two torches burned.

"Father, you and I have never been close, at least not since my childhood, but I felt drawn to come here and work through my latest dilemma. I keep this shrine, as it were, out of some sense of familial bond, although we haven't spoken in millennia."

Shadows from the torches caressed the statue, highlighting the marble and giving it a sort of sentience. It depicted Hermes, a chlamys draped over his left arm, his right hand facing upward as if it could support something. His face bore the slightest smile, almost a smirk, with his eyes staring off at some distant mischief. The snake-entwined winged staff he used to transfer the souls of the dead lay at his feet.

"I held out hope that you would have come to me, at some point, to offer some fatherly advice or scorn, depending on your whim and my activities of the moment. Why, of all the gods, Apollo chooses to live among the mortals, never ceases to amuse me, since you have spent your share of time flitting about wearing the guise of a merchant or grizzled old man." He raised his head toward the cold eyes of the statue. "I would ask why you have forsaken me, but we both know the answer. Shame. You are ashamed of me because I don't uphold your unrealistic Olympeian ideals. Why should I?"

Perhaps it was a play of the light, but the head of the statue seemed to move with Otto's voice as if it were listening to the ramblings of a forsaken demigod. Otto paced the chamber, hands laced together behind his back, taking moments of silence for every moment he shared his thoughts aloud with his father's effigy. He drew his fingers along the stony caduceus, tracing the curves of the serpents and the marble plumage.

"All this power wasted on one who chooses to be subordinate to his brother. If I had inherited your mantle…" He smirked. "Let us just say that my presence would be known the world over."

Otto sat against the wall, facing the statue, eyeing it from head to base over and over.

"So limited." He pushed himself off the wall. "I need to flush out your brother. For a god of *his* power to be so absent must mean he is in hiding. I am certain he has put himself deep within Gaea's warm flesh, far from the view of prying eyes. He must be drawn back into the mortal world so that I can bring him down."

He sat cross-legged before the statue, his palms pressed together, his fingers touching his lips as if he were in prayer.

"I had thought to start another smear campaign against his precious Task Force Division. I have uncovered unease within its ranks, and I could use that to provoke dissension. Not all who work under the aegis of the United Nations are endeared to Paul Fairmont or the task forces. I've been at their meetings and listened to their prattle, unbeknownst to them. Or, I could bring to light how precious Alkinoë plays favorites with her philanthropy. Again. Some groups petition for her aid, and she summarily ignores them for other charities. Alas, though, these would arouse the U.N.'s legal counsel, revealing that which I would not want to be unshadowed."

He closed his eyes and took a few deep breaths.

"So much truth to reveal, O Shining One, and yet, to do so, would more than likely bring more chaos down upon *me* and that which I strive to do. That cannot happen. So, Father, guide me, your wayward son, in my mischief. You who claim to be its master should have no trouble dropping a secret in my ear on how I can scare your brother into the open."

Again, Otto paced the chamber, this time he quickened his movement.

"Come on, Father, share with me your ways! Shall I bring down the Fairmont boys? Perhaps the potter? The geneticist? This very task force has the might to undo my machinations, does it not?" His voice would have echoed in the chamber if the stone walls had permitted it. "Perhaps... Perhaps..."

He clasped his hands together and grinned.

"Oh, by Hekate's crown, I think I have something. It would take aught but Zeus' lightning to crash upon the ground to bring these children of the gods into the public eye. Should something precious be endangered, then they would protect it. It is their sworn duty."

He nodded, his eyes sparkling in the torchlight.

"Thank you, Father. You have inspired me. I knew you would be good for something."

Touching the wall, he opened a door into an empty hallway. When it closed behind him, the tan wall looked seamless. Each step had intent, and he turned the corner toward the main elevator.

Back in the shrine, a figure hovered on winged sandals from the shadows behind the statue. Adorned in similar attire to the stone likeness, he shook his head.

"My dear boy, how little you know. A god of mischief I may be, but I am not one to condone wanton destruction. Whatever inspiration you claim to have received from me, I know not what it is, but I am duty-bound to let this city's protectors know. May the *Moirae* be merciful even to you."

Like a whisper, the figure vanished, and he who was known as Olympos' fool would do what he had not done for many years—involve himself in the affairs of mortals.

Quinn sat tapping away at her glass console when the team hurried into her office, each with the same look of perplexity as they stopped by her desk. The liaison smiled, even though she couldn't see their expressions, nodding her head toward the boardroom table around the corner. Eight legs shuffled across the office, and then Quinn heard her four teammates gasp.

"Hermes!" Sarah clapped her hands together.

Smirking, Aleta put her hand on her hips. "I guess I'm not the only thing with wings they let in here."

The messenger god chuckled. "I am elated to see all of you. It has been far too long."

Brandon took a few steps forward. "Is this about…"

Holding up his hand, Hermes shook his head. "I am afraid I do not have news about your father. I wish I did. But, I do have something to tell you. Please sit."

Quinn stood in the back of the meeting area. Dan looked back and smiled to himself. She cared as much about his father as anyone could.

"Someone who wishes to do great harm upon you has a plan that I fear will bring devastation." Hermes paused to collect himself. "My powers in the mortal realm are limited, so I can only appear when I gather up the energy to do so, like now, or when I am summoned. Unlike your father, who has tethers to the mortal world, I do not. It is that which allows him to stay here. We gods were not expected to live outside of Olympos for long periods. My brother's love for you all, and his wife, have provided that anchor."

"Forgive me, Hermes. But, what does this have to do with this… devastation, as you put it?"

"I am getting to that, Danelos. I was invoked by my son, Autolycos, who then spoke aloud his thoughts, not realizing that I could actually hear him, and it was only because he had called upon me that I can tell you what I heard. He has vengeance planned against your father, and I believe it involves attacking something you all hold dear. He thinks Apollo has sequestered himself away willingly, and by drawing him out, Autolycos would then have the opportunity he seeks. Be ever on your guard. My son is a crafty one."

"I vaguely remember hearing about him, Hermes. What did my father do to him?"

Hermes leaned forward. "I am uncertain, Brandon. I was invoked inside a shrine, and powerful wards were cast to seal it, so I don't know where I was or, better yet, where Autolycos is. I wish I knew more. My son and I have been estranged for a long, long time. As soon as I learned of this, I knew I had to tell you. Be careful. As the son of a trickster god, he has many talents. He can appear as anyone at will."

"Can he become anything other than people?" Aleta glanced at Brandon but directed her question at Hermes.

"That I do not know. He has other skills, though. He has a honeyed tongue and can beguile those who are weak-willed. He will not attack you directly. Against even just one of you, he would not succeed, especially you both." He looked at Dan and Brandon. "He will strike those who cannot fight for themselves."

"So, we wait? There's no scrying we can do? No Olympeian locator spell?"

"Aleta, trust me when I say that Autolycos has hidden himself well in this world. If he has not been seen or heard of until now, then he can stay hidden."

Aleta let out a combined sigh and grunt. "So, we wait."

From across the room, Dan made eye contact with his uncle, and Hermes nodded. As if she could sense that communication, Quinn invited the team to join her at her desk to relay some intel about Akmon's current mission. Dan commented he would join them in a moment. Brandon hesitated, but Dan's expression conveyed it was okay.

"That liaison of yours is as crafty as I am. How does she sense things like that?" Hermes smiled and shook his head.

"It's a gift, I'd imagine. I didn't want to speak with you about Quinn, uncle."

"I know. You want to know how fares Olympos."

Dan shook his head and smiled.

He continued. "I have some intuition as well. Anyway, Zeus is… calmer. Like a potted plant, he stays in his throne lost in thought. I fear not even the *Moirae* know what thoughts go through the mind of Zeus Keraunios."

"Well, I'd imagine since he's *not* the Thunderer right now would frustrate him." Dan leaned back in the leather chair, put one leg over his knee, and rubbed his chin.

"He did live without that for a year. It is not for the loss of his thunderbolt that he broods. He knows he is not destined to be without it. Danelos… he is the self-anointed king of Olympos, the sovereign of the gods, and he is impotent to help his son. I have tried to communicate with him on many occasions. It *is* one of my talents. But, I cannot loosen my father's tongue. Hera has been just as fruitful."

Dan furrowed his brow and pushed out his lower lip. "Hmm. I have never known my grandfather to be so…"

"Depressed." Hermes put his hands behind his curly-locked head. "I am not a healer of the mind, nephew. I know not what will pull my father from this. It is as if he has found himself in his own Tartaros."

Dan sat up, planting both feet on the floor, tapping his fist on the table.

"That's it! Who better to speak about places of torment than Hades? Will you speak with him?"

Hermes nodded. "Hmm, that might work. That Hades does not visit Olympos would be enough reason for him to seek his brother out. Plus, Hades can speak of what his adopted son, Aristeides, has been doing to help your father. Danelos, that was an inspired idea."

"When you're descended of Coeos and Phoebe, intellect runs in the family. I do have my moments." He grinned. Then, he placed one of his hands on that of Hermes and lost his mirth. "Do tell me what happens."

With a gentle nod and wink, the messenger god vanished.

Brandon sat down next to his brother who had resumed his pensive look.

"Everything okay?"

Dan snapped out of his distraction. "Eh? Yeah, I think so. I'll tell you over dinner. Let's get the others and go grab Thai."

They passed by Quinn's desk, and Dan chuckled.

"You're a piece of work." He tapped her desk.

She was busy at her console, but replied, smiling, "I know. Enjoy your dinner. Brandon invited me, but I need to finish some things."

The office door clicked shut, and Hermes appeared at her desk.

"You know more than you're letting on." She slid her fingers across the glass, tapping occasionally.

"You *are* good. And, perhaps I do. No sense in giving them information that may not help them. They need to remain focused. So... how did you know—"

"What? That you were here or that you know more?" Quinn raised her eyebrow and smiled. "To quote someone wise... it *is* one of my talents."

Between Thessaly and Macedonia, in Greece, sits its tallest mountain—Mount Olympos—at just under 10,000 feet. Mountain climbers have tried, since ancient times, to scale this majesty, hoping to reach the ethereal home of the gods, but finding themselves disappointed when they simply see a snow-capped peak that overlooks the surrounding range. One would think that accomplishment alone would be worth celebrating, but when the magic of the gods seems within reach or the hope that it is, anything less can be unsatisfying. No mortal had ever crossed from the mountain of stone to that of divinity. Natural laws held no command over the marble hewn by Gaea, and hallways intertwined in ways no mortal eye could reason. Nestled at the center of the holy sanctuary, the throne room lay open to the sky with only columns forming a boundary between the seats of the gods and the clouds. The largest carved seat belonged to Zeus, one which he slouched in, his arms lying limp on the eagle-headed armrests. His crown hung on the corner of the back of the throne itself.

Beyond the columns flew eagles, hawks, owls, sparrows, and a myriad of other avian creatures who had the heavens as their domain. Helios' sun brightened the airy milieu for them, but it did not dare permeate the space around the sky god. A deep yet soft voice echoed in the chamber, one these halls had not heard for a long time.

"Be wary of the shadows, brother. Like a Siren, they can lull you into their thrall."

Hades, with silent footsteps, stepped up the dais to his brother's throne. With a heavy sigh, he took Hera's chair.

"Your view is so… small. The heavens do not compare to the Fields of Asphodel or the dark purple of the Vale of Mourning."

Among the birds that flitted about, occasionally Pegasus would soar past, neighing as if to express glee. On the other side of the mountain, gryphons nested, and the plaintive cries of the hatchlings could be heard across the skies when the other birds fell silent.

Hades continued. "He is in Gaea's care, brother. She will let no harm come to him."

Zeus didn't reply. He simply stared, glassy-eyed, outward.

"Aristeides works tirelessly to help him mend his mind. I have never known a mortal to be so determined on behalf of a god."

Kronos' youngest child had taken on the pallor of marble, and one might even have thought that he had become a part of the throne itself if not for the soft fluttering of his hoary beard in the breeze that dared waft through the chamber. Hades remained silent for a time, either watching the birds or the fire pit that smoldered, sleeping until its mistress Hesteia would rouse it for a purpose. He left Hera's seat and meandered through the other thrones, his fingers brushing the cool stone as he passed by each. When he reached his, one which he never used, he flashed back to his year of mortality and how he'd longed to be among his brethren, even sitting in that very chair crafted painstakingly by Hephæstos. What he'd gained and lost during that time could fill tomes, and the heartache of not being around his beloved Persephone rose to the surface for a moment, and his icy ichor grew even colder for a mere moment. He understood loss. He had felt Ari's loss when Timaios became a shade. That man had been his only mortal friend. It seemed only fitting that Hades should adopt his son. It filled part of the emptiness, but it could never appease it entirely. When he reached Apollo's golden seat directly across from Zeus and Hera's, the underworld's lord squinted at its radiance. Hades looked down the hall to his brother who had done or said nothing since he arrived. He had to change that.

He sat on Apollo's throne.

At first, Zeus didn't do anything. But, then, he sat up, his thick hands gripping the armrests. In the past, filaments of lightning would arc across his body, signaling that the worst was about to come. But, at this moment, without that power, his eyes burned bright red like lava.

"Do not dare..." Zeus started at a normal tone, but by the time he reached the last word, his voice echoed throughout the skies, with the birds and clouds disappearing.

Hades remained unmoved. Rather, he reclined against the finely sculpted gold, the barest hint of a smile emerging.

Once more, Zeus hurled his words as he would a thunderbolt, and the throne room shook from the stentorian assault. This time, each utterance carried a percussive element that Mankind wouldn't be able to ignore. When Hades didn't budge, Zeus rose to his feet. His eyes locked on his brother, Olympos' king taking calculated steps. Substantive fists clenched, he descended the dais. By the time he reached the floor, that last step shook the chamber.

"If you do not move..."

Hades' smile lay hidden in his dark beard. From behind Zeus' throne, Hera emerged, but Hades shook his head ever so slightly, and the queen retreated to the shadows. This was a conflict between them and them alone.

"Brother, what will you do? You have remained in that chair for, what? Months by mortal standards?" Hades kept his tone level yet insistent. "Your tantrum... well, a *mortal* woman had to take your power away before you all but destroyed Gaea."

Zeus had been taking measured steps until Hades' last comment, and then he stopped.

"Does the world mean that little to you? You lived among them as I did. It changed me, Zeus. I know it changed you too."

Looking away, Olympos' king closed his eyes and took a deep breath. He moved to the center of the chamber and sat on the ring of stones surrounding the fire.

"Turn and face me, brother. You bear this burden alone."

"He is my *son*, Hades."

"Not to diminish your pain, but you have many. Why is Apollo so different?"

Zeus turned toward the glowing embers.

"Of the many, he is the only one who has taught me how to be... better."

Hades leaned forward, raising an eyebrow.

"The day Lismonia came for us, we departed this holy place for the mortal realm, at my son's behest. I indulged him because he seemed so impassioned. I never thought much of the experience." Zeus sighed. "I... misjudged."

Hades' eyes widened.

"I do not think I have ever heard you use that word before."

Zeus glowered. "That year would be an infinitesimal moment in my existence. I began it with indifference, but ended with comprehension."

"You shared little of that time with us, brother. Hera spoke at length about her own experiences in Japan, but she told us that we would have to ask you about yours. You are not known for your reticence."

"When I returned to Olympos to confront our father millennia ago, I spoke with our mother about what had transpired since she had placed me with Amaltheia. Rhea told me how I was destined to take Olympos back from the Titans, kill our father, and then reign over all of Gaea. The prophecy would be fulfilled by me and me alone. When you and the others joined me, you looked to me for guidance, even though I was the youngest."

"And, you led us to glorious victory, brother. I remember well. I still bear the scars of that war. What is your point?" Hades' irritation started showing. He didn't like to remember the Titanomachia.

"My point, brother, is that from that moment on, I had to lead. The *Moirae* would not be swayed, and even though I asked them to switch my fate with yours since I felt you would be a better leader, they were unmoved. So, I stayed on that path. I decided from that moment forward that I would be the king you needed me to be, despite my headstrong ways and unquenchable libido."

Hades exhaled as if he had held his breath. "I... I had no idea you wanted *me* to lead. But, Zeus, despite wherever your path has taken you, you have been that sovereign Olympos needed."

"Did you ever wonder what would have happened if you had drawn the longest straw? How arrogant we all were! You, Poseidon, and me, drawing straws as if assigning dominion over the world was a child's game."

"To us, it was. Our priggishness knew no bounds. And, yes. I have thought about the straws. I drew the shortest one, if you recall."

"Are you still harboring resentment?"

Hades laughed. "No. The underworld is where I need to be. After my sojourn in the mortal realm, that fact was reinforced even more. I seek not to have the crown of Olympos on my brow no more than I should hold the trident of the seas in my grip. We are all where we need to be. This is why I came to see you."

Zeus took steps toward his brother. "I have been a fool."

Hades was about to speak when Zeus stopped walking.

"Before you fervently concur, allow me to finish. I did not regard Python as a threat. I had been watching his movements, but I was unaware of the strain on Apollo's mind. Had that not been the case, I believe my son could have vanquished that serpent once more. Of all the gods, only Apollo carried the weight of two lifetimes with him, and that was too much to ask of any immortal. I am surprised, yet proud, that he lasted as long as he did."

"Your son's fortitude has been tested before, and he has been victorious. Apollo shall overcome this setback as well. He has allies."

"Yes. One of whom was able to remove my power. Clever girl."

"Indeed, brother. She should not be underestimated."

"So, this Aristeides… He is now your son?"

Hades explained everything he knew about Ari's father, Timaios, their conversations, his death, and how Ari became a part of Danelos' life. When he told Zeus about Ari's motivation to help Apollo, Zeus's face softened a little.

"Another age of heroes has come, Zeus. Between Danelos, Kidemonas, Sarah, and Aleta, plus Ari and Esteban, I have hope that the world we once helped nurture may yet thrive. I hear even Hephaestos' son, Akmon, has joined their ranks as well."

"He has. These young heroes keep *my* faith alive, brother. If not for their actions, and their connection to Olympos, I fear that we would melt into the ether. My soul has been touched by the mortals, and for the first time in my entire existence, I understand them."

Hades nodded. "I concur. The underworld is where I choose to be, with Persephone by my side, but I do see how mortality has its own divinity and eminence."

As above, so below.

The realms of Olympos and Hades share brothers whose do-minion looks out over an expansive panorama of immortal lives—the sovereign gods on high, the airy *skia*, or shades, adrift beneath. What connects them both comes from more than their parentage. When the Moirae spun the cords of the gods, they didn't know what would spring forth from the loom. They only knew it would bring about change. The world remains in flux, always shifting, always morphing into something else.

Zeus turned toward the throne of abalone, carved with swirls and eddies, encrusted with coral.

"What of our brother? How does he feel?"

"Poseidon does what he always does. He remains the bridge between us. You are the bringer of the thunderbolt. I, the bringer of shadow. The fluidity of his realm allows us to be who we are. We sons of Kronos govern because Fate has decreed it so. Through our power, the heroes walk their path." Hades stopped for a moment. "When you forgot your place, Zeus, and let grief cloud your judgment—"

"I almost destroyed everything. I know." Zeus returned to his throne. "I am not ready to resume my role as the bringer of the thunderbolt. I know that now. I need to allow myself to feel that which mortals feel until I can move through it and emerge clear. Thank you for helping me through my sorrow, brother. Per-haps we can speak again… more often."

Hades nodded, this time with a reverence not toward his brother, but the king of Olympos, before vanishing into black smoke. Zeus again descended the dais and stood by his son's throne.

"This I swear to you, Phoebos Apollo. I will listen to that which mortality has taught me and let it guide my hand hence-forth."

As within, so without.

That which Zeus thought before, wrestling with his anger and grief, manifested itself in the full power of the storm. What raged inside his mind also raged outside it. To be that which you feel is to succumb to your heart. But, the heart is a powerful part of any being, god or mortal. When one understands the rage within, he can tame the rage without. In Zeus' case, he needed Aleta's help because, despite his omnipotence, he didn't know how to move beyond his immortal heart while feeling such a deeply mortal emo-tion. Gods don't grieve. Not really. They act out when insulted or disrespected, but comprehending loss doesn't come easily to them.

Zeus headed out of the throne room, but just before he left, he uttered, "There must always be balance."

25 | A CITY BESIEGED

B lack marble walls with the pristine sheen of a stagnant sea rose into darkness, enclosing the boardroom of PANOP-TES where a slab of the same material sat in its center, surrounded by twelve black leather chairs. Torchlight introduced both light and shadow. Along the back wall, etched into the marble, was the feather emblem surrounded by the words, in Ancient Greek, *Argus Panoptes knows all and protects the worthy*.

A dozen men and women gathered around the table, six to a side, garbed in standard-issue attire, all in black: turtleneck, pants, belt, and boots. Each of them bore the small feather icon branded to the left wrist and wore a black matte finished wristwatch on the right. Built into the watch was a transponder that let each agent wear a disguise with a voice command. It wasn't more than an illusion, unlike Otto who could change his form, but it gave each agent the ability to blend into any environment or stand out as needed.

A pocket door slid open, and Otto stepped into the room, his hands locked behind his back. All twelve rose in unison, saluting with index and middle fingers in a V-shape placed over the right eye, palm outward. With a single nod from Otto, they returned to their chairs.

"The time of reckoning is upon us. We draw out the son of Zeus. Are all the preparations made?"

An agent raised his finger and nodded.

"Outstanding. How long?"

The same agent replied, "Six hours."

"And the agents who deployed the measure?" Otto raised an eyebrow.

"Self-immolation. No loose ends."

Otto lowered himself into his chair. "Now… we wait. Apollo will surely surface."

Throngs of people, including students, poured into the McKim entrance of The Boston Public Library, many of them headed for the Bates Hall Memorial Reception in honor of library benefactors since the library's opening in 1894. This fundraiser happened every five years, and it brought in artists, authors, professors, and business professionals from all over the world. Bates Hall, part of the Central Building of the library, was renowned for its coffered ceiling and arched windows, dating back to 1895, and was restored in 2005.

At 9:00 a.m, a bomb exploded in the courtyard. The debris flew outward, sending chunks of the building onto the surrounding Boylston, Dartmouth, and Blagden Streets, as well as damaging much of the other side of the building. Emergency crews arrived within minutes, assessing the damage and tending to the wounded. Bodies of those unable to flee protruded from the shattered stone, blood trickling along the ground and splattered on the rubble. Boston Police established a perimeter around the blast site, letting only emergency and police vehicles near the building. A television news van arrived, its crew pouring onto the scene. The woman reporter, a spitfire at 5'5" with wavy salt-and-pepper hair and a defiant stride, located the lead police officers on the scene as well as firefighters, library personnel, and witnesses, not stopping until she had what she needed. Within fifteen minutes, she went live.

"Good morning. This is Etta Dulce from WDDB news reporting live from the Boston Public Library Central building on Boylston Street. A bomb exploded at 9 a.m. in the courtyard, and witnesses on the street say that they heard a massive explosion and saw the walls of the library explode outward with smoke billowing from the blast. The Memorial Reception for benefactors of the library was being held in Bates Hall on the second floor. Sources from the library say approximately four hundred attendees were in the hall at the time of the explosion…"

She blinked as her eyes began to water, turned her head to compose herself, and exhaled sharply.

"Dammit…" she muttered.

Etta stood a little taller and continued.

"We don't yet know how many people were in the building as a whole, but as more information becomes known, we'll be sure to share it. At this time, the names of the victims aren't being released to the public out of respect to the families. This is Etta Dulce, live from WDDB news."

The cameraman signaled when they were off the air. Netty took off her tortoiseshell glasses and dabbed her eyes with a tissue, shaking her head. All around her, emergency crews ushered bodies, injured or in body bags, on gurneys toward ambulances. Sirens wailed everywhere, with a cacophony of shrill voices adding to the disarray. Etta leaned against the news truck, staring up at the sky, a trickle of tears leaving a trail on her cheeks.

"Why… why…" Her words escaped, like a hushed breath.

Next to her, a woman spoke.

"We don't always know why these things happen, but people like you, who care, make a difference, Ms. Dulce."

Shaken from her contemplation, Etta's woeful eyes widened.

"Woo woo! You're Talon. From that task force… Gaea."

With white wings and silver javelin, Talon let out a tiny smile.

"You're an Amazon, right? You are freaking awesome! I know you're here to help, so I won't hold you up, but I want to interview you." She pointed at Talon and adjusted her clothes.

Talon winked. "Maybe later." She spread her wings and leaped into the air toward the fracas. "Just keep doing what you're doing. You have the heart of an Amazon, and it shows in your work."

Surveying the scene, Talon flapped her way around a few city blocks to ensure there was no other damage. At a gathering of police cars, she spied a familiar man and alighted nearby.

"Agent D'Alessio!"

Finishing a conversation with his colleagues, directing them to various places in the area, Task Force: Kappa agent Mike D'Alessio turned to see Talon with her wings folded behind her back. He sipped his coffee before giving her his characteristic smirk.

"Figured you'd show up sooner or later, Doc. Anything from above?"

She shook her head. "The explosion was largely contained to the library. Buildings across the street on all sides suffered cracks and broken windows, but the main body count is limited here." Talon folded her arms. "Anything you can tell me from your end? Boston PD is on scene. What brings you out here?"

He walked her to the yellow crime scene tape that blocked ingress from anyone not tied to law enforcement and pointed toward the McKim Entrance.

"Cameras on all sides of the building have shown nothing out of the ordinary for the last 48 hours. Our CSI team is going through the footage now. Whoever placed that explosive knew what to do to avoid being seen. The bomb squad is in what's left of the courtyard now to find the type of device that could do this much damage. Just spoke with my lead agent, and they're going in with IMS tech to see if they can narrow things down a little. As for what brings me out here?" He scratched the back of his head. "The son of a certain U.N. diplomat was reported as being part of the reception in Bates Hall, and you know what that means."

Talon sighed. "Unfortunately. It's not just a local crime scene. This one has global implications. Does the ambassador think her son was the target?"

Agent D'Alessio slugged the rest of his coffee. "What do *you* think?"

She gazed off at the chaos. "Well, I'll let you do your job, but if you find anything that fits my line of work, you'll let me know?"

"You got it. Anything looks like a minotaur or a unicorn, I'll call you." He winked.

"Smartass." She took off and flew toward the building to see if she could assist. If Task Force: Gaea agent Talon couldn't do anything, Dr. Aleta Halston might be able to.

From near the Old South Church, across from the bombing site, a man in a houndstooth sport coat and glasses crossed Boylston Street and, avoiding law enforcement with the stealth of a shadow, found his way inside the ruined building.

Agent D'Alessio received a call on his radio to enter the crime scene, specifically the remains of the courtyard. Boston PD had cordoned off a path for official personnel to maneuver without disturbing the main area, and when he emerged in what once was a serene outdoor café, he gasped at the devastation. The fountain that once proudly displayed a bronze replica of MacMonnies'

statue, *Bacchante and Infant Faun*, was gone, along with the arcades of arches and columns. Little of the Central Building remained at all. Agent D'Alessio found his team.

"Agent Blake, what do we know?"

A man in his early forties, Boston Blake had examined more bomb scenes than any agent in this task force. What drove him to find answers was something simple—the truth. With every clue he would find, he would push harder until he had learned as much as the evidence would allow.

"Very little." Agent Blake crouched down with his ion mobility spectrometer. "Agent Patterson and I have located the detonation point here, but IMS readings are sketchy at best."

"There's barely any residue at all." Agent Patterson handed Agent D'Alessio a print-out from the IMS. This makes no sense. Even with the extreme heat of a bomb with this blast radius, there would have to be residue, especially at the cellular level."

"Your search for the truth has reached an obstacle, then." Agent D'Alessio returned the paper. "Keep at it. No residue? That's just impossible."

Agent Blake fiddled with the dials on his IMS.

"We're assuming this is a normal bomb. Only a handful of devices out there can cause this much damage without leaving a trace. We'll figure it out."

"Remember, boss, truth is golden. When it shines, we'll see it." Agent Patterson smiled.

Brian Patterson, like Boston Blake, believed in the power of truth, and that it would show itself with the right motivation. Both agents had started with Kappa around the same time, and they'd gained the reputation as relentless investigators. No dead-end or obstacle discouraged them.

"Yeah, well…" Agent D'Alessio checked his watch. "It's almost 10 a.m., and I'd like some answers soon. We have news crews out there hungry for this story, and I want answers before *they* find them."

Leaving his brownstone, a man strolled down Essex Street, waving and smiling at his neighbors enjoying their coffee on the next stoop over. Raising his head to the sky, he inhaled deeply and closed his eyes, taking in the morning sunshine as it shined off the mirror-like windows of the surrounding buildings. His phone buzzed, and he glanced at a reminder for an appointment an hour

later with the Children's Museum to unveil a new wing that focused on children's contributions to the city of Boston. Later in
the day, he was volunteering at the V.A. Hospital in West Rox-
bury. Just as he was about to pass a bagel shop, he raised an eyebrow and popped inside.

"I'll just work it off at the gym later," he muttered to himself.

A few minutes passed, explosions echoed throughout Boston, raining down shattered glass everywhere. The earth shook,
cracking buildings and asphalt, and people clambered into the
streets from businesses and apartments. Car alarms blared in a cacophony, and then distant sirens howled, amplifying the entropy.
The man stepped outside and surveyed the chaos when he heard
the shrill cry of a woman followed by the words "Please! Help my
son!" He dropped his bagel and bolted down the street through
throngs of people, scanning the area for the source of the
woman's plea. Half a block down, he saw her, shrieking, bloodied
hands trying to pull on a sign that had fallen from the flower shop
she'd just exited. Beneath the rubble, the man saw tulips, crushed,
and a small hand, unmoving. Pushing on with purpose, he leaped
over a toppled garbage pail and the hood of a parked car to reach
her. As soon as he did, he saw the terror in her eyes, and she
gripped his arm.

"Please! Oh my God, please. My son is under there! Can you
help?"

Putting a hand on her shoulder, the man replied that he
would try and asked her to stand back. He scanned the debris for
the best place to start, and then he located the edge of the sign
covered with crumbled bricks. Crouching, he put his fingers beneath the metal, seeing the boy's lifeless arm on the sidewalk near
his feet. As he pulled up, his brawny frame compensated, the veins
on his muscled arms popping out from the strain. He grunted, and
the metal sign moved about an inch, not enough to reach the boy.
With his eyes clenched shut, the man continued to lift, and when
he heard the mother shriek that she couldn't lose her son, the man
growled and pulled up with everything he had.

"Hurry! Get him out! Not sure how long I can hold this!" He
grunted, bearing the weight.

A passerby helped the woman carefully extricate the boy, and
when he was free, the man dropped the sign and crouched by the
boy who wasn't breathing. First, he checked to make sure there
were no obvious injuries, and then he initiated chest compressions

and checked for breathing. After a few tries, the boy coughed and then cried. The man noticed the boy's arm looked off. He called for an ambulance.

"Ma'am, I know you want to hold your son, but his arm's broken. From what I can see, he should be okay until the paramedics arrive. Here." He removed his hooded sweatshirt and placed it over the boy. "He may go into shock. It'll be okay."

Leaping onto the scene, Aegis met them both, asking what happened and if everyone was okay.

"There was an explosion, and-and this man came out of nowhere. He saved my Charlie's life." She couldn't hold back the tears and cradled her son's head.

"You're Aegis, from Task Force: Gaea. Wow. It's an honor to meet you, sir." He gripped Aegis' hand.

"It seems the honor's mine. You did a great thing…"

"Dustin. Dustin Dorough. And, hey, I just heard a cry for help and came running. It's what anyone would do. I'm just glad the boy will be okay."

"Considering the damage throughout the city, I don't know when the ambulance will arrive, so I'll take him to the hospital." Aegis drew his sword.

He opened a portal to Children's Hospital and encouraged the mother to go through it. Aegis positioned Charlie so he could lift him without exacerbating his injuries and then turned toward Dustin.

"Hey, thanks for what you did. Just be careful, hero." Aegis nodded.

Smirking, Dustin saluted Aegis just as he passed through the glowing gateway.

As soon as the moment passed, he went inside the florist to make sure everyone was okay before checking other businesses on the street. This would certainly be a day when the citizens of Boston would have their resolve tested, and perhaps others would rise to the challenge, just like this young man. One could only hope.

Another Task Force: Kappa crew arrived and spread across the area to check for other casualties as well as examine the debris. Agents set up a perimeter of yellow caution tape and took readings of the area. One radioed Agent D'Alessio with the same results as Agent Blake—no residue. They were instructed to remain on-site and record as much data as possible on the off chance they could find one iota of evidence.

Sitting on a stoop across from the flower shop, the man in the houndstooth sport coat and glasses glanced over the top of a newspaper. Again, with airy maneuverability, he sought out the debris.

Talon soared above the streets of North Boston, multiple plumes of gray smoke from bombs streaking the afternoon sky. Local firefighters and police had streets cordoned off, keeping the crowds away from the most damaged areas, but the chaos was growing. In a situation like this, her lightning wouldn't help. It would actually make things worse if it struck in the wrong spot. Even though she had taken Zeus' control of the storm from him, she didn't suddenly gain his command over it. The best she could do would be to do surveillance and help those in need.

She crossed the expanse toward Boston Harbor until she circled the aquarium and headed back toward the city. Only three bombs had gone off in this area, and the streets had been cleared of civilians, but as she was about to pass over the Old North Church, she heard a frantic voice. Her eyes picked up a brownstone on Battery Street that had partly crumbled to the sidewalk. Hovering just above the debris, she found the source of the voice—a man was trying to push a piece of a lintel off his leg.

"Hang on, Nikki!" He grunted as he pushed at the stone. "Are the boys okay?"

A muffled woman's voice replied.

"Thank God. Just hang on! I'll be… right… there." Again he pushed, but he didn't have the leverage to move it. "Come on! Move, damn it!"

"Allow me." Talon gripped the massive stone with her feet and, flapping hard, pulled it off the man's leg. She called into her wristcom. "Ambulance needed at the corner of Battery and Hanover, Quinn. I've found a man, mid-forties, with an injured leg, and there are others inside the building."

"Dispatched," replied Quinn. "It might take a few."

Talon put her attention on the man's injury.

"Sir, hold still. I need to look at your leg."

"Don't worry about me! My wife and kids are in there!" He tried to move closer to the collapsed entrance.

"Sir, what's your name? What are their names? If you move, you'll make things worse."

"Can you get them out?" He pushed himself a little closer to the rubble with his good leg, but when he couldn't get farther, he growled. "I'm Rusty Trimble. My wife's name is Nikki. Andrew and Tyler are my boys."

Talon crouched. "Look, your leg is broken, Rusty, but you're not bleeding much, thankfully. The bone didn't break the skin. Stay still until the paramedics arrive. I'll see what I can do about your family."

She assessed where the doorway would have been.

"Don't you have lightning powers or something? Can't you just blast open a hole?" Rusty, despite Talon's warning, tried to get himself closer.

"Not unless I want the whole building coming down." She spied a window a few apartments over on the second floor that had broken glass, but the frame was undamaged. "Nikki, if you can hear me, let me know if you and the boys can move from where you are."

Rusty's wife confirmed that she and her sons could.

"Go to the second-floor landing, if you can, and get to the window."

An ambulance howled a few blocks away. Talon surveyed to ensure it could arrive without a problem. Fortunately, people had evacuated the area, and the street was free of debris.

"Rusty, just relax. It'll be over soon. Hopefully, that's for us. Are you okay?"

"I'll be fine. Just help my family." He had propped himself up on his arms, his bloody hands pressing onto the sidewalk.

Talon kept watch on the window. "How old are your boys?"

"Andrew's eleven. He's built like a football safety. Tyler's five." His voice dropped. "They're my whole world."

She smiled. "You'll see them soon. How did you get trapped outside?"

"When we heard the explosions, I ran out here to take a better look. I was just about to go back inside when a tremor rattled the building, collapsing the doorway and part of the first floor. I didn't know Nikki and the boys were fine until just before you arrived. I thought they could leave through the back door of the building, but she said the parking lot heaved during the tremor, pushing the asphalt up against the door."

"Where's your apartment?"

"On the fifth floor. I guess the stairwell's clear so they could make it down." He stopped. "Shouldn't they have reached the third floor by now?"

At that moment, they heard Nikki's voice.

"Up here!"

Scanning the building, Talon couldn't see them until she looked straight up.

"They're on the roof!" Rusty pointed.

Flying up to them, and hovering, Talon saw that they were all right, except for a few scrapes. Andrew and Tyler clung to their mother.

"Any injuries? Why didn't you go to the third-floor window?"

The boys just stared at this woman with wings.

"No, we're fine. How's Rusty?" She tried to look over the edge, but the boys held onto her. "The front stairs were damaged, so we took the back ones up. There were no windows there, though."

"He has a broken leg, but he'll be fine. I'm going to fly you down one at a time."

She set down on the roof.

"Who's first? It's perfectly safe."

Nikki got eye-level with the boys. "It's okay. You can go with her. I'll be right down with you."

Her youngest, Tyler, approached Talon, examining her wings.

"Do you want to touch them? Would that help?"

She extended a white wing, and he brushed it with his palm, giggling.

"See? It's real." She crouched. "Put your arms around my neck."

Tyler looked back at his mom before complying, also wrapping his legs around Talon's waist.

"Ready? We'll be down in just a moment."

With careful attention and an arm under Tyler, she lifted off and brought him down. The first thing Tyler did was run over to his father who immediately hugged his son.

"I'm so glad you're not hurt." Tears stained his son's shirt as Rusty pulled him close.

"Dad, that was so cool."

Rusty chuckled. "I'm sure it was, kiddo. I'm sure it was."

A moment later, Andrew joined them. Rather than being shaken by what had happened, the boys were just elated to have flown down with Talon. Then, the sound of stone cracking prompted Talon to leap skyward. As she reached the roof, the floor was buckling, and Nikki held onto the edge. The center of the roof was caving in, so Talon had to plan this correctly. Swooping from behind, she put her arms under Nikki's and lifted straight up just as the building collapsed inward. She couldn't see if it would affect Rusty and the boys, but she couldn't get Nikki to safety and attend to them, too. With Nikki across the street, Talon turned to see that the others weren't where they had last been. At first, she thought they'd been buried by the rest of the building, but then she heard Andrew shouting.

"We're over here!"

All three of them, also across the street, sat on the steps of another brownstone.

"How did you get here?" Talon checked them all for injuries.

Nikki wrapped her arms around her husband and the boys.

"Fear." Rusty smiled awkwardly. "With the building cracking, I tried pushing myself away and told the boys to run, but they each grabbed an arm and pulled until I could stand on my good leg and hobble over here. If not for them, I don't think I could have made it."

He tousled Andrew's hair and winked at Tyler. An ambulance pulled up, sirens blaring, and paramedics brought gurneys and medical supplies. Nikki and the boys would ride along with Rusty in the ambulance. Just before they left, Talon gave the boys each a feather from her wing.

"I want you both to remember that you're heroes. You helped get your dad to safety. Thank you for your bravery." She smiled one more time before taking to the skies, waving.

Watching from behind a parked car a block down, the man in the houndstooth coat brought the glasses down and scanned the scene, but hid in shadow when he heard the squeal of tires.

A black van pulled up, and Agent D'Alessio stepped out with Agents Blake and Patterson as well as three others who went off in different directions to investigate. Looking up, he shielded his eyes as he watched Talon head back toward downtown Boston. Smirking, he shook his head.

"Agent D'Alessio!" Agent Patterson handed another IMS readout to him. "This one's different. We're trying variations on the scanner settings, and this time, we registered something metallic, but nothing we've ever seen before."

"So, microscopic trace material. What do you mean you've never seen it before?"

Agent Patterson pointed to the print-out. "Most carbon steel is made of iron and carbon, plus other components. In this composite analysis, we have iron, carbon, other known compounds, plus an unknown element. We've tried isolating it, but our database can't tag it."

Agent D'Alessio huffed. "Ours can't, but I know whose can."

○━━━○

Floating on the air currents, Aether propelled herself toward Boston College, another victim of the bombing. From high above, she saw the carnage that the explosion had caused, people scurrying out of buildings, gathering with others, and some sitting on the ground, in tears, comforting one another. She set herself down by Stokes Hall where campus police and emergency personnel had gathered to assess who should go to a hospital. Residual smoke from Gasson Hall, a building now in ruins, filled the sky. Attending to those she could, guiding the injured toward the paramedics, she saw a young woman running around, in tears. As soon as she saw Aether, she ran up to her.

"Can you help me? Please! I think my friends are stuck in Devlin Hall. The building collapsed, and I can't find them."

"Okay, calm down…"

"Sybrina. I'm sorry. I'm just so freaked out about this."

Aether took the girl's hands and reassured her she would do everything possible. By the time they arrived at Devlin Hall, small crowds had gathered, some shouting names of people they believed to be inside. The steeple had crumbled, pieces of it strewn across O'Neill Plaza, crushing the main entry of the building. Most windows had cracks or had popped out from the nearby explosion, almost destroying a Gothic Revival college landmark that had existed since 1924. Groups of students and school employees huddled together, comforting one another from the loss of the neighboring Gasson Hall, another cornerstone of the college since 1913. Emergency crews ushered away those in need of medical attention and those for whom that attention was no longer necessary. A dark, emotional pall shadowed this majestic hall of learning, and Aether lost her breath as she took it all in.

"They're in there!" Sybrina pointed, her finger shaking.

"You're sure," Aether replied, but her eyes were everywhere else.

"I mean, I *think* so. The last time I saw them, they'd gone to work one of the gallery exhibits."

"Stay here. Let me take a look. What're their names?"

"Thomas Coffin and Brett Rudolph." Sybrina clasped her hands together, wringing them.

Leaping into the air, Aether moved above the campus to avoid the cracked plaza, alighting by the west side of the building, and checked for an entry point to Devlin with the least amount of wreckage.

"Thomas! Brett! Can you hear me?" She moved some of the fallen brickwork with a gesture, careful not to affect the building itself since she didn't know what might cause the structure to crumble.

Aside from the background noise, she heard nothing. The back of the hall had fallen as well, and Aether put her hand to her chest.

"Blessed Gaea…"

With calculated movements, she cleared blocks away. As soon as she determined she could move larger amounts, she took care of a swath of stone, calling for the men. Nothing. Through the front windows, since most of the inner walls had fallen, she spied the plaza and Sybrina, sitting on the ground, rocking, staring at the building. Through the remains of a hallway, Aether took careful steps until she saw a man's body lying beneath a shattered wall. His eyes open, glasses broken on his face, he didn't move. She crouched down and closed his eyes, taking off his tortoiseshell glasses. On the other side of the rubble, another man, also dead. His gray suit was soaked with blood, and part of his head was crushed. As soon as she surveyed everything, she returned to Sybrina who, seeing Aether's pained expressed, burst into tears.

"No… No!" She then wailed even louder.

"I-I'm so sorry." Aether knelt, cradling Sybrina against her. "There was nothing I could do. Do you want these? I found them on one of the men." She held out the glasses.

Sybrina cocked her head, wiping away her tears. "Whose are those?"

"I assume either Thomas or Brett's. They were the only two left inside."

Shaking her head vigorously, Sybrina sat up. "They don't wear these kinds of glasses. What did the other man look like?"

"A gray suit—"

A shriek erupted from Sybrina as she put her hands to her mouth. She started giggling and crying simultaneously. "Those weren't my friends." She hugged Aether.

"Wait. What? What do they look like?"

The description Aether received looked nothing like the men she found. In his mid-thirties, Thomas was a stocky, bald man with a reddish-brown beard—Sybrina called it a rainbow beard— with brown eyes. He was wearing a steampunk vest with black and crimson damask stitching over a black dress shirt, a black kilt, and calf-high black boots. At the other end of the spectrum, Brett, also in his mid-thirties, had blue eyes and wore thin-framed glasses, and was wearing a striped polo shirt with jeans as well as running shoes.

"Your friends may have escaped the building before it collapsed then. I saw no trace of anyone dressed like that, and I would have noticed Thomas' clothes." She smirked.

"They said they would call me if they were leaving Devlin." Sybrina tried calling them, but no answer. "That's odd. Of the two, Thomas usually picks up."

Aether shrugged. "Things have been kind of crazy. I'm sure they will call when they can. Maybe they're stuck somewhere with no signal. These buildings sometimes inhibit phone use."

"The basement! Did you try the basement?" Sybrina gripped Aether's arm.

"I didn't. Do you think they're down there?" She looked back toward Devlin, and her voice lowered. "The damage is extensive."

"Please check. Please!"

With no outer doors that led to a basement, Aether returned inside. A few hallways later, she did see a doorway that led to a stairwell, but it was crushed. Narrowing her eyes, she sent a block of stone through the door itself, standing ready for any fallout. Through the door opening, she could only see blackness and smell traces of smoke. Calling out for the two men, she thought she heard a response, but had a hard time differentiating it from the noises outside. The stairwell itself sustained severe damage, but she was able to move brick and stone from the building to make a path. At the lower level, the door remained intact, although the cement wall above it sustained cracks. The inner part of the building had collapsed from underneath, showing that the foundation itself was damaged from the explosion in Gasson Hall. Sparks from exposed wires, flickering fluorescent and emergency lights, illuminated an otherwise cavernous part of the substructure. A building of such an age wasn't designed to withstand this kind of attack, even laterally. Again, Aether called out, but no response.

"This doesn't bode well." She whispered to herself.

Down one hall, around piles of concrete and steel, she spied another door to a stairwell. This one led down one more level. She had just touched the door to open it when a tremor rattled the building. These stairs had no major damage, so she made it to the lowest level unhindered.

"Thomas! Brett! Are you down here?"

The halls, like on the floor above, had little to no lighting. She had only gone about ten feet when she heard pounding. At the end of the hall, faint voices came through a sealed door. The ceiling support had fallen, blocking the door itself from opening outward. She leaned at the door and heard what sounded like two men's voices.

"Thomas? Brett?"

"Hey! Yes! This is Thomas! We're stuck in this office. Can you get us out?"

"My name's Aether. Are either of you injured?"

"No, just hungry. And I really have to pee."

"Had you listened to me, Brett, when I told you to go—"

Aether started to raise her voice. "Guys! We can take care of all of that later. Right now, I need you to move back from the door, as far back as you can. Is there anything you can position yourself behind?"

"Um, yeah. A table." Thomas made noises as if he was moving it.

"Get behind it, and don't move until I tell you."

The steel beam was beyond her ability, but the walls weren't. However, if she moved any part of the wall to open a passage, she could destabilize the support. With no real debris to use as a tool, she had one other choice—the floor. Beneath the tile would be a subfloor, and beneath that, foundation, and then earth. Kneeling in front of the beam, she put her palms on the floor and closed her eyes. Concentrating, calling her Quarters, she pushed her mind to where she could surpass the physical building and reach the very ground on which this building was constructed. Normally, she had to have visual contact with an element, but the only element she could actually touch was air, and she couldn't use it. She drew upon her connection with Gaea to connect with the earth, forcing it up through the floor. Aether repeated her meditation. Her eyes burst open, flames fluttering from them, and the tiles cracked as two pillars of solid earth protruded through, pressing against the steel beam. With the element in her view, she pulled it from the ground, creating a platform onto which the beam could rest. It would remain solid as long as she concentrated on it. By undulating the dirt, she could move the beam away from the door.

"Thomas! Brett! Let's go!"

Brett could open the door just enough for them to squeeze through. They crawled under the beam to where Aether was. She released her hold on the dirt, and it collapsed, the beam crashing to the ground.

"You're both okay?"

Thomas clapped his hands together. "Heck yeah, thanks to you!"

Brett couldn't stop looking at her auburn hair and green eyes. "I'll say." He smirked.

Thomas smacked him on the back of the head, and Aether just rolled her eyes.

"You both need to head up to the surface. I'll be right behind you, but I need to secure this first or the whole building will cave in."

Grabbing Brett by the arm, Thomas led them both toward the stairs. Aether gave them enough time to clear the area before using her power to fill the sub-basement with dirt. The space wasn't secure enough to leave where people might find it. She also knew that if she supported the structure, a construction crew might eventually salvage it, even if it meant losing part of the basement.

Sybrina threw her arms around Brett and Thomas, and they explained what happened. She pulled them down to the cement steps, sitting between them, hugging one, then the other, every so often. Not long after, another tremor shook the campus, and the outer walls of Devlin Hall fell inward, sending up clouds of dust and smoke. When it cleared, a massive mountain of debris remained. Aether didn't emerge.

Brett jumped up. "Where is she?"

"Hey, I'm sure she's fine. I mean, she can move earth and stuff."

"Not if she's crushed, Thomas." Brett started to move away, but Sybrina pulled his arm.

"There's nothing you can do." She yanked him to a seated position. "But, I'm sure she's okay. Right?"

Ten minutes passed, and it probably felt like an eternity to them, but a fissure opened just behind them, and Aether climbed out of it. As she got closer to the three, she saw both Thomas and Brett tapping their right legs, almost in unison.

"Hey, are you sure you're all right?"

Sybrina and the others jumped right up, all three taking turns hugging her, with Brett's hug a little longer than the others. Aether explained that, despite her best efforts, the building had sustained too much damage, so she had to let it collapse. The best way out was to create a tunnel away from the building.

"Sorry to have scared you. But, I had it under control. I do have to ask you both, why were you in the sub-basement by yourselves?"

Brett and Thomas gave each other the side-eye, gesturing with their eyebrows that the other should tell her. Finally, Thomas sighed.

"Okay, whatever. We were setting up our next Dragon's Lair campaign. We play with a few friends every week, and I'd wanted to go over some details with Brett."

"And?" Brett hopped on his toes.

"We... um, were talking comic books." Thomas chuckled.

Aether smiled. "You'd fit in with Zodiak. He's a huge fan of role-playing games. All right, since you're both fine, I'm going to see how else I can help local law enforcement here. I leave you both in Sybrina's capable hands." She turned toward the young woman. "Don't let them out of your sight."

Sybrina looped an arm through each man's arm. "No worries about that! Thank you for everything."

"By the way, Thomas, love the outfit." Aether winked.

He grinned. "Thanks! Loving that 1960s catsuit."

Aether ran toward the remains of Gasson Hall, checking in with a group of police officers. This building had been reduced to rubble, they told her, as the site of the explosion, and crews had worked for a few hours already to find any survivors, but little hope remained. The best Aether could do was check on the small groups gathered around, and her powers could do nothing to help give solace to the grieving or the survivors. One of the young women within earshot asked her friends, her voice shaking, why anyone would attack the college. Aether gave herself a panoramic of the scene, taking in the carnage and the rest of the quad within her sights. The windows of the O'Neill Library facing Gasson, despite being shielded by trees, had shattered from the blast wave, but the building itself had sustained no visible damage. Engineers had arrived to survey the building, and Aether made mental notes of those coming and going. It would be evening soon, and the area had been cordoned off to prevent unauthorized access. She would return after dark to do a more extensive investigation without the prying eyes of students or the police. This explosion was one of a dozen across the city, and she would need answers as to who and why.

Seated on a bench out of the reach of the blast area, the man in the houndstooth coat and glasses put down his newspaper and sneaked toward Gasson Hall's remains. Vigilant for law enforcement, he crouched down and touched the rough shards of the stone, rubbing his fingers together. Taking in the destroyed campus, he shook his head and returned to the shadows.

26 | THE ACT OF SAVING

Sitting on the open back of the black van on Battery Street, Agent D'Alessio was working on his third latte of the day while Agents Patterson and Blake pored over the data from the ISM inside the van at their mobile lab. Their back-and-forth in technospeak provided background noise while Agent D'Alessio thought about the current bombings and their possible connection to something more than Task Force: Kappa could handle.

"Anything else you can tell me?" he said aloud, his back to the other agents. "I'd like to have something to tell her when she gets here."

"She's here." Talon made a soft landing in front of him, folding her wings behind her back at which point they disappeared.

"Whoa. I didn't know you could do that." He just about choked on his latte.

Talon chuckled. "I figure I'll be here for more than a few minutes, so there's no sense in drawing unnecessary attention to myself. You said you needed my help?"

"Agent Blake? Join us for a moment."

The man emerged from within the van and hopped onto the street, extending his hand.

"Boston Blake. A pleasure."

Talon shook his hand. "Same here. Mike tells me you and your team have some information that you think connects to my line of work?"

"Yes, ma'am." He hesitated. "You're the Amazon on your team." He shook his head and smiled. "It's an honor to meet you."

"How so?" She raised an eyebrow.

"I've studied ancient tribal cultures of the Black Sea, specifically the Amazons of the Thermodon."

"You have a degree in ancient history?"

"No, ma'am. Just as a hobby." He grinned. "The idea of a society of all-female warriors intrigues me. I went on a few digs with your colleague, Aegis, er, Dr. Fairmont, back in graduate school."

"Agent Blake, enough fawning. Get to the point." Agent D'Alessio checked his watch.

"Yessir." He stepped up into the van, extending his hand to Talon.

"This is Agent Patterson. We both took readings at the Central Library and the bombing here, and we have some data we can't parse. From everything we can tell, the bomb was encased in steel, but something about the readout doesn't make sense. Look."

Talon leaned over a microscope.

"Mhmm."

Agent Blake lowered his head toward her. "Find something?"

"Well, this is a steel composite." She adjusted a knob on the viewer. "But, there's an additional substance bonded to it. I'm guessing it's not residue from the accelerant, either. Mind if I take this back to Ashburton Place?" She stood up, looking at both agents.

From the open back doors of the van, Agent D'Alessio, who was still sitting on the edge, replied, "Just let us know what you find." He finished his latte and tossed the cup into a trash bin on the inside of the van.

Agent Patterson handed her a slide sealed in a plastic bag.

Talon smiled. "Thanks for the intel, Mike. If it's what I think it is, we're going to be working together much more."

He laughed. "Oh, good. Can't wait."

Wings spread once more, she took off. Agent Blake followed her flight until she vanished in the clouds, a childlike grin plastered on his face.

Agent D'Alessio closed the back doors and took the driver's seat. Through a small opening into the mobile lab, he told them it was time to head back to HQ to check in with the other Kappa teams.

⊙═╾═⊙

At the corner of Beacon and Arlington Streets in the heart of the city, The Pinkerton Agency sat right on the northwest corner of the Public Gardens in a repurposed brownstone. Exiting the front glass doors, two new employees, a young woman in her early twenties and a man around forty, listened as the president of the company explained more about their job.

"Glad I caught you before you left. We're expanding to a new office in Dallas, and things around here have been quite hectic, but I wanted to touch base about what we're looking for. Technically, you'll both be with us as business analysts, and since we produce everything from conventions to trade shows to concerts, your job description is pretty fluid. As much as I hate to say this, some days, you may just help troubleshoot and put out fires." He laughed. "Questions?"

The young woman asked about the dress code. She made a point of asking because, if the president wore a sport coat, a plaid shirt, jeans, and dingo boots, she just wanted to make sure what was acceptable.

"Great question. Business casual works best for us. Don't get me wrong. You're going to work hard, but I feel you should be comfortable. I'd just save the Godzilla slippers for after work, though." He smirked.

The other new hire nodded and smiled at everything the president said, following up his colleague with an inquiry about professional development. Being new to this field, he wanted to know how much attention this company paid to growth.

"Wow, another awesome question. After your probationary period, you'll be invited to participate in workshops on how to implement enhancements to existing systems, create new systems, and fix defects. We do that quarterly. If there's something you feel you need, please make sure to let me know, and we'll see if we can't make it happen. The last thing I wanted to mention—"

The earth rumbled beneath them, cracking the sidewalk. From a distance, multiple car alarms rang out.

"That sounded like it came from behind this building!" The woman looked all around.

"You both should go back inside and head to our basement. Follow the signs inside the entrance. Since we don't know where

261

that came from, it'd be best to play it safe. Call someone and let them know where you are. I'll be right back."

He hurried down the block toward the sounds and turned the corner. What he'd feared had happened—Boston Preparatory, a school for grades K-6, was the victim of a bombing. The wing closest to him lay in pieces, chunks of the building scattered on the street. Since it was before school began, teachers, parents, and administrators who had been milling about gathered to corral the students arriving on foot or by vehicle. Craning his head over them, the man stood agape at the damage. Anguished cries from parents who couldn't find their children, coupled with the arriving sirens and car alarms, compounded the chaos. With no rescue vehicles on the scene yet, he bolted toward the collapsed wing and got a closer look. Some bodies lay beneath the debris, and a few were children. His eyes bounced around the area, and he helped a teacher and a student who had been knocked over by the blast. They had only suffered mild scrapes and bruises. He then entered the school where the wall had come down and disappeared within the smoky black interior.

Aegis vaulted himself over parked cars and assisted the arriving emergency teams, moving larger chunks of the stonework to free those trapped or to uncover the bodies of those who didn't survive the explosion. He leaped on top of a parked mover's truck to scan the area. From the earlier bombings, he knew that the perpetrator wasn't going to be on the scene or was well-hidden. When he had made a full 360° assessment, Aegis joined the law enforcement officers. Officer Cat Ramirez, who recognized him, brought him up to speed.

"Aegis, I don't know what to tell you other than this is like the other bombings across the city." She looked around. "The bastard targeted children, too. If I catch the son of a—"

Aegis put his hand up. "Easy, Cat. I know how upsetting this is. And, I'm right there with you. Where can I be of the best use for you and your team?"

She shrugged. "Everywhere. Do what you can, and thanks."

He started toward the building when she spoke again.

"Oh, and some people said they saw a guy run into the building right after the explosion. I sent an officer to look for him, but no one's come out yet. I'm not sure who he is, but we'll let you know if we learn something."

Multiple ambulances arrived and went, and gradually, the crowd grew smaller as emergency crews handled the lost, injured, and deceased. Crews of construction teams went inside to assess and shore up the rest of the wing to prevent further damage and injuries. Aegis carried an elderly science teacher to a gurney when he spied someone leaving the building. A soot-covered man in a ripped red plaid shirt held a boy and a girl, one in each arm over his shoulders, and the boy was wrapped in a sport coat.

"I need help over here!" He traversed what remained of the debris and found an emergency worker.

The EMT rolled over one gurney in each hand. "What happened?"

She lowered the child wrapped in the man's coat onto a gurney first, and another EMT arrived to help. Barely conscious, the boy in the coat had scrapes on his arms and face. The other child, a girl, also suffered lacerations, but she was awake.

"I heard the explosion around the corner and came running. You guys weren't here yet, so I went inside to see if I could help." He caught his breath. "I could only get these two."

He watched as the other EMTs tended to the children, and one worker handed the man his coat, asking if he needed any medical attention. Officer Ramirez stepped up to him.

"Sir, I'm Officer Ramirez, Boston PD." She flashed him her badge. "Can I have your name, please?"

"Sure. Shawn Pinkerton." He handed her his identification.

She looked it over, writing down his information. Before she handed it back to him, she held it up to his face. "Can you tell me what you were doing here? A witness said you ran into the building right after it exploded."

Shawn kept his eyes on the children, smiling slightly when he knew they were in good hands as the EMTs rolled them into ambulances.

"As I told the EMT, I heard the explosion from around the corner. I came running to see what had happened, and with all the kids around and no ambulances, I wasn't even thinking before I just ran in there."

Officer Ramirez sized him up. "You could have gotten yourself killed, not to mention these kids. Did you see anything before the explosion?"

"No, unfortunately." He fidgeted with his hands. "I own a business around the corner and came running after what felt like an earthquake. I have witnesses for my whereabouts if you need them."

Officer Ramirez opened her pad and took down the names of Shawn's employees.

"Okay, well, Mr. Pinkerton, just because you're 6'3" and built like a lumberjack doesn't mean you should run into buildings, even if your intentions are good. Understand?"

"Yes, Officer." He cocked his head while she made some notes. "Are you from Texas by any chance?"

She chuckled. "Yep, I've been in Boston for ten years, but I guess I haven't lost my accent. From Amarillo originally."

"Me, too! That is awesome. I don't meet many Texans here." He shrugged. "So… am I free to go, ma'am?"

"Yep, but we may call you if we have other questions."

Aegis joined them. "So, you're the troublemaker. I'm sure Officer Ramirez talked to you about running into buildings and such, but I just wanted to say thank you." He shook Shawn's hand. "You risked a lot, but you did help those two kids."

"Wow. It's an honor to meet you." Shawn gave a toothy smile. "I just wanted to do my part. Can't let you and your teammates have all the fun."

Laughing, Aegis acknowledged Officer Ramirez with a thumbs up and walked with Shawn as he headed back toward his office.

"Well, you were certainly a hero for those two kids. I'll make sure to let you know how they're doing." He patted Shawn on the back. "I wish more people thought the way you do, but be careful about jumping into action like a superhero. Although you do seem to have the makings for one."

He disappeared in a sword portal, and just as it closed, the mystical energy dissipating, Shawn's jaw dropped.

"That… is amazing," he uttered, shaking his head, as he continued walking.

Passing him, the man in the houndstooth headed toward the crime scene, but Shawn didn't notice as he was too preoccupied with getting back to his business. The man scoped out the area, but too many police and emergency workers milled about, so he kept walking, fists clenched.

"Zodiak, since you're the closest, head toward Seaver Street and Blue Hill Avenue. Reported explosion. I'll send you more intel as I get it."

"That's by the zoo. On my way, Quinn."

He hopped off the T as soon as it stopped at Ruggles Station. With rush hour masses, he'd be quicker on foot—well, *four* feet. As soon as he was on Tremont Street, he took on his Sagittarian form and sped down Columbus Avenue until it hit Seaver Street. No doubt the explosion had increased the chaos of later afternoon traffic, forcing him to leap over vehicles wherever possible. Catching a glimpse of smoke through the trees along Seaver between Franklin Park and him, he launched himself over the wrought iron fence, galloping down tree-covered paths until he found the source of the smoke. Resuming his human form, he located firefighters who were attempting to put out a blaze that had consumed much of the area.

"Tell me what I can do."

A firefighter pulled him aside. "We have the fire under control, but we know people were trapped inside in the Tropical Forest exhibit on the other side by the Giraffe Entrance. Boston PD is on scene, Zodiak, but they radioed for a crane."

Zodiak shook his hand. "Keep doing what you're doing. I'm on it."

Again in centaur form, he traversed the park, kicking up dirt as he went. Part of the dome that housed the Tropical Forest exhibit had collapsed, forcing park employees to transport animals away. Bomb squad personnel and police had blocked off the area, only allowing in emergency vehicles, both human and animal ambulances. Zodiak knew the zoo well and looked for one of two people who could give him answers. Dr. Jayme Courtman-Bean was directing helpers when he found her.

"Jayme, what do I need to know?"

She put a hand on his shoulder. "It's horrible. Sadie's badly injured. She was the only gorilla in the enclosure, and when the roof collapsed, well... one of her arms is broken. The stork and anteaters." She put a hand to her eyes. "Crushed. No chance of survivors."

"Baird's tapir?" He cringed.

Dr. Bean shook her head. Zodiak pulled her into a tight hug.

"I'm so sorry. I know how much these animals mean to you. To me. What do you need me to do?"

Pointing to the other side of the Tropical Forest building, and through tears, she asked if he could help locate the animals in each enclosure. She was going to work with the animal rescue vehicles to make sure the other animals received proper medical attention.

"Where are you sending the survivors?"

"Stone Zoo. They can help us until we can find more permanent housing."

"Let me see what I can do, and we'll talk more later." He gently squeezed her shoulder.

With the main entrance crushed, Zodiak found an opening in the metal framework and crawled inside. He could smell the fear of the remaining animals, but he could also smell death. Even though the animals of the zodiac were made from stars, he connected with them as he would any custodian, with compassion and understanding. He'd worked as a zoologist for ten years before he became Zodiak, and he'd done everything from work with designing facilities to maintaining microclimates to caring for sick and wounded animals. Although he wasn't a licensed veterinarian, he had enough training to care for the basic medical needs. He'd even handled syringes and done blood work in the field when he was in Africa and South America. What he looked for in this collection of habitats were simply signs of life.

Through mangled beams and hanging wires, he saw the glass enclosures of the snake exhibits, and flickering lights made it a challenge to see. He put a hand over his amulet and closed his eyes.

"Great Serpens, I need your vision. Allow me to see your kin."

When he opened his eyes, they took on a green glow and settled as vertical slits. Zodiak examined every enclosure, locating first the green anaconda. He opened his hand, letting the snake smell him. Determining he was no threat, the fifteen-foot dark green snake with oval patches and yellow spots wrapped itself around Zodiak's waist with its head near the man's ear, flicking with its tongue.

"No need to thank me, my friend. Now we need to find the others."

As Zodiak maneuvered, the massive snake directed his human rescuer to other spots in the darkened area. Two Kenyan sand boas and a Madagascar tree boa held onto Zodiak's arms, while a Rhinoceros rat snake sat loosely around his neck. He found a way out of the building and approached Dr. Bean who jumped at the sight, but more at Zodiak's snake-like eyes than his companions. Two zoo attendants took great care to place the boas and rat snake in large buckets for transport. Before the anaconda unfurled from her human host, she flicked his ear again.

"She said she can't be in a bucket. Do you have something bigger?"

Dr. Courtman-Bean chuckled.

Zodiak stroked the massive head of the snake before giving her over. "She isn't kidding. Do you have a cage?"

"Of course." A zoo attendant, no more than twenty years old, stammered, scampering about to find a discarded cage they could use.

"I'm going back in for the pygmy hippos, the mandrills, the capybaras, and the ocelots. Have someone follow me with rope to use as leashes." He took off for the building.

He returned a few more times, carrying a grunting pygmy hippo on each of his shoulders, thanks to the strength of Taurus. The mandrills and capybaras followed him out of their own accord. The ocelots needed the rope to keep them from straying, but once outside the building, they eagerly hopped into a cage.

"That's incredible. Thank you." Dr. Courtman-Bean gave him another hug.

"I scouted the rest of the building." He hesitated. "You do have some corpses in there. But, these are all the living creatures. I wish I could have…"

"You did quite a bit. It's appreciated." She wrinkled her nose. "You might want to…"

"Take a shower? Yeah. I know."

They both chuckled before he headed back toward the zoo entrance. As he galloped away, she shook her head.

"That never gets old," she uttered.

Zodiak received three buzzes in succession on his wristcom from Quinn.

"Just got a call from the 9-1-1 dispatcher. Two men are trapped. When the bomb hit, a tremor weakened the restraining wall, and they both fell into the lion enclosure. Possible injuries."

By the time he was on the scene, a few Boston police had tried to put a rope ladder over the edge, but one of the lions was playing with it. The other two cats stood off to the side of the men, roaring.

"Officer, how're the men down there?"

"They seem to be okay. Just spooked. Silly lion wants to play with the ladder."

Zodiak surveyed the area. Rather than shouting at the men, which would get the cats riled up. He put a thumbs up and raised his eyebrows at them. They returned the thumbs up."

"As long as they're okay, I'm going down there to distract the cats. When I tell you to, lower the ladder slowly. If I shake my head at you, stop moving."

"Got it."

While Zodiak could leap from where he was and land with avian grace, he knew that would startle the lions. He climbed down the broken wall, dropping the last few feet. His arrival got the lions' attention, but they didn't move. The closest cat to him, the one who had been batting at the ladder, roared, taking a few steps. Zodiak had his hands up, palms out.

"It's okay, big guy. It's okay."

Another roar, to show his dominance. But, the cat didn't move. He lay down without taking his eyes off Zodiak, whose eyes had taken on the golden hue of the great cat. Channeling Leo, he took steps toward the lion. When Zodiak was within just a few feet of him, the other two moved closer to the men, circling them.

"Wh-What're they doing?" One of the men muttered, moving closer to his friend.

"Don't move." Zodiak's voice remained calm, and he enunciated both words. "Any sudden movement will attract their attention. What's your name?"

"Matthew. Matthew Skipworth." His voice shook as the lions continued to encircle them. "They're not going to attack us, will they?"

"If you remain calm, you should be just fine. You're from England?"

"Uh huh." Matthew pulled his legs in. "Peterborough."

"And your friend?" Zodiak took another step toward the lion.

The other man replied, "Steven Marin. From Brooklyn. We're visiting a friend here in Boston. We were waiting for him to join us when we fell in here."

"You're both doing great. Just keep your voices low and calm."

"What're *you* doin'?" Steven's eyes bounced from one lion to the other as they circled.

Zodiak took another step. "I'm showing him I'm no threat. He's a bit spooked. By drawing on *Leo*, I take strength from the constellation as well as the presence of another lion."

Matthew's eyebrows jumped up. "Hey, I'm a *Leo*!" He realized he was shouting and lowered his voice. "Wish I could do that thing you're doing." He leaned into Steven and whispered. "He's got nice arms."

"You know I can hear you." Zodiak laughed.

"He does." Steven tried for a smile, but he was distracted. "Nice pecs, too."

Sticking his hand out in front of the lion's nose, Zodiak watched for a reaction. A warm, wet tongue slobbered his palm, and he knew this lion at least was comfortable. He gradually was able to scratch the lion's cheek and then rub his mane. Without his connection to *Leo*, Zodiak would not have been as fortunate.

"Okay, one down. Two to go." He crouched down to the lion's level and tousled his mane. "Stay here. Okay? My friends mean you no harm."

Both Matthew and Steven were sitting so close to one another that they were almost in each other's lap. Steven fidgeted with the buckles on his black boots. Both young men locked arms, their faces pale. Matthew pulled a small pad and a pen from his jacket pocket, making quick strokes on the paper. Steven gave him a puzzled look.

"Don't judge me. I draw when I'm nervous." His tongue protruded just slightly from his lips as he concentrated on his drawing.

Steven leaned closer to him. "New Jersey doesn't scare me. *This* scares the crap out of me."

In the distance, another bomb exploded, frightening the lions who roared their disquiet and paced around the two men. Zodiak sighed, dropping his head.

"Really?" He muttered. "Can't I catch a break here? Okay, boys. Here we go."

Putting his fists together, knuckle to knuckle, he took a deep breath and concentrated. The pale green peridot, Leo's gemstone, glowed in his talisman.

"I call upon *Leon*, the great lion of Nemea. Grant me your shape so that I may quell your brethren."

From the skies, a deafening roar thundered, and a few stars sparkled briefly, even in daylight. Zodiak dropped to all fours, and his body grew golden fur that twinkled, then morphed into a lion that stood ten feet tall at his shoulders. The celestial beast raised his head and roared at the other three who continued to pace. More sensitive to the disturbance than humans, they put out a low growl. *Leo* took a few steps. The other three lions moved backward around the men. Matthew and Steven pulled their locked arms tighter. *Leo* took two more steps, swishing his tail. He roared, this time louder than his leonine comrades could, and the three gathered behind the men. *Leo* put himself between them and the lions. He turned his head and growled.

"I-I think he's telling us it's safe to go." Matthew slowly stood up, his arm around Steven's shoulder, and moved toward the rope ladder.

"I'm not gonna argue with a lion the size of my house." Steven glanced over his shoulder to see *Leo* keeping the others at bay.

Once they were out of the enclosure, Matthew shouted down that they were safe. Zoo caretakers entered the area, sedatives at the ready. Rumblings from explosions across the city had faded, but sirens still traversed the distance. *Leo* had lowered himself on all fours, sphinx-like, and the other lions had done the same. They exchanged growls and low roars. Ten minutes passed, and then Zodiak morphed back into human form. He stroked the lions' manes, speaking softly. One rolled over on his back, exposing his underside.

"I've always wanted to do this," Zodiak muttered to himself, rubbing the lion's belly. "It's okay, fellas. You're going to be okay. I promise."

When he joined the caretakers, he told them they wouldn't need their tranquilizers. He had explained to the cats what was happening around the city and that the humans would do everything in their ability to keep the three feline brothers safe.

"You spoke to them?" A caretaker cocked his head.

Laughing to himself, Zodiak used the agility of Cancer and strength of Taurus to jump up and out of the enclosure, finding Matthew and Steven with the police who had given them water and something to eat.

"Are you guys okay?"

Both men nodded, chewing on their food. Matthew took a swig of his water to wash it down and wiped his mouth with the back of his hand.

"One of the officers said your name is Zodiak. You're in Task Force: Gaea, aren't you? I was just telling Steven that I wished we Brits had a group like yours in England. Thanks for what you did."

Zodiak smiled. He saw Steven just staring at his arms. "It's all in a day's work, Matthew. We sometimes cross the pond as needed. So, keep an eye out."

Matthew pulled his pad from his jacket and tore off a piece of paper.

"Here. I drew this while you were, well, you know."

On the paper was a drawing of Zodiak, shirtless, wrestling a lion. Zodiak chuckled.

"Creative license?" Matthew blushed.

"It's great. Thank you." Zodiak shook his head and smirked.

Stepping forward, Steven stammered out, "Can we take a picture with you?"

Making a 'come here' motion with both hands, Zodiak put his arms around the men's shoulders while one of the officers took the photo on Steven's phone.

"I really do need to get going, but hey, don't forget to tag me in that. Zodiak with a 'k'. Take care, guys."

Both Matthew and Steven grinned and continued eating. Before they left the area to meet up with their friend, they looked over the edge of the enclosure to see the lions just lying together, grooming. Even the sirens in the distance didn't seem to bother them. Whatever Zodiak had said to them worked. In the crowd that had gathered, the man in the houndstooth coat stood, blending in. Too many people meant it would be a challenge to get closer.

Back at the Ashburton office, Aleta stood in her white lab coat examining the slide Agent D'Alessio let her take. The whoosh of a sliding door opening and closing made her smile without looking up.

"Glad you could make it, Dan. Check this out. I must say. The Task Force Division has the latest tech."

He looked through the eyepiece. "My doctorate is in archaeology. What am I looking at?"

"Oops. Sorry. That's residue from one of the explosions. What it shows is the microscopic remains of steel, but also something not found on any ordinary table of elements. I'll give you a guess."

Dan looked up, his face turning pale. "It's Earthsteel. That means we're dealing with immortals." He plopped down on the lab stool. "How is this even possible? I thought Earthsteel was impervious to harm. How does it end up in bomb residue?"

Aleta watched his face and muttered to herself, "Wait for it…"

"No way." His eyebrows rose. "An immortal with access to Earthsteel is colluding with humans. Gods don't require bombs."

"Looks like that may not be true. From everything I know about Earthsteel, only Hephaestos and Gaea can forge it. Neither one of them would do this." Aleta shrugged.

"Yeah, it takes a god to work with it. That was my understanding as well. I wish Akmon were around. We could really use him with this, but he was having adjustment issues here. He decided to apprentice with his father for a while."

"A visit to the blacksmith?"

"Nah. Not yet." Dan pulled out his phone. "I do know that, with the right tools, any god can manipulate Earthsteel, but it requires ancient magic. And I do mean ancient. Gaea was the one who showed Hephaestos."

"How about you explore that angle, and I'll check in with Quinn." She put the glass slide in a plastic case.

One sword portal later, Dan left for Delphi. Aleta let Quinn know she was on her way and called in Brandon and Sarah.

27 | BROTHERS

Quinn took the information Aleta had given her and corre-lated it with the database. While the search ran through the petabytes of data stored on the U.N. computers, the four debriefed what they knew about the explosions.

"Guys, I'm going to leave my connection to the police scanner open. We don't yet know how many bombs exist, and if you're needed, I want you to know a-sap." Quinn always pronounced 'asap' as two words.

Sarah, in her latest gray catsuit, had her legs crossed and twirled her ring on her finger. "So far, we know about twelve. With so many simultaneous bombings, we've been spread thin. Law enforcement has been stretched as well."

"Don't forget Kappa. Team leader D'Alessio has kept me in the loop on what his team's been up to, as much as possible. I had the strangest chat with an agent... Patterson? Yeah, that was it. He seemed awfully fascinated with my Amazonian background. I wonder..." Aleta looked away.

Sarah snapped her fingers and smiled. "Hon, you're drifting."

"Anyway, Kappa has its hands full. I can't even imagine the casualties." Aleta shook her head.

"Latest counts were 1,452 dead and 4,613 injured." Quinn spat out the response as her fingers glided across her console.

Both Aleta and Sarah simultaneously turned toward her.

"Are you serious? Over 1400 dead?" Aleta leaned forward, her voice echoing in the office.

Sarah clasped her hands to her mouth. "All this to draw Apollo out?" She wiped her tears with the back of her hand. "I want to find this bastard and shove a bomb down *his* throat!"

Quinn stopped her hands. "Ladies, listen. Right now, every dispensable agency is out there handling what happens. There are only four of you. Even if you went from scene to scene, you can't be everywhere. From what I can tell, you've drastically minimized that body count."

"Any chance at all we can—"

"No, Sarah, No prediction because no discernable pattern. Every time a bomb goes off, that algorithm automatically starts. Trust me. I'm doing all I can."

Sarah leaned back hard in her chair. "Sorry, Quinn. Of course you are."

Brandon joined them, his shirt and pants ripped, and with blood spatter on his face.

"What the hell, Brandon? Are you okay?" Aleta looked him over for external injuries.

"Yeah, yeah. I'm okay. That blood isn't mine. Hey, enough already, I'm okay!" He put up his hands between him and Aleta. "Sorry. Not trying to be a jerk." He took a small towel Sarah handed him and wiped off his face.

He relayed to the three that, on his way into the office, another bomb had gone off at the entrance to the Park Street T station a few blocks away, but when he arrived to help, the police and Kappa had it under control. He had been removing debris to aid them underground by the tracks when the ceiling collapsed. Using his body as a shield, he prevented loss of life, but a chunk of ceiling hit a passerby on the arm, and the wound opened an artery, spurting blood everywhere.

Aleta interjected, "It was probably a brachial artery. Was the person okay?"

"Yeah. Paramedics were already on-site, so the man was helped pretty quickly. It was madness, though."

"Brandon, how is it that a bomb can go off a few blocks away, and we didn't hear or feel anything?" Quinn moved her fingers around, touching certain spots on her console. "It detonated underground, beneath the station, but you should have heard *something*. That's odd. Plus, the satellite didn't alert me of any incendiary devices going off, either."

"Well," Aleta replied, "what if the blast radius was controlled somehow? If it were just enough of an explosion to rattle the station from below, and we all know how old the T stations are, it could have been hidden by the other intel coming in."

Quinn, hearing a repetitive beep, tapped her console, smirking. "*That* was the alert about the train station. Satellite's been glitchy. Good thing you were around, B."

"Yeah. Good thing." He chugged a glass of water. "Wish we knew how to predict these things or discern a pattern."

"Already been down that road, Brandon. Nope." Sarah refilled his glass.

"I feel weird just sitting here. Shouldn't we be out doing something?" Aleta looked out over the Boston Common and Public Garden from the conference window around the corner from Quinn's desk. Dotted across the city, a few plumes of smoke rose, and the streets had become congested due to emergency vehicles. She stared at the crowds of police cars and ambulances clogging Tremont Street by the Park Street station.

"There was nothing else to do, Brandon?" Aleta wrapped her arms around her body.

He stood next to her at the window. "Not really. They had it under control. Boston PD has things well in hand. I have to give them credit. When our team first started, they didn't know what to make of us, but now, we've reached a pretty good synchronicity. The city can't rely solely on us when so many men and women have devoted their lives to this city."

Brandon put his hands on her shoulders and leaned toward her ear.

"We're doing what we can. Let's face it. There may come a time when Task Force: Gaea, or even the whole Division won't be around. The city has to be able to rely on many heroes, not just four."

Quinn's console made a series of noises, and she pulled a Braille report off her printer.

"Kids, when it rains it pours."

All three convened around her desk. At that same moment, Dan emerged through a portal.

"Good timing, bro. How'd it go at Delphi?" Brandon waved Dan over.

"She didn't know." Dan put a hand through his black hair. "Once she gave the secret to Hephaestos, she never told another.

I asked her if he could have told someone, but he made a Stygian Oath to her. Dead end."

"Maybe not." Quinn tapped on the document. "It took some deep searching, but this composite of Earthsteel in the bombs came up with the earlier search we did with SKOPUS and the cameras."

"Oh, please tell me SKOPUS is involved in this." Brandon put his palms together.

Quinn shrugged. "No connection as yet."

"So, how does this help us?" Sarah put her hands on her hips.

"Let's put a pin in that for the moment." Quinn put some images on the screen across from her. "Second piece of info. Satellite picked up these gems, and partial facial recognition tagged them as similar. Apparently, he's been at every single bomb site."

Brandon stepped closer to the screen. "Wait. How is that possible? Many were simultaneous explosions. The only way he could do that…"

Aleta and Dan looked at each other and spoke in unison. "Wait for it…"

"…is if he were an immortal of some kind." Brandon tapped his temple.

Dan gave Aleta an air "high five."

None of them knew who it was, and his face wasn't completely visible. The only connection was the houndstooth coat and the glasses.

"A mysterious stranger who appears at bombings, many of which are synchronous, and we have an Earthsteel residue at the sites. We find him, and we find our bomber." Brandon punched his own fist.

A buzzer told Quinn that a search string had a result. As soon as she touched her console, the stimulus gave her the information.

"Dan, you familiar with Exeter and Blagden? Based on this description, seems our mystery man came up on a surveillance camera a moment ago. He's heading south on Exeter. That was near the library bombing."

"He may be heading toward the Back Bay T station, Quinn. I'll head him off." Dan jumped through a sword portal.

Five minutes passed, and another portal opened with Dan holding the man in question, tied with a black rope, off the ground.

"The more you squirm, the guiltier you appear. Settle down." Dan lowered the man hard in a chair.

The man's hard glare didn't abate until Dan crossed his arms and raised his eyebrows, returning the expression.

"When I saw him, he immediately ran toward the train station. Not the smartest move when I can move through portals." He leaned down into the man's face. "I think he's tried to shift away, but the lasso of Atlas impedes all magic. Basically, you're stuck until I free you. Cooperation is in your best interest."

Dan sat back across from the man, his sword over his knees. The man looked from face to face until he stopped with Sarah. His expression softened, and hers did for a moment, too, until she realized he was playing on her pity. When he couldn't get a response, he exhaled sharply.

"Who are you? Why would you kill all those people?" Quinn's hands moved around her console.

The man turned to her and squinted, examining Quinn's face.

"You're… blind." His soft voice didn't match his scowl.

"And you're brilliant," she replied. "Yet, that answers neither of my questions."

He lowered his head and breathed out. "My name is Dr. Armon Fantiss."

Faster than the eye could follow, Quinn moved her fingers across her console.

"Here we go. Dr. Armon Fantiss, distinguished professor at Berklee College of Music, with advanced degrees in musicology, ancient music, and music therapy. Trustee of the Boston Public Library. Height, 5'10". Weight, 150 lbs. I could go on…" Quinn sat back and put her hands behind her head.

"I'll get to the point." Dan sheathed Thyroros. "We have images that show you at most of the bombing locations, thanks to our ubiquitous cameras. Why did you plant all these bombs?" Dan leaned on the arms of the man's chair, his face close to the man's head. "Why did you *kill* all these innocent people?"

Dr. Fantiss raised his head, making eye contact. Through the glasses, the man's eyes were teary.

"I… I didn't. That wasn't me…" His voice dropped off.

Dan growled then continued. "How do you explain—"

Dr. Fantiss choked out a few unintelligible words.

Moving to the front of her desk, Quinn sat back against it, facing the man who sat quivering.

"Dr. Fantiss, this city has seen more destruction and loss of life in the past month or two than it has in a very long time." Her voice stayed level. "If you know something about who did this, you need to tell us. Who are you protecting?"

He said nothing and pressed his chin against his chest. Brandon pulled the team into the conference area, and Quinn stayed with Dr. Fantiss.

"Look, if Dan can't intimidate this guy into speaking, we need a different approach. My gut tells me he didn't set the bombs. He definitely knows something, though. I'm not comfortable letting him go. Since he's a suspect, we *can* hold him here for forty-eight hours."

Sarah looked back at Dr. Fantiss. "I'm with Brandon. I don't think he did this. Let me try something. Stay here."

She pulled a chair next to the man and placed her hand on his arm.

"May I call you Armon?" She took his silence as permission and continued softly. "Armon, my gut tells me that you didn't set any bombs. But, you do have to admit that you being at so many sites makes you look suspicious. My main concern is stopping more bombs from going off and finding who did this. People have died, Armon. The latest casualty count is 1,452. If you can help us?"

He lifted his head, his eyes shimmering behind his glasses. "I didn't want to believe he could do it. I never thought he would take lives."

Sarah glanced at the others with a look, and they walked back into the room.

"Who, Armon? Who didn't you believe could do this?"

"My... brother." He exhaled hard.

Aleta, brow furrowed, pulled Dan aside.

"This man's brother is Autolycos? Hermes told us that Autolycos was going to try to flush out your father by destroying something valuable to him, namely, this city. Does Autolycos have a brother?"

Dan shook his head. "No idea. I do know someone who can tell us, though. Be right back."

He went to the far end of the conference area and vanished into a portal.

"This brother. Does he have a name?" Sarah raised her eyebrows and cocked her head.

Silence reigned for a few minutes. Dr. Fantiss grimaced and kept his gaze away from the others.

From behind them, in the conference area, they then heard another voice.

"Philammon?"

Dr. Fantiss, at the sound of that name, looked up and his breathing became erratic.

"Her-Hermes? What are you doing here?"

Hermes fluttered over to the man. He lifted Dr. Fantiss' chin. "Philammon, what are *you* doing here?"

"How-How did you know it was me?"

"Your glamour doesn't work on me, my boy. You may appear as a mild-mannered music teacher here in the mortal realm, but I remember you as the energetic son of Apollo who loved to strum his lyre with—"

Brandon stepped closer. "Excuse me? Son of Apollo?"

Hermes sheepishly smiled. "Hmm. You didn't know. Back when your father and I were much, much younger, we both became enamored of a young woman… Chione. Your father seduced her. After he left her sleeping, I visited with her as well. She gave birth to twins, Philammon, by Apollo, and Autolycos, by me."

Dr. Fantiss' face contorted, and his voice shook the room. "*Visited* with her? Hermes, you used your power to keep her asleep and took advantage of her! She didn't even know you had been there until you showed up at our birth. I may not agree with what my brother does, but what you did to *our* mother was… is… reprehensible!"

Hermes' smile hardened into a stoic glare, his eyes flaming, but then he lowered his head and faded back to Olympos.

"Coward!" Dr. Fantiss struggled against the black cord, grunting. "Get this thing off me!"

Dan lifted the chair up by one leg. "Enough! You still haven't explained why you were at bomb locations. Brother or not, you will remain tied up until you do."

"All right! Put me down!"

Stepping back, Dan lowered the chair, letting it drop the last foot. Crossing his arms, he stepped toward the man, but Brandon put out his arm.

"I have been following Autolycos for a long time." Dr. Fantiss wouldn't look at Dan, so he turned toward Sarah. "We have a bond. I have ignored it most of my life, but deep down, I always know where he is, or at least the general area. From childhood, he has wanted to see both Apollo and me suffer. Mostly Apollo."

"Why you?" Sarah sat forward in her chair.

"I was to suffer for being a son of Apollo, I guess." Dr. Fantiss glared at both Dan and Brandon. "Eventually, my brother lost interest in me altogether and focused his attention on Apollo alone. No matter where in the world I went, I could feel his presence lurking around me. I had settled in Boston around the same time Apollo did as Paul Fairmont. I held no resentment for him, but I never knew him as a father, so when he arrived here, I went on with my life."

A heavy silence followed before he continued.

"Where *is* our father? Why hasn't he shown himself? Maybe he just doesn't care about the mortal world the way I thought he did. Pretty selfish, if you ask me, to let all those people die."

Dan kicked the chair across the room, and it slammed into the wall, cracking the drywall. Dr. Fantiss' head hit the wall, leaving an indent in it. As the man recovered, Dan took two strides toward him. Security guards burst into the office, but Brandon put his hand up.

"It's okay, fellas. We've got this."

Dan lifted Dr. Fantiss by the cord wound around him, bringing them face to face.

"Our father can't make his presence known, for his protection and ours! You're so disconnected from things that you probably didn't feel Python sink his fangs into his flesh and pump him full of venom which destroyed his mind. The only Olympeian god to ever choose to live among mortals and help humanity lies—"

"Dan! For all we know he's in league with Autolycos. Watch what you say." Brandon stepped closer.

Whimpering, Dr. Fantiss stopped his struggling. Dan's roaring anger had made his face red and his muscles tight. His other fist was clenched so tightly that blood trickled onto the carpet. He tossed the man to the floor.

Dan leaned over and pointed his bloody finger. "You also don't know that Python used my husband's body to do his evil, and now the man I love more than anything in the world tries desperately to fix what Python shredded. He risks *his* mind to mend *our* father's! This man, a mortal man, who spent an entire year of his life as the damn ferryman of Hades! This man who has only ever acted out of love and compassion for others!" His breathing was so heavy he sounded like a bull about to charge. "With no knowledge of what's gone on around you, you're poking into things you can't possibly understand. Your brother has killed and injured over six thousand people who did nothing wrong other than just trying to live their lives!"

Stepping by the door, Brandon moved a broken side table out of the way.

"Dan. In the hall."

Dan scowled at his brother, but Brandon scowled back.

"Now."

Following his brother out, Brandon closed the door.

"You-You let him do this to me." Dr. Fantiss' breaths were soft and shallow, and his hair had fallen over his glasses. "You're supposed to be heroes."

Sarah crouched next to him, helping him to the couch.

"Can you please take this rope off me?" His eyes pleaded with her.

"Only Dan can. I don't think he's inclined to do anything for you at the moment. I'm sure he'll be back." Her voice countered Dan's with the softness of a morning breeze. "Philammon, how do we find Autolycos?"

"You can't. He has ancient magics and wards in place to protect himself. I only know that he's in the city, and that's because of our bond."

"Didn't you think you'd get caught being at so many bombing sites? Don't you think Autolycos knows you're here?"

Quinn sat back behind her desk.

"Dr. Fan—Philammon, your movements were tracked because you were at multiple crime scenes. That information triggered our satellites and computers. If our technology can see where you are, then Autolycos has the same means. How do we know you're not a spy for him? How do we know that he won't come here, to these headquarters, and destroy us right now in his search for Apollo? Can you even fathom why Dan is as angry as he is?"

Philammon had nothing to say and sat, shoulders slouched. His houndstooth jack torn and his glasses bent, he was a broken man in all ways except physically. Olympeian heritage kept him young and in one piece, despite Dan launching him into a wall. All four sat without speaking for about ten minutes before Dan and Brandon returned with Dan going straight for the window.

Brandon sat next to Philammon who looked over, his face drained of color.

"My brother would like to apologize for his behavior." He exhaled all of that in one breath. "He can sometimes let his temper get the better of him. If you can't help us find Autolycos, what *can* you tell us that could help? We're trying to prevent more loss of life."

Philammon murmured. "The last... The last time I saw him, about ten years ago, he went by the name Otto. Otto Wolf. I don't know if that helps you. Can you now please untie me?"

Dan, without speaking, removed the black cord. As Philammon was at the door, Aleta stopped him with a touch on the shoulder.

"Just remember. Your father needs *all* his sons, you included. Also, those crime scenes? Steer clear of them."

A security guard escorted Philammon to the elevator. As the silver doors closed at the end of the hall, Aleta saw the expression of a man now lost in purpose. She shut the office door and leaned against it.

"Gaea help me..." She whispered, putting her hands together and pressing them against her lips.

Dan fell back into the couch next to Brandon, and Sarah sat on his other side, leaning on his shoulder. Aleta put herself in a chair across from them. The only sounds to surround them were the blips and beeps from Quinn's console. They knew they needed to be out helping the police and emergency response teams, but they also knew they needed a moment, just to collect themselves. Heroes had limits. Although it probably felt like an eternity, ten minutes later, Quinn had finished her task.

"Okay, kids. I need ten minutes. Otto Wolf. Who's ready?"

Stretching out his legs, Dan put his head back and laced his fingers behind it. Brandon leaned forward, his arms on his legs. Aleta swung the chair around to face Quinn. Sarah got a glass of water. Quinn took their silence as her cue to brief them. She learned that Otto Wolf arrived in Boston back when the Task Force Division first began. Records back in the 1960s had only started to be moved onto computer files, as they existed then. Most of the punch cards that the United Nations had used were scanned and put into digitized formats, highly classified ones—codeword clearance only. The U.N. incinerated the cards in only two confidential locations as they were recorded, and within a year, all the data was secured in digital form. During this switch over, Otto Wolf had started his first company.

"Evidently, kids, SKOPUS emerged as the first major corporate entity to produce surveillance equipment, and according to some reports I've unearthed, the first cameras were made of a simple polycarbonate resin, i.e., no Earthsteel. I have the specs right here. The scans of old schematic drawings show a much bulkier design, probably due to a lack of streamlined technology. What I did see, though, is that the peacock feather we saw on the new camera is the same here."

Dan reached over to Quinn. "May I see the report?"

He shared it with the others. Aleta squinted a bit as she looked closer.

"Well, we know from Dan that Hera's not involved." Aleta returned the report to Quinn. "Although I really don't know how she couldn't be with a peacock feather involved."

"I'll broaden the search parameters. Maybe we—"

Dan jumped up. "Don't bother. I don't know why this didn't occur to me earlier. Peacocks didn't always have their eye-shaped design. They were all white. When Argus, the hundred-eyed giant, was watching over Io, a girl-turned-cow, Zeus sent Hermes who lulled Argus to sleep by playing his pipe. When Hera returned to find the cow gone and Argus dead, she took his eyes and placed them on her favorite bird as a memorial. I think we're dealing with something else here."

"Here we go." Quinn's fingers flew over the console. "Argus Panoptes. Argus the All-Seeing. Son of Gaea. I guess your father included him in the Task Force database at some point. Broadening search..."

Dan called Ari to check on the progress with Apollo. Aleta and Brandon watched out the window over the city. Sarah rolled her chair to Quinn's desk.

"I suppose we would know if more bombs had gone off. Seems strange that they all went off in succession, but now, nothing."

Quinn's fingers hit random spots on her console. "It's called a 'first wave'. Autolycos wanted to flush Apollo out, but seeing as that didn't happen, he'll probably regroup and deploy other explosives in more sensitive locations."

"Like hospitals. Aleta! We have to go. Now!"

"What? Why?"

Sarah grimaced. "I'll explain on the way. Quinn, how many hospitals in Boston?"

"Thirty, give or take. I'll send the co-ords to you."

Shoving the phone in his pocket, Dan started to follow them, but Quinn stopped him.

"Where are they going?"

Quinn pulled a printout from behind her desk, her fingers checking the Braille, and she explained the situation. Grunting her disappointment, she shoved the paper at Dan.

"Other than the reference to Argus, 'Panoptes' comes up blank. Damn. We have to find this Otto Wolf." He crumpled the paper.

"I'll keep looking. I've requested a TF-17 on the roof. You and Zodiak should scan the city from above. I'll let you know if I find something."

Sliding her fingers, Quinn tapped into as many databases as she could to find connections. All liaisons had been trained on over two dozen databases, known as 'access points'. Being the only liaison who handled otherworldly threats, she had other resources that she was only supposed to use when absolutely necessary, thanks to Apollo. Using this wasn't without risk, however.

"Open access point 'Owl 1'. Voice authorization, Quinn Reynolds."

An artificial intelligence with a female voice said, *"Command code."*

"Code G434 Alpha."

"Code accepted. Proceed."

"Now, let's see what we can uncover."

About thirty minutes passed before she stopped scrolling through files. She would only have access for an hour at a time without raising suspicion. A different kind of haptic feedback through her fingertips made her pull her fingers back. It was more intense than usual.

"Damn. 'Panoptes' *does* exist somewhere, but this is a high clearance lock. For it to be locked out at this level means only one individual has access." She sat back abruptly. "And he's currently chained."

28 | FOLLY

Otto Wolf brooded in his chamber. Bombs all across the city hadn't borne the fruit he wanted. Seated beneath his father's statue, in the flickering shadows of torchlight, his eyes reflected the flames. The door opened, and Lieutenant Harold stepped through the darkness. When she had interrupted him last time, he knocked her to the ground. This time, she had been summoned.

"You wanted to know if anything had changed."

He lifted his fiery gaze to hers. She lowered hers.

"Nothing. The damage has been contained. Body counts are lower than projected. Should we initiate another—"

"No. They will be expecting a second wave. Let them fester. While Apollo's whelps and their companions scour the city, we'll focus our attention elsewhere."

Adrianna lingered.

"I'll send word when I need you again, Lieutenant. That is all."

Alone again, Otto spoke aloud.

"I'm not certain what you did, Father, but I have a feeling you warned them." He turned his neck from side to side, the bones cracking. "No matter. I have other plans. Apollo has sons who are not part of the United Nations, sons I can use to my advantage."

Talon soared above Tufts Medical Center. Making a wide circle around, she let Aether know that she couldn't tell if any incendiary devices were on property or not. They could be hidden anywhere, and with Earthsteel as a component, they could be smaller than the average bomb. Aether, with an eager lilt to her voice, told Talon to meet her at the observation deck atop the John Hancock Tower, the tallest building in Boston.

Having mastered the ability to glide on air currents, Aether landed on the roof to an awaiting Talon. In her hands, she had a small box.

"Sorry for the delay. I had a stop to make." Aether gestured toward the outer door that led into the observatory, currently closed for the night.

Talon took the cue to arc some lightning at the door panel, shorting out the door lock. Aether knelt in the middle of the floor, the windows overlooking Boston in front of her. Wings retracted, Talon stared out over the city for a moment while Aether got settled, her hands open before. After a deep breath, she called the Quarters.

"I'm ready. Sit across from me." Aether opened a map of the city and pulled a silver chain from her pocket. From the box, she removed a chunk of one of the bomb casings, attaching it to the chain.

"You're going to scry for the bombs. Clever." Talon smirked.

"I'm not just a pretty face." She held the chain above the map. "O Anemoi, ye gods of wind, who blow over sea, mountain, and verdant glade, help me find any weapon of Earthsteel made."

Aether's eyes became white, and the winds outside the observation deck blew from all directions, whistling through any crevice. At the end of the chain, the chunk of bomb twirled one direction then the next. She spoke again, her voice sounding as if multiple beings spoke as one.

"Attend me, Eurus, Zephyros, Notos, and Boreas! I call upon you with the blessing of Thalassa, Khaos, Hesteia, and Gaea. Show me!"

The bomb fragment spun in as wide a circle as the chain would allow, faster and faster, until it shattered, spraying smaller pieces across the map, ten in all. Outside, lights shot up into the sky, like spotlights, and Talon jumped to the window.

"I see some of them. Boston Medical, Brigham & Women's, Boston University Medical…" She checked the map. "Two are moving, and one is right here."

Aether exhaled, shaking the fog from her mind.

"You all right? Wind gods giving you a hard time?"

"Something like that. Not sure why. The ones that are moving are together?"

Talon nodded, her eyes on the map.

"Aegis and Zodiak. Remember, they carry Earthsteel weapons. And here." She smiled, pointing up.

Laughing to herself, Talon shook her head. "Of course. The javelin."

"That leaves eight potential bombs. Quinn was right. You have the locations?"

"Let's go. One question, though. What do we do when we find a bomb?"

"I know what to do." Aether winked.

∘══◆══∘

"Hey, what do you think those are?" Zodiak pointed from the helicopter to the lights shooting into the sky.

Aegis took in the city. "No idea. But, we just lit up like a lightbulb. Magic."

As if on cue, Aether radioed to let them know what they'd discovered, saying they could handle the bombs. Aegis reported no other activity in the city, and he had been listening to police radio as well. The helicopter made a wide arc around the city for another sweep. Quinn informed Aegis of her limited findings, but now they knew that 'Panoptes' *did* exist in a TF database.

"Of course it would be classified with only Dad having access. The one piece of information we need, and it's inaccessible." Zodiak rolled his eyes.

"*When* he's back, we'll have a long talk about access. Until then, we still have to figure out how to find Otto Wolf. I think we need to have a chat with our brothers. Maybe they can help. They've been around a lot longer than we have. Pilot, bring us back to HQ."

∘══◆══∘

At Brigham & Women's Hospital, Aether held out the folded map embedded with Earthsteel shards. Both she and Talon stopped cold when the map lit up.

"Blessed Hesteia... The Neonatal ICU." Aether shivered. "Otto's a monster."

Talon called in the bomb squad that had been waiting outside along with doctors in helmets and Kevlar vests to retrieve the dozen infants in their incubators and bassinets and transport them to another hospital if need be. Those in incubators were connected to portable power sources. Aether moved through the glass-enclosed room until the map glowed brighter. Attached to a warming unit under a bassinet, the bomb looked inconspicuous, and it was no larger than a soda can. They had deduced that it mustn't be motion-sensitive because bassinets get moved around. So, effectively, this bomb could be detonated anywhere on the floor. The Boston bomb squad insisted on being responsible for getting it out of the hospital, but Talon and Aether would take over once it was outside. Since it could be detonated at any time, and since Talon and Aether knew the blast radius, the adjacent hospital wings were evacuated as well. No unnecessary personnel remained.

Once the bomb squad successfully removed the device, Talon placed it in a specially designed foam-insulated case to prevent the bomb from being jostled in transport. Plus, like the conference room at HQ, the foam prevented signals from triggering detonation remotely. Not knowing if and when this bomb would go off had everyone moving in slow motion. This was the seventh to be retrieved, and the last was at Tufts Medical. With cameras everywhere, neither Talon nor Aether knew if Otto would be informed of these removals, but if he were, Talon surmised he might detonate one or more. Nevertheless, they had to do what they could. Talon flew around Brigham & Women's once more to be sure that no other device had been planted before she and Aether headed for Washington Street.

With the hospital built right over the street and only blocks away from Chinatown and the Theater District, an explosion would do a considerable amount of damage. Talon had radioed ahead to the chief of staff, a woman she'd worked with for years, and informed her of the potential danger. Not knowing where the bomb was situated, however, made any evacuation a challenge. Aether's first thought was the Floating Hospital for Children, but that might be too obvious considering where they just found the last bomb. Flying over the campus, Talon noticed the map lit up just over the Ziskind building on the north side. Too many other buildings and the roadway would be caught in the blast, so evacuation would be just about impossible. Aether joined her at the entrance. It took twenty minutes going from floor to floor, but they ultimately found the device in the Hematology Lab attached to a centrifuge. Again, the bomb squad removed the machine from the building, handing over the bomb to Talon and Aether. Latching the case shut gave them all a moment to exhale, but then the next question arose: how to dispose of the devices?

Both Talon and Aether agreed that no one agency could hold these devices. Due to their intricate design and the Earthsteel in the casing, no mortal group could deal with them. With no destination in mind, they brought the case to Spectacle Island, an abandoned island in Boston Harbor. If the bombs did explode, no civilians would be hurt. Looking back at the city, Aether stood quietly thinking while Talon paced.

"We can't stay here, and we can't leave the bombs here. What're you thinking?"

Aether turned toward the ocean.

"We can take a small boat out into the sea. I can lift the case into the sky as high as possible, and you can blow it to bits with lightning."

Thinking for a moment, Talon then shook her head.

"Even if you could get the case high enough, I'm not sure we'd be far enough away not to get caught in the shock wave. Besides, showering debris into the ocean isn't a good idea. I could fly the case higher, but I couldn't get away fast enough before I could blast it."

"Well, then what?"

They both stared off, the eastern horizon spreading before them. Talon took in the skies above while Aether examined the island. They both agreed they couldn't leave the case here, even temporarily. An explosion laced with Earthsteel would have devastating consequences, and its magical properties would have an untold effect on the ocean.

"Earthsteel would have to be contained by someone who had the power to deal with it. Bringing it to Olympos wouldn't work out. I know Hephaestos has worked with this metal, but he hasn't worked with bombs like this. I'd rather not test out his knowledge with risk. This metal predates the gods themselves. An explosion of that magnitude would undoubtedly wreak havoc with the mountain." Talon stared down at the case by her feet.

Raising an eyebrow, Aether smiled. "Well… we would need to find a place that predated Earthsteel, now wouldn't we?"

"We can't ask Gaea to house this. I wouldn't want to risk hurting her."

"Talon, Gaea wouldn't be hurt. She has been around since the beginning of creation. But, that's not what I was thinking."

Aether reached the waterline, put her hands on her hips, and turned her head back toward Talon.

"Ophion. He is a *protogenos*. Not only do I think he could keep these bombs from doing damage, but I also think he knows to remove the Earthsteel from the casings. Then, he could destroy the bombs themselves with no risk to himself or Eurynome."

Talon was just about to offer a rebuttal when she stopped herself.

"You know… that sounds like it would work. How do we get in touch with Ophion?"

"I know how." Aether's voice took on a more serious tone. "Zodiak, this is Aether. I need you on Spectacle Island."

A Task Force A-19 water Jet Ski slid to a halt on the beach half an hour later, with Zodiak hopping off. With his teammates in sight, he couldn't take his eyes off the metal case in Aether's hand. She informed him of what she wanted to do, and, like Talon, he hesitated before agreeing with the idea. He walked into the water until he was waist-deep, touched his palms to the water's surface, and drew on Pisces. After a few minutes, he turned back to Aether and Talon.

"I need to go further. Under the water."

Aether stepped forward. "Are-Are you sure? You can't communicate with Ophion from there?"

Shaking his head, Zodiak walked until he disappeared beneath the surface and continued for a short while. Being in touch with Pisces, he could breathe. Darkness surrounded him, and only the faintest twinkling of stars could pass through. He closed his eyes. The message he sent through the water was simply that they needed Ophion's assistance. If the god would grant them an audience, Zodiak knew he would send his messenger. Zodiak had put himself into a meditative state which made him sensitive to changes in water temperature and movement. He didn't know how much time had passed, but he slowly opened his eyes when he felt a different aura approaching. In the shadowy depth, faint lights shimmered, and before he could see the great fish's eyes, the fifteen-foot-wide maw of razor-sharp teeth appeared out of the haze. Then, the eyes, a pale whitish-gray illuminated. Zodiak's own eyes widened. He had forgotten just how large Carkharos was. If the fish were spotted by anyone above, its sheer magnitude would cause panic being larger than any Megalodon. The shark opened its jaws. Zodiak stood his ground despite how his heartbeat pounded in his head. He had to keep reminding himself that Carkharos was born a man and became a shark to serve Ophion. Inside the shark's mouth was a conch shell the size of a basketball.

Zodiak came back on shore cradling the shell. Talon commented on how pale he looked, and he replied that she would look pale, too, standing in front of that massive beast. Aether put the shell to her ear, and her eyebrows lifted when she heard Ophion's voice.

"What did he say?" Zodiak leaned his hands on his knees, breathing heavily. "Please tell me he'll help. I don't want to think I did all of that for nothing."

Smiling, Aether handed the shell to Talon. "Yes. He said he would help."

"So, how is it that I can communicate with Ophion telepathically, but he has to send his shark to reply?"

Talon grinned. "It's a sign that you're worthy. Remember, you guys couldn't even approach Ophion last time if Jaws didn't approve."

"How do we tell Ophion what we need?" Zodiak dropped to his knees on the sand. "Am I going to have to do that again?"

"Not exactly. Ophion's message said that he knew what we needed and had a response." Aether looked over at the Jet Ski.

Zodiak and Aether took the Jet Ski out farther into the open water. With no lights to guide them, they relied on Talon's directions. When they were sixty miles from the island, they stopped. Talon circled above. Zodiak put his hand in the water and sent the message that they were ready. Being so far out, it didn't take long for a response.

"Guys, something's rising beneath you. I wouldn't look down if I were you."

Aether wanted to know why.

"Well, remember that *Jaws* poster? Imagine you're the swimmer."

"Just tell us when to drop the case." Zodiak's voice shook.

Talon flew back a bit. "Um, I'd say now is as good a time as any."

As the case descended, the gaping mouth closed around it, the markings on the shark glowed for just a moment, and then he was gone. Without waiting for confirmation, Zodiak sped the Jet Ski back to the dock at Squantum Point Park with Talon meeting them there. He commented that he'd had enough of the water for a while. Even though he knew that Carkharos wouldn't have harmed them, he couldn't get the idea of a massive shark beneath them in dark water out of his head. Aether laughed to herself, putting her arm around him. Talon retracted her wings and stared out over the eastern horizon.

"I wonder when we'll know anything," she said softly.

"Sir... Have we moved the devices from the hospitals?"

Major McCallister stepped over to Corporal Francis' station, leaning over the man's shoulder.

"No." The major hardened his expression. "Why?"

"A motion detection alarm pinged my computer. That only happens if the device leaves the premises and activates the GPS. According to the satellite, the secondary devices are no longer where we planted them. Look."

McCallister's stern gaze scanned the screen. He tapped a few keys to show other readouts, but then grunted when he didn't get the results he expected. He pulled out his cell phone, punched two buttons, and shoved it back in his pocket.

"Nice work, corporal. Let me know if anything changes."

The soldier saluted and resumed working. McCallister entered Otto Wolf's private chamber. Cocooned in shadow, the man the major had come to talk to radiated animalistic energy, a palpable frustration that made McCallister lower his head. He had served in the Navy for fifteen years, was a decorated war veteran, and stood a solid 6'2" with a quarterback's frame, but when Otto Wolf stepped into the torchlight, his scowl caused McCallister to take two steps back.

"Why do I sense you come with less than palatable news?" Otto's low voice had an eerie quality that compounded the captain's apprehension.

"We-We have news about the secondary devices. They're... gone."

Otto straightened up. "Excuse me? What do you mean, 'gone'?"

McCallister tried to stand up straight and keep his hands clasped behind his back, but he kept shifting his weight from foot to foot.

"Corporal Francis notified me that the devices were no longer on-premises, but he didn't know where they were."

"I see." Otto waved his hand over a water-filled kylix and images swirled into view. "Our satellite had the last known coordinates of eight devices at Spectacle Island, it seems." He waved his hand again. "Then, they were about sixty miles offshore, and then... nothing." Otto held his hand over the bowl for a moment. "I detect magic. Ancient magic. Beyond that, I cannot see."

He clenched his fist and the water in the kylix boiled to where the clay bowl shattered. Otto moved toe to toe with McCallister and then lifted off the ground to where he was eye to eye.

"Francis failed to notify us sooner. I have difficulty believing that he reported what he knew in a timely fashion. How *I* could detect what happened by tapping into the satellite and he could not means he is useless to us. Deal with it."

Otto lowered himself to the ground.

"Aye, sir." McCallister saluted and returned to the control room.

"Oh, Apollo, your minions have sent my handiwork to the ocean depths. Let us see what happens"—he reassembled the kylix with water and conjured a view of the coordinates—"when I detonate all eight at once. Be ready, Poseidon." He snapped his fingers, leaning closer to the bowl, eyes locked on the water's surface.

The Atlantic at night was strangely calm. Otto's focus turned into a glare with a guttural growl rising into a roar when not even a bevy of air bubbles cracked the surface. Swinging around, he narrowed his eyes at the statue of Hermes, and it crumbled into rubble.

"Et tu, pater?" He crouched and drew his hand through the remnants of marble. "Ironic that you and your brother should be in league together against me. Other brothers will aid me."

Into mist he vanished, his departure moving the dust where he stood.

At Delphi once more, Dan sent a text before drawing his sword. Through one portal after another emerged the Apollonides. Greeting them were the others Dan trusted above all else. Once introductions had been made, Dan led them to a part of the ancient ruins where they could be out of the eye of tourists, the remains of the Sanctuary of Athene Pronaia.

"Why are we meeting here and not at our father's shrine?" Ryuma scowled.

Dan moved to the center of the ruins of the tholos, its circular base still intact.

"Fewer people visit this place. Plus, it seemed fitting that we should meet where wisdom is required. All of Delphi resonates with Apollo."

Jamshid moved through the ruins with a faint smile.

"I remember this place in its prime. The temple to our aunt was something to behold. Always the archeologist, eh, brother?"

Dan chuckled. "Perhaps. Nonetheless, I asked you all here because my team and I need answers. We're hoping you can help."

Lost in the panorama of mountains beyond, Keion returned to the conversation when he heard his name. His expression was one of nostalgia, and he mirrored Jamshid in his appreciation.

"We had a recent conversation with another of our brethren. Philammon. He had been wandering the sights of explosions throughout Boston carried out by Otto Wolf, who we know is Autolycos." Brandon smirked.

Jamshid rolled his eyes. "Now, there's a name I never thought I'd hear again."

"Not a fan?"

"Not exactly, Brandon. He and I had an *encounter* during the Olympeian Age back when I went by Iamos. Let us just say that he is not to be trusted."

"So we've established." Aleta stepped forward. Here's what we know. Tell us what *you* know."

She explained about SKOPUS, the peacock feather, and what they did know about Otto Wolf, which wasn't much. The name SKOPUS sounded familiar to Jamshid and Keion, but Ryuma said he had no recollection of it. He did qualify his response by saying he had been largely disengaged from the world for a long time, so even if he had heard of it, his disinterest would have kept it from his memory. All three knew of Hera's peacock, since no other god had such an affinity for the bird, but beyond that, nothing. Keion put his hand on the word *aletheia* etched on his chest and pulled Dan aside.

"Something is off, brother. As the current guardian of Truth, I know there is more, but even that knowledge is blocked as if by a monolith. Perhaps your sword…"

Dan shook his head. "The sword's power is linked to prophecy, not truth. It was forged by Gaea, not Apollo. I wish I could help you."

"It's an enigmatic sensation, knowing you have access to so much knowledge, truths that the world itself chooses to ignore, and I can't breach this obstacle."

"Magical wards can do that. But, who could be so powerful to block aspects of Truth?"

"Wards are normally meant to protect, so whoever set it up wanted to keep something from our reach. I would wager it's Autolycos."

Dan scratched his chin. "There *is* something we can try." He turned toward the others. "Sarah?"

He explained the situation, and Sarah perked up, saying she knew all about wards. Setting them up required one to be focused and to choose an element from which the ward will emanate, but if the ward were especially strong, it may have been augmented by more than one element. Dan told her that Keion, now the living embodiment of Truth, sensed something blocking the information about Autolycos. Sarah asked Dan to portal her back to her apartment since she needed something.

In the grassy patch at the center of the tholos, Sarah sat before a small kylix she used for certain spells. With her power, she reached into the earth for water to go into the bowl.

"O Thalassa, spirit of the sea, I call upon you to provide this vessel with a connection to your element."

The water swirled a moment.

"O Gaea, mother of all, I call upon you to provide this vessel with a connection to your element." She sprinkled some dirt into the water, and it, too, swirled around.

"O Khaos, of the lower air, I call upon you to provide this vessel with a connection to your element." Rubbing her hands together over the bowl, she opened them and a swirl of air touched the water.

"I need fire."

Keion pulled out a lighter. Sarah drew the fire toward her, letting it swirl over the bowl.

"O Hesteia, of the sacred flames, I call upon you to provide this vessel with a connection to your element."

She gestured for Keion to sit across from her, and they held wrists.

"O Guardians of the Tetrastoikheia, I ask you to remove the barrier to Truth held by this son of Apollo."

The water swirled and bubbled, turning random colors, and Sarah tightened her grip on Keion. She moaned and pushed back against a resistant force. He tried to pull his hands free, but Sarah's eyes turned white and she muttered 'No...' and squeezed harder. Winds blew around the ruins. Her voice growing, she spoke in the Olympeian tongue until finally, she shrieked, flying backward. The kylix settled, now empty of its contents. Aleta rushed to her side.

"She's unconscious." She cradled Sarah's head in her lap. "Are you all right?"

Keion nodded, rubbing his wrists. His copper wrist cuff had left a mark on his skin. He asked if there was anything they could do for Sarah. Brandon touched her cheek and the garnet of Capricorn on his amulet glowed. Sarah's eyes opened, and she sat up.

"Orion." She exhaled hard. "Somehow Orion is working with Otto."

Aleta helped her stand. "Seriously?"

"How is that possible? He's dead." Dan scratched the back of his head. "Now we just need to figure out what the hell is going on."

29 | FIRST CONTACT

Mornings at Grove Psychiatric Hospital had the tenor of a relaxed beehive: active yet not frenetic. Ari's arrival prompted a brief chat with the floor nurse when he signed in, and he always greeted people with a smile. He never knew if he would need assistance, so he understood it was always better to treat people with respect. As an introvert, he struggled with small talk; it became a necessity, however, if he wanted to keep up the rapport. This would be one of those days when he took Esteban to the solarium; the young man had told Ari that he so enjoyed the feeling of sunlight on his face, even if he couldn't see it. The sensation put him at ease. What they were doing required a tremendous amount of psychic energy, and the beneficial properties of natural sunlight could only make their task easier.

As Ari wheeled Esteban to the windows, he noticed a man in a white lab coat sitting with a teenage girl on a bench there for the same reason as he was. The man kept glancing over at Esteban, trying to be subtle, but it was clear he wanted to get a good look. After he locked the wheels of the chair, Ari strolled over.

"Good morning. What a beautiful day, is it not?"

The man collected himself. "Yes, yes, it is."

Ari rocked on his heels with his hands in his pockets, always keeping Esteban in his periphery.

"I could not help but notice you were looking at my patient. Do you know him?"

"He seems familiar, but I am not sure how that could be." Nervously, the man extended his hand. "Dr. Francesc Gómez."

With a firm grip, Ari returned the gesture, never taking his eyes off the man's face.

"Dr. Ari Fairmont. A pleasure." He raised an eyebrow. "Where in Spain are you from?"

Dr. Gómez's eyes widened. "I-I am from Madrid. I specialize in brain trauma. You recognize my accent?"

Nodding, Ari glanced back at Esteban. "Do you know my patient, Dr. Gómez?"

"He reminds me of a man I knew at the Centro de Salud Mental Aranzuela in Madrid. I believe his name was... Reyes, Esteban Reyes."

Ari showed a slight smile and nodded.

"I see. There must simply be a resemblance, then. Did you transfer here, or..."

"My patient suffered severe trauma from a car accident, and her parents requested that I come here to work with her." He looked past Ari again.

"It was a pleasure, Dr. Gómez, but I should tend to my patient. Enjoy the sunshine."

Ari sat on the bench facing Esteban, but he also kept the doctor in his sights. In his mind, he reached out and asked Esteban if he knew the man. Esteban recognized the name, but he had never dealt with the doctor. Ari cut the solarium visit short, and once Esteban was back in his bed, Ari called Dan and asked him to run a background check on the doctor. Within five minutes, Dan called back to let him know that Dr. Gómez had a clean record from Centro de Salud Mental Aranzuela, but he had relocated to Boston recently.

With Esteban comfortable, Ari and he ventured into Apollo's mind. This time, the god was around sixteen. Apollo greeted them, wondering where they had been, but he still spoke only Greek. In his hands was the lyre with many more strings on it, on both sides. He explained that his understanding had strengthened by organizing the strings, and the memories started falling into place. Some he had to leave until later as they were too emotional for him to process in his current state. Remnants of Python's venom remained in places, but much had been destroyed, partly by the fires in his mind, but also because of his mind strengthening. Apollo pulled Ari's arm toward another doorway, one that looked different from the rest.

Venom sealed this opening on all sides, and it had hardened to look like amber. For as much as it looked almost gemlike, they knew how dangerous it was. Apollo opened his palm and concentrated hard.

"Ídou!"

"I *am* beholding." Ari leaned closer.

A flame burst into existence, about the size of a candle fire.

"That is incredible." Ari jumped back a bit. "You can conjure fire!"

Apollo stared at the flame, and it grew to twice its size.

Esteban's mouth fell open. "Increíble! But, does it—"

The young god pushed his palm toward the door, his fingers curled forward slightly, and furrowed his brow. With a grunt, he generated enough of a blast to melt the venom from the door handle. Beads of sweat came together on his forehead and dripped onto the floor. Ari found a torch and burned away the rest.

"Save your strength, Apollo. But, what a terrific success."

The door squeaked open to reveal an armory of a sort with battle-axes, swords, shields, and archery tools. Along the edges of the chamber stood statues of women, some armored, some in less military garb. Strings ensnared each of the statues, some connecting and some wrapped around individuals.

"Are-Are these women Apollo has—"

Apollo tapped Esteban on the shoulder.

"Amazónes." He lifted his eyebrows to reinforce his displeasure.

Traveling the statues, Apollo stopped before one of them and bowed his head. He crouched to where her name had been etched in a plinth, but it had a coating of venom. Ari reached over with the torch, but Apollo stopped him. Mustering his own strength, he conjured a small flame to burn away the poison.

"Danaë." Ari lingered on her face. "I remember stories about her and the Themiskyran Amazons. Apollo once told us during that *other* time when he rescued Danaë and became an ambassador for the Amazons. This was when he learned how to respect women more. In that timeline, it was through Danaë that he met Alkinoë."

Headdresses of other Amazons he had met lined the walls, including one of an eagle.

"That reminds me of Aleta. I do not know when he would have met this tribe."

Apollo unraveled strings from various places around the chamber and strung different sides of the lyre. When he reached the one attached to the eagle headdress, he placed it on the side of the lyre where the current timeline's memories stayed. His experiences with these women didn't seem to be as extensive, and it didn't take him long to attach all of the memories. Most seemed to be from that other timeline. Apollo explained a little about each woman: Cydippe, Astraia, Oritheia, and Taraeis had left stronger impressions with him than the others. He commented to Ari and Esteban how much he had grown to respect those women. With this piece of the puzzle back in place, Apollo smiled to himself. Even though he had not met those particular Amazons in this timeline, he would always remember how they grew to respect *him* as well.

They exited the other side of the stone chamber through an arch that had no door, and then their path illuminated on its own. Instead of another room, what lay before them stretched out as a long corridor, flanked on both sides by niches that contained more statues. Columns that rose higher than they could see stood on either side of each niche. On each column sat a torch, but it was not torchlight that illuminated this space. Rather, it was a luminescence brought by Apollo's presence. More ochre-colored venom covered everything, and what had been a peaceful expression from seeing the chamber grew dour on the god's face. Upturning both palms, he growled. In each palm grew a vibrant flame, larger than before. Without warning, he threw his hands outward to the sides of the corridor, shouting something in Olympeian Greek that Ari could not comprehend. As the fire struck the niches, the venom ignited, and like a fuse, the flames consumed it until it moved into the darkness ahead. Grunting, Apollo fell to his knees.

Through heavy breaths, he muttered, "Kaneís den ponáei sta paidiá mou."

Ari gasped. "He said, 'Nobody touches my children.'"

"This reminds me of the Louvre. An entire wing of statues. These are all his children? How many does he have?"

Chuckling, Ari commented that he had lost count, but he knew only the ones that mattered to him. Together, they walked past the beekeeper Aristaeos holding a hive, the hindquarters of an ass at his feet. Then, Aesculapios with his snake-festooned staff. Dozens of men and women, mortal and immortal, bordered the great hall of Apollo's mind. Eventually, Ari stopped before three statues standing near each other.

"Danelos has told me about Onkios, Erymanthos, and Iamos. These three, plus he and Brandon, are the Apollonides known to exist. I wonder if Danelos knows just how many siblings he has." He chortled, continuing down the line.

Midday at the Arcady, Keion strolled, arms behind his back, around his patrons, engaging new ones and conversing with those he knew. At this point of the day, sunlight hit just the right spots to cast a sparkle on glass pieces while highlighting paintings and sculptures. Some said it was deliberate choices in the architecture to allow for this, and others thought it was some kind of magic. Nevertheless, it gave the gallery an allure that no other one had in London. Nestled in a corner was a cobalt blue velvet chair that curved around a small table. It could seat three comfortably, but a man in the middle of it nursed a martini. Keion leaned over and asked if he needed anything.

"I'd like for you to join me, Onkios." He sipped his drink.

"Of course." Keion signaled one of his employees. "A glass of Pinot Noir and another lemon martini, extra dirty."

The man hesitated mid-sip.

"I make it my business to know my clients, Mr. Wolf."

Otto laughed. "You're good. Then, you must know why I'm here."

"Actually,"—he took the wine from the server's tray—"I haven't a clue. My powers of perception don't include telepathy."

Otto finished his first martini and exchanged his glass for the new one.

"And, please, it's Keion. I haven't been Onkios for a long time. How may I be of assistance?"

Otto and he exchanged pleasantries about the gallery, speaking of art and trends, classical pieces versus modern ones, until Keion's agitation began to show, and he didn't show it often.

"Mr. Wolf, while I revel in discussing art, I know that is not why you're here. If you're anything like your father, you have a motive." He sipped his wine. "Be so kind as to get to the point."

"I like you." Otto plucked an olive from his glass and popped it in his mouth. "That bodes well. I would imagine you have some information that I might... procure from you. And, I am willing to pay handsomely for it."

Leaning back, Keion smirked.

"What information do you wish, and why do you think I have it? Oh. And how handsomely?"

"The whereabouts of your father."

Pausing, Keion gently lowered his glass to the table, leaned back, folding his hands in his lap.

"I reiterate. How handsomely?"

Otto launched himself from his seat and perused the collection of paintings, his hands clasped behind his back. Keion stopped every time he did, rocking back and forth on his heels, waiting for Otto to say something more. He'd smile at patrons as they passed by, but then his expression would return to disdain. After the sixth stop, Keion cleared his throat.

"Oh. Yes. You asked how handsomely." Otto nodded toward a Degas, *The Dancing Class*. "This. This is a masterpiece." His smile spread like that of the Cheshire cat, leaning closer to Keion. "I have more of his works. Works that have never seen the light of day."

An eyebrow on Keion lifted slowly, and he pushed his lower lip out.

"Do tell."

"See that Renoir over there? The *Bal du moulin de la Galette*? There was a companion piece. Well, *is*. I have it."

Looking to each side, Keion stepped closer, signaling a server with a quick look at the same time.

"Cherise, a bottle of Roederer Cristal Gold Medalion to my table, please. Two glasses."

Otto gasped and smiled coyly.

"Mr. Wolff, you spoil me. That is one of the most expensive champagnes in the world. Ah, look, we even share a surname, sort of."

Keion gestured toward a staircase that traversed the wall of windows overlooking the Thames, one that only he and chosen guests could ever climb. They emerged in a circular loft with a wall and ceiling made of one piece of glass, not one seam to interrupt the vista of London. A sofa of golden crushed velvet sat against the wall. Cherise arrived shortly thereafter with a silver tray on top of which rested inscribed silver chalices. She offered the two men their champagne and discretely exited. Keion held up his chalice, its silver edge glinting in the sunlight.

"To our mutual satisfaction."

Otto tapped his chalice to Keion's before sipping.

"I dare say this reminds me of the nectar of the gods."

"Oh, Mr. Wolf, Olympeian nectar has nothing on this. Shall we talk?"

Passing Anios, a Delian king, among other offspring, Ari and Esteban kept an eye on Apollo. Every so often, the young god would stop, touch a plinth, as if to make fatherly contact with his child before moving on to another. His zigzagging down the hall ceased when he stood before two statues that took up one niche. One marble likeness was dressed in a tunic, a chlamys over his shoulder. His right hand rested on the pommel of a sword at his waist, and his left was lifted to eye level, open palm up. On his face, a circle beard. The other man, his hair neatly shorn, had his right hand on the other's shoulder. His left hand hung at his side, gripping a carved chain that held a talisman.

Apollo reached out and touched the plinth again, but he lowered himself to his knees, dropped his head, and wept.

"Who are they? Why do they share one space?" Esteban's eyes traveled the shapes of both marble bodies.

Ari smiled and put his hand on Apollo's quivering shoulder.

"The one on the left is Danelos. My beloved." His glassy eyes lingered for a moment. "His brother Kidemonas stands next to him."

"He acts differently around them. What makes them special?"

A sideways look from Ari took Esteban by surprise.

"I-I mean, why treat them not like the others?"

In a soft voice, Ari replied, staring at the statues.

"Because they are *not* like the others. Of all Apollo's sons, these two live near him, and he has spent more time with them than any of his other children."

A sound came from Apollo, a muffled uttering of words.

"What, Apollo? What did you say?" Ari knelt to his level.

A tear-laden god turned his pained face.

"Eínai kommátia tis kardiás mou."

Esteban closed his eyes and turned away. "They are pieces of his heart. Ari, I can't even imagine what seeing this is doing to him, yet he lingers here."

Caressing the back of the god's blond head, Ari sighed.

"You would, too, if your heart, as well as your mind, lay shattered before you. Soon, Apollo. Soon you will be reunited with them. I swear this to you."

Rising, Apollo levitated to where he could touch both his son's faces.

"Evgeneís polemistés mou…"

He continued toward the exiting arch, with Esteban following, but Ari stayed behind a moment.

"You both *are* indeed his noble warriors. He sees you exactly as you are."

Ari found Esteban standing near Apollo who was stringing his lyre in the arch. Even though he seemed focused on the task, the god was elsewhere. This next chamber was filled with threads to such a degree that one couldn't even walk through the entanglement. The mixture of past and current timeline elements interwoven also had the extra obstacle of venom clinging to everything. Light that emanated from Apollo exposed only a small piece of the knotted mess; he handed the lyre to Esteban. He looked down at closed fists and then opened them. Fire ignited in each palm. In one large outpouring, the venom was consumed, leaving the strings unharmed and Apollo a bit winded. Esteban leaned toward Ari.

"Why does the fire not harm the strings?"

"Remember, this is all a construct of Apollo's mind. The fire is not real. It is a manifestation of his inner power. The strings we see are merely another physical representation of what exists here. In a way, everything we see is Apollo's way of allowing us to aid him. If he did not want our help, his inner mind would have driven us mad."

"So, our presence helps him focus, then."

"I believe so. That you and I believe he can be healed reinforces his will to survive. I am afraid we must go. We have been here longer than usual, and I am getting tired. This chaos is a puzzle we cannot even begin to help him with."

Nodding, they severed their link. Once he was sure Esteban was resting, Ari went to the cafeteria for some coffee. While he stared at the wisps of steam rising from his cup, both hands cradling it, footsteps came from behind and someone sat adjacent to him. Dr. Gómez put his cup down and asked if he could join Ari. The doctor tried to make small talk, and his inquiries always went back to Esteban. As earlier, Ari deflected, never confirming, and always watching the doctor's body language. He redirected the conversation back to the hospital in Madrid, with Dr. Gómez also keeping his answers short and vague. Finally, after about ten minutes, Ari asked why he was interested in his patient. The doctor shrugged it off as just being curious since he thought it was the same man he knew in Spain.

"How would you react if I started asking all sorts of questions about *your* patient?"

"Well, I… I would probably be as evasive as you are, I suppose. Look, I understand you're protective of him. And, you've made your point. Speaking of patients, I need to check on mine." He downed the last of his coffee before leaving.

Watching him go, Ari narrowed his eyes.

Something is not making sense, he thought. *No one is that curious about someone without a reason.*

On his way back to Esteban's room, he stopped in the solarium which showed the late afternoon sun striating the skies with pink and orange. His thoughts returned to Dr. Gómez. Even though Dan had told him the man had nothing in his past, that didn't sit well with him. At the nurse's station, he checked the sign-in sheet. Of course, it didn't mention patient names or room numbers. The nurse on call returned to her station, and Ari paused in thought before stepping over to her.

"Hi, Nancy. How are you this afternoon?" He flashed a smile.

"Oh, just fine Dr. Fairmont." She brushed a curl from her face. "Never a dull moment, right?"

He chuckled. "Of course. So, I was supposed to meet Dr. Gómez to discuss something, but I cannot find him. Is he still here?"

The nurse checked her computer.

"Well, he hasn't signed out yet. You can check room 105, though."

Ari bowed his head and pressed his hands together. "Thank you. I hope the rest of your shift goes well."

"Thanks. Oh, and how's the hubby?"

"He is well, thank you. Busy as usual, but I will tell him you asked about him." Ari waved as he walked backward toward the 100 wing.

At room 105, no chart sat in the folder on the wall, but that wasn't uncommon. Ari tapped his knuckle on the door a few times, and hearing no response, pulled the door open just enough to look inside. The closed blinds let in slivers of light. No one was in the room, and the bed was empty. Visiting hours had ended hours earlier. Sliding into the darkened room, he skulked about. The room seemed as if no one had been there for quite some time. As if sensing something, he returned to Esteban's room.

"Esteban?" He made the connection mentally.

"Sí? ¿Está todo bien?"

Ari exhaled. "Yes. Everything is fine. Can you tell if anyone aside from me has been in this room?"

"No one. I can tell something is wrong. What is it?"

After explaining what had happened with Dr. Gómez and the empty room, Ari didn't want to speculate, but Esteban wanted to know what could happen. Without any other information, Ari didn't feel comfortable talking about things he couldn't prove—yet. He didn't want to say anything to the nurse or Dr. Gómez, either. Arousing suspicion would only make the situation more dangerous.

"I don't know *how* I know this, Ari, but you are not being honest with me. I can sense it. Por favor, dime que estas pensando."

"What I am thinking, Esteban, is that I do not feel comfortable leaving your side. But I do know someone who can help me."

He asked Sarah to come to the hospital. Since visiting hours were over, she couldn't just walk through the front door. She said she'd find a way in and meet him in Esteban's room. An hour later, the room door opened slightly, and Sarah whispered Ari's name.

"Come in, quickly."

In her all-black Emma Peel inspired outfit, she approached the bedside and took in Esteban's peaceful expression, his eyes facing the ceiling.

"This is Esteban, eh? Can he hear me?"

Nodding, Ari told him that Sarah was with them, and he was going to connect her with them. His obol could bridge that consciousness, making it almost like a conference call. Instead of just hearing the voices, Ari created that construct where all three appeared in Esteban's mind as full people. This way, they could see facial expressions and hear tones of voice better.

"It's a pleasure to meet you, Esteban. I have heard so much about you."

"Same here, Sarah. Ari trusts you, so I do too. Ari, why did you call Sarah here?"

"Sarah has the ability not only to sense magic but also to create wards. Do you sense anything at play here?"

She shook her head. "No, no magic at all. Other than the power of your obol, and the innate power within Esteban, nothing else is present."

At ease, Ari asked if she could establish a protective ward around Esteban's room, something that would either prevent intrusion or could alert them if someone tried something. She could do both, but she would have to break the mental link to do it.

Cross-legged on the floor, she removed a small plastic box from her belt. Within its four compartments were water, earth, and a small piece of wood. The empty compartment now had air, and she used a lighter to ignite the wood. All four elements were at her disposal for this ritual.

"Gathered here are elements four,
Whose ancient power I implore,
From Hesteia's fire,
From Khaos' air,
From Thalassa's water,
From Gaea's earth, I ward this room,
Guard this space from all ill will
and all those who wish Esteban doom.
May the Tetrastoikheia perform this task,
O Guardians of the elements, honor this I ask."

In a flash, the fire went out. Sarah touched Esteban's arm and was brought back into the mental landscape. He said he could feel electricity all around him, that he felt more secure. Ari caught her up on what had been happening. Her initial response was to alert Dan and the others, but Ari didn't want everyone involved. He assured her he could handle it. Sarah inquired how Apollo's healing was going. Esteban didn't know what he could or couldn't say to her, so he simply told her it was moving along reasonably well. She commented how happy she was to meet him and told him she would always be available to help if he needed something.

She and Ari left the hospital together, and he went home while she went to Ashburton Place. The second shift had taken over the offices, but she knew Quinn would still be there. As usual, Sarah found her tapping away. After the usual pleasantries, she asked Quinn to check Dr. Gómez's phone records. When Quinn asked why, all Sarah would say is that she wanted to help Ari if she could. While Quinn worked *her* magic, they caught up on the team business.

"So, big glowing shark, eh? I'll bet that's the stuff of nightmares." Quinn smirked. "I mean, I've never *seen* one, but still."

Sarah laughed, plopping into a chair. "I think it bothered Brandon more than he'd like to admit. Carkharos is a mystical creature who used to be a man, but when you're out in the middle of the ocean and see a massive set of teeth rising from the depths, you tend to forget that part."

"I've been meaning to ask you, and feel free to tell me to mind my own business. I don't hear much about either you or Brandon going out at all. Not seeing anyone?"

Groaning a little, Sarah pushed her hair back with both hands.

"Between my pottery, my gallery showings, and this stuff, I don't have time for much of a social life. It's okay, though. I'm much more of an introvert. The manager of the art gallery flirts with me, but he's married, so that's a no-go."

"And Brandon?"

Sarah sat up. "Oh, heavens no. He's like my big brother."

Laughing, Quinn shook her head. "No, I meant is *he* seeing anyone. Trust me. I know you guys are more like siblings than anything else."

"You know, now that you mention it, I really don't know what's happening with him. With his work at the university and the task force, he's a lot like me. He prefers his alone time. I asked him once about it, since he gets hit on constantly by everyone. Jonathan, the barista at The Beanery, has been trying to chat him up for a while now, but he's gotten nowhere. Brandon just smiles and blushes. Sandra on Task Force: Epsilon has had her eye on him, too. Whenever I see her at staff meetings, she always asks about him. All he'll say is that he's happy being single."

"He once told me that his connection to the zodiac is enough. Well, plus you guys. I mean, if I had a dozen celestial creatures to keep me company, I think I'd be pretty busy just trying to keep them all straight in my head."

The console beeped. Quinn's hands tapped the glass a few times.

"Well, well, well… it seems this Dr. Gómez has some unlisted numbers in his phone, both calls and texts." She slid her finger up the glass to scroll. "This same number also appears on someone else's phone."

Sarah leaned forward. "Who?"

"Dr. Fantiss aka Philammon."

"Huh. Any chance that number belongs to Otto Wolf?"

"I'm still checking that part."

Sunsets in Mashhad had a warmer palette of color, at least according to anyone who lived there, and Jamshid lost himself in them as often as he could at his favorite table at Café Aftab. The marketplace remained a bustling hub of activity until late at night, and Jamshid would engage with anyone who would indulge him about politics, culture, or even the weather. Being in the heart of everything gave him great joy. One hand consistently held a cup of coffee—this day, it was Turkish—and the other held a book or newspaper. He and Brandon spoke about how similar they were in this aspect, the only difference being what side of the world they were on. At a certain point just before sundown, strings of round bulbs woven above the patio popped on like small moons. Through the crowded street ambled a boy, about fifteen years old, holding out an upturned baseball cap to the patrons. When he approached Jamshid's table, he was met with a knowing look.

"Did you not think I would know it was you? When you're of our bloodline, it's easy to sense a glamour or disguise." He gestured to the boy to sit.

Once at the table, the youth's façade melted away to reveal an older face.

"I should know better than to try to deceive one who is descended from truth, eh, Mr. Motjaba?"

"Indeed, Mr. Wolf." He threw back his coffee, putting the cup down harder than expected onto the saucer. "How can I help a son of Hermes?"

Otto glanced from side to side and leaned closer.

"Perhaps it's how I can help *you* that we should discuss."

Jamshid with a relaxed smile leaned back and opened his arms.

"What kind of help could you possibly offer me? I have everything I need."

"Let me cut right to the chase. I want to know where Apollo is. Price is no object."

"What makes you think I know where he is? And, if I tell you I don't know, you won't believe me. Even if I knew, there isn't anything I want."

As Otto turned his head in all directions, he would smile slightly when his gaze lingered on patrons.

"Oh, I'd say there is. The lives of everyone in a five-block radius."

Jamshid leaned forward, his palms on the table.

"What... are you saying?"

Curling his fingers, Otto checked out his fingernails before making eye contact.

"You have until sunrise to decide.

"And then?"

"Let's just say that the citizens of Mashhad will meet with an explosive demise." He stood to go. "It would have been much easier if you had something you'd wanted, but I did my homework. You're quite content to live out your life in this sand-laden little town. I'll come back in an hour. If you're smart, you'll deliver what I want."

"All these people will die if I don't tell you where my father is." He scanned the plaza, taking in everyone, bearing witness to their humanity, their everyday existence. "Come back at sunrise."

Gaea's adyton has harbored only one god in its entire existence. Its sole purpose came into being when Gaea needed a place to house the Sacred Scales, and their whooshing lingered in this soundless place like a whisper. In another chamber, the son of Zeus struggled to restring his mind. The external figure looked as he did in the not too distant past, an older adult, while a much younger incarnation roamed the rooms and hallways of his mind. Even in Ari and Esteban's absence, Apollo worked to put right that which Python destroyed. With the haze slowly fading, he was able to make small amounts of progress. He would touch a string, experience the memory, and place it on the correct side of the lyre.

A tedious process to be sure, but one that had to happen, or he would languish for the rest of his existence in Gaea's inner sanctum.

As he concentrated on the strings, he looked for any way to distinguish them from each other so he could expedite the process. To live through each memory, even partly, would take quite a while. Since Ari and Esteban's departure, he had been through a third of the strings, each one pulled taut across the chamber. Some had become tangled with others, but most remained individual strands. Apollo stared at the lyre. If the lyre is part of his mind, does it still work the same way a lyre does, he wondered. He let his fingertips slide across the strings for a moment before he withdrew his hand. Holding the instrument in his lap, he strummed enough to get the strings to vibrate. While he savored the music they made, a sound echoed. Pressing his hand against the lyre strings to stop their sound, he gasped.

The strings from that set of memories around the chamber vibrated as well.

With this revelation, he had a defined direction. Having identified the frequency of the different strings, he untied knots and unraveled the web. This conglomeration of thought had no theme—these were random memories that hadn't attached themselves to a specific place in his mind. It would take less time to work through this, but it would take time.

Ari's cell phone woke him around 5 a.m. The number on his screen was from the Task Force: Gaea office, so it was from Quinn. He managed a "hold on" to her while he lifted Dan's arm from around his torso and slipped out of bed. Closing the bedroom door behind him, he stepped out onto the balcony. Her searching had borne fruit. Quinn had found a voicemail through the phone carrier, and when she did a voice analysis, she learned the caller was a Lieutenant Adrianna Harold. While Ari didn't know who she was, Quinn had accessed her service record. She was a second lieutenant in the American Conglomerate Armed Forces who had been assigned to a private entity a few months earlier. The voicemail message simply said, "Locate target at Grove. Check in at normal time."

Quinn debriefed Ari on what he knew about this doctor, and he began with Dan's overall clearing of the man based on his search. She informed Ari that Dan's search was cursory at best, but her clearance could provide deeper intel. While she had Ari on the phone, she accessed the larger network and came back with a bit more information. It seemed that Dr. Gómez had been at Centro de Salud Mental Aranzuela in Madrid at the same time that Esteban was a patient. Hospital records showed no contact. At least on the network, these two hadn't crossed paths. The doctor had been practicing for only a few years, and the hospital in Madrid had been his first employment. He arrived in Boston a week after Esteban had been moved to Grove. Records showed that his patient, a Catalina Rodrigues, had no medical records until her admittance to Grove. Quinn said she would dig further, but Ari told her not to bother. That was enough to know that Dr. Gómez was not being honest. He would explore on his own, and he ended the call.

Dan entered the living room ten minutes later, scratching his head and yawning, but Ari had already left. His phone buzzed. Quinn relayed everything she knew to him, including the abrupt end to her call with Ari. Dan told her he trusted him, and that he was sure if Ari needed any help, he would ask. As soon as he ended the call, he noticed a text message from Ryuma. He arrived in his brother's medical office shortly thereafter.

"Those portals are certainly convenient." Ryuma was reading a chart as Dan emerged. "You had better sit down for this."

Dan took in the office, including the view of Osaka through the bank of windows.

"Hello?"

"Oh, sorry. I've never been to Osaka. Just admiring the view." He took a seat by the desk.

Ryuma pushed the folder aside. "I appreciate it differently."

"So, what's so urgent?"

"I had a visit from Otto Wolf. He made me an offer. I felt you should know."

"So, he's doing exactly as we said he would, trying to make alliances with you, Keion, and Jamshid to learn Apollo's location."

"I have to admit… It was a tempting offer. He said he had connections that could bring Hyotaru back to me, no strings attached. Not like Eurydice."

Dan leaned back and crossed his arms. "I see." He stared at his brother.

"You want to know what I told him, don't you?" Ryuma's voice was flat. "I told him I would think about it and that he should come back in three days."

"Why three days?"

"I'm a busy man. I heal people. My patient load has spiked recently, and they're my priority."

With a contorted expression, Dan sat up. He was about to speak when Ryuma began again.

"Hyotaru and I had our time together. Don't you think after she died that I did everything in my power to get her back? I spoke to Hades shortly after she left me. He offered to let me see her in Elysium, but I declined. After she drank from Lethe's waters, she wouldn't know who she was. I'd be watching a shade of the woman I loved with no chance to love her the way I used to. I've grieved. I buried that pain deep inside my heart. Hyotaru Kobayashi exists in my memories. I don't know who Otto says he knows, but not even Khaos could bring her back. Death has rules."

Dan's elbows rested on the chair's arms, and his chin sat on his interlaced fingers. He stared off until Ryuma cleared his throat.

"What will you tell Otto? I mean, if you have no intention of telling him anything, why didn't you just say that when you met?"

Ryuma exhaled slowly.

"You were considering telling him? Did you really need time to think about it?" Dan's voice rose.

Even without sight, Ryuma's eyes conveyed emotion. He glared at his brother. His words came out measured and calm, yet his tone was clear.

"You have no idea what it is to lose part of your heart forever. I know all about Ari's sacrifice. You lost each other for a year, but you're together again. Yes, I thought about it. I didn't want to fuel Otto's rage with an immediate denial. I don't want him to harm our father. But, when you've lived for millennia, you learn to ponder, to contemplate, to reason through things."

Standing up, Dan unsheathed his sword. "I'm sorry. You're right. Please let me know how your meeting goes."

Halfway through the portal, Dan turned to see Ryuma nod once.

"Again, I'm sorry."

Brandon had gone to the university to work for a bit when he heard a ringtone he hadn't heard in a while. He checked his phone, but it wasn't that. Someone was trying to reach him through video chat on his computer, but he didn't recognize the name: Violet331. Normally, he'd just disconnect since he didn't give this contact information to many people at all. He hardly used it. Intuition inspired him to accept. On the other end was a man whose face he knew, but in a place he didn't.

"Jamshid? How did you get this information?"

"Just listen, brother. I had a curious visitor who wants to know the whereabouts of a certain missing person."

Eyebrow raised, he nodded. "I see. And how did that go?"

Jamshid exhaled. "A bomb will go off at sunrise my time if I don't tell him what he wants to know."

"What? Where? I'll get the rest of—"

"Brandon, stop. I have a feeling that if you and your team show up, city blocks will *blow* up." Sweat beaded on Jamshid's forehead. "I don't have power, not like I used to. This has to be handled delicately."

Pressing his hands together and putting them against his lips, Brandon looked off for a moment.

"If we give Otto misinformation, he'll detonate." He shook his head. "We can't tell him where Apollo is." Leaning back, grunted. "Damn it. Dan just told me Ryuma had a meeting as well. Haven't heard from Keion yet, but I imagine it's the same."

"If I tell the authorities what's happening and try to evacuate, it'll be chaos." Jamshid looked over his shoulder. "I'm at an internet café in the city. We can't talk much longer."

Brandon told him that he would contact the others and see what they suggested. Going up against Otto would prove to be disastrous, especially after what happened in Boston. Joined with the power of Orion, Brandon added, Otto would be almost unstoppable. The Olympeians, according to Jamshid, while powerful, didn't have a base of worship in the mortal world that they once had. To help, they would have to reveal themselves to the world, and that would open up discussions that they felt mortals couldn't handle just yet. One team of four with connections to the gods was more than enough for them to understand. Their most powerful adversary who had full and clear knowledge that could help them was currently indisposed with Gaea's adyton.

When Brandon's phone buzzed, he saw it was Keion. He told Jamshid he'd get back to him as quickly as he could. Keion had a similar story to share, but his situation wasn't quite as dire.

"He wants to offer art for Apollo's location? That doesn't make sense. Why would Otto threaten to blow up Mashhad but offer you paintings? Is there something about Mashhad that threatens him? Did he say anything else?"

Keion responded with a single, "No."

"Now, I'm stumped. We have only a few hours"—he checked his watch—"actually, less than that, to prevent an explosion in Mashhad."

"So, the Apollonides are helpless. We took on Apollo's power just to watch a madman commit murder."

Brandon thought for a moment.

"I'll call you back."

He texted Dan to see if he could find one of the two individuals, or both, who should be able to help. This was one of those moments when he lamented that none of the zodiac gave him the power to travel like his brother's sword.

A portal closed in the middle of Brandy's Pub in downtown Los Angeles, causing the DJ to stop the music as Dan became the object of everyone's attention. He spied who was needed at a corner table.

"I need your help. Both of you."

Dionysos was swirling a brandy. "Nephew! Come, join us. Perhaps you can settle—"

"No! I need your help. Now. Autolycos has set a bomb to go off in Mashhad. We have maybe thirty minutes. You and Ares are the only two gods I know who can help."

"Autolycos? Hermes' whelp?" Ares chugged the last of his ale. "Can't you handle him?"

Dan leaned closer, locking eyes with his uncle. "Hundreds will die. I need you."

"You'll owe me." He glanced at Dionysos. "Let's go."

"What? You can surely—"

Ares glared and his eyes turned red.

"All right! All right. I'll go with you." Dionysos finished his brandy.

"Take me with you." Dan crossed his arms. "I don't know where the bomb is, but I would imagine you do. If something happens, I can help."

With a nod, all three vanished only to reappear just outside the café where Jamshid had spoken to Otto hours earlier. A minute later, Jamshid stepped up to them.

"We don't have much time left. I have no idea where the bomb is." He shot his eyes everywhere. "I don't have the power to stop it." His face was flushed, sweat on his brow. "Danelos, what should we do?"

After surveying the marketplace, Dan took Jamshid with him and then turned toward his uncles.

"Please. Find that bomb."

The gods never really cared for pretense, unless it served them, so Dionysos levitated himself above the throng of people, not caring who noticed. This world had seen its share of mystical occurrences, but it wasn't an everyday thing. Seeing a man rising above them stopped the people where they stood. Fortunately, it was early morning, so not many people walked the streets. Ares, however, had a different tack. Drawing this sword, he gripped the hilt with both hands, muttering something in ancient Olympeian. With flaming eyes, he lifted the sword with one hand, and it radiated a ring of fire, like a ripple. As soon as it came into contact with the location of the bomb, Ares turned toward it and vanished. Dionysos used his power to radiate calm across those who assembled. As the fruit of the vine has the power to invoke chaos, it also can create peace. With waves of energy passing over Mashhad, the people slowed their travels and became more subdued in their reactions.

Otto stepped out of an all-night convenience store, looked at his watch, and his expression soured. When he arrived at the café, he didn't expect to see two men waiting for him, one he knew.

"Mr. Motjaba, you impress me." He stared at Dan. "This would be your brother."

Dan glowered. "I am."

Otto smiled. "Sunrise has come, and yet…" He waved as if to imply something should be happening. "I didn't realize you were that powerful."

A broad shadow from behind made Otto turn and look up.

"He isn't." Ares dropped the crushed remains of the bomb into Otto's hands. "I am." He made eye contact with Dan. "Remember. You owe me."

With that, he shimmered away in a red mist. Dan sat up.

"Nothing would make me happier than to disembowel you for what you did in Boston."

"Ah, Mr. Fairmont, is it? You have the means to do it, do you not? What's stopping you?"

Dan rose, leaning toward Otto, but then sat back down.

"Ah, not today then. But there is the matter of the information I need." Otto turned his attention to Jamshid. "Until we meet again. Our business is not finished, son of Evadne."

Smirking, Jamshid cocked his head. "Information? Did I say I had information, or did you just assume I did?"

Straightening up with a scowl, Otto disappeared in black smoke. Dan gestured at the server for some coffee. The brothers neither said anything nor looked at each other. After the coffee arrived, Dan handed the server a few *reals*, took a sip, and leaned back in his chair. The noises of the growing market crowds blanketed them, giving each the distraction he needed from what had just transpired. With the third sip, Jamshid looked at Dan.

"Why *didn't* you kill Otto, especially after what happened in your city? You have the power and the weapon."

"Otto has information. He's useful, for now. If I give into my anger, we'll lose any opportunity to find out more." He sipped. "Answer me this. Why would Otto plant a bomb here, in Mashhad? Ryuma could have seen Hyotaru, and Keion was offered valuable art."

"Not sure. He and I had never met before until he approached me."

"I do find it interesting how he referred to you."

"My parentage isn't a secret."

Dan downed the last of his coffee. "Just knowing his fascination with our father, why he didn't refer to you that way."

"It's been a while since I've spoken with my mother. She stayed in Greece. By the Aegean. Something about being closer to her father."

Dan suggested that perhaps he call her and ask about Otto or Autolycos. He followed the idea that the world of immortals is quite small, especially when you're the child of an Olympeian.

Jamshid said he'd call her. Spying an alley or hidden place to use his sword, Dan asked him to keep in touch.

30 | CONNECTIONS

In the basement of her building, Alkinoë glided fluidly around, focusing on an unseen adversary. Her lips revealed a silent mantra. As her arms swung around, she took a variety of stances, controlling her breaths. Fluorescent lights buzzed as her solitary sparring became more intense, and her eyes jumped around. Reaching down, she snatched up a sword, using it to continue her dance. An Arkadeian relic, the sword had seen its fair share of battle, and it was the queen's favorite. It whistled as she swung around this metal extension of her body. Her fervor reached a crescendo, and she plunged the blade through a cement column. Using her toe, she lifted a wooden staff into her waiting hand and twirled it around, jumping and sweeping against that opponent in her mind. Like with the sword, she worked herself into a sweaty frenzy, and then cast the staff aside.

Her hands, weapons in their own right, moved through the silence, casting shadows on the floor and walls, along with her lithe legs, muscles tensing with each movement. Combinations of somersaults led to leaping across the concrete floor, doing backflips a few times before landing on a mat. Using her training by Athene, as well as her more recent Krav Maga, Alkinoë had retained her edge. She put her hands on her knees, her chest heaving. A whooshing sound made her spin around and snatch the towel that flew toward her.

"Everything all right?" Another woman, in a sports bra and shorts, stepped from the shadows, taking sips from a water bottle.

319

"Of course, Diana." Alkinoë chuckled, patting herself down. "Just working off some extra energy."

Diana tossed the bottle toward her.

"If you say so."

Alkinoë narrowed her eyes a little, asking if Diana doubted her. Diana replied that they had known each other for a long time. Part of their sparring arrangement was maintaining honesty. Carrying any kind of emotional burden would get in the way of their work together. She reminded Alkinoë that one of her sovereign duties was to maintain a clear head at all times. Showing distraction, even a little one, could give any adversary an advantage. Alkinoë commented that Diana knew her well and that it was an old friend from her past, someone as close to her as any blood sister.

Alkinoë spoke of how she had met this friend from another city when they were children on a hunting expedition. Another party, solely made up of women and girls, would occasionally meet in the woods outside of Tegea and join the Arkadeian hunting parties. The alliance between Themiskyra and Arkadeia had been one of the strongest in all of Greece. Similar in age, Alkinoë and her friend often paired off, and a friendship developed.

"Years later, within months of each other, she and I competed in tournaments in our respective cities where we each became queens. Our sisterhood remained strong. Then, I moved here with Apollo and Kidemonas."

"Who was this woman that lingers in your thoughts?"

"Danaë, Amazon queen of Themiskyra."

"She just suddenly came to mind?" Diana stretched in preparation for sparring.

Alkinoë shook her head. "Something about the memory troubled me. One of the moments in my mind that lingers is meeting Apollo through Danaë. *That* is not how it happened, though."

"Are you sure? I mean, it *has* been a long time."

"I think I know my own mind. It must be connected to what my son-in-law and his friend are doing to piece together Apollo's memories. My husband must have somehow tapped into that moment from the other timeline."

"And because of your deep connection and love, you are privy to that memory?"

Alkinoë nodded. "But, why? The Danaë he met and the one I know are different women. Or, are they?"

Diana took her staff and tossed another one to Alkinoë.

"How *did* you meet Apollo?"

"That, my friend, is a story for another day." She took a sparring stance. "Be ready."

Otto Wolf, sequestered in his private meeting space, paced, clenching and unclenching his fists. Against the wall, in a niche, sat the remains of his father's statue. With each pass around the room, he glowered at it, but there wasn't anything more he could do to the dust. Otto railed on about what he had done to evoke Apollo from wherever he could be hiding as if repeating his failures brought some clarity. At times, it didn't seem as if he were talking to anyone in particular, and other times, he was directing his comments.

His voice would change inflection, and he would speak of his reasons for drawing Apollo out from wherever he was. Those explosions across Boston were supposed to invoke a god's wrath, he said, but instead, all they did was bring the city of Boston together, along with the Task Force Division and the police, making heroes of ordinary mortals. He spun around toward an object sitting on a stone.

"I did this for you, and to lure Apollo out into the open! I sent souls to Hades, took human lives, all to appease your spirit, as tribute, Orion. You were the greatest hunter the world had ever known, and I thought by channeling your power, I could hunt my prey, but an Atlantaean witch can apparently undo all that. What good is this to me?"

The object shimmered in the ambient light, offering no reply.

"With a mortal mother and a bastard for a father, the scope of my power is limited. As for that Atlantaean, the Tetrastoikheia protect her. That wretched group of miscreants will soon figure out where I am! I have few resources… and fewer allies. If I can just learn Apollo's whereabouts, I can remove him from the equation."

Catching the pulverized marble in his view, Otto sighed and lifted a finger, coalescing some of the dust into the head of Hermes' statue.

"My father." Otto nodded his head. "My father, yes."

Through the maze that was Apollo's mind, Ari and Esteban scrutinized as the god plucked the strings of memory and placed them on different sides of the lyre. So many memories, Ari whispered to Esteban. How Apollo could keep track of which ones were from the other timeline and which ones were from the current one eluded him. Esteban concurred. At one point, Apollo stopped before a tangled mess of strands and ran his hands over it. In a way, it looked like he was making music only he could hear. With the slightest touch to bring out each string's resonance, he moved his fingers. One finger lingered on a particular string, and he pulled it taut. With this other hand, Apollo summoned Ari, placing the man's finger on the string. Ari gasped as the memory filled his head. His hand trembled, but Apollo held it to the string.

"Y-You are speaking with my father. I did not know that you knew him. I am there, too, as a two-year-old. My father is telling you of thieves who had stolen items from the Temple of Hades, including vessels of holy wine for sanctification. Sometimes, my father would perform the necromanteia, where mourners can speak with the dead. The wine was part of the ritual."

Ari wiped away some tears.

"You are now reassuring my father that you will protect him, and me, from further thievery. Then... Then, the prince... Kidemonas is coming in to play with me while the men speak." Ari smiled.

Esteban then saw Ari's expression harden, and he wrenched his hand from the string.

"You lied. You lied to Timaios. To me. You did not protect my father. Danelos told me that my father languished after I disappeared. I could not go back to Arkadeia to see him. My father injured himself to attract the Eurynomoi who would then devour him. He was looking for an escape from his suffering."

Esteban put a hand on Ari's shoulder. "Did they save him?"

"No. Kidemonas, who had gone back to Arkadeia with Danelos, took him from the temple where the Eurynomoi were, but his wound was too great. He bled to death."

Ari's voice grew deeper, interrupted by sighs. He put his hand back on the string and squeezed it between his fingers before he wrapped his hand around it and tried to pull it, shaking the web-like configuration. It wouldn't come loose. Apollo turned to Ari, confused. Before the young god could do anything, Esteban stepped in front of Ari.

"Stop. This is *his* memory. He didn't know you would be hurt by it, and he doesn't understand what has happened."

Again, Ari pulled at the string, ignoring Esteban and Apollo. The next thing Ari knew, he was standing over Esteban's bed.

"What did you do?" Ari growled. "What—"

In his mind, he heard Esteban.

"Enough! I pulled us from Apollo's mind because I didn't know what you would do. The Apollo we see in his mind has no idea what you know. What did you think you were doing, pulling on the string?"

His hands clamped on the bed rail, Ari squeezed until the metal gave way but stopped before he could do serious damage.

"I-I just wanted that memory to end."

It was a few minutes later that Esteban commented that he knew what it felt like to be disappointed by Apollo. He also reminded Ari that when Dan and Brandon had traveled to the past, Apollo wasn't there anymore, so there was nothing he could have done to protect Timaios. If he wanted to be angry at Apollo, he could. He couldn't and wouldn't take that away from Ari, but if that anger got in the way of Apollo's recovery, then he would have to put that anger aside until Apollo could receive it. Reluctantly, Ari agreed. Plus, Esteban added, his anger wouldn't bring Timaios back. Ari said nothing. Esteban said they should convene the next day after Ari had had some time to cool off. Without responding, Ari left the hospital.

Dan came home to see Ari asleep on the sofa. He planted a soft kiss on Ari's forehead, and Ari's eyes fluttered open. As soon as he saw his husband, he threw his arms around him and squeezed. Dan asked what was wrong, but Ari just held on, pressing his chin on Dan's shoulder. Dan leaned back on the couch, his arm around Ari. They didn't talk for a while. When Ari wanted to talk, Dan knew he would. That night, when they went to bed, Dan was sitting against the headboard with Ari lying against his chest. Feeling Dan's arms around him, he fell asleep soon after. They hadn't talked about what happened, but whatever it was, Dan knew he could handle it.

Around 9 a.m., Ari returned to Esteban's bedside and apologized for how he had acted. Esteban thanked him but said that it was Apollo, the version in the god's mind, who deserved the apology. They found Apollo in yet another string-strewn, venom-coated chamber. As soon as Apollo saw Ari, he threw his arms around him, asking why he had left. Ari knew he had to be honest, so he explained everything. Apollo lowered his head, saying he didn't really remember Timaios that well at this point, but he said he could empathize with the anguish Timaios must have endured dying without his son near him. Ari apologized for his anger, saying that he understood how Apollo couldn't have stopped Timaios from killing himself since the god wasn't in Arkadeia at the time. This adolescent Apollo didn't have those recollections, but he assured Ari that he would do something to honor Timaios once he regained his full faculties.

Using his own flames, Apollo burned off the venom in the chamber. Esteban commented that the torches were no longer needed if Apollo could do this on his own. He must be getting stronger, Ari added. As if anticipating the question, Apollo said he would not be able to burn off all the venom at once. To attempt such a thing could be disastrous. He went back to stringing his lyre.

Ari pulled Esteban aside and asked if he thought Apollo should know more about what was happening in the outside world. Perhaps knowing the impending danger might intensify Apollo's motivation to clear his mind. Esteban reflected on when Apollo had been inside *his* mind in Madrid and told Ari that things have to happen in their own time. Not only did Apollo need to sort out his memories, but he would also have to get stronger. While Ari agreed, he wasn't sure keeping things from Apollo was a good idea. It took a little while for Apollo to clear the chamber of strings. His smile of satisfaction lifted the spirits of the others. In the next chamber, the god continued his task with a bit more alacrity. As he worked, he commented that he was happy to have both of them with him. It had given him a positive anchor. In their absence, he didn't work with the same intent. Esteban offered the idea that perhaps Apollo liked having someone bear witness to his task, to give it more meaning. The god turned toward him and grinned, nodding.

With another chamber cleared, Apollo stepped toward a metal door with a green patina and multiple locks around the edge. A symbol embossed in the center made Apollo gasp.

"What is it?" Ari got closer to it. "I do not recognize this symbol." He reached up to touch it.

"No!" Apollo pulled Ari's hand back. "Kíndynos."

"Danger? Why would you have such a place in your own mind?" The way Ari asked, he didn't expect to get a response.

The blue-gray eyes of Apollo latched onto the symbol. He exhaled hard.

"We cannot go on."

Both Ari and Esteban swung around with those words.

Pacing before the door, eyeing the seam between the metal and the surrounding stone, Apollo let his fingers graze the edge of the copper door.

"Apollo, no!" Ari reached to pull the god's arm back, but Apollo put up his other hand.

"It is all right. Stand back."

Igniting flames in his hands, he pressed them onto the door. The fires consumed the entirety of it, eventually dwindling until they burned out. Apollo stepped back to reveal the glimmering copper door, free of its age. The symbol stood out clearly: a skull with a serpent wrapped around it.

"What in the name of Olympos is that?" Ari's face quivered, and his eyes widened.

"The symbol of Python. Beyond this door lies memories tied to the son of Gaea, both in the past and recently."

Esteban moved closer. "Apollo, if I may be so bold, how is it you're speaking English now?"

When Alkinoë responded to the knock on her door, she saw Sarah, and her expression softened as she beamed. It had been so long, she whispered, since they had spent any time together. Before Sarah knew what was happening, Alkinoë put a cup of Darjeeling in her hand and gestured toward the living room sofa. Sarah commented on how much she always enjoyed being in her home, that it created such a soothing atmosphere. Alkinoë blushed as they sat. More small talk about pottery exhibits and volunteer work with a children's hospital followed, and by the third cup of tea, they were laughing like old school friends. Sarah thanked her hostess for the invitation, adding it had been months since they had spent any quality time together. With another sip, it was the eyes of a warrior queen peering over the edge of the china cup and not just the wife of Apollo.

"This has been quite enjoyable, but…" She placed the cup on the saucer and leaned back. "Something is on your mind. What is it?"

Sarah's cup made a tik as it touched the saucer, and she sighed.

"Well, yes, I did come to ask you something. How did you know?"

"I used to be able to read the slight expressions of my captain of the guard from across the battlefield."

"Okay. Well, then... Do you know if Apollo keeps any information on the ancient gods? Things like prophecies or other old texts?"

Alkinoë cocked her head. "What are you looking for exactly?"

"We have some connections between Autolycos and Orion-"

Alkinoë sat up, her soft aspect tightening.

"...and I thought I would ask—" Sarah stopped when her friend's demeanor changed.

As if it were a sign, Alkinoë took Sarah's pause to head toward the kitchen. Sarah's head tilted to one side and then followed.

"What I am to show you know cannot be shared, not even with my sons."

"Of-Of course." Sarah trailed Alkinoë up a staircase behind the kitchen.

The winding wooden stairs had lights along the floor to guide them, something atypical in a building that had been around since the early 1900s. Sarah asked if they were headed to the roof. Three upward turns later in silence, they stopped at a landing, and the stairs continued up. A dark wooden door before them looked no different than the others in the building except that it lacked a doorknob. Alkinoë asked if Sarah knew how to open a mystical lock, a *magikí kleidariá*. Sarah smirked. Putting her palm on the door, she closed her eyes.

"The door is indestructible. I can feel the energy it gives off, but Apollo kept the lock simple. Old magic. I suppose he didn't expect anyone to try." Her eyes turned bright orange. A word from a language that hadn't been spoken in eons came from her mouth.

After a few clicks, the door vanished, revealing a small chamber of stones lined with old, wooden shelves piled with scrolls and objects. A small square table in the center lay stacked with books, more scrolls, and a lamp that ignited as soon as they entered. Alkinoë said that she had never been in the room, but Apollo had spoken of it. She had a feeling that, if anyone could open it, Sarah could.

When Sarah inquired as to why Apollo never showed her what was inside, the once-queen replied that everyone had secrets. This room, she added, wasn't a room. It was on another dimensional plane, like Olympos. She started to ask Sarah if she knew what she was looking for to which Sarah replied that she would know it when she saw it. From the ancient stories of her Atlantaean ancestors, high priests kept scrolls sealed with special locking mechanisms that would only unlock for the worthy. Sarah cleared a place on the table and unfurled a cloth that held a thin chain with a crystal. She held up the crystal to her mouth and whispered to it. The crystal pulsed with light and swung back and forth. Calling forth a piece of the lamp's fire, she said Orion's name aloud and blew the flame at the crystal. Five beams of light struck different parts of the chamber.

"Quickly, collect the objects touched by the light before it fades."

Five scrolls. That would be the bounty of the light. Each scroll was bound with an intricately inscribed ring.

"These locked scrolls all contain the name of Orion. We need the *key*." Sarah examined each one, her fingers brushing the mechanisms ever so lightly.

As if she had had an epiphany, Alkinoë stood taller and commented that, in Arkadeia, similar locks only opened in sunlight or moonlight. Sarah scooped up the scrolls and headed toward the roof. Alkinoë found Sarah placing the scrolls on the tar paper. Looking at the sky, she grimaced.

"It's a cloudy day, but," her voice lilted, "I can fix that."

Lifting her arms and face to the sky, she found the spot in the clouds where the sun should be. She pressed her palms together and muttered to herself. The diamond on her ring gleamed white.

"Khaos of the lower air, I invoke you! Great Mother of the Protogenoi, part these clouds so that Helios may be seen!"

At first, nothing happened. Gradually, the air moved around them until their hair whipped around. Air currents tousled the trees along the streets, and flags flapped as if maddened. The gray clouds dissipated, and beams of sunlight shot through as if shot by a celestial bow. Showered in light, the metallic bands on the scrolls buzzed with electricity, clicking until each one popped

327

open. Sarah and Alkinoë returned to the chamber and unfurled each scroll with care so that the parchment wouldn't crack.

"Of *course* they're in ancient Greek." Sarah rolled her eyes.

Alkinoë stepped in. "Allow me." She scanned the scrolls. "These first two speak of Orion's exploits, probably from a priest of Hephaestos. This third one might be what you're looking for. See these symbols? They speak of how Orion's bow was placed with him in the heavens when Zeus made him into a constellation. To retrieve anything from the heavens requires one of two things. One is the Eye of Ouranos that Brandon has, and the other is..." She ran her finger across the symbols. "I can't make it out."

"What is it?" Sarah narrowed her eyes over the parchment as if to learn something.

"I wonder... Perhaps Autolycos' purpose is to sacrifice Apollo using the bow. The woman who bore Autolycos—"

"I know about Chione. Her son Philammon told us what happened."

Alkinoë looked toward the shelves of scrolls. "Perhaps Autolycos is jealous because Philammon was born of love, so he wishes to punish him. To kill his *own* father would bring the wrath of the Erinyes, however."

"But, to do what he did to Boston? All to draw Apollo out? All of those lives..."

"Autolycos *is* the greatest thief known to the world. It wouldn't surprise me if he found some arcane magic to take the bow from Orion's celestial grip. Touched by Ouranos, the bow would have power beyond reckoning. Perhaps that information is what's missing from the parchment."

"Are you saying that it was the bow's power that gave Autolycos what he needed to attack Boston on such a grand scale?" Sarah paled.

Alkinoë clenched her fists. "If he could tap into it, yes."

"From what I know, the gods abhor human sacrifice. Tantalus tried to feed the gods his son Pelops—"

"And Tantalus is in Tartaros. That is where Autolycos belongs. I wonder if he thinks he can reach Apollo where he lies with such a weapon."

"Then, we need to find out what ancient enchantment was used to break the heavens' hold on the bow so we can undo it. Those deaths should be avenged."

Alkinoë shivered and found a place to sit. She placed her hands over her mouth and clenched her eyes shut. Tears still found a way out. Sarah put an arm around her, feeling the woman's body tighten and release with each sob.

"It's okay. We'll figure it out."

Something flickered in the light from the hall and landed on the table. Through teary eyes, Alkinoë noticed and reached out.

"Meleia!" The little owl hopped onto Alkinoë's finger. "You are my hope, tiny one. Athene be praised! There is hope yet, Sarah." She wiped her eyes. "I was thinking of her, and she appeared."

Sarah returned the scrolls to their designated space in the chamber.

"I need to go. Are you all right?" She placed a hand on Alkinoë's shoulder and smiled at Meleia.

Nodding, Alkinoë brought the owl into the hallway with Sarah following. As soon as the chamber was empty once more, it sealed. Back in the apartment, Alkinoë brought Meleia onto the balcony where the little owl perched on a branch of the potted olive tree.

"I'll keep you posted." Sarah hugged her friend.

"What are you going to do?"

Sarah turned back just before she left. "Talk to Brandon."

Enjoying a cup of coffee on the balcony, Dan leaned on the rail to watch the activity around the Charles River and the skyline beyond it. Breezes played with the ends of his hair. The glass door opened from the living room. Brandon fell back into a lounge chair, exhaling, putting his hands behind his head. Dan looked over and smirked.

"Well, there goes *that* serene moment." He laughed and sat next to his brother. "What's on your mind?"

"Just thought I'd stop by and say hi. Everything going well at the university?"

"My archaeology students are raising money to go on a dig to Egypt or Machu Picchu, whichever they can afford first. I told them I'd help them make the arrangements."

"You gonna go?"

He took a deep breath. "I don't know yet. It's been ages since I've been on a dig. Might do me some good. It's contingent on a few things."

Brandon stared at him. "Like Dad? I wouldn't think you'd go before Dad returns."

"Of course, I'd wait for Dad. You're kidding, right?"

Tapping his fists against his legs, Brandon gazed off at the skyline.

"Maybe."

"What is this about, Brandon? You didn't come here to bust my chops, did you?"

Brandon swung his legs around to face Dan.

"And this is about Otto." Dan shook his head. "You want to know why I didn't just kill him. Oh, don't shrug at me. You know we have a rule against that, right? If I had, you don't think he wouldn't have a contingency? We know nothing about them. Nothing. And you're pissed because I didn't take him out."

They sat in silence for a little while. Out of the corner of his eye, Dan looked at his brother. Brandon did the same thing. Finally, Brandon blurted out that he didn't understand why Otto wanted their father so badly. Apollo had never even mentioned him. After a swig of coffee, Dan said maybe they should meet him and find out. Brandon glared.

"Meet him? He doesn't get a social call when he killed thousands of people. Seriously? If we meet him, we put him in some sort of prison that could hold him."

"Look, Otto's had millennia as a demigod. He knows how to manipulate people. I just don't think we're ready or able to take him in. He's been able to stay hidden this long. Plus, he's not above taking lives. The next ones could be ours. I'm not suggesting we sit down and laugh about our dysfunctional Olympeian ancestry. I'm just saying we should *talk*. I have faith that Ari and Esteban are making progress in helping Dad. Once Dad's better, he can help us with Otto."

"That's an awfully unclear time frame you have there. That could be… months? Even years before Dad's back to himself. So, how do you expect to meet Otto? Is there even neutral ground?"

Dan raised his voice, wanting his brother to tell him when he thought they should meet. Was there somewhere where Otto wouldn't try something? Brandon looked away. More silence settled between them. He said he didn't know under his breath. Dan asked what he'd said.

"I don't know! I'm not as worldly traveled as you are. This," he pointed to his amulet, "doesn't open doors to places."

Dan clenched his fist so hard he broke his coffee mug. Brandon's eyes widened, and he stood up slowly.

"Hey, if we're gonna fight, let's not do it up here." He smirked.

Dan shook his head and laughed.

"I don't want to fight with you. Our fight is with Otto. He's not even here, and he's got us going after each other." He looked down. "And that was my favorite mug too."

After hugging it out, they went inside. While Dan threw away the mug's pieces, he said the way to keep Otto from doing anything when they met was to invoke a sacred truce. That was what Apollo had done in Arkadeia. It would give them a few hours to meet, and neither side could do anything to the other. The enchantment was old but reliable. Even Otto's associates, since he would have some, wouldn't be able to do anything. After the truce ended, all bets would be off, though. Just then, Sarah called Brandon. All Dan heard was him agreeing to do something, and then he said he had to go. Sarah had a plan she wanted to try. Before he left, Brandon suggested a location for the truce since it would be far from anyone to harm, if things went awry.

Apollo, without taking his eyes off the door, said that something about the door must have broken the barrier between ancient Greek and his ability to speak English. That must mean he's getting closer to fixing the problem with his memory. He also said that getting through this next chamber would be even more difficult than the others.

"Why?" Esteban looked between Ari and Apollo.

"I faced Python when I was younger... and more recently. That first time, I expended a great deal of energy going up against a son of Gaea and needed to rest for quite a while. You know what happened this last time."

Ari fixed his eyes on the door. "What should we expect?"

Apollo shook his head. "This door has none of the venom, but that might not be a good thing. We have to tread carefully."

"But this is your mind—"

"Esteban, we are in a god's mind. This is uncharted territory." Ari shrugged.

Extending his hands toward the door, Apollo said he knew why they both needed to be with him. They each put a hand on his shoulders. When Apollo's palms made contact with the copper, his eyes became like tiny suns. His voice grew louder as the ancient words poured out. The mental landscape shook all around them. Emanating from his hands, fire spread, melting the copper door. In its place remained a black opening into the unknown. Glacial air rushed past them, extinguishing the flames, and the pools of copper solidified beneath them. Apollo breathed heavily, his head lowered.

"Now what?" Esteban craned his neck to look into the emptiness.

"Now we go in." Apollo took their hands and all three became enveloped by the darkness.

Sunderson's Farm lay broken, the remains of the wooden barn and fence worn down. Weeds grew through openings in the debris, claiming what remained. The land, once fertile, was now fallow due to neglect and time. Dan stood in the middle of a field.

"I wonder if Hermes was able to get a message to Otto?" Dan said aloud, kicking scraps of broken wood. He crouched down to pull a handful of weeds. "I also want to know if he'll honor the truce."

Hermes materialized in overalls, a plaid shirt, and his hair looked like a 1950's movie actor. Dan joked that Hermes always had to play the part. The messenger had been able to communicate the truce to Otto through Morpheos. Dan muttered that he didn't realize a man like Otto would even dream. Hermes gave Dan a dagger of Helios and a small iron bowl. Both must draw blood into the bowl and invoke the truce. He was insistent that the truce would only last 2 hours, one per participant. Even if they accomplished what they sought out to do, they must wait for the time to elapse.

The winds shifted in direction.

"He's coming." Hermes vanished.

Through the expired field, Otto got closer, wearing overalls and a farm hat, a piece of hay in his mouth. Dan rolled his eyes.

He kicked the ground with his toe. "I didn't think you would come."

Pointing at Dan with the wheat, Otto replied, "Curiosity."

They drew the blade across their palms, and the crimson liquid pooled in the bowl, the rim of the bowl turning white for a moment. Dan looked at him, and together, they said, "Anakochí." *Truce.* An energy field formed around them.

"I guess the clock starts now." Otto tipped his hat.

Otto asked about the truce and commented on how clever it was that his father had used Morpheos to get into his dreams to convey the invitation. Dreaming was something he had allowed himself to do since it allowed him to live out his desires in full, he told Dan.

"What do you want with Apollo?"

Otto chucked. "I'm supposed to reveal all my secrets to you? Is that how this works?"

"The Boston bombings," Dan growled. "They were supposed to draw out my father. Does that loss of life not even matter to you? Parents are grieving for their children!"

Following loud laughter, Otto ranted about how life, especially mortal life, was inconsequential. To a demigod, who had lived centuries, life was tedium, a perpetual state of ennui. With time crashing all around like one wave after another, he had grown impatient with each sunrise, each sunset, and all of the moments in between. Entertainment became harder and harder to achieve. His own existence, he offered, was quite frankly a waste of cosmic energy. And, yet he could not bring about his own end. Even with the right tools, he wouldn't be able to extricate himself from the Moirae's threads. He was forever bound to them, to the world as a whole, and because of this, he had to focus on something even more important.

"What happened in Boston… well, that was *partly* meant to draw out your father. When you want to catch something, you use a lure." Otto spit a piece of the wheat out. "*Should* it matter? Mortals live lives of self-indulgence and hedonism. Within the bubble of their own interests, they thrive. Outside of it, they fail." He spat again. "I've been watching your father for an exceptionally long time. I wanted eyes everywhere." He spread his hands out.

Standing taller, Dan glowered. "Wait. What did you just say?"

Otto raised his eyebrow. "Didn't you hear me? I said I wanted to watch Apollo." He enunciated that second sentence.

"No, you said you wanted eyes everywhere. Oh, I wish Brandon could have heard you."

Dan laughed. "Those cameras *are* everywhere. The letters I saw on the camera casing." He stooped and wrote ΠΛ… O… T… S in the dirt with his finger. "Based on the spacing, and what you just said, I'd bet my sword that they spell PANOPTES. As in Argus Panoptes. Argus, the All-Seeing."

He stood and wiped his hand on his jeans.

"And the feather. It all makes sense now."

Smirking, Otto sat cross-legged and adjusted his hat. "You reasoned it out. Clever boy. *Now* what will you do?"

Dan said aloud, "I wonder why the computer couldn't determine the name from the letters and spacing. I mean, it's Greek. Probably some kind of ward of protection which, I'd imagine, no longer exists. It does not need to now."

Otto's smug expression melted into a pout. "You're not the only ones who can reason something out. Apollo's in hiding. He's not on Olympos. I've checked. He's not in Hades, either. Tartaros, perhaps? Oh, if wishing made it so. I offered your brothers various treasures, even threatened Mashhad, for the information. I have other ways. Other connections. Since I cannot find him, he must be somewhere where no search could find... Oh, now that's good..."

Sarah had asked Brandon to meet her at the Public Garden in Boston and awaited him at the edge of the pond. She entertained herself by playing with water, passing it from hand to hand in small streams.

"Simpler times, eh?" Brandon came up next to her, his hands in his pockets.

Smiling, she sent the water back into the pond. "Yeah. I didn't ask you here to reminisce about easier days, though. Come sit with me."

"Is everything okay?"

"When you were in Arkadeia, you found a shrine to Akmonides, right?"

"Wow, you're getting right to the point." He chuckled. "Yeah, why do you ask?"

"Alkinoë and I found some ancient scrolls that say the only way Autolycos could get Orion's bow, which it seems like he's using to augment his power, is either with your amulet or something else equally as powerful. Now, I know he didn't use the Eye of Ouranos, so can you think of anything else that could summon a celestial object?"

Brandon leaned back on his hands. "Hmm. And you're thinking that Autolycos went to Akmonides' shrine and found something. I never saw anything there, except Leto."

She put a hand on his shoulder and smiled, a glint in her eye. "We should go there."

"You're serious. Wow. Well, I guess we could, but I don't know how. Dan's never been, so he couldn't use his sword."

Sarah nodded toward his chest. Under his shirt was the amulet, although it didn't show because of a glamour she had used once their original glamour from Apollo had faded. "With your connection to the amulet, maybe it can give the sword the image it needs?"

"I suppose it's worth a shot." He texted Dan. "He'll get this after he meets with Otto."

"Excuse me?" Sarah put her hands on her hips.

"Yeah… let me explain that."

Dan stood taller and his face hardened. "You think you know, do you? And these connections. Who? Hermes?" Dan crossed his arms. "You think he'll help you? Or, do you think you can force him to? And just where do you think my father is?"

Otto grinned. "You needn't worry about what I can or cannot do, child. My arsenal contains things that would make even Zeus grow pale."

Dan growled, jumping toward Otto, but he stopped himself. "No. The truce is almost up. Otto, the sons of Apollo won't help you. Any of them."

The moment the magical truce ended, Dan portalled himself back to Task Force headquarters. Otto roared with laughter and vanished.

Once the portal closed behind them, Dan told Quinn he needed to go to Olympos if anyone was looking for him. He gave her the information he had figured out while talking to Otto so she could add it to their files.

He found Hermes flitting about in the throne room with Zeus seated, lost in thought. He told Hermes what happened and that he could be in grave danger. Hermes laughed, asking how Autolycos could possibly hurt him. Dan relayed that Otto had things in his arsenal that would make even the king of the gods grow pale. Zeus perked up. Dan explained that Brandon had been taken hostage a year earlier by a man who thought he could steal the zodiac amulet. The man used something called tharma-kondios, the "bane of Zeus." Olympos' king shot up. Hermes asked how that was even possible. That arcane substance was impossible to find. Dan brought them back to the moment, saying that it didn't matter how Otto got it, but that it seemed as if it were the most obvious thing for Otto to try. Zeus wasn't sure if there was anything that could counteract the poison. Magical herbs were not his forte. Hermes perked up and hovered closer to Dan.

"I know only one expert on magical herbs. But it will come at a price."

"There's another problem. Otto thinks he knows where Apollo is. What scares me, and you know it takes a lot to do that, is I think he knows too. Now it's a race against time."

Hermes blanched. "He… There is nothing he can do. Even if he found Gaea's adyton, he cannot enter it."

"I wouldn't put anything past him, Hermes. Grandfather, can you think of any way Otto could breach Gaea's inner sanctum?"

Zeus looked off for a moment and then shook his head. "But Danelos, that does not mean he will not try. He is a child of folly, and folly has a way of outthinking reason when it wants to. This enigma belongs to you and your team."

The messenger of the gods tightened the grip on his staff and melted away. Dan returned home, saw Brandon's text, and radioed Sarah about his conversation with Hermes. She said she needed to see him and would find him after his class.

Brandon and Sarah waited outside the lecture hall where Dan taught. For his job, he traded his T-shirt and jeans for khakis and an Oxford shirt. Dan knew that his secret identity, as it were, was basically nonexistent, but he acted on the premise that it was largely intact. People still had a difficult time believing in that which they couldn't explain, so those who knew Dan and his team never publicly outed them. It was more of a general curiosity. Dr. Dan Fairmont had been a professor long before he became a member of Task Force: Gaea. In some ways, he had convinced himself that Aegis and Dan Fairmont were two distinct people.

"It gets harder and harder to do my job with what we deal with." Dan brushed back his hair with one hand as he escorted them down the hall to his office. The mahogany-framed doors and ages-old plaster walls of the university were a stark contrast to the streamlined Task Force building. Once inside, he gestured for them to sit. "What's up?"

"Well," Sarah began, "I'm *not* going to ask you about your meeting with Otto." She glared at Brandon and then at Dan. "But… we do have a favor. We need you to send us to Greece."

Dan laughed. "You two going on a vacation?"

"Ha. Ha. No. Your mom and I found some scrolls that said Autolycos would need some ancient magic to retrieve Orion's bow from the heavens, and we think visiting Akmonides' shrine could give us some answers."

"Mhmm. You know I've never been there, right?"

Brandon sat forward. "That's where my amulet comes in. If we can somehow use its power to feed the image to the sword, maybe it can open a portal there. What do you think?"

"I suppose it's worth a shot. But, best not to do it here. I know where we can go."

The portal closed, putting them on the roof of Apollo and Alkinoë's building. It was tall enough to avoid the curious. Brandon put one hand on the amulet, the other on the sword, and closed his eyes. The gemstone in the amulet turned bright red and shone on the blue gem in the sword's pommel. The sword itself took on a reddish hue, and Dan took that as his cue to open a portal. As he finished the opening, the smell of ancient magic came through, and Brandon recognized the ruins of the shrine he had visited in the past. Dan wished them luck and told them to signal him when they wanted to return.

Remnants of the circular shrine remained, and the cypress trees that had once girdled it had long perished. Nothing of the past lived in this place. Within the crumbled remains lay the fire pit, its edges jagged from the erosive elements. Both Brandon and Sarah examined this once-holy space in silence. This site atop Mount Parthenion had a vantage overlooking a valley peppered with wildflowers and grasses, as if it chose to isolate itself from humanity and all its foibles. No sounds except that of the winds brushing past them broke the stillness. Brandon stepped to the edge of the mountain.

"I climbed up here from the valley once." He wasn't even sure Sarah was close enough to hear him. "Coming to terms with my Arkadeian heritage came with a price."

Dirt crunched under Sarah's feet. "And what was that?"

"I could no longer hide behind any boundaries, externally or internally. Accepting who you are means you have to accept every single thing. Being here back then challenged so much of what I knew. Learning that Akmonides and Ouranos were one and the same was one thing I had to wrap my brain around."

"And what else? Well, you said 'one thing'. I assume there were other things."

Brandon nodded, gazing out at the valley. "The voice of the shrine turned out to be my grandmother's. The Hidden One. I understood more about my introversion once I knew that my own kin chose to remain out of sight of the world."

She leaned against his shoulder, squeezing his forearm.

"It's a shame that she can't be here now to help us."

Smiling, Brandon put his arm around her.

"Yeah. Come on. Let's see what we can find."

Unlike a temple that had inner chambers, this austere shrine had a fire ring and nothing else, even in its original form. It had no roof or doors. Its purpose was to allow the celestial tapestry to shine through and offer the unfiltered light of the stars and moon to purify anything in its presence—a bridge to the stars from the Earth itself. Brandon clutched his amulet while he examined the ruins. As he made his way around the circumference, he sat on the part of the fire ring that was still intact. In the center, where a fire would burn, lay nothing but dust and withered leaves. Sarah returned to the ring as well, standing on the opposite side where Brandon was. She leaned closer, narrowing her eyes, and blew toward the center. The wind moved some of the dirt.

"What're you looking at?" Brandon's voice barely broke a whisper.

"I see something." Making a gesture with her fingers, she created a small whirlwind that carried the object to her waiting palm. "It's a piece of burned parchment. Recently burned, too."

Brandon joined her. "How recent?" He scrutinized the paper.

"Not sure. But, this couldn't have survived since ancient times."

She moved the air around the fire ring, nudging the debris away more. Two more pieces of parchment lay beneath the dust. Examining each one, Sarah deduced they were from the same larger piece, but she saw no words or symbols. She commented that she didn't know of any reconstruction spells to bring the parchment back to its original state or even show them what was

338

on it, but perhaps there was someone who could help. Sarah texted Dan.

Half an hour elapsed before they saw something circling above them. Wings spread wide, it flew above the fire ring before settling on it. It was an owl, species *Athene noctua*, and it transformed into its namesake.

"Thank you for coming." Sarah bowed her head.

Athene smiled. "Of course. It has been a while, hasn't it, Kidemonas."

Brandon nodded. "Indeed it has. The last time I saw you was before I was about to climb to this very spot."

"I have not been here since then, either." She gestured for Sarah to give her the pieces of parchment.

In the presence of mortals, she would appear as the circumstances demanded it. To Odysseus, she appeared in her resplendent armor. For this moment, she wore a simple shift bound around the waist with a belt made up of metallic owl faces and leather thong sandals. Her hair was pulled back with a comb. Athene placed the pieces on the ground and stretched her hand above them.

"Apokalýptoun ta mystiká sas." *Reveal your secrets.*

The edges of the parchment grew outward until all three were bound to where they were originally. Symbols appeared one by one.

Brandon leaned over. "That's not in any version of Greek I would know."

The goddess picked up the parchment. "It is not. It is not even in Olympeian Greek. These symbols are from an early Protogenoi tongue. How Autolycos could read this astounds even me."

"He is a thief. Who knows what he came by that would enable him to understand it, let alone say it." Sarah shook her head. "None of this even looks familiar, and I've studied ancient Atlantean as well."

"Can you read it?"

Athene shook her head. "Alas, no. I don't even think Zeus could. The only ones who could would be a Protogenos, and the only living and present one would be Gaea. She wouldn't, not for one such as Autolycos."

Brandon sighed. "He's a master of disguise, but I don't think he could fool Gaea. Could he? Who would he have impersonated to get her to translate this?"

Athene said she could surround the shrine in a temporal bubble and cast another revelation enchantment to show the images of who had been at the shrine, but it would take a little time to prepare as she would need to meditate. Brandon told Sarah that, even though Athene was an Olympeian, working within the tapestry of time was tricky business. This was why Apollo was careful about sending him back to the past. He had had to prepare for three days just to invoke the power to do it. Sarah wondered why Brandon never really tapped into his own powers as a demigod and preferred to use the amulet. His answer was simple: fear. Giving in to his Olympeian side meant learning how to use enchantments. Having access to that level of power had responsibilities tied to it. He liked having more control over his life than giving himself over to powers beyond his understanding. Dan had dabbled in it, he told her, and he also decided it was best to use the sword as his instrument.

"Dan told me that, in that other timeline, Zeus tried to kidnap him when he was born because he wanted Dan to become an Olympeian. Later, Demetrios was sent to free Ares from Tartaros to maintain balance on Olympos. Even in that other time, Dan didn't have aspirations of being a god. He enjoyed humanity way too much.

"With my Atlantean ancestry, I'm tied to primordial forces too. Like you both, I prefer being human, but with access to the power we do have. Whatever godly power may have brought about the Atlanteans and my ancestors was so diluted over time and the humanity in my ancestry. I couldn't even imagine being a goddess." She looked over at Athene sitting on the remnant of a pillar. "She must bear quite a heavy burden."

It took about an hour for Athene to finish her meditation. She instructed them to stand behind her as she created the temporal bubble.

"Be prepared for what you might see. Remember, though, that this is simply the past playing back. You cannot change anything."

"How far back do you need to go?" Sarah twirled her finger in a backward motion.

"The enchantment will move swiftly through time until it comes across those who have been to this shrine, and then it will slow down. I would imagine that no one comes here, not even tourists. This is not a spot heavily known by mortals."

Extending her hands, Athene began the enchantment. Once she finished, a shimmering barrier formed around the entirety of the shrine. They could see inside it, but nothing could enter it. Light and shadow moved as days and nights transpired. As she said, no one visited the shrine. Hours passed, with Brandon and Sarah pacing around the barrier. Athene asked them to be patient. One couldn't make time go any faster than it wanted to. The sun eventually set, so Sarah set up makeshift torches around the perimeter. Brandon was staring off into the skies when he heard Athene's voice.

"Watch."

A figure approached the fire ring. In the torchlight, they could make out a decidedly male form. As he moved toward the ring, his face came into view. Sarah gasped.

"Autolycos posed as *you*, Brandon. How could Gaea not know it wasn't you, though?"

Athene froze the activity within the bubble. "He has access to magics older than the gods if he can fool a Protogenos. I do not even know where he would get that."

Sarah got closer to the bubble to see the doppelgänger of Brandon. As she moved around the scene, a shadow behind him caught her attention.

"Athene, please continue showing who was here. I think we're missing something."

"As you wish." She gestured, and the activity continued.

"Look behind the figure of Brandon. There's someone else with him." Sarah pointed to the shadow.

Athene made some other gestures. "Stand back. I will expand the bubble."

The shimmering boundary moved outward, capturing more of the space. Sarah gasped and put her hand over her mouth. Athene stopped the progression.

Sarah stepped closer. "If I didn't see this with my own eyes, I wouldn't believe it."

"That's... That's *Ari*." Brandon's eyes narrowed. "How is that possible?"

Athene moved into the bubble and examined the figure of Ari, looking closely at his face.

"No. It is not him. It is someone using his body. I can see a presence behind his eyes that is not human."

Sarah's jaw fell open. "Python back when he inhabited Ari's body. This happened months ago before Apollo was bitten. Autolycos has been planning this for a while, then." She pulled out her phone and snapped a photo. "Will the picture last after you remove this enchantment?"

Athene nodded. "That would explain how Autolycos had the power to fool Gaea. Python is her son, and he had managed to manipulate her."

"And since Python is trapped in the heavens, we won't know what the parchment said."

Brandon scratched his head. "Well... technically... I *could* reach out to Python through the amulet. But it's risky. If he tries to assert himself, he might escape."

Athene stood taller. "Then, you cannot. You will have to find-"

"Gaea. We can just ask *her*. We obviously don't intend to use the incantation. We just need to know what it says so we can find a way to counter it."

"Sarah, is your connection to her that strong?" Brandon crossed his arms.

"There's only one way to find out."

Glancing to the sky, Athene raised an eyebrow, thinking for a moment.

"You need not speak with Gaea. In fact, you do not need to know what that parchment contained."

Sarah shared a look with Brandon. "I'm not sure I understand-"

"We know that Autolycos posed as Brandon to get Gaea to show him the enchantment to release the bow from the heavens. But, Brandon, you do not need any enchantment to take things from the heavens, do you?" Her question sounded more like a statement.

"I've never actually taken anything *from* the heavens-"

"However," Athene held up a finger, "you *have* placed things in the heavens."

◦━✦━◦

Upon returning to Boston, Sarah remembered her conversation with Dan about what transpired on Olympos with Hermes and Zeus. She had one more journey to make, one that could put her in great peril. Dealing with the world of the gods always meant a price would be exacted for any favor. Immortals rarely, if ever, acted beneficently. If you wanted something, you had to be willing to pay what they wanted, and the cost was non-negotiable. Dan knew Sarah could handle herself, so that was never in question. He knew well, though, who she needed to talk to, and that individual didn't always play fair. Those who broker in magic seem to have no problem taking advantage when it suits them.

31 | BRINGING THE FIGHT

The glowing portal opened onto a lush, green meadow, carpeted with random patches of wildflowers, and the rolling landscape rippled in the sea breeze. As soon as the opening vanished, the smells of the Task Force office were wafted away, replaced with the cloying perfume of jasmine and rose. Boulders and trees, some fringed with ferns, sat amid the grasses. Hovering above, iridescent blue dragonflies danced on the wind with blue jays, warblers, or cormorants. In the background, atop a distant mountain almost obscured by clouds, rested a white marble shrine. Following some steppingstones, Sarah placed a small copper bowl on the grass and put in birch bark, lemon balm, and angelica.

"Daughter of Perseis, Daughter of Helios, I give this offering in peace. I come without malice."

Breezes blew across the fields, bringing the scent of lavender and lilac. So much floral perfume left a heady aroma lingering on the landscape. A white snake slithered through the grass toward her. Sarah lowered her head, gesturing toward the bowl. The snake made its way up her extended arm, flicking in one ear and then the other, moving down her other arm, and disappearing into the meadow.

The grasses parted before a woman whose white himation covered her head. "Welcome to Aeaea, daughter of Annabeth, descendant of Syra. Rise."

Sarah stood but kept her head lowered.

"Look me in the eye, girl. I wish to see the bold eyes of she who came all this way."

The woman removed her himation, and her deep brown hair was braided around her head, a metal comb, like a crown jutting forth. Along the top edge of the comb were silhouettes of animals. She extended her hands, and Sarah took them. The woman lifted them up, and she noticed the ring.

"So, you are the one worthy enough to direct the Tetrastoikheia. A sister of the craft. How may I help you?"

"Goddess, I ask for something from your garden. A snipping."

The woman nodded, understanding the request, gently squeezing Sarah's hands. "Protection... for whom? *From* whom?"

"Hermes, from Autolycos."

She laughed. "Father and son, a pair of fools. Why?"

"I fear Autolycos may try to harm his father to find the whereabouts of Apollo. He has already killed many innocents to find out."

"No one is *truly* innocent, sister. But, I understand. I ask a price."

"And I am willing to give what you ask."

"Be careful. You do not even know what I ask."

"To keep Hermes and Apollo safe, no price is too high."

"Noble and brave. Fitting for a daughter of Atlantis. Very well. Upon Apollo's return, come and spend one lunar cycle with me." She looked out over the land. "Syra came. As did her mother. We learned much from one another."

Sarah smiled. "Of course, goddess. It would be my honor."

"Please. We are sisters of the craft. You may call me by my name."

Dan had told her how to let him know she needed a portal to return, but instead of going to the Task Force division office, she went straight to Olympos. Hermes was most pleased to see her and that she had acquired the herb. He asked the price.

"Safeguard the ring. Circe is nothing if not cunning."

Sarah stared at her finger. The ring, in the ambient light of the Hall of Tribunals, took on a luster unseen back home. Each gemstone pulsed with energy as if it had sentience. Perhaps, like the gemstone in the pommel of Dan's sword, an immortal figure actually resided in each of the four stones. She knew that the power of Thalassa, Gaea, Khaos, and Hesteia could not be contained, but it would be easy to think that something lived within the crystalline structures.

"The ring is bound to me and only me. Surely, Circe knows that."

"Indeed." Hermes' smile illuminated his entire face. "But she would do everything in her vast power to wrest that from you. Do not underestimate her, despite that she may have called you 'sister'."

Sarah's eyes moved right to Hermes' face and narrowed. He laughed.

"I know things. Did she take your hands?"

Her expression made him laugh again.

"She tried to undo the binding enchantment on the ring while she held your hand. It will just mean she will try harder when you visit her." He held up the snippet of the herb. "Thank you for getting this. If it works as well as it did on Odysseus, then Autolycos will assuredly be... confounded."

"This is the third time you are here, doctor. What have you learned?" Otto crossed his arms and lowered his eyes a little.

Dr. Goméz wrung his hands, trying to make eye contact, but avoiding his direct gaze as if looking into Otto's eyes would burn his retinas like looking directly into the sun. His face twitched as beads of sweat eventually trickled down his temples.

"Not much, I'm afraid. Dr. Fairmont visits Esteban daily, and they spend hours in his room." He pulled his collar from his neck.

"Does he *say* anything?"

"No. I don't know what he's doing in there. Occasionally, he brings Esteban to the solarium." He stopped as if anticipating what Otto was going to ask. "I did try to speak with Esteban, to see if he was truly unreachable. He sat glassy-eyed. I have never heard him speak. I honestly don't think he can."

"Then why does Dr. Fairmont linger there? Why?" Otto's eyes flared orange.

"I don't know… Sir, I am afraid that he will figure something out about me. I can tell he watches what I do. Is there something else you want me to do besides observe? I will try to get into Esteban's room."

"See that you do."

"If I may… why does Esteban Reyes matter?"

Again, Otto's eyes shimmered a little and then returned to normal. "He matters to Dr. Fairmont, and Dr. Fairmont matters to his husband, a son of Apollo, and Apollo matters to *me*. See how that works? Your usefulness is waning, doctor. Fix that."

Cowering, Dr. Gómez left by shuffling out backward. Otto rebuilt the statue to his father with a gesture. "Now onto more pressing matters."

Standing over the fire pit, Otto's face took on the hues of the flames while his eyes glimmered like glass. He flicked his finger, and the image of a sphere hovered before him.

"How to find you, Apollo. The heart of Gaea remains a secret. That would be the only place where you could hide from me. Uncharted on any divine map, only those invited or permitted by the Earth Mother herself can enter. Had Python still held thrall over you, I could have used *him*, but now… I have to find other means."

The globe dissipated into the air, and Otto backed away from the ring into the shadows, chuckling to himself.

◦━━◆━━◦

Apollo and the others edged into the obscured, algid chamber. The son of Zeus ignited a palm fire, its plasma undulating. Only two threads traversed the space, and Apollo considered them both.

"Only two threads?" Esteban stepped closer.

"Yes." Apollo's voice was soft. "Make no mistake. There may only be two, but these memories have terrible power. One is from my first meeting with Python. The other, from my last."

"My father told me the story of how you defeated Python at Delphi, making the shrine yours. Would that not be a good memory? Why do you seem reluctant to relive it?"

"Ari, the battle lasted for an entire lunar cycle. Yes, I was victorious, but at a great cost. I was different then. This was before I left Arkadeia. Before I lived as a mortal." He moved around the chamber, never taking his eyes off the strings that sparkled with an almost radioactive presence. "I had yet to learn compassion. Being a son of Zeus, I used power to solve my problems. Even reason had its limits."

Esteban thought for a moment. "If both strings are from the same timeline, why not just attach them to the lyre and move on?"

"I would have to touch them to do that. Experiencing the emotional and physical toll they took on me… it's excruciating. Mortals bury difficult remembrances for a reason. When I was mortal, I had great difficulty doing that. Many, many sleepless nights."

"Can we simply return to this place after you have dealt with other less painful moments?"

Apollo shook his head. "There's an order to things. This chamber lies in our path now because my mind deems it so. Even if we tried to pass through this chamber without doing anything, we'd end up here." He took a deep breath. "You need to bear witness. That's why you're here. I understand that now."

"Do you want us to do anything to help you?"

"No, Ari. Just be here." Apollo closed his hand around one of the threads. He gasped. "Th-This is the first battle."

As the memory took hold, he started to sweat, and he lurched as if being struck. Scratches appeared on his face, and red ichor dripped to the floor. His other hand took hold of the string as he reacted to the battle. Bruises showed up on his arms and legs, his clothing ripped, and he fell to his knees with a grunt. A shrill cry shook the space around them, and the scene unfolded for Ari and Esteban to see. Apollo's clothing changed to battle-worn gold armor, the apparition of Python rising before them. This was how the serpent looked during those ancient days, so many of his scales shimmering. Thyroros in hand, Apollo deflected Python's tail and fangs. The Delphic shrine sat partly in ruins around them. Fang against sword. With one of Python's strikes, a fang snapped against the blade, but it grew back. Where the severed venom-filled piece landed, it scarred the earth.

Apollo's skill as a warrior would almost rival his sister Athene, his techniques fluid and powerful. At one point in the melee, however, Python pinned him down, moving his scaly head closer to his adversary. Venom dripped onto Apollo's cheek, burning it.

"I will make sssssure Gaea paysss homage to me. I will break her ssssspirit, son of Zeus!"

Apollo loosed a gut-wrenching scream, shaking the land and remains of the shrine. From his core, he glowed like a small sun, sending Python slithering into the shadows. As the light faded, his cheek had healed, and the sword's gems were afire.

"I will destroy you, Python. And, Gaea, your mother, will aid me!"

Amid hisses, the serpent laughed and returned to the open air. "She will never harm her own. Yet, she will ssserve me!" His tail knocked Thyroros away.

He reared up to strike, and Apollo took the advantage of seeing his adversary's vulnerability, firing three fiery arrows into the serpent's belly. His writhing ceased, and then Python breathed his last. His scaly corpse melted into the earth, leaving a dark stain. The scene then changed to Apollo, with Gaea's help, rebuilding Delphi. He remembered kneeling before her as she gave him the temple. As he assessed the damage, he found the high priest, a mortal he had known for decades, lying dead, yet another casualty of Python. He closed the man's eyes and put a coin under his tongue for Charon.

Ari and Esteban froze after witnessing such a spectacle. The image melted away. Apollo yanked the string free and put it on the lyre. His wounds then healed. As he reached for the other string, Esteban put his hand on Apollo's arm.

"If this is your mind, you should be able to set the terms. Why should you have to suffer?"

Apollo lowered his head. "Lying in Gaea's adyton, this is the memory that repeats, keeping me in writhing torment more than anything else." He whispered, his voice trembling, "Blessed Gaea, why must I suffer?"

Esteban narrowed his eyes at the other string, how it pulsed with energy, and then he looked over at Apollo, the anguish surrounding him, oscillating like a heartbeat. Without a second thought, he pulled the string free, allowing the memory to play in his mind. Apollo jumped, his mouth agape. Ari begged him to help Esteban, but Esteban shook his head and held up his hand as he dropped to his knees. With a tremulous voice, he uttered that he needed to understand. As Apollo had said, he would bear witness. Unlike the other memory that physically tortured Apollo, this one didn't affect Esteban the same. His face told a different story, however. Something was happening in his mind.

Time didn't pass the same way in Apollo's consciousness, so it was unclear how much had elapsed before the memory faded from Esteban's mind. Once the images faded, he fell back on the floor, his chest heaving. Ari helped him up. Esteban put the string on the lyre the way he had seen Apollo do it.

"You suffered through that moment long enough. Hopefully, now, you will have some peace. Come on. We have more to do."

⚬━◆━⚬

"Hello, father. You found me." Otto sat at the fire ring, the embers glowing. "I felt a disturbance in the Force as you arrived." He chuckled to himself.

Otto put on a gas mask before sprinkling something into the fire.

"I am sorry to do this, but I need information." His voice was muffled.

The embers sent up sparks as the dust ignited, and the chamber grew hazy. Hermes was at the other side of the ring, staring.

"Autolycos, my son…"

"Your son? You hold me in contempt! You *raped* my mother, and then you abandoned us."

"I-I do not know what to do or say. The past is what it was. I do not revel in that moment, and I have lived with that shame ever since. Believe that or not. I know that does not soften what happened or even remove the pain. Nothing can. *That* Hermes has not existed for thousands of years."

"You lived with shame, but do you know that my mother lived with shame as well? You took her innocence from her. You stole from her something that she could never, ever regain. And, then, like *your* father, you left her with child, without a care or shred of decency. You will pay for that. Soon."

Hermes sat on the ring. "You are right. I shall pay for what I did. But not by your hand. Only the Moirae know how that will unfold."

"Wait… What's happening?" Otto straightened up. "Why aren't you succumbing? You should be wheezing and covered in oozing pustules!"

Hermes pulled a small sprig from a pouch and held it out over the embers.

"As the closest Olympeian to you, the only one you could hope to see, you wanted to force me to reveal a secret by poisoning me with 'the bane of Zeus'." His voice deepened. "You may be my son, but you are a *hemitheos*. Chione, may her soul be at peace in Elysium, was a mortal. As clever as you are, you cannot surpass me." His eyes glowed red.

Otto stared at the sprig. "Moly… Damned witch. I'll—"

Hermes laughed. "You are no match for Circe. Abandon your quest, Autolycos. If you do not, rest assured, when you *do* see my brother, it may be the last thing you see." With that, he shimmered away, and the moly dropped into the embers, its essence eradicating the *tharmakondios*. Otto pulled off his gas mask with disgust and threw it in the embers. It melted along with his plan.

∘══✦══∘

Dan and the team arrived at the Ashburton office after being summoned by Quinn. She put an envelope on the table bearing the letters ΕΑΓ — epsilon alpha gamma. Dan said it was the initials for Task Force: GAEA in Greek. He removed a piece of paper with the word PANOPTES, also in Greek, an address, and 'Paraskeví. Mesiméri.' *Friday. Noon.* No name or any identifying information accompanied it, and they didn't think it was Otto.

"Clever. PANOPTES is the name Otto must have given to something, like a business, since we have an address." Dan gritted his teeth. "In three days, we find out."

∘══✦══∘

Once the team left, Quinn did what she did best: research and update the Division database. A decade earlier, when she first joined the Task Force Division, Quinn Reynolds entered as a field agent. She was 23, just out of the American Conglomerate Armed Forces, and looking for a new experience. Her technology background caught the eye of the Division tech officer who put together a thorough dossier on her before giving it to the United Nations liaison, Paul Fairmont. He sat down across from her at a café in Paris where she had gone for some time away and told her she looked like she would be the best person for the job he wanted to offer.

With a dual degree in World History and Computers, plus her military background, she would have the requisite skill set to be a part of the Task Force Division of the United Nations. Initially assigned to Task Force: Kappa, she went into the training program to work with international security, the purview of Kappa. Her first missions involved covert operations in countries or regions that were "hot," or ripe for security issues within governmental systems and commerce. She and her team would parachute into problem zones, determine the source of the complication,

352

and with the precision of a surgeon, extricate the people or tech-nology that was causing the disturbance. Within two years, she became a Squadron Leader gaining code key clearance at some of the upper echelons. Three missions came through the team's liai-son, and Quinn delegated which subteams would go on which one. She reserved the mission to South America for a few of her most trusted team members and herself. Due to the covert nature of the mission, only a few higher-ups even knew who was on the team.

Dropping into the compound of a major drug cartel under the cover of night, Quinn's team found the personnel and infor-mation needed and was awaiting transport just out the compound when a spy from the cartel saw them and launched a shoulder-fired missile at the TF-18 copter, blasting into shrapnel. Having managed to get most of her team to safety before the explosion, Quinn was too close to the copter when it was hit, and shards of metal struck her face. Unable to retrieve her because she was too close to the compound, and without a means of escape, the team left her behind, assuming she would be killed by the cartel's militia once located. It wouldn't make sense to risk more lives for one team member. The team had what it needed and had to bring it back to headquarters. With an SOS call over encrypted channels, another TF-18 extricated the team. Quinn was left for dead.

While lying in a tent, covered with a tarp like the other dead, flies buzzing all around, Quinn regained consciousness. She had no radio on her, and her injuries kept her from moving. Even if she tried to escape, she had no idea where to go or how to get help. All she could do was wait and see what happened.

When the Kappa team arrived back in Boston, the second in command sent in her report, documenting that Quinn was unfor-tunately lost in the escape attempt. The paperwork had to go through proper channels, one of which was the Division Liaison before it could be processed, and that took a few days. As soon as Paul saw this, he noticed the coordinates from the report and van-ished in a burst of light. When he reappeared, he was in the com-pound just a few feet from the tent where Quinn was, but he didn't know that. While he assessed the area, he spied someone in military garb and a pilot's mask skulking around with an M4 car-bine, a magazine-fed rifle. Just as Paul appeared behind this per-son, the individual swung around, pointing the barrel inches from Paul's head, but the aim was a little off. Using his innate ability to discern truth, he realized it was Quinn and told her he was there to rescue her. Not understanding how he had even gotten there, she stepped back, and the moonlight illuminated her face. That was when Paul saw the dried blood on her face. He gave her the codeword needed to identify a team member in the field. Once she recognized the codeword and his voice, he told her to trust him.

They both materialized in Commonwealth Military Hospital in Boston where Paul, using his United Nations credentials, had her admitted. Despite many surgical attempts to repair her eyes, nothing worked. The damage was too severe. Paul was heartsore. He wanted to heal her, but if he did, there would be too many questions. His identity as Apollo was known only to a few people, and the world hadn't experienced any otherworldly events that would give rise to explanations of a magical origin. Memory tampering was messy as well, and not always permanent. The gods weren't worshipped in the *Oikoumene Broteios*, the world of Mortals, and he had been drawing power from the well of all Olympeian power, the mountain itself and Olympeia, the mountain spirit. What he could do, though, was make her comfortable.

While Quinn convalesced, Paul decided to tell her who he was. Surprisingly, she took it well and said she had always surmised there was something different about him. He explained why he couldn't heal her outright and that he felt responsible for what happened. She agreed that it would raise suspicions, and the Task Force Division had its share of secrets already but did not agree with his assessment that what had happened to her was his fault. The nature of the job, she said. One thing he was able to do for her was to have someone teach her Braille as well as move her to his department, an agency yet unnamed, but prophecy had foretold of a team that would come to be that would see to things beyond the mortal scope in an otherwise human world. In the meantime, she would work for Paul Fairmont. A year after he had found her, he told her he wanted to take her someplace special. When they ended up on the roof of the building, she questioned where he was taking her, but he simply opened a doorway and stepped through, holding her arm.

Quinn immediately took a deep breath and realized she was no longer on top of the Task Force Division in Boston. She said the air smelled of electricity and roses, of all things. As they traveled the marble landscape of Olympos, Quinn swore she could see things, at least shapes of things. A little while later, she was walking on her own without Paul to guide her. When she asked what was happening, Paul explained that while he couldn't heal her, bringing her to Olympos would enhance her senses a little. The purity of the air, pulsing with life and power, would redefine her ocular abilities to be more intuitive. When she eventually returned to her office, she held up her palms as if feeling the essence of her surroundings in a whole new way. Paul and she developed a routine of coffee whenever he was in town, and their friendship grew from then on.

Where she had once been a boots-on-the-ground agent, now she made sure one of the most complex teams in the Division had all its intel. Pulling up her search screen, she typed in:

show /demigods

Her cursor flashed for a few seconds before generating a list:
/demigods
> */Apollo*
>> */Danelos Fairmont aka AEGIS*
>> */Brandon Jeffries aka ZODIAK*
>> */Dr. Ryuma Taiyo aka Erymanthos*
>> */Jamshid Motjaba aka Iamos*
>> */Keion Wolff aka Onkios*
>> */Dr. Armon Fantiss aka Philammon*
> */Hermes*
>> */Autolycos aka Otto Wolf*

Quinn opened the notes file for this meeting:

Team GAEA Notes: Team concerns that Otto Wolf aka Autolycos (see "Hermes") could possibly find a loophole or means to access the adyton (see "Gaea"). Connection to Olympeian power levels (see "Olympos") could present a bigger problem. AEGIS expressed concerns over relying too much on Paul Fairmont (see "Apollo"). When/If PF returns, he wants to establish different boundaries. TALON suggested that other demigods might join GAEA to expand the membership since AKMON [can discern the composition of objects] took a leave of absence to build his relationship with his father (see "Hephaestos"). Not clear yet how many are out in the world, but AETHER expressed interest in looking. Vetting procedures for any new demigod members must include a deep search into the past (including otherworldly places, via AEGIS or trusted proxy).

When she had finished the official business, she opened a separate file for her journal:

QReynolds: I'm worried about Paul. Dan says that he's okay enough, or he would have heard something. The damage by Python was enough to break down some sort of neural pathways between parts of his brain, if Olympeian's even have brains. I remember him telling me a while back, before GAEA team, that he'd suffered from occasional migraines, a side effect of both keeping those sets of memories as well as living in the mortal world. Had he remained on Olympos, he would have been fine. He chose a life with mortality which includes his wife and sons. He says they sustain him more than any Olympeian energy would. Not sure what'll happen if he doesn't return. Can't think about that. He's been there for me more times than I can count. I'll do what I can to keep GAEA team up to speed. End journal.

At the requested time, Task Force: Gaea arrived at the address—a rundown warehouse in an abandoned industrial park. Even the parking areas sustained damage as if the earth itself had buckled beneath it. Aether sent a leaf toward the building, and it disintegrated denoting a forcefield. Aegis started to pull his sword, but Aether commented that that would tip their hand. While they considered their options, from around the side of the building, a man in a sweatshirt and jeans approached. The team took a defensive posture. The man pulled back his hood.

"Philammon?" Aether lowered her fiery hand. "What are you doing here?"

"I'm here to retrieve something. I've been thinking a lot since our last meeting. I can't simply stand by and watch my brother destroy everything he touches while looking for my father." He turned to Aegis. "*Our* father. I know the last time we met, things didn't go well. Trust me when I say that I want to help."

Aegis nodded, and they shook hands.

"You said you're here to retrieve something."

Philammon didn't have to answer. His face told Aether all she needed to know.

"How did you know about the bow?"

"I may not live as a demigod as my brother does, but I have access to knowledge."

"Philammon, it's not safe. Your brother has taken human lives. Leave this to us." She touched his arm.

He looked as if he were going to say something, but then he just shook his head.

"Philammon, please—"

"Sar—Aether, I can handle it. Trust me. I know where the bow is and how to access it. Once I have it, Otto can no longer use its power. I have to make this right." His jaw stiffened.

They each made an impassioned plea to change his mind, but he was insistent. Finally, Philammon changed the subject by asking what they would do with Otto when they found him. This time, Aegis did draw Thyroros.

"He'll be punished for his crimes. Don't worry."

"My brother is cunning. I don't even think Tartaros could hold him. Expect anything from him." Philammon pulled his hood back over his head.

Zodiak stepped forward. "How do we get past the forcefield without setting off any alarms?"

Philammon pulled a keycard from his pocket. It had blood on it. Aether asked how acquired it, but Philammon said it was best that she not ask. He wouldn't look her in the eye.

"Humans are off-limits." Talon leaned forward, her eagle eyes fixed on him.

He got nose to nose with her. "We don't play by the same rules."

"We don't have time to argue about this. It's time." Aegis put his sword away and nodded toward the building.

"I'll get the bow and meet you back at your headquarters. Don't wait for me." Philammon swiped the keycard.

The door opened into a darkened corridor with red pin lights along the floor, and they moved inside.

Otto spoke to someone in silhouette.

"You know I don't like hurting people. I didn't want to kill all those people in Boston. Your knowledge, though, is too valuable to me. Being as close to them as you are, you know where I can find Apollo. At first, I would have just manipulated him a little, toyed with him, made him suffer. But now, the world needs to experience the loss of Apollo. How you could have been so blind to what he did… yes, blind. You don't see things the same way others do, do you? Rest assured, when this is all over, you will see things clearly again. I know they are coming for me. I am counting on it."

◦═━━═◦

Apollo held up the lyre. "I can tell we're nearing the end of this task. A fog still clouds my mind in places, and other memories are equally as troubling to me, perhaps more so than Python. Are you sure you are ready to continue this journey with me?"

Without hesitation, Ari and Esteban nodded. "We've come this far, Apollo. We're with you until the end." Esteban smiled.

"No mortals have ever done so much for me, ever."

"I'm not entirely mortal." Esteban shrugged, smirking. "You know, I haven't thought much about Orphne since the truth became known."

Apollo put his hand on Esteban's shoulder. "When the time is right, you may wish to see her."

"She's a daughter of Nyx, like Lismonia, and that makes me kin to that monstrosity as well."

"Esteban, you are also linked to Zeus. Focus on that." Ari smiled.

Apollo chuckled. "It's certainly an interesting turn of events when one should be thankful to be a descendant of Zeus. My father may have changed since being mortal, but he is still the king of Olympos with an ego the size of it."

Ari asked what lay ahead that could be more troubling than Python. Apollo sighed. He had borne witness to much in humanity and did nothing. Murder. Genocide. Plagues. As a younger god, he fell prey to arrogance and pettiness. Living as a mortal opened his eyes too much, but he couldn't erase the past. There were no Sacred Scales to realign this time to wipe away his sins. Leaving the empty chamber, they traversed another great corridor flanked with tapestries of events throughout history. Almost everyone depicted a heinous act that Apollo participated in or witnessed and did nothing about.

"There are no threads to attach to the lyre." Ari turned his head all around.

Esteban looked closer at one of the tapestries.

"Yes, there are, aren't there? Each of these is woven with threads that come together and create these frozen moments. Do you have to unravel them?"

Apollo shook his head, his glassy eyes staring at each one as they walked past. Halfway down the hall, he lifted the lyre up toward them. They unfurled on their own, threads attaching themselves to the pegs on the lyre. Apollo's knees buckled, but he didn't fall or let go of the instrument of his sanity. As the threads found their place, Apollo stared off at where each tapestry used to hang.

"There is much I should atone for. And, I will."

Ari cocked his head. "What do you mean?"

The last of the tapestries deconstructed and became a part of the lyre. Apollo didn't respond, but he continued his thoughts.

"I have watched disease ravage the human body and spirit. I have even sent plagues to destroy city-states that challenged Olympos. I have shot quivers of arrows into the hearts of those who did nothing more than stand up for themselves, but as a god, I took their lives… because I could." Apollo dropped to his knees.

Ari knelt next to Apollo, trying to look him in the eye.

"You have also done much good in the world. Your healing touch has saved many. The plague that afflicted Sparta, the pestilence that destroyed the fields on Mycenae, the curse of the Thessalians… My father told me much about how you have brought light and hope to those in need. You are correct. You cannot erase the past or wish it away. You can only learn from it. Grieve for the fallen. Even shed a tear for every single life, mortal or otherwise, that you have hurt. Living in the past will not change anything."

Apollo cradled Ari's face. "Efcharistó."

He looked over at Esteban. "Thank you *both*. Return to your world. I have much to do, and your faith in me, not as a god but as someone who has a place in this world, gives me the strength to move forward."

Moving through the corridors of the PANOPTES compound, Task Force: Gaea reached a door in their path that slid open vertically with a whoosh. On the other side, a phalanx of two dozen agents, men and women in black uniforms, filled the corridor. With such close quarters and no room for a sword or a javelin to maneuver well, Aegis and the others would engage the group in hand-to-hand combat.

"These people are stronger than I expected. I have to watch my strength if they're human." Aegis grunted at Zodiak, who tossed a man over his shoulder.

Zodiak then crouched to avoid another man who dove for him, letting the man's movements make him crash into the wall.

"They're *Myrmidons*. That's why. Didn't you see the ant tattoo on their neck?" Zodiak saw a man coming up from behind Aegis. "Duck!" A roundhouse kick sent the man flying.

"Thanks. Myrmidons, eh? Good to know." Aegis used his manacle to block a kick from one of the women.

According to legend, Zeus changed ants into men, and they became the first Myrmidons. Like their insect counterparts, they can lift many times their own body weight, in a sense, making them superhuman.

"They fight well, almost like Athene trained them." Zodiak engaged two agents at once, slamming them together.

Aegis moved so his back was against his brother's. "They haven't, but we *have*."

As soon as a few agents fell, more would arrive, much like ants in a colony. Aegis and the others had made some ground, but each new wave of agents kept them from moving forward any faster. Talon, whose bones were hollow as an eagle's, knew *how* to fight, but she had to keep herself from sustaining injury.

"I'd be much better if I could use my wings. I'm not much use here." She used her javelin to deflect what she could.

Aether brought her knee up into an agent's thorax and then thumped him on the back with both hands. "Yeah, I know. Just do what you can for now. You use any lightning, we could all be fried."

An agent caught Zodiak off guard, elbowing him in the stomach and then flipping him over. With the man's foot on his chest, Zodiak drew on Taurus for strength, and pushed the man's leg up, cracking it. Using one of his own legs, Zodiak knocked his assailant away. Two agents held the injured man under his shoulders and ushered him through a panel in the wall. These Myrmidons said nothing, but they acted as a honed unit as if they had prepared for this very day. As the team pushed their way around a corner, a shot rang out, and Aegis lifted his manacle to deflect a bullet. Two more shots ricocheted off his arm and lodged into the wall. He caught the eyes of the shooter, a woman in a military uniform with a small patch that read LT. HAROLD on her chest. Staring at him, she took her SIG Sauer P320 in both hands and fired again, and Aegis moved his wrist to deflect the shots, sending them back at her leg. With a grunt, she dropped her weapon and pressed on the wound while an unnamed agent grabbed her and opened a wall opening to take her through, but Aegis lassoed her, tugging hard enough to get the agent to release her. The man disappeared through the opening. Agents tried to cut the cord to free her, but when Aegis arrived, he threw them down the hall, one by one. Lt. Harold lay bleeding against the wall.

"Where's Otto?" Aegis lifted her by the cord, kicking away an agent trying to attack him from behind.

She grunted and turned her head, trying to push against him, and it was then he saw the mark on her wrist.

"A ward of loyalty. If you told me what I wanted to know, you'd die."

He lowered her to the floor and drew Thyroros.

Glaring down at her, he pointed the sword. "*Don't* think about where Otto is."

The letters on the sword turned white as did Aegis' eyes.

"Thank you." He grinned and opened a portal.

Before the portal could close, he felt a sharp pain in his calf. She had stabbed him. Once he was through, he removed the blade.

"Hephaesteian steel. Dammit."

Philammon skulked through the corridors on another side of the compound free of the fighting. Alarms blared all around, the red pin lights along the edges of the corridor flashing. He located a keypad and slid the bloodstained ID card. He heard a click, and the door slid upward. When it closed behind him, the dark walls lining the corridor gave off a pale, phosphorescence. Fifty feet ahead, he saw another locking mechanism, one with no keypad. Taking a deep breath, he took out a small piece of paper with a few phrases in ancient Greek. He placed his hand over the lock and concentrated, his lips mumbling the words. It took three tries to get the intonation right, but he then heard the click before the door slid upward. This time, yet another door barred his way ten feet in front of him. On a narrow shelf beside the door sat a small blade etched with ancient glyphs. In the center of the door was a copper square that shimmered as if liquid. Philammon sighed.

"A blood lock. If it's attuned to my brother alone, this is in vain." He sliced his left palm with the blade to get the ichor flowing and pressed his hand against the copper. Ichor dripped down the cold metal and then was absorbed by it. Nothing happened.

He pressed his bleeding palm against the copper once more, reciting something in a whisper. His pupils turned silver, and a mist emanated from his mouth. Removing his hand, he watched the mist mix with the blood and get absorbed. The door crackled until the darker metal fell away, leaving one entirely of copper. When the last fragment came free, the copper door parted down the middle, revealing what he had sought—the treasury of Autolycos.

A room the size of a football field sprawled before him, pedestals jutting forth that supported treasures from antiquity to the modern-day. Along the wall, illuminated niches held even more.

"By the gods… this is the kylix that Dionysos had given to the Spartans as a gift. And here," he moved to another niche, "this is armor used by an Amazon queen, still bearing the bloodstains of its long-dead user."

A few more niches held other timeworn treasures: the dagger Clytemnestra used to kill Agamemnon, a war-battered shield from a Trojan soldier that had sat in Menelaus' sacred vault, among other pieces of historical value. Each piece Philammon knew had a place in the grand scheme, and each piece stolen by his brother, largely out of spite or to prove he *could* steal it. He wandered through the objects until he reached a niche holding a silver bow that sparkled with fragments of stars sitting next to a quiver of silver arrows whose fletchings also twinkled. Looking side to side, he put the quiver strap over his shoulder and examined the shimmering bow before returning to the door. A soldier blocked his path, his gun drawn.

32 | EDGE OF DARKNESS

S hades pass through the iron gates of the underworld, and they must pass by Cerberos to reach the three judges who will determine their ultimate fate. The skiff of Charon reached the shore of Acheron where the souls disembarked for the dusty path toward their eternal life, and a throng of airy phantasms hovered in silence. Towering above, the Hound of Hades sniffed, discerning the substance of the spirits of the dead. Hades would say they have the distinct aroma of lilac mixed with sulfur, something that differentiated them from the more magical beings who resided in this place. After they drank of the river Lethe, they smelled of dust and mold, the floral lilac fading into memory. Once passed the three-headed canine, they moved en masse toward the temple of Rhadamanthys, Aeacus, and Minos. One shade separated from them and floated across the Vale of Asphodel toward the black palace of Hades.

In the throne room, Persephone slept on a black velvet chaise with legs of polished marble. The shade hovered by the queen before resuming his physical form and uncorked a silver vial from which emanated a pungency so powerful it rendered her unconscious. He lifted her limp body and left the palace, skulking toward the thick Grove of the Repentant, a group of silvery trees. Sprinkling a purple powder over Persephone's mouth, he fused her lips until no trace of her mouth could be seen. From a black rucksack, he stuck rods of iron in the ground around her, reciting an incantation. The rods began to glow like embers. As he returned to the palace, he chuckled.

⊙━━◆━━⊙

Upon entering the shadow-ensconced throne room, a deep voice caught his ear, and he hid behind a pillar, watching the lord of the underworld cater to his duties. Soon, a ruckus came from outside, and daimones scurried to surround their king, saying that the queen had been found imprisoned and could not be roused. It was at this point that Otto strolled before Hades, smirking.

"What does one say upon greeting you? Good day? Good night? It's so hard to know the protocol when visiting this dank corner of the world."

Hades glowered. "You. You dare raise a hand against the queen of the dead?" He reached out his hand, and across the chamber, Otto grabbed for his own throat.

"Harm me… and she… will remain as she is," he coughed.

With a growl, Hades released his hold, sending Otto to the floor. He felt his neck, twisting it back and forth.

"What did you do to her?" Hades' words caused every spiritual entity within earshot to scatter.

"It's a Hephaesteian cage. Quite brilliant, actually. The iron rods, aided by some old Titan magic, prevent whoever they encircle from leaving their confinement. You'd think one could step over the rods, but not without excruciating pain."

Hades took a few steps forward, but Otto put up his hand.

"Harm me, and she will remain there for eternity. Only I can release the enchantment. I would also need to unseal her lips."

Roaring like a lion about to pounce, Hades' emotions shook the ground upon which they stood.

"What. Do. You. Want?"

Otto sauntered up to him, leaning in. "Directions to Gaea's adyton."

Hades bore into Otto with the darkest of eyes. The air around them moved as if the dust itself was sentient.

"And if I give you directions, you will free Persephone."

Otto laughed. "Well, a way *in* would be good."

This time it was Hades whose laughter filled the chamber.

"Only Gaea can do that. Even if you stood at the very point of entry, without her permission, you stay where you stand."

"Hmm. So, that part is true. How about this? *You* gain me entry into her adyton, or she remains in her current situation for all time."

With the faintest of smiles, Hades climbed the dais to his throne where he drank from a gem-encrusted chalice.

"Gaea will not yield to me. Besides, the one who seeks access is the only one she would allow to enter. So, even if *I* could get her to open the adyton, *you* could not go inside. But…" He conjured a small ball of light. "Follow the light. It will bring you to the gateway. Be careful, son of Hermes. Time passes differently here. Your travels may take you a few hours or a year. But, if that is what you wish, as they say in the mortal world… have a party."

"When I do gain entry, make a place here for the Shining One." Otto followed the light from the palace and headed through the Vale of Mourning toward the Caves of Tears.

After brooding for a bit, Hades sought one of the chambers in his palace where he would go to think, a sacred space not even his wife would go. Once inside, thick darkness enveloped him. In this darkness, the king knelt.

"I seek your counsel, Erebos. You have advised me well over the millennia. You have no allegiance to any save yourself and therefore have no bias. I am not one to admit I need aid, but when it comes to Persephone… well, I am here."

A son of Khaos, he took the amorphous shape of dark energy that accompanied Nyx on her journey over the earth to bring the night to Gaea. With no mortal features, he communicated to Hades in his mind.

"Autolycos has imprisoned my queen in a Hephaesteian cage with Titan magic to keep her from escaping. I am a son of Titans, so my power is not as powerful. Can you, keeper of the dark, aid me in freeing her?"

In his mind, Hades heard the reply, "Son of Kronos, I am forbidden to intervene. Protogenoi existed before the Titans. You have all you need. History reveals all."

When he returned to his throne room, Hades sank into his great chair to ponder Erebos' words. If history revealed all, then it would be history he would have to revisit.

Like those who had traveled the path before him, Otto could see nothing. The ball of light provided him something to follow, but it did not reveal the path before him. For that, he would have to trust. No sound existed in this place, not even the crunching of the dirt beneath his boots. Left to himself, he started to hum, but it didn't take long for him to stop. A demigod of mischief he might be, but even this place can bear down upon those whose purview is mirth and folly. Hermes knew much of this realm by being the soul-bringer, but Autolycos had never been before. His understanding came from stories and the experiences of others.

Thoughts and memories teemed in his mind: his plans for what he wanted to do once he found Apollo and how he would continue his legacy of mischief. He smiled recalling moments when he was a boy thief running through towns, surreptitiously placing fruit or jewels in his pocket. His ability to take on any disguise had afforded him luxuries that a son of Hermes should have had, instead of those a half-mortal in a world that had all but forgotten the gods was able to have. He muttered that the hours, or was it days, dragged on and on. To pass the time, he changed into different individuals: gods, mortals, and creatures. None of those forms gave him any solace, except his own. At times, he had no thoughts at all, putting one foot in front of the other as if in a trance. Being half-mortal, he could be affected by immortal constructs like time more easily, despite how he tried to focus. Hades was right—the perception of time was lost.

The journey ended when the ball of light stopped moving. Otto put his hand into the blackness and a cold firmness met it. Despite the temperature, a heartbeat was discernible. It was not Apollo's, but Gaea's. He had arrived at the adyton. He glided his hand along the stone, learning each bump and crack, each bit of texture.

"Beyond this wall lies what I seek," he whispered to himself.

He pressed his entire body as if to embrace Gaea.

"O Great Mother, I beseech you. Let me enter your treasured place, your inner sanctum. He will trouble you no longer once I dispatch him. I know no face I wear will trick you." He stepped back from the wall. "Python, your misunderstood son, lies *imprisoned* in the heavens by a son of Apollo. It was Apollo himself who *killed* Python in ages past. Surely, keeping him safe is an affront to all you hold dear."

Otto transformed into Apollo as Paul Fairmont.

"See? Doesn't this face disgust you? His chiseled jaw, his blond hair, his penetrating gaze. He destroyed your son."

He looked around with an expectant, hopeful face. When no reply came, his expression hardened.

"Remember Boston? Did you feel it when those souls entered the underworld, their lives ceased by the bombs that created ragged, human shrapnel? Did you shudder when their blood oozed into your earth? When their cold bodies... bodies of mothers, fathers, and children lay forever gone? Apollo did that. If you wish to put the blame, put it on the son of Zeus."

Otto leaned against the stone and giggled.

"I can always do it in another city. Perhaps New York. Or Athens. Every time a mortal dies, it's because of Apollo. See how this works? And I take pleasure in knowing that Hermes must release each soul before it can cross over. Apollo has been a blight to the gods, to humanity. Even to you, Gaea. Especially to you."

Eyes flared crimson.

"Let me in!" His voice grew with each word, and had he been in a normal stony enclosure, the rock would crumble from the reverberations.

Jumping to his feet, he grunted and shrieked as he pummeled the wall before him, and each strike made his voice like gravel. Again and again, fist met stone, and his roar grew increasingly more guttural.

Covered in sweat, his hands and legs dripping with blood, Otto hobbled to the throne room of the dark palace, laughing to himself. Shades and other creatures scattered as he approached, making his way toward the ebony marble throne where Hades sat scepter in hand engaged with one of his minions. As Otto took a step up the dais, Hades put up his palm.

"A fruitless endeavor, it would seem."

Wiping his face with a bloody hand, Otto chuckled.

"It doesn't matter. Knowing that you will never see—"

From behind Hades' throne came Persephone, her lips as present as always.

"That's impossible! That Hephaesteian cage—"

Hades nodded to his wife who took her throne.

"Titan magic, yes, I know."

"But, how..." Otto narrowed his brows.

Hades glanced over at his bident, his two-pronged scepter.

"Ancient history, Autolycos. When Erebos ruled this realm, this bident was forged for him. After the Titanomachia, when I took over as king, I claimed it. It predates your 'Titan magic' since it is older than the Titans themselves."

"Your queen's lips should still be sealed. Surely, the bident didn't undo *that*."

"I am not the only one of power here. She who sits among the *Lampades* unwove your enchantment."

Otto growled, "Hekate."

"So, it seems you leave unsuccessful. I must commend you, though, on taking the form of a shade. You truly do have your father's talent at artifice. If it were up to me, Tartaros would be a fitting place for you, among the likes of Sisyphus or Tantalus, but the *Moirae* have other plans for you."

Hades tapped the scepter once on the marble floor, and the ball of light that guided Otto earlier swirled around him, returning him to the mortal realm.

33 | CLOSING IN

A ri stepped into the hall to see Dr. Gómez sitting just out-side it, rubbing his palms on his legs. The doctor started interrogating him, asking what he had been doing in there for so long, hours in fact, and why; Ari stepped forward to move past him. Dr. Gómez blocked him chest to chest, close enough that Ari could look into the man's eyes and feel his breath. He said he didn't want to hurt him or Esteban; he just needed to know. Ari replied that it was none of his business at which point the doctor put his hand on Ari's arm.

"Remove your hand."

"Or?"

Ari lifted Dr. Gómez by his collar and slid him up the wall.

"Put me down!" He wriggled in Ari's grip, but he remained just where he was. "How are you so strong? *What* are you?"

"This man is under my protection." He lowered Dr. Gómez.

The doctor fixed his shirt and walked away in a huff, but then turned back.

"That door wasn't just locked. I asked a custodian to open it, and he couldn't. Why?"

"That is not your concern."

Dr. Gómez took one step forward. "Well, it *is* actually." He showed Ari a gun he had in his coat pocket. "Take me inside."

Ari hesitated, but the doctor pointed the gun at him, keeping it close to his body.

"You will need to leave the gun outside the room."

369

"I'm the one with the gun. I'll decide where it goes." His voice shook, looking down both sides of the hallway.

"Do not say I did not warn you." He moved to Esteban's bed.

The doctor couldn't enter the room, despite a few attempts. Ari could see he was contemplating putting the gun on the chair in the hall. "What's happening? What did you do?"

"I did nothing. No harm can come to us in this room. Put the gun down."

Dr. Gómez reluctantly put the gun on the chair, craning his neck down the hall for any people. He stepped toward the threshold, but he couldn't pass through. He pushed with his palms.

"It seems, doctor, that you wish to harm either Esteban or me... or both." Ari shrugged.

Snatching the gun from the chair, Dr. Gómez stormed off. "This isn't over!"

"They're getting close. I'm not sure how they knew how to find me, but it was inevitable, I suppose. Esteban Reyes is under *someone's* protection, a ward I can't break. I wonder why... No matter. I have dispatched someone to take care of Dr. Fairmont." Otto smiled.

A muffled voice.

"That concerns you, doesn't it?" He holds up a cell phone. "Tell me what I want to know, and I just have to make a call. Up to you."

Silence.

"Have it your way. No matter. By now, one of that precious task force has been compromised. My own special blend of poison. Nasty stuff."

Apollo's chained body writhed within the dark adyton. He sat up, his eyes glossy, and pulled against his bonds, his muscles flexing, and the chains tightening but not relinquishing their hold. Red ichor ran from where the manacles cut into his flesh. Sweat dripped off him with each attempt, and the links clanked, one in particular bending from the strain. As if aware of this small victory, Apollo pulled harder.

Esteban cautioned Ari about Dr. Gómez, and Ari assured him he would be careful. He pulled a silver cylinder from his pocket, squeezed his hand around it, and it extended into a quarterstaff. Another squeeze collapsed it back into the cylinder which he returned to his pocket. He'd be fine, he reiterated. Within Apollo's mindscape again, they saw him as a much older god, as he appeared in the mortal world most recently. Ari's cheeks puffed from his grin.

Apollo told Ari he must return because there was danger. Ari informed him about Dr. Gómez, his connection to the Madrid hospital, and that something wasn't right about him. Apollo said his mind had been clearing, and he sensed something sinister about the doctor, but he couldn't be sure if it was the doctor himself or those connected to him. Truth was hard to reconcile when one's mind was addled, he added. He had more to do, he said, having removed much more of the venom in their absence. He felt he could see the end of the journey. Esteban wanted to remain in the mindscape, but Apollo said it wasn't advisable without Ari as the anchor.

"I know you feel deflated and powerless, Esteban, but if you were to get lost in my mind, you wouldn't be able to leave. I have enough trouble managing one persona in here, let alone two. We are too close to finishing this."

"I understand." Esteban smiled. "I know we'll all get through this."

"Ari, remember you're *not* human." Apollo nodded and smiled.

Once the link was broken, Esteban asked Ari what Apollo meant by that. Ari simply replied that he knew what he had to do.

On his way toward the T station near the hospital that meandered through a small park, Ari's face changed to that of recognition, and he slowed down. He shook the cylinder, extending his staff, and resumed his pace. He hadn't gone ten more steps when Dr. Gómez came from behind a tree, the gun close to his body, and pointed at Ari.

"What are you doing with Esteban? Tell me."

Ari took a moment before responding. "Why are *you* so interested in Esteban?"

"I need to know your connection to him." The doctor flexed his fingers around the gun's grip. "I don't want to hurt you. Just tell me what I need to know, and I will let you go."

"Did someone from the hospital in Madrid send you?"

Dr. Gómez kept the gun on Ari, his hand trembling. Ari leaned forward on one foot, and the gun went off. Ari deflected the bullet with the staff. The doctor gasped and let off two more shots, both deflected, and Ari knocked the gun from his hand. Dr. Gómez stooped to grab it. Ari placed the tip of the staff at the man's throat, forcing him to walk backward toward a bench. He pushed against the doctor's chest until Dr. Gómez was sitting and instructed him not to move. Using his other hand, Ari called Dan, but it went to voicemail. The doctor tried to get up, but Ari put his foot on the bench between the man's legs.

"What part of not moving is difficult?"

"W-What are you going to do to me?"

Ari ignored the man and spoke to who answered.

"Quinn, this is Ari. Can you send agents to apprehend Dr. Gómez? I think Dan would say to use the jeeps, no… GPS on my phone. Thank you."

A few minutes passed and two agents in street clothes walked right up to Ari. He explained what happened and pointed where the gun should be, and one of the agents retrieved it before taking Dr. Gómez into custody. Quinn called back to let him know that the agents should be there in a few minutes. He sighed and said that two agents were already there and took Dr. Gómez. She asked if they identified themselves, and he said no; he had just assumed. She told him task force agents always show their identification. Ari was going to try to follow them, but Quinn dissuaded him, saying they would find another way to get to the doctor.

The men ushered the handcuffed doctor into an alley a few blocks away. Dr. Gómez's phone rang, and an agent pulled it from the doctor's coat pocket and placed it next to his ear.

"You are no longer useful, Dr. Gómez. Adios."

Philammon stepped over the body of the soldier who had an arrow in his leg, lying next to his broken radio. Skulking down the hall, Philammon headed back the way he came. A pair of soldiers stepped out in front of him, and his eyes glowed, sending them into the wall, rendering them unconscious. As he sidestepped them, he adjusted the bow and quiver over his shoulder. Another soldier jumped out from a wall opening, gun drawn. With a finger gesture, Philammon sent the gun flying from the soldier's hand.

The man pulled a knife from his boot, but another gesture embedded it in his leg. Philammon bolted down hallways, trying to remember where the exit was. He recognized the markings of the hallway he needed, looking back every few seconds to see if he was being followed. At the door, he punched numbers on the keypad, but they didn't work. He muttered, "Come on!" It happened again. "By the gods…" Then, he remembered a key card needed to be inserted. Just as he pushed the last numbers in and heard a beep, he turned back to see a soldier at the end of the hall.

"Stop where you are!"

Philammon pushed the door open.

"Did they think backing us into an office would help?" Aether slammed the soldiers into walls with bursts of air. "Did you see where Aegis went?"

"Nope." Zodiak hurled a soldier over a desk, but he jumped back up.

Four more piled onto Zodiak, and Aether turned to help, but she heard a growl and then saw the four fly across the room.

"Gotta love Taurus and Leo both." He cracked his neck from side to side.

The melee stopped for a few seconds before three soldiers jumped into the fray, brandishing Hephaesteian knives. Zodiak threw a metal desk at them which delayed their advance before they resumed their attack. A dozen more soldiers surrounded them.

"What sign can get us out of *this*?"

Zodiak shook his head and drew his retractable quarterstaff from a pocket. Aether saw a lighter on a desk next to her and snatched it, smiling, striking the flint. Once lit, she grew the flames in each hand.

"Much better."

In an underground passage of polished marble walls with iron torches, Aegis had clamped one hand on his leg as he hobbled. His breathing grew erratic, and he winced with each step. When he checked the wound, it dribbled greenish pus.

"That can't be good."

He bounced his eyes all around before the path opened into a cavern. Up ahead, more shadowy passages. Taking Thyroros in both hands, he closed his eyes, clenching his jaw. The letters turned white and faded.

"Something's blocking my ability to use the sword." He grunted. "And my healing power isn't working." He took a deep breath. "I'm coming for you, Otto. Assuming I don't die first."

Soldiers blocked Talon from both directions in a corridor. She put her hands up, and they approached, never taking their eyes off her. A muffled rumbling came from above, shaking the building. Ceiling tiles fell, forcing the soldiers to cover their heads. A flash of light broke through, and when it subsided, she held her javelin, arcs of electricity traveling up and down its length. Most of the soldiers had managed to protect themselves, but a few lay on the floor under debris. A gun went off, but a filament of lightning incinerated it. She turned toward the soldier, another filament disarming the woman who threw a knife. Talon screamed, gripping her shoulder, but she couldn't remove the knife, and the wound sizzled around the blade. As she saw herself becoming outnumbered, she relinquished the javelin to the skies before two soldiers grabbed her.

A cell with invisible walls held Aether, Zodiak, and Talon, all three bandaged from knife wounds. A dozen dark-clad soldiers stood guard. Major McAllister stepped forward.

"Valiant effort. Just not valiant enough. If you haven't guessed, the blades are not of this world. Your wounds will heal. Eventually."

Zodiak rubbed his arm. "What's on the blades? Hydra venom? Medusa's blood? Tharmakondios?"

McAllister laughed. "If you must know, it's a derivative of dog spit. Cerberos, I was told. Each mouth, it seems, has a unique kind of saliva that, when mixed with a touch of aconite, becomes a metaphysical suppressant."

"You nullified our powers with it." Talon turned back toward her friends. "Of course. Cerberos guards the gates of Hades. His bite dissolves shades who try to venture beyond the gate back to the world of the living because they're mystical. Actually, in humans, it has no real effect since humans don't try to enter Hades." She threw up her hands.

McAllister opened a file. "You, Dr. Halston, are of Amazonian descent. Ms. Jacobs is Atlantean, and Mr. Jeffries is divine. Well, half-divine. We've done our homework."

"How long do you plan on keeping us down here?" Aether rubbed her shoulder.

Zodiak got as close to McAllister as the cell would allow. "Where's Aegis?"

The major laughed and left.

Boston Police located a naked body along the Charles River whose extremities, including his head, had dissolved with a toxin they couldn't identify on scene. The officer on duty called in Task Force: Theta since their purview was drug enforcement, thinking it could be a new street drug. Director Paula Gunther said she needed a DNA report as well as the chemical composition of the toxin. Using a portable DNA scanner, the office collected a sample and directed the results to Director Gunther. The DNA came back as a Dr. Francesc Gómez, but the toxin had no known origin. Gunther forwarded the results and chemical composition to a TF forensic team, and they concurred that this substance was unknown to science. Crime scene agents did send photos of the remains, but Gunther forwarded them directly to the forensic team. A short time later, she received a phone call. Under the man's arm, near the armpit, was a tattoo: a tiny feather. A peacock feather, to be exact. She sent an alert to Quinn, but there was no response. This sounded like something Quinn had mentioned during their staff meeting.

Aegis staggered through another forked passage. He stabbed the ground with Thyroros and gripped the pommel with both hands.

"Gaea, I need your help. I-I can't heal myself."

The stone in the blade turned a bright blue, and then flickered into its dark sapphire.

"Gaea… please." He fell to his knees, wincing, but still holding the sword.

Aegis' breathing became shallower, and his hands shook. Ripping the fabric of his jeans, he exposed the wound to the air.

"Ari… I love you." His words came out in a soft breath before he collapsed.

As he neared unconsciousness, his eyes fluttered. The blue light returned, pulsing like a heartbeat.

"Wha-Is someone th-there?" He coughed into the dirt.

Growing brighter, the blue light faded in and out as it bathed him. Slight tremors shook the ground, and Aegis pushed one hand against the dirt to lift himself. His other arm wobbled to do the same. He raised his head toward the light, and once his eyes met it, the light stopped pulsing and shone on him, becoming more intense. As it struck his wound, the pus melted away. From within the cut, a black liquid seeped out onto the ground, evaporating on contact. With the opening sealing, Aegis brought himself to a seated position, his breathing getting deeper. He extended his leg to see the gash had healed completely. The ground ceased its shaking, and the light dimmed, but the gem remained illuminated.

"Thank you for healing me. Whatever that was, it hurt."

A flash in Aegis' mind made him gasp.

"Cerberus saliva and aconite? That would dull my powers. That's why I couldn't heal myself. For a minute, I thought Autolycos did something to affect *you*."

More tremors started, and Aegis' eyes flashed white.

"Wait, what? How is that possible, Gaea? Captured? Can you show me the way?"

The blue light shot from the gem, striking his eyes.

"Yes, I see the path. Thank you, Great Mother."

The passage narrowed to where only one person could travel, and Aegis' frame struggled to move through. He squeezed through a few tight spots until the path widened a bit. Without the poison in his system, he moved with bigger strides. Every few steps, he stopped, pressing his hands against the stone walls, connecting himself with Gaea. A voice in the distance stopped him in his tracks.

"I'm coming for you, Otto."

The directions Gaea gave him had him moving at a good pace; he just had to traverse quite a bit of ground without knowing how far he had to go. Eventually, the path opened up into a larger space and he stood behind a stone, keeping himself in the shadows, once he could hear this voice. He moved to another shadow, and then another.

"Time grows short for you, dear woman. I'm certain you must know another way to enter Gaea's adyton. You *will* tell me, or you will die."

Aegis peeked just enough to see someone chained to the wall, but his angle prevented him from seeing who it was.

Otto continued. "Your connection to that U.N. task force must have given you the knowledge I seek. Will you tell me or not?"

Aegis moved into the light. "Not. It's over, Otto. Let Quinn go. She won't tell you anything."

Otto laughed. "Dear boy. Quinn? Her death wouldn't have the impact I'm looking for."

Aegis moved in. Otto made the torches flanking the body grow in intensity.

"What? No! Let my mother go. Now!"

"Ah ah… see those blades hovering in front of her? They are of Hephaesteian iron." He stepped over to Alkinoë. "One more step and I will perforate her. Ever seen a human sieve? It's quite striking. Now, if you'd like to spare her, for now, *you* can tell me how to breach the inner sanctum. You're his *son*. You would know."

Talon, Zodiak, and Aether sat on a metal bench in the cell. Zodiak made eye contact and nodded ever so slightly. Aether moved toward the forcefield.

"Major, what's going to happen to us?"

He approached, his hands behind his back. "That depends on what Mr. Wolf wants. My orders were to incapacitate and detain you."

Talon smiled. "If this dog spit wears off, are you going to stab us again?"

"I was assured it would last quite a while, Dr. Halston. I wouldn't worry about that. And, in answer to your questions, yes. I would."

Zodiak stared up toward the ceiling, and his breathing slowed. The lights flickered for a moment.

"Lieutenant, go check on that," McAllister ordered.

A young man left. It happened again. On a table behind the cell sat Aether's ring and Zodiak's talisman. The red gem in the center began to glow. McAllister started to order another soldier, but he stopped mid-sentence when the building rumbled. Zodiak's eyes turned white. The rumbling got louder, and the ceiling cracked just before the power flickered. Then, darkness. Zodiak stood up.

"Stand next to me," he told Aether and Talon.

"What did you do?" Aether whispered.

"I freed the zoo."

⊶⬥⊷

Ari returned to the hospital and explained what happened with Dr. Gómez before trying to reconnect to Apollo's mind. Blocked. He tried again, but he couldn't move beyond a thick fog-like barrier. Esteban sensed Ari's frustration, but he smiled. He said that Apollo didn't need them anymore. It was a *good* thing. Ari squeezed his hand. He didn't know what to say, but he supposed it was only a matter of time.

"I won't forget this time we have spent together, Ari. You have been my only true friend."

Ari nodded. "I couldn't have done this without you, Esteban, mi amigo querido."

⊶⬥⊷

Through the ceiling came eleven celestial animals, looking much like their real counterparts, just with flickering starry points of light, and attacked the soldiers who were left guarding the cell. The force field remained intact.

"Must be on a different power source," Talon said.

Zodiak pressed their hands between his. From his chest, a bright light enveloped all of them. They walked through the cell wall, and the energy faded. Aether took her ring and gave Zodiak back his amulet.

Aether followed her teammates into the hall. "How could you do that with the poison?"

Zodiak grinned. "Remember when I was taken captive a year ago? Even without my amulet, I'm still connected to the zodiac. That poison may have suppressed my Arkadeian strength or dem-igod qualities, but it couldn't stop my mind which is bound to the celestial signs. Virgo protects me. She's removed the poison from all of us."

With the power out, Talon tried her communicator to reach Aegis. He didn't reply, but she had a feeling she knew where he was. Once they made sure to subdue the rest of the soldiers near them, they traversed the corridors.

"What will happen to the zodiac?" Aether asked.

"They can't be harmed. They'll keep the soldiers occupied for a while and then return to the heavens." Zodiak winked.

Aether flicked the lighter and grew a softball-sized fireball in her palm. She put up her other hand to block their movement.

378

"Hang on a moment." She closed her eyes for a second. "Gaea told me how to reach Aegis. Hopefully, we'll run into Philammon before we get there."

"You killed innocent people to get to my father!" Aegis's voice echoed. "Those people had done nothing to you."

Otto laughed. "It was a gamble. It didn't work."

"Didn't work? Didn't *work*? Human lives are not expendable! All that destruction. I swear on all that is holy when this is over, and I get my hands on you, you will beg for mercy. Not that I'll give it."

"Boy, do you really want to threaten me? Your mother's life literally hangs on my whim. So, what's your plan? Distract me somehow? One thought, and she's a blood fountain."

Aether had split off from the others and found an exit. She mused aloud to herself that the zodiac animals must have kept the other soldiers busy since she hadn't seen any in a while. It was nighttime when she opened the door, and no alarm sounded. She was able to radio Quinn and update her, but she couldn't see Philammon. He was supposed to get the bow and wait outside. In the moonlight, she noticed something glossy on the pavement. Blood. A trail brought her to the side of the building where Philammon was leaning. His breathing was shallow. She tended to his wound, cauterizing it shut, but he said that he had lost too much blood. Aether figured the bullet he was struck with must have been poisoned with the same substance used on the knives. Next to him was the sparkling bow and quiver, lying in a crimson puddle. Aether stayed with him, but he said it was too late, and she should go find her friends to finish Otto. He made her promise that she would return the bow to the heavens, and then he breathed his last. Not wanting to leave him, she radioed for anyone on the team to go to her, but no one could respond inside the building. Stopping Otto was the priority. Placing a coin under Philammon's tongue, Aether returned inside with the bow and quiver.

Talon and Zodiak found a door that opened into the cavern. Zodiak put his finger to his mouth, and then he pointed toward where he heard voices. Talon launched herself into the air, avoiding the torches so she wouldn't give herself away with shadows. She perched on a rock close enough where she could see Aegis and Otto. Zodiak skulked around by the rocks, hiding as Aegis had earlier. The first to see Alkinoë was Talon, and she landed by Zodiak.

"We can't get close enough without those blades killing her."

"Can you use lightning?"

"It doesn't work like that. Plus, I could incinerate her."

"Then, *what*?"

Aether found them, showed them the bow, and told them about Philammon.

Talon scowled. "Dear Gaea. Now *what*, indeed."

34 | PARADOX REVISITED

In Gaea's adyton, two chains lay on stone, their links twisted and broken.

⟨━✦━⟩

Z odiak took the bow and held it up.
    "Spirit of Ouranos, take back into your keeping what was removed. Let celestial balance be restored."
    The twinkling bow and quiver rose above them and passed through the stone. After a few moments, the red gem in his amulet glowed and faded.

"It's done. The bow has been returned to Orion's hands."

From within the cavern, they heard Otto scream.

"Wh-What happened? My power… The bow… I can't feel it anymore."

They followed his echoing voice to the cavern where Aegis stood, sword in hand, and Otto flailed his arms around in theatrical fashion. Aether gasped when she saw Alkinoë strung against the wall. Gathering fire from the iron torches in one hand, she took up some water from a nearby pool in another. Talon summoned her javelin, causing lightning to strike through the stone ceiling, sending fragments everywhere. Zodiak clenched his fists, bringing the celestial zoo, and the animals hovered around him. Otto recovered from his ranting long enough to laugh.

"Take one step, and the once-queen of Arkadeia will resemble Julius Caesar."

A dozen Hephaesteian blades pointing at Alkinoë hovered in the air. With Task Force: Gaea keeping Otto in their sights, and Otto doing the same with them, no one saw her pull one arm at a time free from its chains, with her landing on both feet.

Otto swung his head around. "No!" He threw his arm in her direction, and the blades shot forward.

Aegis hurled Thyroros toward her, and she snatched it from the air. With both hands around the hilt, she deflected each of the blades, the clang echoing as a dozen knives lodged in the walls around her. Pointing the sword at Otto, she took steps forward.

"Once the bow was returned, your hold on me diminished enough for me to assert myself. May the gods pity you, Autolycos." She snarled.

Another voice, one none had heard for months, entered the fray, filling the space around them.

"The archer's paradox. Clever, Autolycos. Since you can't aim directly for me, you aim for someone close to me, hoping to strike your target."

Otto's laughter shook the cavern. "You're here, aren't you? So, I'd say it worked."

Apollo stepped out of the shadows, dressed in mortal garb.

"Not exactly. My arrival just happened to coincide with my wife's escape."

"Dad? Is that you?" Aegis looked around.

Apollo, in an Oxford shirt and slacks, moved into the light. "Soon, my son."

He gestured, and Alkinoë vanished.

A throng of soldiers poured into the cavern like an ant colony, true to their Myrmidon roots, gathering behind Otto. A wall of black, they filled the space. Dozens of pairs of eyes glared under brows darkened by purpose. Otto stepped back into the mass of people, vanishing, and once he had been enveloped, they all stampeded forward toward Task Force: Gaea uttering no sound.

Skulking back into the shadows, Otto giggled to himself until he heard Apollo again.

"Tell me, Autolycos. What did I ever do to you?"

Otto pressed himself against the stone walls, looking around for the source of the voice, his breathing erratic, sweat beading on his face. A niche in the wall suited his needs to cloak himself.

"Chione went mad, you know, after what your brother did to her. You were the better brother. How's that for irony? I know your history before you became mortal and grew a conscience. I kept my eye on you because it fed my jealousy… it became hatred. I despised you because everything you touch turns to gold. For millennia, I kept watch. A vigil on the almighty Apollo. And, your sons Ryuma, Jamshid, Keion, Danelos, Kidemonas, and Philammon… they all have thrived, haven't they? None of them would give you up. Not a one. How do you warrant such loyalty? Meanwhile… meanwhile, I'm a thief. I live in disguise after disguise underground. All because of you."

Otto darted his eyes everywhere, clenching and unclenching his fists.

"Your resentment is misplaced. You and I have never crossed paths. I have had no direct influence on how your life has gone. Deep down, you know that to be true. Autolycos… Philammon is dead."

Wide-eyed, Otto held his breath.

Apollo's voice lowered. "He was shot. *Your* poisoned bullets took my son away, a son who had led a quiet, unassuming life."

Taking deep breaths, Otto moved so that the ambient light struck half his face.

"How... unfortunate. Had he stayed out of trouble, perhaps this wouldn't have happened. Ah, well." The moment he stopped speaking, the ground rumbled, fragments of rock fell everywhere.

"Do you feel the same about Mestra? Alekos? Are you so dispassionate about those you love?"

"Don't you dare speak their names! You have no right!"

"Alekos was three when he died, Autolycos. You must have mourned for him. How terrible to lose a child, at any age. That lack of control when you can do absolutely nothing to change the fate of one so young, so innocent."

Otto screamed so loud that the cavern shook, dislodging pieces of rock that fell like hail. His guttural growl that followed made him sound feral, unhinged. His face twitched, moving between despair and paranoia. He reached out as if to console an absent individual, and then he pulled his arms tight to his chest. A small earthquake returned him to a calmer state, and he straightened, shifting back to the present. As the ground trembled, Otto pressed himself against the walls.

"Is that the worst you can do, Apollo?" Otto chuckled. "Perhaps Philammon inherited his impotence from you and that brought about his downfall."

"Not in your most vivid thoughts could you imagine the worst I could do. But this isn't my fight. I leave you to those who shall mete justice for your crimes."

As Apollo's voice faded, so did the shaking. Otto brushed himself off, taking measured steps along the darkened walls. In the distance, the fracas of his soldiers against the task force reverberated, and the corner of his mouth lifted into part of a smile.

The multitude in black poured forward, trying to use their sheer numbers against four. Aegis crouched lower and lower as a dozen soldiers fell on him until he could no longer be seen. Zodiak tried to move away from his own adversaries to help his brother but stopped in his tracks as the soldiers covering Aegis flew in all directions as the team leader popped up and roared, his arms spread. Using the animal menagerie, Zodiak pushed forward, taking down another twenty soldiers who had no means to fight against the twinkling zoo. Most got right back up but couldn't get past the starry creatures or their custodian. Rising above the fray in his equine form of Sagittarius, Zodiak bucked behind him and climbed over those rendered unconscious. Otto's minions advanced from unseen openings, numbering in the dozens.

In another part of the cavern, Aether brought up her hands, bringing an earthen wall up to keep most of their adversaries at bay.

"I need some cover! I have to cast."

Talon flew toward the wall, extending her hands. The ceiling cracked and fell in huge chunks as lightning striated across the space, pulverizing the stone and showering the soldiers in debris.

Aether clasped her hands, closed her eyes, and moved her lips. Otto's soldiers started recovering from the cascade of stone. When Aether opened her eyes, she spread her arms, and a wave of pale yellow light, like a ripple, moved outward. The Myrmidons were unaffected, and Talon landed by her teammate.

"Whatever you did didn't work." She smirked.

"That wasn't meant for them. It's an enchantment that will keep Otto from leaving his underground stronghold. He can't transport beyond the walls."

"And these guys?" She shot her hand toward the approaching militia.

Aether crouched, pressing her palms on the ground.

"There's an aquifer below."

Making a punching motion toward the wall, the rock receded. Twice more she did this before it collapsed, exposing the interior hallway in the compound. With clenched fists in front of her, Aether pulled her hands apart. A crevasse opened before the soldiers, stopping their advance. With a swift upward movement, a geyser exploded into the cavern, sweeping the soldiers toward the hallway. She manipulated the water to flush those remaining into the building before sealing the hole.

"There. At least we don't need to deal with *them* for a while."

Talon stood agape.

"Man, you're good."

Aether shrugged and smiled.

"Let's see if we can find Aegis and Zodiak.

Zodiak used his Sagittarian bow to wound as many soldiers as he had arrows, but that didn't stop more than twenty. He watched as Aegis lassoed a group and swung them around, using the sheer mass of people to take down others, yet the Myrmidons replenished themselves. The only way to stop this onslaught, Aegis shouted, was to take down Otto. Zodiak remembered that there was one constellation he hadn't thought to use, but it might help them. His amulet glowed red for a moment. As soon as he made contact, he gasped, but then he smiled. Over his wristcom came a call from Talon.

"Hey! Did you do something? I just saw a flash of a white eagle in my mind and then stars. Why are you in my head?"

"Relax. It's the constellation, Aquila. I didn't realize he'd be linked to you until I felt another presence aside from his. But, that would make sense since he's the eagle of Zeus."

"Well, it's weird, so stop it."

"Wait. Don't fight it. By any chance, can you see through walls?"

"Are you out of your—" She stopped talking. "I'll be damned. I *can*. You want me to see if I can find Otto?"

"You read my mind." Zodiak laughed.

She went quiet for a few minutes.

"I think I see him. He's running through the cavern, trying to teleport out, but he can't. Aether's enchantment worked. If he can take on any disguise, the moment he even suspects we're close, he'll become a rock or something."

Aether's voice came next.

"Zodiak, I have an idea, but I need to talk to Aegis. Is he busy?"

"Hey!" Zodiak shouted. "Aether needs to talk to you."

"Can't you see…" Aegis spun around, kicking one soldier into six others, knocking them over. "…I'm busy? Hang on."

Once he had a momentary reprieve while the soldiers recovered, he pulled his sword. As a group of them closed on his position, within feet of reaching him, he created a portal. Unable to stop themselves, they all disappeared through the opening. He hustled over to Zodiak.

"Where'd they go?"

Aegis laughed. "Do you really want to know?"

"Nope. Aether needs you."

"What's up?" Aegis spoke into his wristcom.

"So, Proteus was able to assume any shape, like Otto, but if he were bound, he couldn't. I don't know if the same rule applies here, though."

The lasso made of Atlas' hair was unbreakable, Aegis told her, but if he changed into something bigger, he could loosen it and slip free. Aether thought for a moment and came back with an idea, but she would need Ari's help. She would seek out Hypnos, the god of sleep. It was said that his tears compelled anyone they touched to follow the command of whoever used them. Aegis gave her his position so he could send her to the underworld. Once she was gone, they would need to stall by keeping the Myrmidons busy, and there was no telling how long she would need.

The portal closed at the base of the stairs to the ebony and gold-streaked palace; a guard in black armor escorted her to the throne room. As she approached, Hades scolded her about Dan circumventing protocol regarding entering his realm. The underworld didn't have an open-door policy where anyone with an enchanted sword could just use portals capriciously. Persephone hushed him after seeing the urgency on Aether's face. Once he knew her mission, he relented, giving her the direction to go to find Hypnos. He wasn't deceased, nor was he being punished; rather, he just preferred the solitude of Hades' realm.

On her way out, she passed Rhadamanthus, Aeacus, and Minos, the judges of the dead. Aether had heard about them, but she had never seen them before. She knew of Minos and Rhadamanthus, brothers, and both kings of Crete, from a meeting briefing once, but she knew little of Aeacus. Even though she was not there to be judged, she shivered as they walked by.

Most of the underworld looked similar to the land of the living in that it had expansive grassy areas over rolling hills, patches of white asphodel and purple aconite, although the trees looked more like husks of their earthly counterparts. Passing the aconite, Aether glared, remembering what had happened with McCallister. Wispy shades and gauzy spirits floated about, and the breeze carried the stale scent of death mixed with the pungent perfume of asphodel. At the edges of the field began the caves where daimones resided. While this place already had a winter's chill, this part had dark patches of ice covering parts of the stone.

Aether located the cave of Hypnos, as Hades had directed, marked by a single iron torch hanging in a ring just outside the opening. The flames themselves had an altogether different hue than normal Hadaean fire which had a grayish tint. They were almost an emerald green, flickering and sputtering. The god of sleep sat cross-legged on the ground with a sparkling mist around him, his wings curled around him like a tent.

"I cannot help you, mortal."

Initially startled, Aether then joined him on the ground. Peering between his wings, she saw he had no features except darker spots where the eyes and mouth would be.

"Son of Nyx, I know that you'd be reluctant since my friends and I imprisoned your sister Lismonia, but time isn't on our side."

Hypnos said nothing. She tried to make eye contact, but she couldn't find a place to look. Aether huffed, leaning in closer to his featureless face.

"Maybe you're content to sit here in the dark, but I have a job to do, to help people. All I'm asking for is a few of your tears. What do I have to do to be worthy? I know things like this come with a price."

He closed his wings around himself. "I no longer involve myself with the mortal world."

"I understand. You and the other immortals no longer have the divine energy from worship or even belief. If it helps, I *do* believe. I wouldn't be here otherwise. What is your price, and I will pay it. Please. The mortal world you no longer involve yourself with needs help, and that is why I do what I do."

She sat back, crossed her legs, twirled her ring in silence. Aether reached out to touch his wing but then withdrew her hand.

Creeping along the ground at the cave entrance, a gelid air blew, bringing in a fog that rolled in much like Lismonia would have moved. It surrounded them.

"*Æther*..." Hypnos sat taller, pulling his wings back a little.

Aether leaned closer to Hypnos, but she realized he was addressing the fog and not her. It was then she understood she was in the presence of a Protogenos.

She leaned over and covered her eyes. "You. You're the one I named myself after." Her voice trembled. "We've officially never met." She then breathed the words, "thank you."

Like his sister Lismonia and mother, Nyx, *Æther* spoke in their minds. The amorphous entity swirled around Hypnos, turning in on itself and moving with the air, then it surrounded her before filling the space around them. Wisps of electricity surged throughout.

Hypnos pulled his wings back as Talon would. "Ah, I see. So *you* are she who controls the Tetrastoikheia. Word of your exploits has passed Hades' lips. My brother says you are to be trusted. I will this once."

Æther evanesced. Hypnos turned his featureless face toward her, revealing his true appearance: a smooth countenance with icy blue eyes. His cheeks gave the slightest hint of a smile, and he nodded. Leaning his head back, he touched each of his eyes with a finger and presented two teardrops to her. Aether held up a vial to catch them and thanked him. He had asked for nothing, but she knew that he would consider her in his debt and might need to call upon her at some point.

She was lost in thought on the path back, staring at the vials that twinkled in her palm. Aether hadn't moved far from the cave when *Æther* returned, encircling her like a soft cyclone. She lifted her head and watched him weave around her body, speaking with her. She pressed her fingers to her lips and blinked away a few tears.

"Yes, I will come back and visit you. I didn't know you were so lonely."

Like a playful puppy, he danced around her, as if his mood had been lifted. The gray smoke turned iridescent colors, twinkling like a constellation-filled sky.

"You'll teach me how to use your essence like I use Khaos'? That would be spectacular. Thank you!"

Aether returned to the palace. After thanking Hades for his help, she also thanked him for sending *Æther* to her. Hades nodded with the faintest smile and sent his regards to Ari before opening a portal to where her team was.

Otto hid amongst the structures of the cave, toying with those who sought him. As soon as Talon could find him using Aquila's eyes, he would seem to disappear. He announced that he could leave at any time, and they would never find him, but yet he continued to play. Aegis said to his team that, if he was able to leave, he would have. He probably assumed he could transport himself without needing a real exit. Aegis gave Aether the lasso. Using an enchantment, she bonded the tears to the rope. All they had to do was bring Autolycos out in the open. Aether had no other power that could help them. He was still a demigod, so he had formidable power, but so did Aegis and Zodiak. There were only so many places he could go or hide.

Apollo, dressed in a suit, entered Grove Psychiatric Hospital wearing a badge that said Dr. Andrew Paolo. He signed in at the front desk, made small talk with the nurses on duty, and headed toward Esteban's room. Pausing, he took a deep breath, a habit he picked up from being mortal. The first thing he did was close the blinds to darken the room. At Esteban's bedside, he brushed the young man's cheek with the back of his hand.

"I am so sorry it has taken me this long to make this right."

Pressing his palm on Esteban's head, he closed his eyes. Light emanated from beneath his hand and then subsided. The young man's own eyes, which had been open, fluttered. He gasped and exhaled sharply. Apollo touched his arm.

"Slowly. It's all right. Just breathe."

When Esteban saw Apollo's face, tears flowed into his pillow.

"I have healed your mind. It will take a little time for you to fully recover. Can you sit up?"

Esteban never stopped looking at Apollo and tightened his grip on the god's arm. Apollo took the man's other hand and slowly helped him sit on the edge of the bed, his legs dangling. His body had been kept alive with a feeding tube and physical therapy, and he would need time to regain his full musculature. The gown hung on him like a sheet on a scarecrow.

"Just sit for a moment. There's no rush." Apollo kept his hand on Esteban's arm, removing the feeding tube with a glance.

They didn't speak while Esteban looked around the room, his eyes adjusting to taking in his surroundings. Then, he reached out, his arms shaking, and Apollo leaned forward. Even though Esteban didn't have his full strength, he closed his frail arms around Apollo and pulled him as close as his ability would allow.

From the moment they made contact, both man and god released their emotions at the same time, sobbing and heaving.

"Lo siento mucho, Esteban. I am so, so sorry." Apollo managed to say through his outpouring. "No podía ayudarte antes… but I can help you now. " He squeezed a little tighter. "Forgive me…"

⌐══◆══⌐

He wheeled Esteban to the solarium. As they passed the nurse's station, the nurses gasped, clutching hand to mouth, and cried to themselves seeing him look back at them and smile. The sunlight seemed to shine brighter at the windows, and both Apollo and Esteban bathed in it.

"Let it wash over you, Esteban. Let its healing power permeate your whole body."

Within just a half-hour, some of his musculature returned. His face, once sunken and pallid, looked softer, pinker, and filled out. Even his black hair regained its luster. They talked a little about what Esteban wanted to do, and Apollo advised him not to rush his recovery. He had been catatonic for quite a while, and even the power of the god of healing needed time to restore Esteban to his former self. He asked Esteban if he could walk on his own, but he shook his head. Apollo helped him dress, and a car waited for them. He didn't want to just start magically transporting the young man around.

"What do you want to do first?"

Esteban put his hand on his belly. "Eat."

⌐══◆══⌐

Zodiak grumbled to Aether why Gaea couldn't just tell them where Otto was, and she replied that he should know that Gaea was capricious. Who she helped and when could never be predicted at all. Task Force: *Gaea* had to live up to its mission. Aether had been sending minor waves of energy through the cave floor to show them where Otto could be hiding. At the very least, his disguise might diminish for a split second. Quinn radioed to let them know she had sent some other task force groups to surround their coordinates and to apprehend anyone they saw leaving until they could be interrogated. With the perimeter secured, the team would redouble their efforts. Talon moved alongside Aether. She had an idea that might give them an advantage. Careful not to announce the idea too loudly, she intimated to the others what she wanted to do and be prepared. This time, when Aether would send out her energy, Talon would piggyback it with an electric current. At the very least, she said, it would amp up the reaction, although it more than likely wouldn't stop Otto. The problem was, it would also be uncomfortable for anyone else within the range of the burst. Talon and Aether did a 1-2-3 and sent out their power. Aegis and Zodiak winced. Farther down, the sound of pain was coupled with slight movement. Aegis lassoed the source, a rocky outcrop near the wall.

"Return to your regular form and remain that way. You *must* obey."

Rock rippled and shifted back to humanoid form, and Otto writhed within the lasso's hold.

"Wh-What? How did you compel me to do that?"

Aegis secured more of the black cord around him. "What now? Where can we put him?"

"With Lismonia in the Ptinotrofeio?" Zodiak smirked at Otto.

The demigod's face went white. "No! Please! She'll destroy me. You know what her power is!" Then, his face darkened, and he smiled. "I-I know what this is, this power you used…"

Aegis pointed his sword at Otto's neck.

"Release me, son of Zeus. You *must* obey."

The hand that held the rope quivered, and Aegis started to lower his sword.

"Aegis? Oh no, he's figured it out. Fight it, Aegis!" Aether put her hand on his arm.

With his sword arm lowered, Thyroros clanged against the stone. Aegis' face showed the struggle of fighting against the power of the tears, and his other hand slackened on the rope. Otto's sinister smile grew for a moment, but then it melted away when he saw the Sagittarian arrow aimed at his throat. Zodiak in equine form towered over them.

"If your next word isn't 'stop', your throat will feel my arrow. Rest assured, it can puncture demigod flesh."

"Let me—"

Shaking off the hypnotic suggestion with Otto lying on the ground, bleeding ichor, Aegis lifted Hermes' son over his head with one hand, heading for the way they entered.

"I know where you need to go."

Gaea's adyton

Aegis closed the shackles on Otto's wrists and removed the lasso. Hermes hovered in shadow.

"You have no power here, Autolycos." Aegis stepped away.

Holding the wound on his throat, he shouted, "I will escape! And when I do—"

Aegis swung around and got into Otto's face.

"This is the adyton of Gaea. No one leaves without *her* consent."

Once he was gone, Otto sat, pulled his knees close, and laughed.

"Well played, father. You'll let me out, won't you? You wouldn't let your son languish here for eternity."

"We *all* have consequences to answer for, my son. Farewell." Hermes shimmered away.

Task Force Division, Office of Task Force: Gaea

Quinn gathered the others around the conference table to debrief two days later. Local authorities had reported that repairs were underway from the attack on the city, and the mayor was going to hold a memorial service for those who had lost their lives. A monument had been designed and would be built in the Public Garden. Official commendations would go out to those civilians who had risked their lives to help. The abandoned warehouse that had been PANOPTES was under lockdown, and the soldiers under Otto's command were in police custody and would be held until trial in a facility designed to hold those with superhuman abilities. McCallister and Harold would be dishonorably discharged and stand trial for their crimes.

Ari arrived and sat next to Dan. The team erupted in cheers for his work in helping Apollo regain his mental faculties. While they finally had the chance to catch up with him, Quinn excused herself.

"I cannot believe that Autolycos is finally gone." Ari squeezed Dan's hand. "I feel horrible for the part I played in this—"

Dan put a finger up to Ari's mouth. "Stop. *You* did nothing. That was Python. I don't want to hear any more about it." He replaced his finger with a peck on the lips.

Sarah put her arms around Ari from behind.

"I am so proud of you."

"We all are, Pookie." Aleta reached across the table and took his hand. "You're a hero, kiddo."

Blushing, Ari lowered his face. "It was not just me. Esteban deserves a lot of credit. Without him, I could not have done it."

In the outer office, Quinn could be heard talking to a familiar voice. As she returned to the conference table, Apollo, wearing his name badge that read Paul Fairmont, followed. Both Dan and Brandon started to get up, but then Dan looked back at Ari, and he signaled his brother. Then, Dan nodded at his husband.

"You go. You deserve it."

While Apollo and Ari had their moment complete with a hug, Dan and Brandon stepped up, and both brothers took their father into their arms. As Apollo fully entered the conference area, a beaming Sarah and teary-eyed Aleta had their turn. All of their voices became a tumult, but then Apollo held up his hands.

"Okay, okay, I want to tell you about what happened, but first…"

He gestured toward Quinn's area, and Esteban slowly came into view in a T-shirt and jeans. His body had almost returned to its healthy form. Ari gasped. Esteban walked right up to him, looked right into his eyes, and pulled him close. Both men had their catharsis after all this time. Ari then introduced him to the others.

"I'm sure you all wouldn't have minded that I made a stop on the way here." Apollo grinned, stepping back.

Delphi

By the ancient ruins just after sunrise, Apollo appeared in a burst of light with Dan and Brandon waiting. Ryuma, Keion, and Jamshid, one by one, arrived, joining their brothers. Upon seeing their father, all of them smiled, even Ryuma. Apollo held up a hand, palm facing them, and said something in ancient Greek. The words singed into all of their flesh turned to smoke, and his fingers closed.

"I'm whole again." Apollo took a deep breath. "Thank you all for containing my power until I could return. You will never know just how much that meant."

Jamshid hugged his father, Keion clasped Apollo's wrists, and Ryuma nodded with a faint smile and then went over to Dan and Brandon.

"I want to apologize for my attitude. You both have done more for the world than I could ever hope to do. I wanted to sincerely thank you. If I can ever help again, please don't hesitate to ask me."

Dan and Brandon exchanged a look of surprise.

Apollo gathered them around him.

"I asked you to come to Delphi because this is the seat of my power on Earth. From this place, I fed many a prophecy through Pythia. While there is no need for an oracle anymore, Delphi brings me peace. Dan, you have become the closest thing to a Delphic oracle in this modern world."

He crouched closer to the ground.

"This is the very spot where I took out Python the first time." Jamshid knelt next to his father.

"Are you truly all right? Your ordeal—"

Smiling, Apollo rose.

"I am more than all right. It has been a long, long time since I have made sense of my own existence. Bearing the weight of those other memories caused me so much anguish that I didn't realize I was feeling. It was a constant dull ache that I didn't know was there until it was gone. When Python's venom broke the barrier, there was actually some relief. The pressure was gone. But it wasn't a good kind of relief. I needed the help of others to find my path back to true reason."

"Did you ask us here because you wanted to reclaim your power at your own temple?" Keion sat next to Brandon. "Father, I don't mean to be harsh, but why ask us *here*? Surely, we could have met anywhere. London. Mashhad. Tokyo. Boston."

Apollo stared into the sunlight as if he was absorbing the very energy itself into his being. All five men looked at each other, shrugging shoulders. Without turning his head, he answered.

"I have walked the Earth as a mortal not once, but twice. The first was a punishment, with my Olympeian power stripped away, the second, a conscious decision to see what made mortality what it was in a world I had never seen. Those experiences pale, though, when I think of other days in my existence." He turned toward the five men. "Days that brought you into my life."

He held out his palm, and a golden urn appeared.

"In answer to your question, Keion, I asked you here because this will be the final resting place of your brother, Philammon."

Keion turned away and muttered, "Now I feel like an absolute ass."

"Your brother led a quiet life, even millennia ago. He never quarreled with anyone. Those who knew him loved him. His singing could inspire the Muses. I regret that he and I didn't see enough of one another, either in the past or present. I commend his ashes to the valley of Phocis, where he used to play as a child."

The lid of the urn opened, and the winds took the ashes of Philammon deep into the valley, and as the air moved, it was almost as if they could hear the son of Apollo sing one last time. Dan, Brandon, Keion, Ryuma, and Jamshid stood together overlooking the valley, watching as the remains of their brother settled among the flora. Shortly thereafter, saying their goodbyes, each left the shrine, with Apollo gazing out, his eyes glistening with regret.

A few days later, Apollo, Ari, and Esteban walked by the Charles until they reached Ari's favorite bench that gave him a spectacular view of the river. Ari hung on every word the man said, and hearing him speak aloud brought him abundant joy. He had told Esteban earlier that day that, even though he could hear him in the hospital while they were connected via the obol, actually experiencing him speak and act was one of the finest things he had ever seen.

"Do you want to return to Spain?" Ari leaned forward on his knees.

Esteban was gazing out over the river, smiling. "No. There is nothing for me there. I want to remain here, in Boston. Apollo invited me to live with him and his wife so that I can acclimate better. Alkinoë arranged for me to work with a charity she supports helping orphans."

"And Orphne?"

Esteban shook his head. "Not yet. I'm not ready. I want to remain in the company of mortals."

Apollo leaned back, his elbows on the bench. "I know exactly what you mean."

"I know I'm not mortal myself, but I need to come to terms with what that means now that I'm no longer catatonic."

Excusing himself, Apollo vanished.

"Ari, thank you for everything. I've never truly had a friend before, and now I have so many."

"We will figure these things out together, mi amigo."

Mount Olympos

Hermes stood by the fire ring in the center of the throne room, watching the flames flutter and flicker. Thunder rumbled beyond, and then lightning struck the dais, leaving its master in its wake. Zeus took his seat.

"You wish to see me."

"I do." The messenger walked up the steps toward his father.

"You seemed troubled, my son. I am not used to such melancholy on your face."

Hermes, with slow footfalls, approached the golden throne and knelt. He removed his winged helmet and placed it on the floor, and then he put his caduceus down.

"Long ago, I put my desires before the will of a woman, fair Chione. I lulled her to sleep with a song, and then, in her hazy slumber, I lay with her. From that union came our son, Autolycos. I am ashamed of my actions, and I seek punishment."

Zeus leaned forward but said nothing. Pondering for a moment, he nodded.

"Strip me of my godhood." Hermes choked out. "Send me to live among mortals until such is my time. I will take nothing from Olympos." He couldn't even face his father.

The king of the gods sat back on his throne, placing his mighty hands on the golden arms of the majestic chair. Again, the heavens trembled far off, and lightning scattered. In the shadow of his father, Hermes shook. Time had no place on Olympos, so it was unclear as to how long it took Zeus to think about his son's request, but he was ready to issue his response. Unlike his normal stentorian voice, his words came out as soft as a breath.

"I will grant your request. You may resume the life you once lived as Mark Phillips. I will place you where you lived, in the mortal city of Los Angeles. You will have to fend for yourself. And…"

A bolt of lightning struck Hermes, and when it subsided, a wheelchair remained, and seated within was a man who looked nothing like the son of Zeus and Maia. This man had to live out his days as a paraplegic. No longer would he wear wings.

"Goodbye, Father." Even the voice was different.

Another bolt sent the man Mark Phillips from the sacred halls he would not see again.

Sometime later, Zeus, Athene, and Apollo stood next to Hermes' throne, a seat that the messenger rarely used, but one that marked his role as an Olympeian. The king of the gods wept, placing the caduceus on the arm of the chair. Athene leaned against her father.

"He is not gone forever, Father. His choice was the right one. Someday, you will see him again."

"Perhaps. With his absence, there is another. He played a vital role in the cosmos as Hermes Psychopompos. We shall need a new guide for the souls of the deceased to the underworld."

Apollo's fingers grazed the caduceus. "The raven Velos, who used to deliver my prophecies to Delphi, will function as psychopomp until we can replace my brother."

"Very well." Zeus turned to his son. "You have lost both a son and a brother after having so recently returned to us. I am so sorry." He squeezed Apollo's shoulder.

"He is not dead, Father, although he is gone from us. I will keep watch over him, but fear not, I will not intervene. He made his choice, and we need to respect that."

As Dan slept with Ari wrapped in his arms, moonlight struck through the window, bathing the sword Thyroros in Selene's silver luminescence. The inscription turned white, and a triple voice of Maiden, Mother, and Crone of the Moirae ushered in a new prophecy:

With Reason restored,
And Truth enthroned,
Purpose becomes the way.
What was once possessed:

Must now be lost,
And a new dawn becomes the day.

That which guides the four,
That which parts time and space
That which summons the sky
That which guards the twelve
Yields to the iron shears,
And a path unseen
Must now unfold
For the remainder of the years.

Invisible to the mortal eye, the raven Velos made his first journey as a psychopomp, traversing the globe, until he found the body. Los Angeles Police had cordoned off the intersection, and the EMTs wheeled the gurney toward the ambulance. Before they lifted it inside, Velos swooped down, invisible to the mortal eye, touching the body with his beak. As he headed toward Hades' realm with the soul, one of the EMTs asked if there was any identification on the deceased.

"Poor guy was struck by a car as he was wheeling himself across. His ID says 'Mark Phillips'."

35 | DECISIONS

Months later

The shrieking bark, its shrillness dispersing nearby murmuration of starlings who scattered like shrapnel, echoed across the wheat fields, now partially trampled into what resembled something akin to haphazard crop circles. A group of local farmers who gathered by a nearby farmhouse pointed and took photos on their phones of the furry monstrosity whose surprise presence had caused quite the tumult, and one that local Kansans had never seen the likes of. Attempting to contain the creature, Aegis and Aether found themselves befuddled by the canine's elusiveness.

"You'd think a fox the size of a barn would be easier to detain," Aether spoke into her wristcom.

A football field away, Aegis found himself uncharacteristically winded.

"I told you," he panted, "this is the Teumessian Fox. It can't be caught by conventional means."

"So how do you suppose we be unconventional?"

Moving with superhuman speed, Aegis caught up to the fox and tried to launch himself onto the creature's back. Living up to its reputation, the four-legged one turned just before Aegis could grab hold, and the man hurtled to the ground, having the wind knocked from him. Grunting, he jumped again, this time landing

399

on the back of the fox's neck, gripping the bristle-like hair. Before the fox could fling him off, Aegis dug his knees into the animal's neck to maintain his hold. Talon soared above, taking in the situation and relating to Aegis the larger scope. So far, the fox had only torn up fields, but if left to its own, it would trample farmhouses and farm equipment, endangering lives. Zodiak did crowd control, as townsfolk and farmers were a curious lot, and disregarded his warnings, trying to get a selfie with the fox somewhere in the background. Local law enforcement wasn't much help as they were as intrigued as everyone else. Aether caught the fox heading back in her direction, called her quarters, and positioned herself.

"I'll set up an earthen barrier to keep this thing away from people, but you're going to have to contain it."

Her arms outstretched, she closed her eyes and lifted her arms. Nothing happened. Again, she tried, but the ground didn't budge at all. She asked Aegis if the fox could suppress magic, and he said he didn't think so. Before she responded, she spied a water tower and reached out for it, hoping to draw the contents to her instead.

"Something's wrong!" Aether's voice cracked over the wristcom to her team. "I can't move earth or summon water." Examining her ring, she made sure all the gemstones were intact, and they were. "My ring isn't working."

"Hang on, honey, I'll take care of this. I'll have to be careful not to set the fields on fire." Talon soared higher toward and reached up to summon her javelin. "What the hell?"

She flew even higher, higher than usual, but it was no use. Her silver javelin wouldn't come. Seeing Aegis about to be thrown off, she sped toward him, able to catch him as the fox shook him loose. They set down by the police barrier where Zodiak stood guard.

"These police don't know what to do. The most they've dealt with are drunk guys or the occasional loose cow wandering down the street. You're not having any more luck, I can see."

"Why don't *you* try something? I can't summon the javelin, and Aether can't use her powers it seems. Aegis?"

"My strength is intact. This fox is just wily and quick. I could try knocking it down, but I can't contain it."

Aether stared down at her hand. "Your lasso? The fox can't break it."

Zodiak put his hand on her shoulder. "We'll figure this out. Don't worry. Hey," he turned toward Aegis, "Can you just open a portal and send it somewhere?"

Aegis shook his head. "I don't know where it came from to send it back. It just appeared out of nowhere."

An officer approached, his hat askew. "Are you all gonna keep jabbering or are you gonna do something about that... thing... before it hurts somebody?"

Talon rolled her eyes. Gathering herself, Aether assured the officer they were doing their best and just strategizing. For the moment, the fox was just sniffing around, so they were using that time to figure out a plan. The man stuck out his lower lip, nodded, and returned to the crowd. Talon pulled Aether aside.

"Hey, kiddo. You okay?"

Aether had her arms wrapped around herself as if she were cold, her gaze toward the ground. Talon squeezed her shoulder a little.

"I can't touch it, Aleta. That connection is gone."

"Can't touch what?"

Crouching down, Aether put some dirt in her hand and held out her palm.

"Watch."

After a few seconds, she sighed.

"Nothing happened."

"Exactly. I willed the earth to move, and it's like it doesn't hear me. Oh, Gaea, I hope I haven't offended you."

Talon pulled her close. "There has to be a reason for this. Once we take care of this capricious canine, we'll figure it out." They started to walk back, and Talon stopped. "Do something else."

"Like what?"

"Something magical that doesn't require the ring." She saw a piece of rusted metal from an old tractor lying in front of them. "I have a thought."

Aether brushed her palms together to remove the dirt. Centering herself once more, she twirled her pointer fingers around each other in a winding motion and then pulled them apart while looking at the metal strip. Following her magical gestures, the piece of metal tied itself into a knot. Aether laughed while crying.

"You did it. I think I know what the problem is. Your ring isn't working. I couldn't summon the javelin. Come on."

She told Aegis and Zodiak what happened, and Aegis unsheathed Thyroros and swiped at a tree stump. As if through butter, the blade slid through, the chunk of wood sliding to the ground.

"Sword seems okay."

Talon shook her head. "Your sword is made from Earthsteel by Gaea."

Before they could continue, screams erupted as the fox started scampering in their direction. If it weren't stopped, it would destroy the farmhouse, nearby houses, and the people too stubborn to leave. The ground shook as the beast came closer. Aegis told Talon what he wanted to do, and she lifted him with her feet by his shoulders. Sword in hand, he signaled when they were in the right position, and he concentrated on the sword to cut a portal as Talon brought him up and around in a large enough circle to make an appropriate gateway. By the time they were at the same height as the fox's head, the animal crashed into them, sending both Aegis and Talon to the ground, Thyroros spiraling across the ground. Zodiak ran over.

"You okay? Damn, what happened?" He lifted Talon then looked to his brother.

Aegis brushed himself off and scanned for his sword. Summoning it back to his hand, he examined the entire length of it.

"Sword's fine. But, I couldn't open a portal. Like you were saying, Talon, the sword functioned as a sword would. It cuts just fine, but its magical tie to Ianos who opens those gateways is gone."

A woman with her teenage son near the border of police cars waved Aether over and pulled her aside. At first, Aether thought they were hurt, but then the woman said something to her that made her eyes widen. Using her wristcom, she brought Zodiak over.

"Hey, what's up? You folks okay?"

"Ma'am, tell him what you just told me. It's okay."

The woman, her head wrapped in a kerchief and wearing a floral dress, clasped her fingers together and told Zodiak. He looked over at Aether, also surprised.

"You're saying that you were hanging up your clothes when you looked up and saw something fall from the sky."

She nodded. "Yessir. It-It looked all sparkly like before it hit the ground, but when I saw it, moving around, you know, it just looked like a normal fox. Well, much, much bigger."

Aether and Zodiak thanked them and returned to their team who had been keeping an eye on the fox's scampering. As if on cue, Talon said, staring at the fox, "Wish I knew where it came from?"

Zodiak cleared his throat. "I know where." He glanced up and pointed toward the sky.

The others hung on his words, waiting for the explanation. It hadn't dawned on him until he heard what the woman told him. If his hunch was right, he knew how to handle it, but he wasn't sure it would work, especially if Talon's javelin and Aether's ring weren't working. Aegis upturned his hands as if to say, "Well?"

"Aegis, you said this is the Teumessian fox. I thought it sounded familiar, but we've fought so many things, I just figured we'd heard about it somewhere. This fox came from the stars. We would know it as Canis Minor." Zodiak gazed skyward.

"Wait. *This* is Canis Minor? How is that possible?"

"Aether, foxes are in the Canidae family. They're related to dogs." Zodiak looked out to where the fox was sniffing and digging.

"Okay, silly question, then. Who's Canis *Major*?"

"That would be Laelaps, a dog who could always catch his quarry. He was sent to chase the fox, but this fox couldn't be caught. Ultimately, Zeus turned them to stone and later placed them in the heavens."

Zodiak walked toward the field, through ears of corn toward the fox, and closed his eyes. After a little while, he returned to his team, and Aether recognized that look.

"It… didn't work. I couldn't connect through the amulet." He pressed his hand over it and squeezed. "I couldn't even feel my connection to Ouranos."

The four of them stood separate from the police and locals, working through options until someone exited the cornfield on the other side. He made a hand gesture, and the fox looked in his direction before regaining its sparkly shimmer and rising back to the heavens. With another gesture, the fields and damaged structures returned to normal. Without saying a word, he approached the team and whisked them away in a flash.

Only the hum of the fluorescent lights made any sound in the conference area. The team stared off, and Apollo, his arms crossed and brow furrowed, stood at the head of the oblong, walnut table. Raindrops meandered down the plate glass windows overlooking Boston. In the background, Quinn opened the door to the outer office where her desk was and joined the solemn gathering.

"I don't mean to interrupt." She spoke in a funereal tone. "Is there anything I can do or help with?"

Apollo shook his head ever so slightly and then breathed the word "No." Nodding, she returned to her desk. After a little more time had elapsed, Apollo turned and left through conventional means without saying anything.

Her eyes looking nowhere in particular, Aleta said, flatly, she could still fly.

Dan came out of his reverie. "Hmm? What was that?"

"Whatever's happening hasn't changed the fact that I can still fly. My eagle side is intact. My vision hasn't changed, either."

Sarah fidgeted with her fingers. The ring sat on the table in front of her.

"I can still conjure. My connection with magic hasn't left."

Dan added that he still had his strength and healing ability, and the sword could still cut. Slouching in his chair, Brandon's elbows rested on the arm of his chair with his fingers interlaced. He rubbed a knuckle against his nose.

In a breathy exhale, he said, "I can't do anything."

"You still have your strength and healing ability, like me." Dan leaned forward. "You're more than your connection to the stars."

Brandon shook his head. "My codename is Zodiak for a reason. Without my connection to *that*, I'm just... nothing."

Apollo entered the shrine of the Moirae, his jaw tight and eyes flaring in the corners.

"Show yourselves."

The iron torches that encircled the chamber remained lit at all times, but with his words, they seemed to dim ever so slightly.

"Show yourselves!" His voice reverberated, and the flames extinguished.

Apollo's face housed the only visible illumination. Even without the torches, the temple had its own pale iridescence in hues of silver and blue. The last time he had visited the three sisters they removed him with a word. With his mental faculties clearer than they had been in a long time, he knew he could handle whatever they would throw at him.

"You may control the thread, but having lived with *two* lifetimes, I have gained knowledge that could affect your power, Sisters Three. Ignore me, and that knowledge stays locked away."

The absence of sound in an immortal realm is unlike anything experienced by mortals. It is like being in a vacuum devoid of anything.

"So be it."

He dissolved into mist.

The torches burst into flame once more, and from the shadows came the three sisters, meeting at the center of the circular shrine.

"Do you think it was wise to ignore him, sisters? If what he says is true, that knowledge could—"

"Be at ease, Clotho. It *is* true. Apollo does not speak in falsehoods. However, what we know about the sacred tools must never be shared. If he wishes to know more, he will have to find others to tell him. We are bound by the rules of prophecy."

Clotho nodded to her elder sister. "What say you, Atropos, to Lachesis?"

The eldest of the Fates, the crone, tapped her gnarled fingers against her withered lips.

"If we are meant to know what the son of Zeus *thinks*, then we shall. Our motherly sister speaks true. Prophecy dictates we keep certain things unspoken. Even now I will not utter the words for fear they would betray us and seek out Apollo Klêdônes, He of the Omens in Words and Sounds."

"For now and all time, we must be tight-lipped. Our vow must be upheld."

Hammer against anvil vibrated through the cavern, and billowing black smoke hovered at the roof of the forge. Light and shadow were as playmates in this place, and the lame smith smiled to himself as he sensed who had arrived.

"Brother, what brings you to the realm of soot and smudge cloths?" He wiped his hands on his apron and turned on his stool.

Apollo's feet hovered over the dirt. Hephaestos gestured toward the ground near him, and the earth itself cleared itself of dust and debris.

"I have a dilemma. The Moirae will not see me, and I need answers. The sacred tools of my sons and their friends have ceased working, and I don't know why. As a metalworker, and one who works with divinely enchanted pieces, can you give me any reason as to why?"

Cocking his head, Hephaestos pushed out his lower lip and thought, fidgeting with a bronze coin in one hand.

"I assume you would know if they had committed some atrocity to offend the gods or something, so, hmm… I know that the sword and amulet were forged by Gaea. The javelin and ring are my handiwork. Let me look at something…"

He swiveled back to his anvil and pulled a leather tome from a shelf next to him, blowing off the layer of time and dirt. Inscribed into the leather with silver ink were arcane glyphs and markings. Hephaestos waved his hand over the book, and its pages fluttered open. When they ceased moving, the smith gestured upward, and the words floated up from the parchment toward Apollo.

"This is the only mention of the Ierá Ergaleía."

"Sacred tools? What does that have to do with this?"

Hephaestos shrugged. "There is an entry here about four sacred tools that have been shared over the millennia with those who are worthy and righteous."

"Does it say anything about them not working?" Apollo's gruffness made his brother lean back a little.

Hephaestos smirked. "Do not, as mortals say, shoot the messenger, brother. You can see the words as plain as I. The entry says—"

"'Those who have been found worthy may bear these tools for the causes of justice and righteousness,'" Apollo spoke the words as they floated by. "'And upon the cessation of their need, they will become inert until needed once more.'" He shooed the words away as if they were pesky insects. "Now, what in Gaea's name does *that* mean?"

"Your sons and their friends are still needed in their role in the outer world, yes? Is this tied to prophecy?"

Shaking his head, Apollo crossed his arms and squinted. "No. I have never heard of such a prophecy, and if I haven't, neither has Dan. 'Cessation of their need'... How can that be so?"

The smith examined the book more. No other reference to these tools existed, and if it were to be anywhere, it would be there. I wish I had more resources for you."

"Gaea doesn't know either, and that is not a common occurrence. I had never heard of a time limit on tools or weapons. I do have one other I can consult." Apollo patted his brother's shoulder. "Many thanks. If I figure it out, I will let you know."

"*When* you find out, you mean..." Hephaestos' face widened in a broad grin.

Nodding, Apollo vanished.

Looking out over the balustrade into the skies of Olympos, Athene smiled to herself.

"It is good to see you back to yourself, Apollo. The wonders of mortals never cease to amaze. We did not speak about this the last time we saw each other."

He stepped up to the marble rail and leaned his hands on it, taking in the vastness of the clouds that paraded by the Olympeian halls at this highest part of the sacred mountain.

"Technically, Esteban is hemitheos. His mother is a Lampad maiden who herself is a daughter of Nyx."

"I was referring to Aristeides. It is not often that mortals impress me, as you know. His selflessness and cunning are truly inspiring." She held up her arm, and an owl landed. "How may I be of service?"

Apollo explained what had happened with Dan and the others as well as what he had found out from Hephaestos' tome. She, too, seemed troubled by the time limit on such tools, especially since she was the one who gave the javelin to the Amazons who passed it down to Aleta.

"When I asked our ash-laden brother to forge it, I said nothing of a time limit. And, even Zeus does not do such things. A gift *is* a gift."

"Then, I am perplexed. It's not often that a mystery lies unsolvable, especially from one who deciphers prophecy. Dan and the others are shaken, and rightfully so. I don't know how to help them."

Athene nuzzled her nose against the grey owl's beak before sending it off and took her brother's hands in hers.

"Some mysteries remain unsolved, at least for a time. When the answer is ready to reveal itself, I am certain it will. In the meantime, I know that you will do what you do best and encourage them to be who they *can* be." She kissed Apollo on the forehead.

Ari's eyes squinted open just as the sun leaked into the bedroom behind the curtains, leaving a looming silhouette between him and the window. Once his vision adjusted, he realized it was Dan sitting on the edge of the bed. He reached over and pressed his hand against Dan's back.

"Are you okay?" His morning voice squeaked.

Turning, Dan took Ari's hand and brought it to his lips. His eyes were in shadow, but when he turned a little, his cheek twinkled. Ari sat up and wrapped his arms around Dan's shoulders from behind him.

"Have you been crying? O polemistís mou…"

Dan exhaled hard through his nose and stifled a chuckle.

"I love when you call me your warrior. I'm okay. Just a rough night's sleep."

He cast his eyes on the scabbard lying on the table, the splinters of light showing its shape and twinkling against the gem in the pommel.

Ari rested his head on Dan's shoulder. "You know that you are more than that piece of metal. Danelos Fairmont has much more meaning and purpose. You were *you* before Apollo gave that to you, and you will still be you even if you can no longer open portals." He pecked his husband on the cheek.

Without answering, Dan stood up, and Ari took in the magnificence of the man he married. Eos' morning light had grown brighter, and now Dan's body doffed the shadow and took on a glow from the window's illumination. Pulling on a pair of sweat shorts, he nodded to Ari to join him for coffee. They would have a little time together before Dan had to go to the university. When he told Ari about the sword two days earlier, he said he was at least glad to know he still had his purpose of teaching others about archaeology and history. Ari opened the French doors onto the balcony and walked to the rail, and it was then that Dan realized Ari hadn't put on any shorts. He started the coffee-making process and shouted from the kitchen.

"You know we have neighbors across the street, right?"

Ari walked in, stuck his tongue out, went into the bedroom, and returned with shorts. While they drank their coffee on the balcony, Ari pried a bit more into how Dan was feeling. Dan logically knew that he was more than the man who could open gateways. All told, he didn't use the sword for that purpose every time they fought against an adversary, but the absence of that power left a pocket of emptiness inside. He felt incomplete. Ari interjected that Dan was not like ancient heroes like Perseus who *needed* his magical sword and helmet of invisibility to accomplish his task. Dan rolled his eyes.

"I see what you're saying. We can discuss the victim-blaming of Medusa some other time."

Ari sipped his coffee, taking his time to put the cup down.

"Calm yourself. I was not talking about Medusa. My point was—"

"I know. Sorry. I didn't mean to get snippy."

Ari pointed out that Perseus had no gods-given physical strength like his great-grandson Herakles. He then commented that it was strange that he was also Herakles' half-brother as they were both Zeus' sons.

"But, I digress. Mourn the loss of the sword's power, but just remember that it has nothing to do with who *you* are as a hero. You have strength, healing ability, tactical knowledge, a sword that can cut into anything, and a team. Do not forget the team."

Dan nodded and knocked back the rest of his coffee. As he got dressed for the university, he mentioned he would be covering funeral rites of the ancient world soon, and asked if Ari might want to be a guest speaker. He wouldn't be able to say he was speaking from experience, since it would be difficult to explain to his students how Ari was actually from the past and came through a portal into the present. Ari said he would think about it, but he did need things to do when he wasn't helping Esteban acclimate. Just then, Dan's phone rang. It was Sarah. She wanted him to know that Brandon had taken this whole situation harder than the others, and she asked if he could speak with his brother. She had tried, but he was being his typical introverted self and not putting his own needs first. Saying he would talk to Brandon, he also asked how she was doing. Knowing she could still cast spells and use other magical abilities made her feel at least a little better. The ring was in her jewelry box because she didn't need the constant reminder of it not working. Sarah turned the question back to Dan, and he replied that Ari was there to be his support and blew Ari a kiss. Before she hung up, she added that Brandon wasn't picking up his phone. Dan knew a few places to look for his brother when he wasn't in a good headspace.

<hr>

Alkinoë threw her arms around Brandon at the door of her condo and said how it had been too long since they had seen each other. He profusely apologized and told her he had needed some alone time. She playfully added that *now* he needed his mother, and he rolled his eyes with a half-smile. He did, in fact, need his mother, but not for consoling him. She gave him a knowing look, and then she noticed his gym bag.

"I know what you want. Are you sure? I won't hold back." Alkinoë pinched his cheek.

Moving to the fireplace in the dining room, Brandon asked why they weren't going into the basement. She held up her finger. Touching one of the bricks, the entire fireplace shimmered away leaving a rough wooden door with an iron ring in its wake. Gesturing for him to open it, he pushed the door by the ring, and it swung open, revealing a short tunnel that led to an open area. Once through the tunnel, Brandon dropped his gym bag, and his jaw fell open.

"Your father created this dimensional space for me. I wanted something bigger than the basement."

Brandon chuckled. "You and Diana did some damage in the basement, didn't you?"

She smiled and shrugged. "Anyway... this is a colosseum-sized sparring arena. You and the others are always welcome to use it. Maybe you'll visit me more then." She blew him a kiss.

Above them spread the bluest skies with wisps of clouds made brighter by the sun above. This was a truly realistic place, down the stadium surrounding them, albeit devoid of spectators.

"You know, this whole cutesy mother routine would be more believable if I didn't think you were about to kick my ass."

She elbowed him. "Go change into your 'I'm about to get my ass kicked by my mother' gear."

The ancient stadium seating appeared to be of stone, as it would have been. Along the perimeter where the seating ended was a tall wall on which hung weapons: battle axes, quarterstaffs, swords, shields, etc., each real and quite hefty. Brandon spied a staff and tossed one to his mother who had changed into a tank top, shorts, and athletic shoes. Her long black hair had been pulled into a tight braid. He preferred to be shirtless with only a pair of running shorts and athletic shoes. They circled one another, flipping around and spinning their staffs, each never taking his or her eyes off the other. Giving her son a "come on" gesture, Alkinoë positioned herself. The mock melee that ensued began slowly, more of a warm-up, and she commented that if he were holding back because she was his mother, he should reconsider that strategy. In response, he leaped forward, swinging his staff around, only to be met by hers, and the thrusting and parrying ensued. Finding her rhythm, Alkinoë moved with precision, anticipating his strikes, and when he attempted to sweep her legs out from under her, she somersaulted over him, thwapping her staff against his back. Brandon stumbled a little, found his footing, and swung around, expecting to catch her as she landed, but she must have anticipated that maneuver because she swooped her staff up under his ankle, causing him to fall on his side.

Sweat coating his brow, he snarled and leaped from his back to his feet. He took some steps back, considering his next move. She used her forearm to remove the sweat from her brow, planting her staff on the ground.

"You've been practicing." She twirled her staff around her hand. "I'm glad to see you're not going easy on me. Now, if only you were actually trying."

Spurred on by her jab, he launched himself toward her, and just before he reached her, he jumped over her, landed, and spun around, taking out her legs. She stumbled but didn't fall.

"See? You could easily have knocked me down. Water break."

Next to the array of weapons was a wooden chest filled with an anachronism of water bottles. After he finished an entire bottle, Brandon crushed it in one hand and dropped it in a basket.

"Do you think I'm really going easy on you?" He sat on a bench near the wall.

Alkinoë drank about half her bottle before putting it on the ground.

"I don't think you're going on easy on *me*. I think you're going easy on *yourself*."

"Not following you."

"Brandon, when you went to Arkadeia, you said you came back with a better understanding of what it meant to be Arkadeian. I think you did learn the responsibilities of being a member of the royal family. What you didn't learn, however, is what it means to be an Arkadeian. I want you to think about something. Our people come from the union of Apollo and Gaea millennia ago. That means we're not human in the true mortal sense. You're a hemitheos, but you're closer to fully immortal than you realize. Over the years of being on your team, you've never really embraced that side of yourself. I don't think you want to."

She finished off her bottle of water and took a seat by him. He had leaned forward, resting his arms on his knees, clasping his hands together. Sweat dripped from his nose, leaving wet spots on the ground.

"It... It scares me, Mom. When I use the amulet, I know it has limitations. I can connect with the zodiac and other constellations, I can draw strength or ability from them. Leo and Taurus... their strength is finite. I know their upper limits, and when I combine signs, those limitations keep me focused. Even becoming Sagittarius. That centaur is a singular being. It has a set form. But—"

Mother put her hand on her son's shoulder and pulled him closer.

"But, if you gave yourself over to the immortal that you *could* be, you wouldn't know the limitations. You might even be tempted to do things, to reach beyond yourself, and do things that could hurt people."

He turned to face her.

"How-How is it that you know these things? It's like you've read my thoughts." He sighed.

Alkinoë laughed to herself, rubbing his back.

"No, my son. I know these things because of your father. Have you ever truly wondered why he doesn't take his place on Olympos?"

"He told me once that it was because of his love of you. He wanted to be with you, and that place was in the mortal realm."

"Perhaps some of that rings true. But, Apollo was the only Olympeian to live as a human being, until recently, that is. Not acting like one. *Living* as one. Even though that timeline no longer exists, his memories of those experiences exist. Those were real to him. When you are born a child of Zeus, you bear the weight of expectation. Living in the *Oikoumene Broteos* gives him self-imposed limitations. He doesn't want to be like his father. He never did."

Brandon sat up and inhaled deeply. He let out his breath slowly.

"In the ancient world, your father wielded his power much more than he does now. The expectation was that gods were above mortals. To dally with humanity was a hobby, a pastime. After he and Gaea created Arkadeia, he started to understand what it meant to be responsible. Gaea wouldn't have let him use her people as playthings. For the first time in his existence, he had limits put on him. That was when he took his Asulos Pistis and swore himself to Gaea, to be her protector. He took an oath to protect his people, to nurture them, to treat them with compassion and love."

"Wow. I had no idea of any of this. He doesn't talk about his past much. So, Dad wanted limits so he could find purpose."

His mother nodded and smiled.

"Purpose beyond worship. Don't fear your immortal side. You're not suddenly going to explode with power and lose yourself in it. As an Arkadeian, you have heightened strength and healing. As an Olympeian, you have much more, but you have to figure out what that means for *you*. The man known as Zodiak can still be a hero, but perhaps a different one. Who knows? Maybe a better one. Now, I'm just getting warmed up. Are you ready for round two?"

Brandon pulled his mother into a tight embrace.

"Thank you. I love you. And, yes, I need to show you what I am made of."

Alkinoë snatched a sword belt from the weapon rack, attached it around her waist, and moved to the center of the arena. When Brandon joined her, he did so walking a little taller.

A white eagle with a twenty-foot wingspan spiraled down toward the roof of the Task Force building, met by Sarah. Just before she landed, the eagle shrank and resumed human form—human form with wings, that is. As her human feet touched the roof, her smaller wings vanished.

"That felt good. *So* good." Aleta gulped down water, wiping her mouth with the back of her hand.

"See? You can do more than just thunder and lighting." Sarah had her hands on her hips.

"That's the thing, though. When I was up there, I... I could still feel that power. It was weaker, sort of like static electricity, but it was there."

They headed toward the roof door back into the building when Aleta turned back and looked into the afternoon sky as one does when searching for a long-lost friend. She split off from Sarah to go to the locker room for a shower, shouting back that she'd meet back up in Quinn's office. Stopping at the coffee station in the hall, Sarah poured a cup, lingering over the liquid as it swirled around. With a heavy sigh, she drank some, opting for a few sugars. Quinn wasn't at her desk when Sarah arrived, but the office door was unlocked. Back in the conference area, Quinn faced the windows, her arms behind her back. Her brows narrowed, Sarah asked if she was okay. Quinn replied with a soft, "Mhmm."

"Aleta will be around soon. You sure you're all right?"

Quinn just nodded.

"Well, I'm just going to browse some of our files until Aleta comes." Sarah took a tablet from its charging dock and sat on the couch, tucking her legs under her body. A few taps later, she lost herself in a case file.

Returning to her desk a little while later, Quinn worked quietly. The barely audible tapping of her fingers on the glass console and Sarah's quiet sipping of coffee were the only sounds in the room. Every so often, Sarah glanced at Quinn but then returned to her reading. She could tell that something weighed on her comrade just from her expression, and she knew better than to pry. Quinn wasn't one for idle chatter, and if she wasn't talking, she was working. At one point, Sarah repositioned herself on the couch, taking the opportunity to move a little closer.

"You know we're not going anywhere," Sarah said, matter-of-factly, not taking her eyes off the tablet.

At first, Quinn didn't respond. After a longer pause, she simply replied, "Mhmm."

Sarah smirked to herself. "Just checking."

Through the door, Aleta strode, dressed more like Dr. Halston with her white lab coat. She, too, had a coffee in hand and plopped right next to Sarah.

"She knows we're not going anywhere, right?" Aleta was looking at Quinn but speaking to Sarah.

"Mhmm." Sarah's response imitated Quinn's tone, and she had hoped it would get some kind of reaction from her, but the liaison remained undisturbed.

"What are you looking at?" Aleta leaned forward toward the tablet.

Sarah giggled. "Sudoku, actually."

Then, from Quinn's desk, "She's hoping that I'll want to talk about what's going on." Her face never left the console.

Both Sarah and Aleta laughed.

"Honey, if you don't want to talk about it, then don't, but we know you're concerned your job might change if our team can't function the way it used to." Aleta finished her coffee.

Quinn continued to work without responding. The other two women chatted a little bit longer before Sarah had to prepare for a gallery opening for her work, and Aleta had to go back to the lab. As soon as she was alone, Quinn sat back in her chair, her exhale quivering.

"You're staying right where you are."

"I knew you'd show up. You always seem to know when I'm… a little off." She sat forward.

Apollo pulled a chair up to her desk. He asked to look into some things regarding the sacred tools to see if, in the Division's history, there had been anything that would help him understand what was happening. They tried different keywords and phrases, random words, and even ancient prophecies that he might have shared just to see what would pop up. Nothing. Quinn asked why he referred to the items as tools and not weapons.

"A tool makes a *change*. Just the word 'weapon' itself implies something violent or warlike. Thyroros may be a sword, which can obviously be used as something violent, but it has always been a tool of portals, hence the name PortalBearer. The javelin isn't like a spear. The former is used in athletic competition and training, and the latter is for battle or the hunt. The amulet is supposed to channel the vastness of the heavens like a hub, allowing its bearer to use that power. The ring is the same, giving the bearer access to the Tetrastoikheia."

"And, suddenly, they're just not able to use these tools. I wonder why *now* of all times."

Apollo nodded. "I wonder that as well. The Moirae won't speak to me, and Hephaestos didn't help too much."

While she typed, she just started speaking to herself. "Tools are used by craftspeople after much training. They master their skill using their tools. Sometimes, they have to upgrade once they've mastered—"

Apollo jumped up. "That's it!" He leaned over and kissed her on the forehead. "Thank you!" He paced quickly around, tapping his mouth with a finger. "Summon the team."

⚬━━✦━━⚬

At the head of the conference table, Apollo leaned on his hands as each member of the team came in and sat down. Ari accompanied Dan since they had been at dinner. Brandon was the last to arrive, still looking the most dejected of them all, his hands shoved into his pockets.

"Thanks for coming in on such short notice, but I think I have something. I don't know why I didn't think of this before. Thanks to Quinn, I think I know what's happening." He paused. "Your tools were given to you with specific guidance as to how to use them, and you've trained for years as this team. Over time, you've learned how to gain mastery over your abilities. I think that the reason why your tools no longer work for you is that you no longer need them."

All four teammates started asking him questions, talking over one another until he put up a hand.

"I know you have questions. Like, why now? Or, how can you do what you've been doing without access to those abilities? I think you still *can*. You've been so used to using those tools that you don't know what to do without them."

Aleta wagged her finger at him. "So, you're saying that I can still summon thunder and lightning? Even without the javelin?"

Apollo nodded. "I am. Think of the javelin like… training wheels that you've now outgrown."

"But, Dad. Thyroros was *your* sword before it was mine. I don't understand—"

Rounding the table to meet his son, Apollo leaned against the wall. "The sword was always meant to be yours, Danelos. Gaea forged it for me, but not because I needed it. So I could pass it down to *you*."

"So, are you saying that my ring has no connection to the Tetrastoikheia? No link to Thalassa, Khaos, Hesteia, or Gaea?" Sarah could barely get the words out.

Nodding, Apollo exhaled through his nose. "That's what I'm saying. I don't know if Syra or the Atlantaeans knew that. Perhaps, for them, that's how it worked, but you've surpassed Syra and her ancestors."

Sarah gasped. "H-How do you know that?" Her face paled.

"I think sometimes you all forget how old I am. I had visited ancient Atlantis. I had met Syra. She was a skilled sorceress, there's no doubt about that. But, you've gone way past her level of power and understanding."

"Why didn't you ever tell me?" Sarah's tears streamed into her lap. "How come I didn't *know* that?"

"Sarah, there wasn't a need to tell you. What purpose would that have served?" Apollo returned to the head of the table. "The ring was sort of like Aleta's javelin. It was intended for the chosen one of the Atlantaeans. It allowed you to unlock what you had inside you all along. You believed it was the source of your elemental powers, so it functioned that way."

Before he continued, he turned toward Brandon.

"Didn't you ever wonder why you were drawn to animals as a child? Didn't it ever cross your mind that there was a reason why you had an affinity for the zoo? You told me that Max and Evelyn used to take you there as a child. You have been the cosmic zookeeper long before you ever received that amulet. Think about that orange cat in Arkadeia that found you."

Brandon's eyes widened, and he sat up. He pressed his hands onto his head, then slid them down to his cheeks.

"I guess I've always known that. So, somewhere deep inside each of us, you're saying we can still access our powers?"

Apollo arrived home after midnight and found Alkinoë reading on the sofa. He was wearing normal business attire, with his tie pulled open a little and his hair a little windblown. He fell next to her, putting his hands over his face.

"You used the front door." She kept her eyes on the book. "Let me guess. You needed to walk."

He leaned his head against her shoulder.

"They didn't take it well. They think you betrayed them."

He raised both eyebrows. "Oh, so you're psychic now?"

"Look, you're the god of truth, just not the god of 'I'll tell you all the truth right now'. Trust me. I understand. The thing is, do they?"

Apollo smirked. "I think Dan and Brandon do. Sarah wouldn't make eye contact with me."

"Aleta?" She turned the page.

"She's still dealing with the loss from returning Zeus' powers. She went from supreme storm goddess to 'just a bird.' Her words, not mine."

He stared straight ahead, not really in the room, while she kept reading. Every so often, he glanced her way. Finally, she put the book down, commenting she had wanted to finish the chapter. Alkinoë leaned her head into his and put her hand over his.

"I think... you need to step back from the task force, at least for a while. You've been—"

"I agree."

Alkinoë picked up her book again, nodding. Silence has different qualities, depending on where it is. The absence of sound in the depths of the underworld has been known to bring about madness for those who are not prepared for it. Even parts of Tartaros have a silence that is like the darkest black possible. High atop Olympos, the silence is thin and tenuous, just barely keeping out the sounds from the skies that surround it.

Here, in Apollo and Alkinoë's home, this pregnant silence bears a heavy weight—some might even say a cost—because what comes from it will change the entirety of the cosmos. Now that he could think without obstacle, without the extra energy expended to keep a mental barrier in place, Apollo could allow himself the luxury of relaxing his mind and simply enjoying the reverie and peace that daydreaming allows.

As Alkinoë closed the book following its last chapter, she kissed her husband whose head was leaning against her, the god of reason and prophecy, who had given himself permission to sleep.

⸺⸱⟝⸺

Exiting the elevator of an office building that Ari had been to a few times, he patted Esteban's shoulder, letting him know that he was proud for taking this step. It would do more than anything any Olympeian could do for him. Before Ari could knock, a man opened the door.

"Ari, it's good to see you again. You must be Esteban." He shook the man's hand. "Nice to meet you. Please, come in."

The familiarity of the artwork he remembered made him smile, and Ari craned his head around to see what if anything might have changed since his last visit. The man brought over a tray with a Japanese teapot and three cups.

"I've been told you'll be able to help me move past some of my issues, Dr. Bean." Esteban sipped his tea.

"More like move through. We can't move past anything until we deal with it and the emotional effect it's had."

Esteban smiled. "Of course. And you're familiar with the circumstances of my… origin?" He sipped more tea, keeping the cup in front of his face.

"Intimately. And, please. Call me Scott. It's my understanding that you want Ari here. We'll be diving into a lot of personal experiences, so I want to be certain you're okay—"

"Scott, Ari has literally been in my mind." He laughed a little. "I have no secrets from him." He smiled at Ari.

Ari patted Esteban's shoulder. "We will take one visit at a time. If at any point either of you wants to step out, let me know."

Scott tipped back his teacup, his eyes going from Ari to Esteban.

"It's been so long since I've had tea this good. What kind is it?" Ari reached for the pot to pour more, but Scott insisted on doing it.

"It's a White Lotus blend I've always enjoyed." The floral aroma filled the office as the fire agates and other stones on the wall seemed to come alive as the sunbeams touched them through the windows.

After the general inquiries as to Esteban's well-being, Scott leaned forward, his elbows resting on his knees, and his fingers interlaced.

"So how have you processed everything you've learned? Ari didn't go into details when he called me, but he intimated that you've been confronted with quite a bit of family history."

Esteban sat up, fidgeted in his seat, and rubbed his palms against his pants. As he started the breadth of his experiences, he kept checking Scott's face for any signs of confusion or lack of understanding, but none came. With that unspoken cue, that underlying sense that he could speak openly, he let everything spill forth about Orphne and his connection to Nyx. His body language settled, but he kept glancing over to Ari. Before Scott could say anything, Ari excused himself, saying that he had to call Dan. A quick, undetectable head nod toward Scott signaled he'd be gone for a while. Scott gestured that Esteban should continue, although Ari's sudden departure had made him tongue-tied. With a few erratic starts, eventually Esteban returned to talking about Orphne.

"When was the last time you saw your mother?"

"Not since I was a child. One day, I woke up to find her gone. But, she has spoken to me… in dreams. She was the one who told me that Ari had become the ferryman."

"Why did she tell you?"

"I'm not entirely sure. I was still in the hospital in Spain, and I think she knew no one spent any time with me. She wasn't able to visit, so she made an agreement with Morpheos."

"Did she just come out and tell you, or was it part of some larger conversation?"

"My dreams were foggy at best, and she spoke in brief statements. I know from Ari that the five rivers tried to lead a revolt because of Charon's absence, but it was unsuccessful. While Ari could maintain the influx of souls, he doesn't have the power of Charon who is himself a child of Nyx and Erebos. I *am* connected to darkness."

"How does that make you feel?" Scott leaned back and crossed his legs.

"Do all counselors ask that?" Esteban laughed a little. "I don't know how I feel. I really don't. I never really knew my father, although I know he is in Zeus' line. I guess that makes me some sort of immortal." He took a deep breath. "I never really felt accepted or understood until I met Ari. He promised me that Apollo would help me, and he kept his word. The cloud of confusion I have around me is not as frustrating knowing I have a friend like him."

"You were once angry at Apollo for leaving you in a catatonic state. How do you feel now?"

"Grateful. I know why he did that now, and it makes sense. I also think he fears me a little."

Scott's face changed to one of confusion. "Why do you think that?"

"I haven't fully awakened as an immortal. I'm of Nyx's and Zeus' lineage. Ari explained to me that I could choose to live as I always have, a human, or I can self-actualize and, in time, grow into my potential. Before you ask, I don't know how I feel about that. I don't think every offspring of immortals has to live as one. I could relinquish my birthright and be wholly human."

"Is that what you want?"

Esteban lingered on Scott's face. He and Ari had talked about this. Being attached to the magic of the gods had been something he'd always known, but at a distance, until Lismonia and, later, being in Apollo's mind. Before that, it was like he was in a fog. The name *El Maldito* had stuck with him in the back of his mind, lingering, holding on to every ounce of his soul. It was like a sickness or cancer that clung to him in its viscous embrace. Ari had told him that darkness and evil weren't the same. He could be attached to the absence of light yet still be a force for good. The question that loomed was: did he want to accept the responsibility of the primordial energy inside him or shed it? Could he be truly happy expunging that which was a part of him? Would he feel the loss? Mourn for it?

"Not right now. I have to think about it more. I *do* know that I'm not ready to be more than human."

"You sound confident in that decision. I can hear it in your voice."

"You understand the push and pull, don't you? The allure of two sides and what they offer."

Although he didn't turn around to look at it, in his mind, Scott was thinking of the painting on the wall behind him of the two kites: the one flying in the breeze and the one tied to the tree stump. Two potent forces vying for control, and he had always chosen the one that represented peace and love.

Scott smiled. "I do." He moved to the wall of plate glass that gave him a vibrant view of Boston. Sunset moved closer, casting its red and gold hues across the city, almost like liquid fire. His face took on the amber glow of the light.

Ari joined them, apologizing for being gone so long, and asked how things had been going. Scott replied that Esteban could tell him if he wanted to and that their time was almost up. He asked how things were going with Ari since they hadn't talked earlier, but more out of a friendly inquiry than a therapeutic one. Ari didn't want to get into what was happening with Dan and the other team members since that would be Dan's choice to share, so he focused more on his helping Dan as a guest speaker at the university as well as being hired on to the team as a consultant. After helping Apollo, he decided he wanted to be available to help the team more, using his abilities as he could. Esteban thanked Scott for his time and set up another appointment, adding that he knew he had more to work on after what he had endured. In the elevator, he had the hint of a smile.

"What is it?" Ari couldn't help but smile as well.

"I've made a decision." He bounced on the balls of his feet. "I'm going to visit my mother, and I will need your help."

36 | TITANS

Tartaros

Crouched in the corner of the cave-like cell, his arms attached to the wall above him with Hephaesteian iron chains and manacles, the shade once a Titan moaned to himself as drops of poison trickled down his form, sending up wisps of smoke. His long, scraggly brown hair hung over his drooping head. Across his chest was a burn mark from where Zeus' thunderbolt had struck him and sent him into the underworld. In a jolt, he lifted his head and sunken eyes dragged from one side of the cave to another.

"It's lavender and myrrh." A honeyed voice shattered the quiet. "The first step to freedom is having the scent of the upper world." A shrouded female figure stepped into the cave.

"H-How…" The shade's husky voice breathed the word, and it was the first he'd uttered in millennia.

"Shhh. Let me work."

Uncovering her head, she revealed dark brown hair, a braid coiled like a serpent around her head. The right side of her face from her forehead to her chin bore an intricate design at the center of which on her cheek was the glyph of bull's horns. From within the folds of her peplos, she pulled a copper dagger. Without hesitation, she dragged the tip across her hand, and blood pooled. Closing her fist over it, she uttered some words, and when she opened her hand, a copper key sat where the blood had been. She unlocked the manacles, but his wrists didn't budge.

"Clever, Zeus. But…"

She twirled the dagger around so the tip was down, and it morphed into a copper serpent. Positioning the serpent's head over the shade's wrists, she let drops of venom drip from its fangs. Grunts came from the shade as the coppery liquid trickled to where the manacle made contact. With a few words uttered, she caused the iron to lose its cohesion and melt away. The shade's arms fell into his lap, and he pressed them to his chest. He still hadn't lifted his head.

"One more thing." She removed a miniature amphora from thin air, lifted his chin with her finger, using her thumb to pry open his mouth, and emptied the contents down his throat.

It took only a few seconds to work, but soon the shade stood, towering over her. He brushed his hair back and twisted his neck around.

"Thank you." His voice had gained resonance. "For someone to risk her life to free me from Tartaros, she either has a death wish or she has a good reason."

She turned to leave the cave. "The latter, I assure you. We must hurry before Tartaros reveals your absence to Hades."

The shade who hadn't walked in thousands of years stumbled his first steps but soon regained the ability. The woman led the way, a small glowing ball of light in her upturned palm. Eventually, after traveling through offshoots of caves and pathways, they reached the river Acheron.

"Charon does not transport shades back across the river. Also, how did we bypass Cerberos?"

Laughing to herself, the woman gestured toward the river of woe, and a path of ice crackled its way to the other side. She moved across without even checking on the shade behind her until she stepped off the icy bridge. They meandered through small passages up stony stairs, twisting and turning their way farther from the depths of Tartaros. The shade tried to engage her, but she remained silent. At some point, they descended, and the pathway took on an altogether different smell. Fire mixed with agony. At the shores of Phlegethon, they stopped.

"Where are we going?"

She turned around, but she didn't remove her hood. Twirling her index finger, she summoned the tiniest thread of fire from the river until it became a ball the size of a marble. She gestured for his hand and placed the ball in his palm, closing his fingers around it. He cried out in agony as the flames entered him, and soon the fire made its way through all his limbs and his head. Somehow, his shrieks weren't heard above the conflagration flowing by them. Collapsed onto the ground, he gradually stood, a guttural growl in the back of his throat.

She nodded slightly. "Welcome back to the land of the living. Now, we must hurry."

Again, she drew the copper dagger across her palm, but this time she turned her hand to let the blood sink into the dirt by the river. Turning in a circle, she made a pattern of blood around them. The man spied the dagger more closely as she waved it like a wand. She squeezed his hand and told him to close his eyes and hold his breath. The dirt within the blood circle bubbled beneath their feet, and they sank as if through quicksand.

Just beyond a set of ruins, the ground gurgled, and two figures climbed free, covered in bloody dirt. The woman entered a large tent adorned with tassels and flowers. By the time the man had as well, she was sitting in a small pool surrounded by white silk in the center of the space with glowing orbs illuminating everything. He wandered around while two young maidens poured amphorae of water over her, washing away the bloody dirt. She started to tell him why the inside of the tent looked so much larger when he interrupted.

"It's magic. You forget. I'm a Titan. We created magic."

The maidens rubbed her with scented oils reminiscent of those the man had smelled earlier. Only when she was dressed in a new peplos and donned her hood did she join him, gesturing toward the pool. While he bathed, he asked the woman questions, but she remained silent. He stepped from the silk-shrouded pool into the tent naked. The woman sat before a scrying bowl.

"I left clothes for you on the table. I assumed your size."

When he met her by the bowl, he was wearing dark leather pants, leather boots, and a leather vest adorned with small metal rings. His hair had regained its natural curls. He stroked his chin.

"I did not even realize your maidens had trimmed my beard. I only had my eyes closed for a moment."

As she had done before, she giggled and smiled. With a wave of her hand, the image in the pool vanished, and she turned to face him.

"Welcome back, Menoetes, son of Iapetos. I have a proposition for you."

This time, it was his turn to laugh. As he crossed his arms, their muscled tone having returned, the leather squeaking and stretching.

"I may be inclined to agree, but first, I would like to know who my benefactor is."

Removing her hood, her eyes twinkled in the torchlight.

"My name is Pasiphaë, the daughter of Helios."

A grin filled Menoetes' face as he puffed out his chest. She pointed to the bowl and the image reappeared.

"And who are they?"

"Two sons of Apollo, an Amazon, and a sorceress."

"What is this proposition? And what does it have to do with them?"

Pasiphaë smiled. "I want you to help me kill them."

37 | JUSTICE

The Underworld

Walking into the throne room of Hades and Persephone, a figure who had not been seen in this dark place in millennia approached the dais. Hades' eyes widened, and he rose.

"Brother? What brings you to this place? Had you summoned me, I would have gone to Olympos."

Zeus looked past him to see Persephone, whose face grew even more pallid as if she knew the reason for his visit, then he returned his gaze to his brother.

"I must speak with you." His voice didn't have the deep timber of the king of gods, but rather the tremble of one in torment.

⚜

The Hall of Tribunals, Olympos

Roaring thunder, heard across the globe, was a clarion call to all immortals to heed their king with immediacy. As many as could fit in the marbled hall awaited in silence the audience of the summoner. In this place, no thrones sat, so when Zeus and Hera entered, they did so at the same level of the rest of the pantheon. Winged gods hovered above while others gathered below with their heads tilted forward ever so slightly. Apollo and Artemis stood the closest in front of their father.

"I bid thee welcome." Zeus' soft, timid words sent a shiver through the throng of immortals. He held Hera's hand tightly.

"When I believed my son was lost,"—he turned his eyes to Apollo—"I felt as if my heart had burst, and I allowed my grief to overtake my reason. In doing so, I caused the death of many. If not for the intervention of Prometheos, more would have perished." He stopped for a moment. "Not even Hades can restore those souls. And they need justice to be served on their behalf. I lived among mortals, as did you all, for a year, and the lessons learned changed me. Perspective brought humility and understanding."

Hades stepped forward from behind his brother.

"I am to be punished for my actions." Zeus lowered his head and stepped back.

"Zeus sought my counsel as to what kind of punishment would fit such a heinous act. I spoke with the three judges, and they agreed. Zeus will be placed in a separate part of Tartaros where he will endure watching the deaths of the mortals his actions caused."

A collective gasp and subsequent chatter spread among the throng. Zeus stepped forward again.

"Silence. This decision was not made without great care and the input of my queen. Olympos must stay strong. I cannot dissolve the Olympeian Pact that Poseidon, Hades, and I created after the Titanomachia. I must be king for that to remain in effect, for the sake of Olympos. However, I *can* choose one who will act in my stead. As such, Hera will rule over the pantheon. I do not know when, or if, I will return to these gilded halls. Long have we acted without consequence to those we wronged in ages past. That must stop."

Artemis stepped forward. "Father, does your decision have anything to do with that of Hermes?"

"My son, when faced with his actions from the past, chose to live among mortals and could not wear the mantle of godhood anymore. Whether his death was of his own design or an accident is yet unknown. Like him, I knew I had to face the consequences of my actions."

Hades put a hand on his brother's shoulder, and they both vanished in black, billowy smoke. With nothing more to be said, Hera dismissed those assembled and remained in the hall with Apollo and his sister.

Hera descended the dais to stand in front of them.

"And you, son of Zeus. Your thoughts?"

"My father's thoughtless behavior, even if caused by his own heart's grief, required justice. I don't know what other punishment would have been suitable, but this seems... appropriate."

"In all the millennia I have known him, I have never seen such an act on behalf of humanity from him. Moving forward, all Olympos will need to learn from this and change."

"Indeed, my queen. Indeed."

ABOUT THE AUTHOR

David Berger fell in love with books when he was 8 years old, and from that point on, his life's journey would never be without a book in his hand. An English teacher since 1993, he continues to share his love of literature with his students. His first novel series, *Task Force: Gaea*, started his writing career in 2012, and he has published numerous pieces of short fiction in anthologies in addition to The DragonHawk Cycle, a Celtic fantasy trilogy. He currently lives in Tampa Bay, FL with his sidekick, his dog, Argos.

www.ingramcontent.com/pod-product-compliance
Lightning Source LLC
Chambersburg PA
CBHW030539260626
47157CB00006B/2098